# THE LAST PENDRAGON

THE LAST
PENDRAGON
Jeanette T. Queen

Book Cover and Formatting by Rose at Melting Roses Designs

Editing by Devon Atwood

First edition 2024

# DEDICATION

This book would not have been possible without the unwavering support of my Aunt Dianna. Who was my first fan, and the first person to read every chapter, even the ones that didn't make into the final version. She has been my ride or die throughout this entire writing journey, and for that, I am truly grateful.

To my children, who are the light of my life and my reason for pursuing my dream. I want you to know that dreams can come true, no matter your age or circumstance, if you truly believe.

Thank you all, I love you!

# CONTENTS INCLUDE

This book contains content which may be triggering to some readers. These include:

- Adult language
- Adult situation
- Mention of sex and blood slaves
- Unwanted sexual advances
- Abduction
- Forced captivity
- Fantasy violence
- Decapitation
- Death of a pregnant woman and her unborn child (past, not an MC)
- Mention of pregnancy due to rape (past, not an MC)

Avalon

# TABLE OF CONTENTS

# PROLOGUE

He stood in front of the enormous stone columns that he had been searching for, for the last ten years. Christopher Madison knew in his gut that this site had not suffered destruction, burning, or reclamation by the ocean. Archaeologists had been searching for centuries with no clue it had been moved to an entirely different realm.

Despite this being a significant archaeological discovery, he wasn't interested in the structure itself, but in what he hoped the great library of Alexandria contained.

The archaeologist in him, of course, would have loved to explore this wonder. He would have loved to explore and figure out how the great library had been moved. Sadly, he didn't have time for that now. He was on a mission, and time was not a luxury he had much of. The spell he had used to get here was a tricky one, and he needed to make sure he was back before his daughter got home from school.

Although he was powerful, he had limited magical knowledge. Most of it, he had learned from books he'd found in his mother's library since she was only willing to teach him the basics. He was pretty sure she would have kept that information to herself if he hadn't started showing signs; he possessed magic of his own.

For his daughter, he would do anything, and that included learning all he could about the magic that flowed through their veins. His daughter was also the reason he now found himself standing in front of a historical stone structure in a different realm, looking for an ancient magical relic.

He'd overheard a conversation between his mother and her oldest friend, Nicholas Black, that had given him all the information he'd needed. They had talked about an ancient artifact that, if found by the wrong hands, could be detrimental to all. They had theorized that it was housed here, in the Ancient World's greatest library. However, neither of them had truly believed it was here. His mother seemed sure it was hidden in the human realm.

Christopher continued up the last few stone steps, past the columns to the set of massive wooden doors that led inside. It had taken him ten years of research, back-alley dealings with other world creatures, and good old-fashioned luck to get him here.

He took a few minutes to connect with his magic and sense if there were any traps for the unsuspecting traveler. When he sensed none, he continued.

As he approached, the enormous doors flung open, and a gust of wind pushed him through. The doors then slammed behind him. He attempted to open the doors, but he quickly realized they were locked. "Damn!" he yelled, banging his fist against the wood in vain.

"I am afraid you will not be able to return that way," a voice whispered in the wind. Christopher turned sharply, looking for where the voice had come from. But there was no one else. He was alone.

"Hello!" he yelled, only hearing his echo repeated back to him. He moved further into the great library. Maybe he was hearing things. He shook his head and pulled his travel pack from his back. He opened it and pulled out his journal.

Christopher had never met his father, the greatest wizard in history, or so the stories say. But he did inherit his gift of sight. Christopher had seen his quarry in a vision. He knew it was here. He had to find the location that matched the sketch in his journal.

For a library that was thousands of years old, it was in remarkably good condition. There wasn't a grain of dust on any of the surfaces. The only sound was the echo of his boots on the stone floor as he moved further into the massive open space filled with rows upon rows of shelves.

He walked through aisles of rolled papyrus, amazingly preserved. Shelves filled with rolls of ancient paper stretched out in all directions. He felt an itch as an archaeologist to examine each roll and read the many wonders that had been lost for generations. But he couldn't, as he had his mission, and he knew that what he was searching for wouldn't be found on a piece of papyrus.

He held up the sketch in the journal, looking for the statue holding the simple wooden box that housed the one artifact he was desperate to find. He knew he was not the one in his family line that would be chosen to wield the legendary sword when it finally decided to awaken and make its presence known. No,

Excalibur was still resting in its hiding place, where it had been for over fifteen hundred years.

He thought for a moment. Perhaps the sword was in this great library as well. The thought quickly left him. It didn't matter where the sword was. All that mattered was finding what he came for. The longer the sword slept, the better.

He found a row of marble statues lined up against a back wall. However, none of them matched his sketch. "Where are you hiding, sweet lady?" He continued his search, going down aisle after aisle of lost treasures, works of art, and manuscripts that would turn the modern world on its head. Yet none of the treasures he passed were the artifact he was searching for.

Suddenly, he could have sworn he saw movement in the corner of his eye. He yelled, "Hello?" He walked toward where he thought he'd seen the movement. Then, there was a loud bang, one he knew he hadn't caused. He picked up his pace and quickly turned the corner. He expected to find someone standing there, or at least, an overturned statue.

He was surprised when he found neither. What he did find was a statue of Queen Cleopatra holding a simple wooden box. The one he had been searching for. He looked around, and again, there was no one else.

This was it—the past ten years of sacrificing time with his beautiful daughter, Elizabeth. All for this small wooden box. However, if this box contained what he thought it did, it would all be worth it. Because it was all for her, his sweet little princess.

He knew he wasn't the chosen Pendragon, but he knew in his gut *she* was. He would do everything he could to help her before her destiny was thrust upon her. Finding the fabled dragon stone was part of that.

Excalibur was the only weapon that could kill an immortal. An immortal like the demon queen, mother of all vampires, and anything purely evil, Lilith. There would come a day when his amazing, precious girl would need to face Lilith. The prophecy had spoken of it.

Finding the dragon stone would ensure that Lilith couldn't get her hands on it. The dragon stone was the only power in the known realms that could heal a wound caused by Excalibur. And Excalibur was the only known weapon that could stop Lilith.

Christopher reached for the box, but the box wouldn't budge. He tried to pry it from the marble queen's hands. He pulled out a pocket knife and tried to wedge it between the box and the hands of the statue. Still, the box didn't budge.

"*Stop*!"

He flinched when he heard a loud voice. There was a bright light. He then felt like he was floating. "What the..."

"Welcome, Christopher Madison. I have been expecting

you."

Christopher looked around and suddenly found that he was no longer in the library. Now, he found himself in an empty white room. No, that wasn't right; it wasn't empty because before him stood a figure, neither male nor female, but a corporal form of light. "Where am I? Who are you?"

"I am the library," the being stated flatly.

"You're a building?" Christopher asked skeptically.

"It's been so long since I have encountered a being from your realm. I had forgotten how limited your scope of the world is."

"I'm pretty sure you just insulted me."

The being laughed. "No insult—simple facts." Christopher had no idea how to respond to that. "Tell me, Christopher Madison, why do you seek the dragon stone?"

He shuffled his feet. "Ok, moving on, I see. I need it. I need to keep it safe."

"And you feel it is not safe here?"

"Well, I found it, didn't I? So could others."

"Have you?"

"Have I what?"

"Have you found what you are looking for?"

"What game are you playing? Of course, I found it. It's in the box." He was getting annoyed.

"Perhaps, but do you have the box in your possession?"

"No, not yet."

"Then it is still safe, is it not?"

"Look, maybe you don't know what's going on out there." He gestured with his hands, waving them around to indicate the outside world. "But I don't have time for your games. If Lilith gets her hands on this stone, then all is lost."

"You wish to keep the stone from Lilith?"

"*Yes*!" He threw his hands up in the air. They were getting nowhere.

"What are you willing to give up to ensure the stone stays safe?"

"What? What do you mean, give up?"

"It's not that difficult of a question. I feel you already know the answer, too."

Christopher weighed the words of the being as he paced back and forth. He knew what was being asked of him. He somehow always knew. Without hesitation, he answered. "Everything."

"Are you sure about that?"

"Yes, for my daughter, I would give up everything. I know in my soul that this stone needs to be kept away from Lilith to ensure my daughter has a chance to fulfill her destiny." He ran his hands through his hair, thinking of the weight his daughter would one day need to carry.

"Very well, Christopher Madison, your sacrifice is accepted."

He lowered his head and nodded as tears began to fall. He prayed that Lizzy would understand why he had made this sacrifice for her.

"We agree, and we will take your everything in exchange for keeping the stone safe and away from Lilith. We will ensure Elizabeth Madison comes into her power when the time is right, so she might fulfill her destiny."

"What will happen to her without me?" Christopher asked through tears.

"Only time will tell. But have faith that all is as it should be."

And with that, all went dark.

# ONE

*Ten years later*

Elizabeth Madison stood in line at her favorite coffee cart on campus. It was a cool morning for the month of May. She really wished she had remembered to grab a light jacket. She had been a student at John Hopkins University for the past four years, and she still hadn't gotten the weather patterns down pat. Maryland could be freezing in the morning and then have you sweating like a reverse harem in church by lunch.

The students in front of her ordered their fancy foam lattes and caramel mocha whatever. She never understood the need for fifteen million options. A simple cup of coffee with a splash of French vanilla creamer was all she needed, and boy, was she going to need it today.

Her time as a student was officially over. She had graduated with honors, received her bachelor's degree, and was now expected to move off campus and start her life or enroll in a master's program somewhere. That was the problem. She didn't know what she wanted to do.

"Good morning." Elizabeth looked up and saw the smiling face of the barista, Tommy. "The usual? Or have you finally decided to spice it up a little?" He smirked, flashing one dimple on his left cheek. Elizabeth was sure his smile must have more than one girl melting for his charm.

"No, thank you, my usual with two plain blacks, please," she replied. Tommy always flirted with her and probably every other female on campus. Elizabeth never took it seriously. She was really bad at flirting, anyway. She had spent the last four years with her head buried in a book. She had no desire to date, even if it was supposed to be part of the college experience.

No, she'd had a taste of love in high school, and when it had gone away. It had nearly destroyed her. She didn't need a repeat. She knew most men in college were after one thing, and that wasn't what she was looking for. Not after tasting the possibilities of forever. Being old-fashioned that way, she knew she could never settle for a fling.

While her peers were out partying on the weekends, she had spent hers mostly alone with her books. Escaping into the pages of a novel had always been her secret pleasure. Who needed just one boyfriend when she could have several in one week? Who cared if they were fictional and completely unrealistic?

"Here you go," Tommy said, pulling her out of her thoughts as he handed Elizabeth a disposable cup holder with the three cups filled with the steaming liquid gold she craved.

"Thank you," she replied, taking the tray from him with both hands and inhaling the sweet aroma. There was nothing like the smell of fresh coffee.

She noticed the few remaining students loading cars and trucks with their belongings as she walked back to her apartment to finish packing. The movers her grandmother had hired would be there around lunchtime, and there were still a few things that needed to be boxed up. And then she'd have the fun-filled task of cleaning the apartment she had called home for the last four years.

Elizabeth's pace quickened as she felt a shiver shoot up her spine, the feeling of eyes suddenly bearing down on the back of her head. As she approached her apartment building, she glanced behind her to make sure she wasn't being followed and nearly ran right into the man exiting the building. Two strong arms grabbed and steadied her before she could spill the hot coffee all over him.

"Whoa, there, speedy. Where's the fire?" Elizabeth looked up into the hazel eyes of her next-door neighbor.

"Oh, my God, Tyler! I'm sorry."

Tyler's boyfriend, Jonathon, laughed from where he stood behind Tyler. "It is going to take more than a speedy brunette with hot coffee to knock him off his feet,".

"I'm fine, love. How about you?" Tyler asked. "You're the one who raced in here like a bat out of Hell."

"I'm sorry, I'm fine. I had this weird feeling, like I was being followed or something." Elizabeth looked behind her and then back at Tyler. "It freaked me out for a minute."

Both men looked at each other in silent communication. "I'll go check it out." Jonathan walked outside.

"Anything to make him feel like a soldier again. Jonathan is great at spotting creepers. If you're being followed, love, he'll take care of it." Tyler put his arm around her shoulder. "Now, about all these coffees, were you reading all night again? Or did you go out to a fabulous post grad party and forgot to invite your favorite person... me?"

"Oh, sorry, these are for you guys." She handed him one of the black coffees. "Crazy how we all moved in here four years ago on the same day and now we are moving out on the same day."

"Yes, crazy how fate works," he smiled sheepishly before quickly turning toward the door.

The front door opened, and Jonathan walked back in, alert in his soldier mode, as Tyler called it. He had been special ops or something, but had then chosen to take the academic route when he'd met and fallen in love with Tyler, who had already been pre-med at John Hopkins. "I didn't see anyone out of the norm. Not that that necessarily means anything."

"Thank you for checking; I'm sure it's nothing. Probably moving jitters or something. I'll be fine." She smiled as she handed Jonathan the other black coffee. He nodded in thanks as he took it from her hands.

"We will be in and out all day if you need anything. Plus, Rick the sup is on the premises today." Tyler squeezed her shoulder.

"Thank you, I appreciate that. But I'm sure it was nothing. My movers will be here soon, and then I'm headed home." She frowned. "I am going to miss you guys so much."

"Hey, now, no frowns. You have our numbers. We will stay in contact." Tyler lifted her chin to face him. "Who knows; you might be surprised where we turn up at."

Elizabeth hoped that was true. Tyler and Jonathan had been her only real college friends, forcing her out of her comfort zone whenever they could. Which wasn't often. Most of the time, they just hung out and talked about books. Tyler loved a spicy romance as much as she did. She didn't know if they would remain close. But she really hoped they did.

She didn't have many friends. Growing up, she'd mainly had tutors since her father and grandmother had traveled the world for work, and they'd insisted on taking her along. She'd gotten to see the world but had never had a chance to make real friends. Not until... no, she wasn't going to go there. Not today.

The three hugged it out and said their goodbyes. With her eyes filled with tears, Elizabeth headed to her apartment to finish packing.

A few hours later, Elizabeth still had an uneasy feeling as she washed out the kitchen sink. Even though Jonathan had assured her there was nothing to worry about, she still wasn't so sure. Trying not to think about it, she threw herself into cleaning.

Her grandmother had offered to hire a cleaning service, which Elizabeth had declined. *Stupid idea,* she thought to herself. Did she really need the closure that cleaning her empty apartment would offer her?

Her life was at a crossroads. *Maybe that's the reason I feel off*, she thought as she wiped out the refrigerator. The smell of bleach burned her nose, causing her eyes to water. She didn't know which road she was meant to go down. The unknown was causing her to feel unsure and afraid. That had to be it. It made more sense than having someone following her, anyway. *Right?*

She had moved on to the bathroom with her cleaning rag and bleach when there was a knock at the door. She wiped some sweat from her brow with the back of her hand, then walked to the door. Still feeling a little unnerved, she opened the door a crack with the chain lock still fastened.

She found two of the largest men she had ever seen in her life standing outside her door. They were wearing matching black T-shirts and jeans. One was holding a clipboard.

"Elizabeth Madison?" one asked in a deep baritone.

"Um...Yes... I am, and you are?" She stumbled over her words.

"I'm Jake, and this is Bob." He pointed his thumb towards his partner. "We are with Black Industries."

She stared at the two men with a blank expression. She was familiar with Black Industries. They were a high-tech medical facility back home, but she couldn't fathom why two of their employees would be standing at her front door.

The one called Jake spoke again. "Apologies, we were told you would be expecting us."

"For what?" she asked.

Jake smiled. "We are here to move your belongings to..." He looked at the clipboard. "To Graystone Manor in Madison."

"You're the movers? The ones my grandmother hired?" Elizabeth was confused.

Jake shifted his stance. "Yes, Ma'am, we were sent by Mr. Black himself."

*When did Black Industries get into the moving business? Are high-tech pharmaceuticals not paying out what they once did?* She thought to herself. "I don't mean to be rude, but I need to make a phone call. Please, wait out here." Elizabeth shut the door before either could respond.

There was no way those two mountainous men were movers. Something felt off, adding to her unease. Elizabeth found her phone on the now spotless kitchen counter and dialed the one person who could shed some light on what was happening.

Her grandmother, Lady Lorraine, answered the phone cheerfully, as usual. "Happy moving day, darling."

"Good morning, Gram," Elizabeth answered, not nearly as cheerfully. "Question. Where did you hire the movers from?"

"Oh, yes, about that. I meant to tell you, I was speaking

with Nicholas, who generously offered to take care of it."

"Gram," Elizabeth said, exasperated.

"What? Is there a problem? Are they running late? I'm sure they will be there soon. No stress needed." Lady Lorraine spoke with her polished English accent.

"Um... No ...they're here, I guess. I mean, you know how I feel about Nicholas."

"Elizabeth." She could hear the frustration in her grandmother's voice. "Nicolas Black is one of my oldest friends, and he has always tried to do what was best for us."

"Sure, if you consider breaking my heart, doing what was best for us."

"No need to be snarky. We are not getting into this again. What happened was for both your own good. One day, you will understand. Besides, I think it was lovely of Nicholas to want to make sure you made it home safely. You can't be too careful these days."

Elizabeth looked at the closed front door and then lowered her voice. "These guys, well, they don't look like movers."

"Okay, what should a mover look like?" Lady Lorraine asked with amusement.

"Not like mercenaries minus weapons," Elizabeth said, rolling her eyes.

"Elizabeth, I'm sure it's fine. But if you want, I can call Nicholas, and we can hire a different company. One that has men that *actually look* like movers, if you wish."

"Ugh... it's fine, Gram. It's been a weird day and then to have bodyguards sent to move me..." Elizabeth trailed off.

"Sweetheart, he sees you as family; you know he just wants what's best for you."

"If you say so," Elizabeth said under her breath.

"What was that, dear?"

Um... nothing, Gram. I better go. I have to let the two movers in so they can complete this job that I am sure is way below their pay grade."

"Wonderful, I will see you home for dinner. Grace is making your favorite—meatloaf with all the trimmings."

"Ok, thank you. I'll see you then. Love you." Hanging up the phone, she walked over to open the front door.

Jake and Bob, if those were even their real names, were leaning against the wall, looking at their phones. They both casually looked up at her when she opened the door.

Jake smirked. "Do we check out?"

"Sure." She moved aside and let both men pass. She was surprised they fit through the door with the amount of muscles they were packing.

For possible mercenaries, they made quick work of her apartment. They didn't let her help, even though it was her stuff, which she pointed out several times. Jake only shrugged and continued doing what he was doing.

When there were only three boxes left, she decided it should be ok for her to carry a small box. This way, they wouldn't need to come back in. Jake stopped her before she could grab it.

"Seriously?" Putting her hands on her hips, she looked up and stared him down.

His lips twisted up. "Boss's orders. We can't have a future doctor hurting herself by doing manual labor, now, can we?"

She rolled her eyes at him, then relented. She was tired of everyone, and she meant everyone, assuming she was at John Hopkins to become a doctor. No one seemed to realize this school had other degree programs that were not medical related. John Hopkins had one of the best archaeological programs in the world. But she wasn't about to debate that fact with Jake, the mercenary mover.

Jake grabbed all three boxes like they were nothing, then turned to her. "If that's everything, we will wait for you in the van."

"There is no need to wait for me. I am going to do a quick walk-through to make sure we didn't forget anything. You guys can head out."

"Boss's orders, ma'am. We were told to follow you back to your grandmother's house."

"Seriously?" She rolled her eyes. "I'm twenty-three years old. I think I can find my way home without an escort."

"Even so, ma'am, orders are orders."

"Fine, I will only be a minute." She turned and walked toward the bedrooms, hoping he would get the hint and leave. A few seconds later, she heard the door shut. Elizabeth walked through each room, opening every closet and cupboard and ensuring that nothing had been left behind.

Elizabeth left her keys to the apartment on the kitchen counter, grabbed her purse, and took one last look at the place that had been her first *on her own* home. She thought she would be more emotional at this moment. After all, it was the end of a huge part of her life. Shrugging her shoulders, she shut the door and locked it for the last time.

Elizabeth walked across the parking lot toward her truck. She waved to Jake and Bob, signaling that she was ready to go. Thankfully, the feeling of someone watching her was gone.

She slid into the front seat of her old 2001 pickup truck, which had affectionately been named Alex. The truck had originally belonged to her dad, who had been obsessed with Alexander the Great, or rather The Great Library of Alexandria. So, naming his prized possession after his obsession had made sense at the time. At least, to her dad, it had.

She felt close to him whenever she was sitting in the same worn leather driver's seat he used to frequently occupy. While opening the GPS app on her phone, she noticed a missed text.

*Nicholas:*

*Liz, call me when you get home. I have a summer job opportunity if you're interested.*

This was probably her grandmother's doing. She hadn't spoken to Nicholas Black in years. Not since that awful day when he had a hand in ripped her heart out. Sure, he had helped with the movers just now. But that didn't obligate her to speak with him. On the other hand, she really did need a summer job. Could she work for him? Was she ready to allow him back into her life?

She didn't dwell on that day anymore. She didn't wake up feeling the loss of what could've been, what should have been, anymore. Perhaps she could at least hear him out. It wasn't like she had anything else lined up. And she did need to work, or she would go insane with nothing to occupy her mind.

Not wanting to think about it anymore, she popped in the Firehouse CD and cranked up the volume to "I live my life for you." This was the song that she and her dad would rock out to while driving. She needed to be close to him today.

Glancing in her rearview mirror, she noticed the Black Industry van right behind her. "Alrighty, then, time to go home," she said to herself as she patted the steering wheel.

# TWO

The next morning, Elizabeth stared out the window of her childhood bedroom, which overlooked one of the many gardens of Greystone Manor. It had been late when she arrived home. The mercenary movers had helped with her few boxes before they took her larger items to a storage unit.

Her grandmother, Lady Lorraine, had been there to meet her. Due to her exhaustion from the long drive and the weirdness of the day, Elizabeth had been unable to fully enjoy the company of her only family, her grandmother Lady Lorraine. Retreating to the sanctuary of her room, shortly after dinner, she'd assured her grandmother they would catch up the next day.

So, here she was, unpacking her suitcase, filling up the drawers of the wooden dresser she'd had since childhood, unpacking her toiletries in her still extremely pink, very girly bathroom, and hanging up clothes in her walk-in closet. She tried to avoid the black dress bag in the back, which held the prom dress she'd never gotten to wear.

This was home—her room, just as she had left it. But it was also a place she had avoided for the past several years. She couldn't be here without thinking of her father and how things had been before his sudden disappearance years earlier.

Christopher Madison had always said he wanted his daughter to follow in his and her grandmother's footsteps. They were both world-renowned archeologists. Lady Lorraine was the foremost authority on all things King Arthur. She was the archeologist who had discovered the site of King Arthur's Camelot, proving the legend was true.

It had always been her father's dream to travel the globe with Elizabeth in search of adventures and lost treasures. She wasn't sure if it had ever really been her dream or a way to keep her father's memory alive. Now that school was completed, she needed to make some decisions regarding her future.

As she looked out over the garden, Elizabeth found herself fixated on a large shadow in the distance. It hadn't moved in the few minutes she had been looking out the window, but she couldn't figure out what was causing the shadow. A cold chill crept up her spine, and that uneasy feeling returned. Elizabeth shook her head. Surely it was due to being home after all this time, which had caused her nerves to be a little unsettled. Nothing to worry about. She needed to get ready, and she desperately needed coffee.

After getting dressed, Elizabeth stopped to check her reflection in her mirror. She smiled as she remembered the gangly teen who used to look back at her. Gone were the braces, bean pole body, and eyes that were too big for her face. Now she saw a young woman with a curvy figure, straight teeth, and perfectly proportioned, emerald-green eyes. Her long, wavy brown hair had been pulled up into a messy bun, and she'd applied some light makeup. Feeling pleased with her appearance, she exited her bedroom, which was on the second floor of the grand manor house. She walked down the long hallway with huge windows on one side, which allowed the sunlight to flow in, lighting the hallway. She came to the top of the grand staircase, which led to the lower level, and she could smell the alluring scent of freshly brewed coffee.

Even though her method of choice growing up had been to slide down the large wooden banister, especially after it had been polished, Elizabeth walked down the staircase. A flood of memories came back to her—sliding down the banister and giggling the entire way down, her father being at the bottom, beaming from ear to ear, and Lady Lorraine reminding her that ladies didn't slide down banisters. A lifetime of memories filled this house.

Elizabeth followed the smell of coffee into the kitchen where she grabbed a mug from the cabinet above the coffeepot and filled it with the hot liquid. She poured in a splash of French vanilla creamer, and then slowly raised the mug to her nose, sniffing the wonderful aroma before taking a sip.

*Ah, now this is the stuff. The elixir of the Gods. No one can make a cup of coffee like Grace,* Elizabeth thought to herself. Grace had a secret ingredient that she refused to tell Elizabeth. She'd once said it was her way of making sure Elizabeth would come home, and she was right. This coffee was one thing that she looked forward to whenever at Greystone.

After a few more sips of the glorious coffee, she looked around and realized she was alone. No sign of Grace or Lady Lorraine. Elizabeth walked over to a round, white table that sat in the kitchen corner, looking out onto the gardens through a large, floor-to-ceiling window. There, she found a note in familiar handwriting next to a small package. No one wrote like Lady Lorraine; she had such a beautiful, almost otherworldly script.

*My Dearest Elizabeth,*

*I apologize for not being with you this morning. I have an early meeting and did not wish to wake you. Grace had to go out of town because of a family emergency. She wished for me to relay that the coffee is fresh, and she has pumpkin scones in the warming oven waiting for you, so enjoy. I hope to be home so we can have a proper tea together. I want to hear all about your meeting with Nicholas.*

*All my love and more,*

*Lady Lorraine*

*P.S. Grace found this package on the front stoop addressed to you.*

Elizabeth smiled as she read the letter from her grandmother. She then picked up the package. It was a small box wrapped in brown paper. It had no return address and no postal markings to indicate where it had come from. *Weird*, Elizabeth thought to herself. She hadn't been expecting anything.

She opened the package to find a black velvet jewelry box with a crest featuring two golden dragons back-to-back.

"Now, where have I seen this crest before?" Elizabeth asked out loud, running her fingers across the top of the box. Once opened, she found a silver chain with a funny-shaped silver cross inside. The proportions didn't fit a typical religious cross. The top portion felt shorter, not as long across as typically seen, while the elongated portion felt a bit too long. It was stunning. The detailed work on something so small was incredible. The top portion of the cross had a very fine strand of silver wound around in a Celtic knot type of design. Looking at it from various angles, one could mistake it for a sword. But that was a silly thought. Who would wear a sword necklace? Okay, maybe a goth chick, but she most definitely was not one of those.

There was no note or card to indicate who might have sent it. Elizabeth touched the cross and felt a shock of electricity shoot up her arm and through her entire body. "What the hell?" she yelled as the box fell to the floor. The shock didn't exactly hurt her, but it wasn't pleasant either. Elizabeth took a minute to get her bearings. *That was some strong static electricity,* she thought as she bent down to retrieve the box and noticed some words written on the bottom.

"The light will overshadow the dark," Elizabeth read out loud. "What does that mean? And seriously, who puts a message on the bottom of a box?"

Elizabeth then realized where she had seen the crest of the two dragons before. It was spattered all over her grandmother's office. The family crest of the legendary Pendragons.

She checked the packaging again to make sure it was her name; it had been addressed to her and not Lady Lorraine. Strange that someone would send her anything with the Pendragon crest. After all, it was Lady Lorraine who had built her entire career on King Arthur and the Pendragons.

Deciding not to think too much about the strange message or the family crest until she could speak with her grandmother, she examined the necklace again. Despite the necklace not being her normal taste, she felt drawn to the simple piece of jewelry. Like it was speaking to her soul and begging her to put it on. She tentatively touched the funny-shaped cross, preparing for another jolting shock, but thankfully, it didn't happen a second time. She fastened the silver chain around her neck, and something seemed to click inside her. It felt right, like it had always meant to be hers.

Movement from out in the garden caught her eye. *Was that a large shadow?* Slowly, Elizabeth moved towards the window to peer outside. However, when she looked out, there was nothing there. Again, a chill went up her back, and she rubbed her arms to rid herself of the goosebumps which had appeared. Elizabeth wasn't the type to scare easily, but something continued to feel off. She couldn't seem to shake the uneasiness.

Her nose was assaulted with the overwhelming smell of wet dogs and burnt toast. Not a pleasant combination. When did Lady Lorraine get a dog, and where was it? As quickly as the scent had appeared, it disappeared. "Ok, that was weird," she said out loud as she looked around, trying to see what could have caused the strange smell.

The doorbell rang, startling Elizabeth and causing her to jump. Uncle Nicky was sending a car and driver to take her into the office that morning. Which, of course, she had forgotten about.

They had talked briefly via text last night to make the arrangements. This had been due to her grandmother's insistence that it was time to move on from her 'childish grudge,' as she'd put it.

Not wanting to think too much about the morning's weird events, Elizabeth quickly grabbed a cream-colored jacket and her light brown purse from the hall closet and ran to the door as the doorbell rang again.

Opening the door, she found a young woman, not much older than herself, standing there in a black pantsuit and dark sunglasses. She had her strange-colored hair pulled back in a ponytail without a single hair out of place. One side was jet black and the other pure white with a perfect part down the middle.

She was tall and slender. The thin line of her lips displayed her lack of enthusiasm about waiting. After a long moment of silence, the young woman spoke. "Are you Elizabeth Madison?" she asked sharply, like she was already not a fan of Elizabeth even though they had never met.

Elizabeth responded, "Yes, that's me, and you are?"

The other woman ignored Elizabeth's question, but responded by saying, "Well then, let's go. Mr. Black is waiting for you back at HQ."

"Yeah, I'm going to need some kind of ID before I jump into a vehicle with you." Elizabeth didn't mean to be rude, but she had been having that uneasy feeling for over a day now. She wasn't about to take any chances. Being kidnapped was not on her bucket list.

The woman flashed a Black Industries badge with her picture on it. Elizabeth didn't quite catch her name because the print was small. She was, however, familiar with the Black Industries badges, and she felt confident that Uncle Nicky had sent this car to pick her up.

Elizabeth nodded and followed the other woman to a black SUV sitting in the driveway. It had dark-tinted windows and was intimidating to look at. This was a vehicle that, if the Men in Black were real, was what they would drive around in, she was sure of it.

The other woman opened the back door and then looked from Elizabeth to the now-open door, silently instructing her to get in. Once Elizabeth was in the vehicle, the other woman let out a small huff before shutting the door and walking around the other side. She then slid into the front driver's seat and Elizabeth was sure she heard her say something under her breath about not being a freaking babysitter.

The drive was painfully silent. Elizabeth was relieved when the SUV pulled in front of a large gray brick building with a sign that said Black Industries. At least she had been brought to the right place and not left in a ditch on the side of the road somewhere, or worse.

The other woman opened the door before she had a chance. Boy, she was fast. Elizabeth hadn't even seen her move around the car before the door was opened. Gearing herself up for more negative vibes from this strange woman, she stepped out of the SUV. The woman stepped to the side, revealing a familiar face now standing in front of her.

Nicholas Black was a tall man, well over 6 feet. He had a full head of sleek black hair, which was always kept short, and beautiful dark brown eyes. His olive skin was a little paler than she remembered. Probably from spending too much time indoors.

She wasn't sure how she was going to feel seeing him again

after all these years. He had been instrumental in one of the biggest heartbreaks of her young life. One that had repercussions, she was still dealing with to this day.

He wasn't her real uncle, however, she'd grown up calling him uncle. She'd known him for as long as she could remember. He was her grandmother's oldest friend. He had always seemed to be there whenever Lady Lorraine had needed him, no questions asked. This had also included moving with his orphaned nephew Shane to the States from England to help after Elizabeth's father had gone missing. He had always been there, an intricate part of her childhood.

He had been there for her crazy teenage years when she and Shane had developed a connection, becoming best friends, and doing everything together. It shouldn't have been that big of a surprise when Elizabeth and Shane had fallen hard for each other, but apparently, it had been. Even more surprising was when Nicholas had forbidden them from being together.

Uncle Nicky had even taken the extreme step of sending Shane away to a military boarding school right before junior prom. Elizabeth had never been the same since. Shane had been the first bright spot in her life since her dad, and his leaving had been devastating.

Elizabeth didn't think she would ever get over it or forgive Nicholas for the pain he had helped cause her. Thankfully, life did move on, and old wounds might not heal, but they at least got a protective scab. When Uncle Nicky had reached out regarding a summer job offer, she had decided, with some coaxing from her grandmother, that it was time to accept the olive branch. She had avoided him long enough; it was time to grow up and move past old hurts. After all, he wasn't completely at fault. There was another who had helped the pain linger, even after all these years.

"Elizabeth, my dear child, I am so happy you are here; I hope the ride was pleasant for you," he said with a smile. He then turned his head slightly and looked at the other woman, who was still standing behind Elizabeth. "Luna, that will be all, thank you. I can take care of Miss Madison from here," he said to the unpleasant woman as he put Elizabeth's arm through his and led her to the front doors.

Nicholas led her to an elevator where he hit the button for the 8th floor. She hadn't realized from the outside that the building was that tall.

"Thank you for your kind offer, and of course, for helping with my move home."

"Of course, anything for you. I hope you know that I only have ever had your best interest at heart. Your future is very important," he said, patting her arm.

She nodded. She knew he wasn't talking about sending her

the mercenary movers. He was talking about the past— a past she didn't want to think about right now. Instead, she changed direction and asked about his business.

She listened to him as he told her about the company. She already knew that Black Industries was at the top of their field in medical technology, having developed the formula for the first synthetic blood which was now used worldwide for blood transfusions, which had also eliminated the need for human blood donors. But she listened anyway as he filled her in.

Exiting the elevator, she followed him as he led her toward the larger office in the corner. As they walked, she noticed there were pictures of various people lining the walls, depicting staff members from here and other countries. But one, in particular, caught her eye, causing her to come to a halt.

It was a picture of a young man wearing a suit and tie, looking very professional. His hair was a little darker, more golden than the last time she had seen him. His eyes, however, were the same ocean blue, which she remembered clearly, and which appeared to be staring back at her from the elaborate frame on the wall. He looked tall and commanding, like a leader. Which, she guessed, was a good thing, since the title under the picture said Shane Black, London CEO. She felt the blush on her cheeks as she looked at the picture. Why, after all these years, did this man still have such an effect on her?

Elizabeth was lost in her thoughts for a moment until she heard Nicholas speak. "He's grown into a fine young man. He has helped our London profits double since he took over as CEO earlier this year. I couldn't be prouder of him. Unfortunately, London keeps him busy, so he never gets to travel home. I must go there if I want to see him."

Elizabeth nodded, knowing exactly what he was trying to convey between the lines. She didn't know if she felt upset that Shane was far away or relieved to know that their paths would probably never cross again, even with them both working for the same company.

Never knowing her mother, losing her father, and then Shane being sent away had caused her to be detached. She never allowed herself to get close to anyone.

She used Shane's memory and their brief time together as an excuse to avoid any man who showed any interest in her. Plenty had wanted to date her, but none had enticed her, none had produced a spark. Maybe she was being silly. Electricity and sparks between two people only happened in the books she read. She hadn't even had that with Shane, yet they did have something, a connection, or at least she had thought they had. Maybe not the passion she now craved, but she had loved him, and she'd thought he loved her.

Hadn't he promised her forever? Then he'd left and never

once had tried to contact her again, even after he turned eighteen. She had been holding onto a promise made by teenagers. A promise he had failed to keep. She decided that it was a good thing he was an ocean away.

# THREE

The meeting with Nicholas went by quickly, going over the basics of what she would be doing while she filled out a mountain of paperwork. He showed her to the cubicle, which would be hers.

Funny enough, they both knew she was way overqualified for the entry-level office position he was offering her. However, it was a temporary summer job and nothing more. Elizabeth needed time to get her bearings and figure out her life plan. He seemed to understand that. She had been on autopilot for what seemed like forever, and she didn't want to live that way anymore. It was time that she took control of her life and figured out what she wanted to do with the rest of it.

The position offered little to no challenge, and it involved answering phones and office-type duties. It was all something that would require minimal effort on Elizabeth's part. The money wasn't that great, but honestly, she didn't need it. She had been left a nice-sized trust fund by her father, and her grandmother had always taken care of Elizabeth, providing her with whatever she needed. Right now, she needed some direction and maybe a little divine intervention.

Once Elizabeth was ready to leave the office, Nicholas offered to have his driver take her home. She declined. The town center was only a few blocks away, so no need to waste gas. Also, she did not want to deal with the unpleasant Luna again. She offered a smile as she assured him that she wanted to walk around town and maybe visit the bookstore.

He was silent for a minute, looking as if he were deep in thought. He finally spoke. "Be careful, Lizzy," he said, using her childhood nickname. "Things aren't as," he paused for a second, "safe as they used to be. Be cautious of your surroundings, and

I—" another pause. "Trust your gut. If something feels wrong, get out and try to get home before dark. Nothing good happens in this town when the sun goes down."

Elizabeth wasn't sure how to take his warning. "I will," she said with a smile. "Don't worry, I'm not a naïve schoolgirl anymore. I know not to talk to strangers offering candy or puppies." She offered him a wink as she walked over to him, giving him a light peck on his cheek.

He gently grabbed her hand, stopping her from backing away from him. "You were born to shine, Elizabeth, in more ways than you can imagine. Your gift of knowing things will serve you well. Use that and trust in your intuition to guide you, and you will be fine."

"Um... Okay... Thank you."

"I know. I sound like a cryptic old man." He laughed as he walked her to the door. "Go, enjoy your day. We will talk more in the morning."

Elizabeth was still deep in thought a few minutes later when the elevator door opened into the lobby. She hadn't heard of any trouble in town. Surely, Lady Lorraine would have mentioned it. And what was that about trusting her intuition? She was sure he had wanted to say more before he laughed it off.

She pushed the thoughts from her mind, choosing not to worry about it now. Elizabeth would talk to Lady Lorraine about it later.

The small town of Madison was exactly the same as she remembered it. A feeling of nostalgia soon took over, easing any unsettled feelings she still had after Uncle Nicky's warning.

Her Grandfather George had been born and raised here, and he had lived all his life in Madison until he had joined the Marines. They had shipped him off to London as a young, fresh-faced soldier during the war, and it was during this time that he'd met a young, aristocratic woman named Lady Lorraine. It had been love at first sight. Unfortunately, their love story had been short-lived.

Elizabeth passed the church where all the Madisons had been buried, all except for one. Several additions had been made to the red brick structure over the years, going from a small, one-room building to a grand, multi-level house of worship.

She walked through the beautifully landscaped cemetery with its artistically crafted headstones. The more ornate ones went all the way back to the 1700s. She paused as she looked up at the large pillar marked with the family crest and the name Madison carved into it.

Fresh flowers were always present at George and his parents' graves thanks to Lady Lorraine, who insisted on a fresh bouquet of lilies to be laid on the headstones weekly. She had also ensured that wild lavender and meadowsweet would be grown around the actual graves, which, according to Lady Lorraine, had been common in Arthurian times, and she felt it was fitting. Elizabeth herself had never really understood the need for fresh flowers in a place few ever visited. But Lady Lorraine always insisted, and Elizabeth had to agree that it did add a bit of cheerfulness to a normally sad, dreary place.

George's last gift to his new bride had been to pay for the fare so Lady Lorraine could travel to the USA to his family farm in Madison until he would have been able to join her after the war. Sadly, he never returned home. He never got to meet his son, Christopher, Elizabeth's father, who had been born a few months later.

Elizabeth bent down and swept a few fallen petals from the headstone of George's parents. If it hadn't been for them, Lady Lorraine would never have become the world-renowned archeologist she was now, which had clearly been her destiny.

That woman had an uncanny ability to locate lost sites of King Arthur's time, like Lyonnesse, Camelot, and the battlefield of Glastonbury. It was as if she had lived during that time because no one else had been nearly as successful as her in locating many Arthurian locations, long believed to be lost to time. Before Lady Lorraine, most people had still thought of King Arthur as merely a legend. She had proved he was a real historical figure.

Elizabeth placed her hands on the headstone she had really come to visit, even though she knew it was an empty crypt below her. The body had never been recovered. The funeral had been full of pictures and people talking fondly about her father, but with no body, it had always left her with a little hope that one day, he would find his way home, and this would all have been a horrible misunderstanding.

She wiped the tears that fell. "Hi, Dad." She sat down cross-legged, staring at his name and the words "Beloved Son and Father," engraved in shimmery white stone. "Well, I did it like we planned. I got my degree in archaeology. I'm not sure what to do now. I don't feel like that's what I'm meant to do—not without you. I feel like there's something more I should be doing; I just don't know what." Bowing her head, she whispered, "I wish you were here."

She didn't know what she was expecting. But all she got was the sound of birds chirping and bugs buzzing. How she longed to hear his laugh or his voice offering some kind of wisdom, telling her it was okay, and she would find her way.

She stayed there in silent contemplation for a while longer. Then she leaned over and kissed her father's headstone, offering a silent, "I love you," before she rose to her feet. She headed to the one place that could always cheer her up.

Her grandmother was a bit of a local legend, so, it wasn't a huge surprise to Elizabeth when she walked into the bookstore in town simply called Madison Books and saw an entire wall dedicated to Lady Lorraine. Everyone loved her here.

There weren't too many people in the bookstore at this time of day. She noticed a few teenagers at a round table with books piled high, more than likely gearing up for exams. There was a blond woman in her late twenties with two small children checking out the children's section, and then there was the lovely older woman behind the counter, staring daggers at the cover of a magazine she held in her hand.

The older woman was not too tall, with a slender frame, long, pure white hair, and bright, teal-colored eyes the likes of which Elizabeth had never seen on anyone else except this woman. She was a woman that Elizabeth knew well. Charlotte looked up, and as her gaze caught Elizabeth's, a warm smile came to the woman's face.

Charlotte quickly flipped over the magazine she had been glaring at. Stepping around the counter, she walked over to Elizabeth with the grace of a trained dancer, looking her up and down and nodding with approval. "You get more beautiful every time I see you, my sweet Lizzy girl." She opened her arms to give Elizabeth a big hug. Elizabeth wrapped her arms and squeezed the older woman tightly. She smiled even though her eyes filled with tears.

"Oh, Charlotte, I didn't realize how much I missed you and this place until now," Elizabeth said while Charlotte patted Elizabeth on the back.

Charlotte gently said, "There, there child, it's okay. I have missed you, too, but you're here now. You're home." Charlotte released Elizabeth and then took her by the hand before leading her toward a cart filled with books. "We can chat while I put these books away."

"Sure, but first, what had you trying to shoot daggers from

your eyes at this defenseless magazine?" Elizabeth chuckled as she moved around the older woman to get to the counter. She picked up the flipped-over magazine, and then her gaze shot up to find the concerned look on Charlotte's face. "Oh, I see," Elizabeth murmured. In large print, the article read, "*Playboy CEO and his latest conquest.*" Below that was a picture of Shane Black with a beautiful redhead who was looking adoringly up at him. Elizabeth tossed the magazine down.

"Lizzy, don't pay any mind to that. It's probably just gossip to sell more magazines."

"It's fine, really. It's been years since I even talked to him. I have no say in what he does or who he spends his time with."

"But still... It can't be easy to see him splattered across the cover like that."

"You said something about putting books away. Can I help?" Elizabeth asked, eager to change the subject.

"Like I would ever turn down free labor from my favorite former employee," Charlotte smiled as she handed a book from the cart to Elizabeth.

The two women worked with a finesse and familiarity of years of practice. Charlotte filled Elizabeth in on a remodel she was planning. However, Elizabeth became lost in thought, reminiscing about the first time she had entered the bookstore, merely searching for a refuge. She had been told her father wasn't coming back. The grief-stricken Elizabeth had fled Greystone Manor and ran and ran and ran until her little legs couldn't run anymore.

That was when she had found herself in front of the little bookstore, looking through the window at all the books inside. Charlotte had seen a trembling Elizabeth outside the window before she had opened the door and invited the young girl in, offering her some hot cocoa. Elizabeth had known not to talk to or accept anything from strangers, but there had been something about this woman that made her trust her. She had known in her soul that she was safe with this woman.

Charlotte had introduced herself as the owner of the bookstore, but not the books inside because the books were waiting for their true owners to come and find them.

This little bookstore became Elizabeth's haven from the outside world. She would come here after school every day and read. She allowed herself to get lost in stories about kings and queens, wizards and elves, until it was time to close, and even then, Charlotte would let Elizabeth stay while she cleaned up.

Elizabeth knew the bookstore like the back of her hand. It was a second home for her and the only place she could escape the memories and the feelings of loss.

Elizabeth had never known her real mother, so Charlotte helped fill that void a little with female compassion and advice.

It was Charlotte who had helped Elizabeth deal with so much loss in her young life. Even now, it was hard to think back on that time. It was too painful.

"I heard you might be back in town and perhaps going to work for Nicholas Black instead of pursuing a career in archeology or coming back here?" she asked, waving a book in Elizabeth's direction as she talked. As usual, nothing got past Charlotte. She always knew what was going on in this town.

Elizabeth examined the book in her own hand before turning away from Charlotte. It was titled *The Mists of Avalon*. Putting the book in its proper place, she then turned back toward Charlotte. Elizabeth filled the older woman in on what was happening in her life and confessed that working at Black Industries was temporary until she could get her bearings.

"Don't get lost in the past, my sweet Lizzy girl. You are stronger than you might know. You have a power inside you that will guide you. Listen to your inner voice, and it will never lead you astray."

The two women continued working and chatting. Then the sound of a bell on the door alerted them to someone entering the store. Two sizable men, whom Elizabeth had never seen before, entered. They were both dressed in head-to-toe black with black hoods covering their faces.

Elizabeth could feel the tension in the room as the men scanned the area and looked at everyone in the store. She noticed everyone had frozen. The woman in the children's section had put herself in front of her two small children as if to protect them. Elizabeth saw Charlotte close her eyes and say a few words under her breath before getting up and turning to her.

"Lizzy, I need you to stay here. Do not move, no matter what." Charlotte's voice had a seriousness about it. Before Elizabeth could answer, Charlotte was up and walking towards the men.

Elizabeth hid behind the bookshelf and peered out to observe as Charlotte walked over to the two men and appeared to wave her right hand in front of them and say something, but Elizabeth could not make out what was being said. The two men turned around and walked out. Charlotte quickly followed, locking the door, then switching the sign to "closed." She turned back and looked at Elizabeth, and then looked at everyone else in the store.

She announced in a loud voice so anyone in the store could hear, "I'm sorry, but the store is closing, and you all need to leave. Please get to your homes as quickly as possible and lock up. Go now!"

Once everyone was gone and only Charlotte and Elizabeth were left, Charlotte looked at Elizabeth with a worried expression. "I am sorry, but it's not safe in town, and you need to get home."

"What is going on here? Who were those men?" Elizabeth demanded.

"I am afraid evil is being unleashed into our world, and I do not have time to explain it to you right now. I am needed elsewhere tonight. Trust me, those are terrible men who you need to avoid at all costs. They did not see you, thankfully. I was able to send them away temporarily, but they will be back." Charlotte hurried behind the counter to grab a few items.

Charlotte walked back over to Elizabeth and was about to say something when the silver cross necklace around Elizabeth's neck caught her attention. "When did you get this?" she asked, her eyes as big as saucers.

"This morning. It arrived with no note. I have no idea where it came from. Do you know where it came from or who might have sent it?"

"It truly is beginning," Charlotte said out loud, but mainly to herself.

"What is truly beginning? And what do you mean evil has been unleashed?"

"Never mind that. Trust that this is no ordinary necklace. It is ancient and quite powerful. It has a way of finding the person who is meant to have it while remaining hidden from those who wish to abuse its power. It has chosen you, and it will keep you safe. I wish I could explain more, but you will find the answers in time. Always wear it, and when the time is right, it will reveal its true magic to you. Have faith."

Elizabeth touched the necklace. "I don't understand. What do you mean by magic? What is happening here?"

Charlotte didn't answer her. Instead, she began talking out loud to someone else. "I know you're here; I sensed you as soon as you entered. Can you please make sure she gets home safely?"

Before Elizabeth could ask whom she was talking about, a cloaked figure stepped out from behind a bookshelf. The figure was dressed in all black, with a hooded cape covering everything except for a small strand of raven black hair.

A small gasp escaped Elizabeth's mouth as she realized it was Luna, the unpleasant driver who had given her a ride to Black Industries that morning.

"Yes, that's why I am here. Mr. Black asked me to keep an eye on Miss Madison."

"Can someone please tell me what is happening here?" Elizabeth put her hand on her hips as she eyed both women, waiting for an answer.

It was Luna who responded. "I am going to take you home now, Miss Madison. I parked my vehicle outback. If you would please follow me?"

Elizabeth didn't move. Instead, she turned to face Charlotte, begging for answers with her expression. Charlotte put her hands on Elizabeth's shoulders and looked deep into her eyes for a long moment before she spoke. "Oh, my darling girl, we shall see each other again. Hopefully, we will have time then for answers to all your questions. At least, the ones I can answer. I have a feeling you will have more to ask when that time comes, but for now, you must trust this young woman to get you home safely." Before Elizabeth could utter another word, Charlotte hugged her quickly, then stepped back and disappeared in a puff of purple smoke.

"What the hell?" Elizabeth yelled in shock and disbelief. "She vanished!"

"Miss Madison, please," Luna said, unfazed by what they had seen. "We have to go now." Luna grabbed Elizabeth's arm and dragged her toward the back door.

"Hey, that hurts, get your strong-ass man hands off me, please!" Elizabeth protested, shocked at how strong the thinned-framed woman was.

But Luna did not stop, at least not until they came to the back door where she halted and released Elizabeth from her grip. Luna looked at Elizabeth, putting a finger to her lips, indicating for her to be quiet. Then, opening the door slowly, she peered out, scanning the area for any movement. Seemingly convinced that there was no immediate threat outside, Luna slightly pushed Elizabeth towards the black SUV. It was the same one she had ridden in that morning.

Once Elizabeth was safely inside the SUV, Luna quickly moved to the driver's seat. She then looked back at Elizabeth and said, "Buckle up. This might get a little bumpy." With that, they were off.

# FOUR

Luna was right; the ride did get a little bumpy as she weaved through side streets and back alleys at speeds higher than Elizabeth could have navigated. If she hadn't buckled up, it would have thrown her all over the backseat of the SUV. Despite the chaos, the ride had been eerily silent after Luna had advised her there was no time for chit-chat.

More than likely, she didn't want to entertain the five million questions now rolling around in Elizabeth's head. Which, of course, was causing a headache to come on. She was confused. Who were those men back at the bookshop, and how and why did Charlotte send them away? How the hell had Charlotte disappeared in a puff of purple smoke?

Maybe Elizabeth had inhaled some of that purple smoke and was now on some kind of drug-induced trip. Well, if that was what it was, then she hoped she would come down from this wacky high sooner rather than later.

Finally, Elizabeth felt relieved when she saw a familiar turn as Luna maneuvered the SUV down the long, winding driveway toward the main house. Greystone Manor came into view, and Elizabeth had never been so happy to see the grand manor house she had called home her entire life.

She had a troubled history with the elegant stone structure. It was filled with memories of the past, good and bad, but at this moment, it was her home, and God, it was good to be home.

She needed to see her grandmother, to feel her warm arms embrace her. It had been such a crazy day. She was sure Lady Lorraine would be able to shed some light on what was happening.

Luna pulled up to the front of the manor house and jumped out of the front seat, moving with cat-like grace. She rushed to open Elizabeth's door, but before Elizabeth could get out, Luna put a hand up to stop her.

"Wait, something's not right," she said as she scanned the area, tilting her head as if she was listening for something.

Suddenly, Luna shoved Elizabeth onto the floor of the SUV, yelling, "*Get Down!*" Luna then jumped into the backseat, positioning her body over Elizabeth and forcing both their faces down toward the floor.

Before Elizabeth could protest Luna's rough treatment, a bright blue light filled the air with its neon glow. Elizabeth lifted her head and stared at the light through the windows just before a loud explosion rocked the ground. Stone chunks flew everywhere while smoke and dust polluted the air.

The force of the explosion sent the SUV flying into the air. As it hit the ground, it kept rolling and rolling. The two women inside were thrown all over the place. The SUV finally came to rest, thankfully landing on all four wheels in the middle of an open field.

Luna quickly looked over at Elizabeth and scanned her. "Are you hurt?" She asked with concern.

Elizabeth, too shocked to speak, shook her head. No. She felt shaky all over, and there was a ringing in her ears. If she looked under her clothes, she was sure there would be plenty of bruises, but nothing major. They could have died. She could have died. *What the hell is happening?*

"Good, we have got to keep moving. It's not safe here out in the open like this." Luna offered Elizabeth a hand.

Both women climbed out of the SUV. Elizabeth was starting to calm down a little when she realized what the other woman had said.

"Wait! What? Leave? We can't leave!" Elizabeth shouted. "My grandmother was in that house. We can't leave her. We need to go get help," Elizabeth managed to say before the tears in her eyes rolled down her cheeks and she started to shake all over.

Luna was silent for a moment, looking as if she was gathering her thoughts. When she spoke, what she said didn't surprise Elizabeth; she was trying not to think the same thing, trying not to let her mind go there. But when Luna spoke, it was with a softness and concern that surprised Elizabeth. "Elizabeth, there is nothing left. I'm sorry, but no one could have survived that blast." Luna gently grabbed her hands. "We barely survived. If it hadn't been for the shielding technology in this SUV, we would have been blown to bits as well."

"But, what if—"

"Look, we don't know for sure if anyone was even in the house. Let's not start jumping to conclusions before we have all the facts. We, on the other hand, are not safe. We need to get moving."

Elizabeth knew Luna was right. They weren't safe standing here out in the open. But she couldn't stop shaking. She wrapped her arms around her waist as she watched Luna taking in the surrounding field. She appeared to be sniffing the air and touching the ground. Elizabeth was not sure how to react to what Luna was doing. She had never seen a person sniffing the air before. It was weird.

"Is there somewhere close we can get to? A place to lie low while I gather my bearings?" Luna asked.

Elizabeth thought for a moment, trying to figure out where she was. "Yes," she finally said. "My family has an old homestead farm over that way. It's been abandoned for decades. Most people don't even know it exists anymore. Plus, it has an old bomb shelter under the main house."

Luna looked over at Elizabeth, nodded, and said, "That will do. Let's get moving before whoever attacked your house realizes we survived the blast and comes looking for us."

Elizabeth looked at the SUV. "What are the chances of this thing still running?"

Luna shook her head. "Doubtful. Plus, it would be too noisy. I have a localized transporter we can use. It's limited to how far we can travel, but it should get us to your farmhouse with no trouble."

"A what?" Elizabeth asked, unsure what a localized transporter was.

"It's technology that can get us from point A to point B quickly." Luna pointed to her wrist at a device that looked like a large smart watch, but with extra buttons. Elizabeth nodded, and Luna started messing with the buttons on the device. "That is, if it's not too damaged from our SUV ride in the sky. If not, I guess we'll make our way over there on foot," she said with an awkward smile.

Luna jerked back and peered into the woods off in the distance. Elizabeth followed her gaze and saw something move in the distance. Before either of them could react, they heard a whistling sound just as an arrow hit Luna in the shoulder.

"Shit," Luna hissed as purple liquid flowed out of the wound.

"What the—"

"Get down!" Luna yelled.

Elizabeth did as ordered. Luna broke off the shaft of the arrow but left most of it in the wound to stop what Elizabeth assumed was her purple blood from escaping. But who or what had purple blood? Yeah, she was going to have to stick a pin in that thought for later when they weren't in immediate danger, and she could have a proper freakout.

They were both crouched down behind the SUV when they

heard loud, heavy footsteps coming their way. Elizabeth looked at Luna, praying she had a plan, but Luna's normally expressionless face looked as lost as Elizabeth felt. Frantically, she continued to try to get the device on her wrist to work, punching the buttons more feverishly.

Elizabeth smelled the distinct odor of a wet dog and burned toast. Her internal alarm bells were ringing off the hook. Elizabeth gasped as two monstrous creatures entered her line of sight. Both were over 7 feet tall and bulky, with large heads. Green skin and dark hair covered their bodies. Long, dangling arms hung below their knees. Their grossly exaggerated eyes zeroed in on them. One was carrying a bow with arrows strapped in a quiver to his back.

"Well, well, well, what do we have here?" the larger of the two beasts said.

"It looks like dinner to me," said the other one.

Looking around, Elizabeth could see red, glowing eyes appear out of the darkness. They were surrounded. Terrified, she looked over at Luna, whose bright blue eyes were staring at the creatures. Her expression was not of fear, but defiance. She would not give these things, whatever they were, the satisfaction of seeing her afraid.

Unfortunately, Elizabeth did not have the same luxury. She was scared shitless, and they could probably smell the fear radiating off of her.

The larger of the two sniffed the surrounding air. "We got ourselves a pretty little kitty cat," he said, sniffing Luna. "I haven't had me some kitty chops in a long, long time."

Luna spit in his face. "I hope you choke to death on these kitty chops, you disgusting troll!" The revulsion in her voice was clear. "Don't you have a bridge you should be guarding?"

*Um... troll... Is she serious? A freaking troll.*

This made the larger troll laugh out loud, and his grin widened, showing off his yellowed teeth. Walking over to Elizabeth, he sniffed the air next to her. Looking down at her in confusion, he then sniffed a little harder.

He got in Elizabeth's face. "Why can't I smell you, human?" he screeched her face. She turned her head away from him, almost passing out from the stench on his breath. It was foul.

Elizabeth whimpered, "Sorry, I showered today." Luna tried to hide a little chuckle that escaped her lips.

The larger troll growled, "It won't matter. I'm sure you will taste delicious, regardless. We aren't picky, are we boys?"

Laughter and howling erupted from all around them. The red glowing eyes moved; large black dogs creeped into view alongside the trolls. Terror filled Elizabeth as she realized what these creatures were. She had studied them in her ancient mythology class. They were freaking hellhounds. Guardians of the gates of Hell.

This was it; she had never really thought about how she was going to die, but being dinner for a group of mythological beings would never have even made the list. She stared at the scary-ass creatures surrounding her. The troll's long, sharp teeth peeked out as he ran his long, black tongue over them, saliva dripping down his chin. His dry, cracked lips stretched into a gross smile.

Elizabeth shuddered as her fear morphed into a very different emotion. She was pissed. Instead of fear, anger coursed through her veins. Anger at these monsters for destroying her home and for wanting to eat her. Anger at herself for being weak and not knowing how to get the hell out of this situation because she was not ready to die. Not now, not today, and most definitely not as something's dinner.

Suddenly, a warming sensation rose from deep inside her, moving along both her arms and into her hands. It was like nothing she had ever felt; it was comforting and protective in a strange way. She looked at the trolls as they now backed away from her. She heard Luna gasp, and as she looked over at Luna, there was the most beautiful blue-green light that had appeared before them.

The hellhounds howled as they followed their masters' lead. Elizabeth looked down at her hands, shocked to see them glowing the same blue-green color. That light was coming from her, but how? A jet of blue-green fire shot from her hands and blasted the trolls and hounds into the sky. "What the hell?"

She stood up, and another blast shot from her hands toward the glowing red eyes in the distance. She heard whimpers, and then the glowing red eyes disappeared. Elizabeth looked down at her hands in disbelief. Had she really done that? She looked over at Luna, but before she could say anything, Elizabeth felt completely drained of all energy. Everything around her went black.

A sharp pain was all she felt as she began to come to. It felt like a marching band had taken up permanent residence in her head. Despite feeling woozy, she sat up slowly. *What happened?* She rubbed her temples, hoping to relieve some of the pain. Taking in her surroundings, she realized she was lying on a small cot in a room that smelled old and musty.

The only light came from a single candle sitting on a table in the middle of the small dust-covered room. Once her eyes had adjusted to the limited light, she was able to see shelves of canned goods and boxes of supplies. Realization dawned on her. It was her family's old farmhouse, or rather, the bomb shelter underneath the farmhouse. *How did I get here?*

Her head hurt badly, and she couldn't think. A creak from across the room diverted her attention, and there was movement as Luna sat up into the candlelight.

There was an old military first aid kit sitting next to her. She was wrapping bandages over her wounded shoulder. Elizabeth could see specks of her dried purple blood on her fingers and all over the cot.

Remembering the arrow, she looked at Luna with concern. "Are you ok?"

Luna nodded. "I'll survive." She stood up and walked over to Elizabeth slowly, handing her a bottle of water and some pills. "These will hopefully help with your headache. They're old but should still be somewhat effective." She sat back down on the cot she had previously occupied.

"Thank you." Elizabeth swallowed the pills and drank some of the water. She looked at Luna, who was staring at her.

"Um, how did we get here? Why is your blood purple? Oh my God, there were trolls and hellhounds!" Elizabeth shot up, then quickly sat back down as her head started to spin.

Luna raised an eyebrow. "Relax, before you pass out."

"Relax? Seriously, relax? That's what you have to say?" Elizabeth huffed. "We... you and me—" Elizabeth motioned with her hands frantically between the two. "—were almost eaten by storybook villains, and you're telling me to relax?

"Yes," Luna replied, "and remember to breathe."

"Fine." Elizabeth took a deep, cleansing breath. "Holy shit... then there was that beautiful blue-green light. Oh, crap!" Elizabeth ran her hands through her hair. "Oh, shit! That... that light came from me! I blasted those freaking monsters in the air. How did I do that?"

"You tell me."

"Tell you what?"

"How did you do it?"

"I don't know. All of this, I have no clue." Taking a deep breath to calm her racing heart, Elizabeth ran her hand through her tangled hair. "Trolls and hellhounds are real?"

"Yeah, trolls and hellhounds are real, and not a good sign." Luna rubbed her shoulder and grunted. "Look, I understand that this is all a shock to you. We keep the existence of the supernatural world hidden from humans for a reason which I will not get into now, but what you need to know is that neither the trolls nor their hellhounds would have been here on their own accord. They aren't that smart. They do the bidding of a more sinister monster— usually vampires or a high-level demon."

All the color drained from Elizabeth's face, and she felt a shiver as she digested this information. Realization hit her, and she looked up at Luna. "Those men in the bookstore, they were vampires or demons, weren't they?"

Luna nodded. "The question is, why would they send trolls to your house? They had to be looking for something or someone," Luna said, looking straight at Elizabeth. "And that brings us back to my first question. How in all the realms did you, a human, manage to call upon dragon fire? You saved my life, so of course I'm not complaining, but the most powerful mystics have yet to figure out how to call upon that power. Only dragons, as far as I know, can wield dragon fire, and you do not look like a dragon shifter to me. So, what are you?"

Elizabeth had no clue how to answer her. "Dragon fire, that's what it's called? I have no idea where it came from." Elizabeth stared intently at her water bottle, pulling at the wrapper. "I was scared, and then I became so angry. I didn't want to die. Not like that, not as something's freaking dinner. As far as I'm aware, I am as human as the next person. Well, maybe not as human as you. You have purple blood, so what does that make you?"

Luna rubbed her temples and looked at Elizabeth. "I am a feline shifter. Now, back to you. Your eyes glowed the same blue-green as the dragon fire before it shot from your hands. I know it came from you. I guess the question is, how?"

There was a long pause. "I don't know," Elizabeth finally answered and shrugged. "I have never even heard of dragon fire, or what did you say you are, a feline shifter, until now?"

Not wanting to think about it anymore, she stood and paced the floor. "But more concerning is, what do we do now? How long have we been here, and how did we get here? Are those trolls still looking for us? How are we going to get out of here, and where are we going to go?" Elizabeth, feeling completely overwhelmed, put her head in her hands.

"Ok, take another deep breath." Luna put her hands up. "One question at a time, please."

Elizabeth looked up from her hands.

"After you blasted those disgusting trolls away with the dragon fire from nowhere," Luna looked at Elizabeth with one eyebrow raised as if contemplating if she believed her or not, "you passed out. I checked to make sure you were breathing, of course, then I sent out a distress signal from the SUV with instructions on where to find us. I was finally able to get my transporter working and brought us here. Now, we wait for backup to come get us."

Luna leaned back against the wall behind her cot.

"As far as the trolls, I doubt they will be back here anytime soon. It's their master we should be worried about. The stupid trolls will report what happened here, and I'm afraid you may have painted a large target on your back."

"Why is that?"

Dragon fire is an ancient, powerful magic that many will want to get their hands on. For your safety, the fewer people who know what you can do, the better. We will need to let the commander know and let him decide how we proceed.

"Hopefully, he can help you," Luna said.

# FIVE

Elizabeth wanted to ask more, like who was this commander person? There were many thoughts swirling through her head. Before she could start her next round of questions, a bright light flashed, and then two men in black uniforms appeared out of nowhere. A tall man with dark hair and crystal blue eyes flashed a bright smile toward Elizabeth, causing two deep dimples to appear on his cheeks. Another man, a little shorter with black hair, walked toward Luna. “The commander sent us to retrieve you. Are you okay?”

“We’re fine,” Luna said. “I have a scratch that needs tending to thanks to a stupid troll’s arrow.”

“A troll? This close to town?” Dimples replied.

“Yes, with hellhounds in tow, but never mind that now. Let’s get out of this place.” She motioned to Elizabeth and pointed to Dimples. “You will need to hold on to Chad here.” Luna rolled her eyes when she mentioned his name. “He will get you back to HQ.”

Elizabeth nodded to Chad —although he did not look like a Chad—as he pulled her close to his side. He winked, flashing his bright smile again. “Hang on tight. The first time is always the worst.”

Before Elizabeth could ask what he meant by that, the bright light flashed again. Elizabeth closed her eyes and held on to Chad with a death grip. She felt like she was flying, yet her feet never left solid ground. Her stomach was doing somersaults, as if she was in a car hill hopping. She did not dare open her eyes for fear of vomiting all over poor Chad. The sensation only lasted a minute, but it was a long minute.

Once the flying sensation had stopped, Elizabeth felt Chad lower his hand from her waist. Slowly opening her eyes, she released her death grip from him. Elizabeth still felt disoriented as Chad helped her over to a chair, and she sat down heavily. Walking over to a small, clear faced refrigerator, Chad pulled out a bottle of water and handed it to her.

"Thank you." She downed the water.

Looking around, she found herself in a conference room. She was seated at the head of a generic-looking wooden table with six black leather chairs positioned around it. Behind her was a white marbled counter, white cabinet, and the mini fridge.

"Um... where are we?"

"Black Industries," Chad said as he took the seat next to her.

"As in, the company owned by Nicholas Black?"

Chad shrugged.

"Where is Luna?"

"She is probably with the commander."

"Why would your commander be here at Black Industries, a medical supply company?"

"I'm sure someone will brief you on everything you need to know. Until then, just know that you are safe."

"Ok, now what?"

"Now, we wait."

"Wait for what?"

"Wait for orders from the commander." He shrugged, as if it was obvious.

"Wait... what? I'm supposed to sit here and wait for some mysterious commander to decide what comes next? I don't think so." Elizabeth stood and walked to the door. Chad watched her with an annoying smirk on his face. She reached for the doorknob, and of course, the damn thing was locked.

"You need to let me out of here."

"Look, I'm sorry, I can't," he said, rising from his seat. "Please don't hurt yourself by banging on the door or anything. It's soundproof. No one will hear you."

"Of course it is." She let her forehead thud against the door.

"Look, I know, it's not ideal, and for that, I'm sorry. As soon as I can let you out of here, I will. It's my job to keep you safe."

"Your idea of keeping me safe is locking me in a small room with only my thoughts and you to distract me?"

He shrugged, then walked over to the marble counter, opened a drawer, and pulled out a handful of magazines before tossing them on the table. "You can read one of these. It might help pass the time."

"I was almost eaten by creatures from a Grimm's fairytale, I have no idea where my grandmother is, and you're asking me to sit down, be quiet, and read a freaking gossip magazine."

"Yes, ma'am," he replied, flashing his damn dimples again as he smirked at her. Crossing his arms over his chest, leaning back in his chair, he propped his black combat boots on the table and then closed his eyes. "Or you could take a nap."

She returned to her seat. "Look, I know you are only doing your job, but I can't stay here. I need answers. I am either losing my freaking mind or I experience something that I can't even put into words." She laid her head on the table, covering it with her arms.

"You will have answers soon, I'm sure of it. You need to be a little patient," he replied without opening his eyes.

"Patience has never been one of my virtues."

"You don't say," he smirked.

"Fine," she huffed. She turned her attention to the pile of magazines sitting on the table in front of her, flipping through the pile and reading the covers as she went. She learned that Hollywood's latest "it" couple had broken up, a new superhero movie had been recently released—and flopped—the country was in a recession, and apparently, they were calling for a shit ton of snow in the Midwest.

Sometime later, she huffed out a long, exaggerated sigh.

"Everything alright?" Chad asked as he opened one eye.

"No, Chad, everything is not alright." She glared at him, flopping back in the chair and crossing her arms around her waist. "How could it be? This has been one of the worst days of my life."

"Would you like to talk about it? Sometimes it helps."

"Why, so you can think I'm as crazy as I think I am?"

"Trust me, I won't think you're crazy."

"Famous last words, Chad. Remember, you asked for it."

He nodded for her to continue.

"Fine." She took a deep breath before she spoke. "Just today, I saw my home explode in front of me. Mythological monsters attacked me. Who, by the way, wanted to eat me. I then saw someone bleed purple blood. Purple, Chad. That's not normal. Then, blue-green fire shot from my hands, and as if that's not enough, I'm now stuck in a tiny room with only you and my crazy thoughts."

Chad nodded. "Feel better?"

"A little, thank you. But now I'm starving. I would sell you on eBay for a humongous cheeseburger and small fry right about now."

Chad started laughing. "Why a big burger and a *small* fry?"

"Isn't it obvious? I don't want to look like a pig. Did you miss the part where the burger was ginormous?"

"Small fry. You are something else, let me tell you, and crazy isn't one of them."

Elizabeth was about to respond but stopped when the door opened, and in walked Luna with a tray of food. "I figured you might be hungry after the evening you had."

"Luna, you're a freaking goddess! I could hug you."

"I prefer you didn't," Luna said dryly.

Elizabeth laughed, "It's okay. I figured you weren't the hugging type."

"I'm not."

"Anyway, thank you. Your timing is perfect. I'm starving." She tilted her head toward Luna's injured shoulder. "You haven't had that looked at, yet?"

Luna brushed it off. "I've had worse; besides, I needed to speak with the commander. And then I wanted to make sure you got some food in your system. Magic takes a lot of energy, and you conjured a lot of magic. So, eat. Then the commander will want to see you."

"Is my uncle Nicky here? I mean, Mr. Black?"

Luna glanced at Chad with an odd expression before she answered. "Yes, you will see him soon. But for now, please stay here and eat. Chad will stay with you, and if there is anything you need, let him know." Chad nodded.

"Where are you going?" Elizabeth asked.

"To the infirmary, but don't worry; you're in good hands." She glanced at Chad before she walked out the door, shutting it behind her.

Elizabeth looked down at the tray Luna had brought her. There was enough food to feed a small village. Sadly, no burger or fries, but there was a plate with some kind of casserole that smelled divine, mashed potatoes with gravy, green beans, mac and cheese, a bowl of salad, a ham and cheese sandwich, a bowl of soup, and crusty bread, as well as chocolate cake and a piece of apple pie.

"Well, I hope you're hungry, because there is no way I am eating all this."

Chad smiled and grabbed the apple pie, not waiting for her before he dug in.

# SIX

Elizabeth was deep in thought, enjoying the last of her chocolate cake, when she heard Chad say, "Yes, sir," out of nowhere. She looked around, but there was no one else there but them. She looked over at Chad in confusion. He then said, "Right away, sir. I'll bring her right now." Looking at Elizabeth, he said, "The commander is ready for you, Ms. Madison."

"Please, call me Elizabeth or Lizzy. Were you talking to the commander just now?" She looked at the closed door.

"Yes," he said with a grin that showed off his dimples.

"How?" she asked, confused.

"There is a communicator that is embedded in my ear. We all have them here. You can't see it with the naked eye, but it's there. It offers two-way communication without getting in the way or interfering with other devices. It's modern tech for the military."

"Oh, ok," she said.

Chad opened the door, gesturing for her to follow. "Shall we?"

She followed him while thinking it odd that Uncle Nicky had not come to find her yet. She wondered if they had informed him about the explosion at Greystone and if he knew about her grandmother.

Elizabeth was so lost in thought, she didn't even realize when they walked into the elevator or when it stopped. They got off on a familiar floor, and she absent-mindedly followed Chad till they were standing in front of an open office door.

"Commander," Chad said and then did a slight salute before escorting Elizabeth to a chair in the office. She was shocked to see whom Chad had addressed as commander.

The commander spoke. "That will be all, Lieutenant, thank you."

Chad turned, offering Elizabeth a quick wink before walking out of the office and shutting the door behind him. Once again, Elizabeth was left confused, this time staring at the commander, or rather Nicholas Black.

Elizabeth wanted to talk, but she was speechless. Nicholas Black walked over, pulled her to her feet, and hugged her. She hadn't known how much she'd needed that hug; she was drained, confused and didn't even know where to start. She let him comfort her until he broke the silence.

"Oh, sweetheart, I am sorry." With those words and his warm embrace, Elizabeth let the tears fall, and she cried into his shoulder. "That's it," he said warmly. "Let it out. Sometimes the best medicine is a good cry."

So, she did. She let it all out. She cried because she knew in her heart that her life would never be the same.

Nicholas Black held her and let her cry until she had no more tears to shed. When she was finished, she stepped out of Nicholas's embrace and sat down. He sat down in a chair next to her and held her hand. She looked into his dark brown eyes and asked, "What is going on? Am I losing my mind? Did that all really happen?"

"Where to start?" he said, more to himself. "You know the story of Lilith, the mother of demons, vampires, and pretty much all things evil."

"I assume you are referring to the Lilith who, according to legend, was Adam's first wife, who refused to submit to him and then was kicked out of Eden."

"That's a condensed version of events, but yes, that Lilith. Well, for far too many years to recall, she has been plotting and planning her revenge on all of humankind. She believed that Eve was her mortal enemy and had somehow stolen Adam from her. As if anyone could make that man do anything he didn't want to." Nicholas rose from his seat and paced in front of her, his hands linked behind his back. "For years, the supernatural communities have been working together—well, mostly together—trying to keep her at bay and protect the human world from her wrath."

"Legend has it that King Arthur and his knights imprisoned Lilith thousands of years ago. So, how is she doing all that?" Elizabeth asked.

"True," he said, "for the most part. They imprisoned her in her home realm. She had been unable to travel anywhere else until about fifteen years ago, when she escaped, breaking through the magical wards which kept her in place for centuries. Dianna, the immortal queen, is getting weaker. She had been using her magic and energy for thousands of years to maintain a protective boundary between the supernatural and human realms, plus the one that kept Lilith prisoner."

"Um... did you say the immortal queen? As in, she lives forever?"

Nicholas nodded, then continued. "It's taking its toll on her. She is one of the original immortals, a race of beings sent here by the Creator or, as some call him, God, with the sole purpose of protecting humans. As Dianna's power weakens, Lilith's evil powers grow. Her dark magic may soon be strong enough to overpower the queen altogether. If that happens, I can't even begin to imagine the hell on earth we will all face.

"Her demons have been creating minor breaches in the boundary to allow some of her vampires into the human realm. We are not sure how they are getting through, but they are. Tonight, they even got an entire group of hellhounds and trolls through." He ran his hand through his hair, and Elizabeth could see the frustration in his eyes. "I am the commander of the Immortal Queen's Military; I am to protect the human realm, and I can't even figure out how they are getting through to my territory."

Elizabeth asked, "What about Black Industries? How can you run a company and the Immortal Queen's Military at the same time?"

"An excellent question," he said, smiling. "Black Industries is a front for the military. All of our research and technology has been to aid the military or the supernatural world."

"Oh."

"Not all vampires are bad, nor do they all wish to follow Lilith. Many of them want to live normal lives and have families and careers without relying on human blood to sustain them."

"You're saying vampires want to live like humans?" Elizabeth's eyes widened.

"Yes, some do. We originally invented synthetic blood to help them live those normal lives. We helped many vampires escape and set them up with a new life, away from Lilith. Now, with war brewing, even more vampires want out, but it's getting harder for us to get to them. Also, the demon raids are happening more regularly, and our attention needs to be here in the human realm."

"You're telling me that vampires, demons, trolls, hellhounds and lord knows what else are all real? They actually exist?"

"Yes, they do."

"And Adam's first wife is evil? She controls most demons and vampires and other mythological creatures hell-bent on destroying the human realms?"

"Yes."

"There are other realms?"

"Yes."

"Um... okay. And you're sure about all this?"

"I am," he smiled warmly at her.

Elizabeth rubbed her temples, trying to release some of the pressure that was building behind her eyes.

"As for you, Elizabeth," he continued, his gaze softening. "We never wanted you to know these dark truths, at least not yet. We wanted you to live a normal life as long as possible. But as it is, time is not on our side. I'm not sure why the trolls were at Greystone. They were looking for something; I'm just not sure what. I had my men do a thorough sweep of the area, and there was no sign of your grandmother or anyone else. There were, however, a few dead hellhounds. This means Lady Lorraine wasn't there when the house exploded."

Elizabeth grabbed his arm and asked, "Really?" A sliver of hope returned to her.

"There are many things that you do not know, and it's not my place to tell you, but know this: your grandmother is a fighter and one of the strongest people I have ever known. It's going to take more than a few trolls or even a vampire army to take that woman down," he said, smiling and patting her hand. "She will find us when it's safe for her to do so. Of that, I am sure. But right now, my dear, we need to concentrate on you."

"Me?" Elizabeth asked, "What about me?"

"You can harness dragon fire, which is ancient magic that usually only a dragon can wield. Once knowledge of how you handled things tonight gets out, I'm sure Lilith will be looking for the human who can call upon the dragon fire. We need to make sure she can't find you. At least not yet—not until you're ready. We also need to make sure as few people as possible know about it."

"What do you mean, 'until I'm ready?' Ready for what?"

"All in good time. You have been through a great deal this evening, and I prefer not to overwhelm you."

"You do realize that everything you just said is terrifying," Elizabeth commented. "Where can I possibly go?" She was feeling lightheaded at the thought of a blood-sucking queen coming after her.

"There is only one place where you can learn about your power that the vampires or whoever else Lilith sends shouldn't be able to touch you, and that's Fireside, the realm of the dragons. They don't normally allow humans in their territory, but I think Queen Surraya might make an exception for you," Nicholas said reassuringly.

"Wait, what? Dragons? Dragons are real also?" She shook her head. "What if they want to roast me and eat me for a snack?"

Nicholas looked at her before he burst out laughing. "Lizzy, you have been watching too many movies. No dragon is going to eat you." He continued to smile. "Like I said, you have been through a lot today and I'm sure you're exhausted. We can talk more in the morning."

"Wait, I have so many questions. Did Gram know about all this?"

"Your questions can wait until morning. It's time for you to rest. I will make the arrangements for your travel to Fireside, and we will talk more in the morning," Nicholas said as he waved for Chad, who was suddenly standing in the doorway. "Please see Elizabeth to her suite."

Chad bowed to his commander and then smiled as he motioned for Elizabeth to follow him. Elizabeth hugged Nicholas before following Chad out.

They walked in silence, Elizabeth's mind reeling from all that she had learned. Dragons and vampires were real. How many other supernatural creatures were there?

Chad led her to a room on one of the lower levels. This building was freaking huge. He opened the door for her and then followed her in. Elizabeth couldn't believe her eyes. This room was gorgeous. It had a huge king-sized bed with tons of soft-looking pillows and a down comforter. She wanted to run over to the bed and jump in like she was a five-year-old.

The room was colored in a calming light, lavender and pale teal. There was a beautiful wooden desk and a chair in one corner. Then, a sitting area with a couch, coffee table, and comfy-looking wing-backed chair nestled on the other side of the room.

Elizabeth was still taking in the room when she heard Chad clear his throat. She had completely forgotten he was here. "Ms. Madison," he started, but she stopped him by putting her hand up.

"Please, for the love of all that is holy, do not call me Ms. Madison."

"If you insist, Small Fry," he said with a wink. "There is a phone on the desk. Dial zero if you need anything. I will come to get you at 0700 hours to escort you to breakfast."

"I'm sorry." She stopped him. "0700, as in seven am? Are you nuts?"

He flashed her a smile. "I apologize, but the commander insists on getting an early start tomorrow, and you will need to eat something."

"Do you know what he has planned for tomorrow?"

"No, but I'm sure he wants to prepare you for your trip before we head out."

"Oh, will you be traveling with me?"

He raised an eyebrow. "Is that okay with you if I do?"

"Of course it is. It will be nice to have a familiar face when I travel to the belly of the beast." She tried to offer a believable smile.

He touched her shoulder. "It will be ok. From what I know of the dragons, they keep to themselves, and they are not violent."

"I pray you're right," she said.

"Well, if that is all, I will leave you to get some rest. Sleepwear and a change of clothes have been provided. You will find them in the closet over there. You will find fresh towels and toiletries in your bathroom behind that door." He pointed to a closed door across the room. "If you require anything else, ask the guard and they will take care of it. Good night and sweet dreams, Small Fry." He smiled as he exited her room.

*He was cute*, Elizabeth thought to herself. Maybe a bit too flirtatious, and was he planning on calling her Small Fry from now on? She shook her head and smiled. She felt good knowing that he would be coming with her tomorrow. Lord knew she needed all the friends she could get.

# SEVEN

Elizabeth tossed and turned all night with visions of trolls and red glowing eyes invading her dreams. When sleep finally came, she heard knocking at her door. Throwing a pillow at the door, she mumbled, "Go away."

The door opened, and in walked an unapologetic Luna. "The commander asked that I bring you these." She held up an outfit with a pair of black leather boots. "I believe your outfit from yesterday would not be appropriate for traveling to another realm. This fabric is lightweight, and it will keep you cool or warm depending on what is required. Additionally, we have enchanted it with protection magic which will keep you safe from most magical attacks, including dragon fire."

The terrified look on Elizabeth's face must have said it all because Luna quickly responded, "Not that I think you will need it. It's a bonus feature. Now, hurry. Chad will be here shortly to escort you to breakfast."

Before Elizabeth could even say thank you, Luna had laid the items on the bed and was out the door. Looking over at the digital clock, which was sitting on a wooden nightstand next to her bed, she moaned when she saw the time. 6:00 am. *Freaking 6:00 am.* The sun wasn't even up yet. But then she remembered Chad said he would pick her up at 7:00 am. She decided it was best to get up and start moving.

Remembering what was happening today, she felt an onset of nervous energy as she paced around her room, wringing her hands. She was going to the realm of the dragons and would meet real freaking dragons. Her stomach was doing flip-flops. Was she excited or terrified? Maybe a little of both. Before yesterday, she would have never even dreamed that dragons existed, let alone all the other supernatural creatures that were real. And she was going to meet some today, face-to-face.

Grabbing the outfit that Luna had left on her bed, she headed to the bathroom. She jumped into the shower, hoping the warm water would help her wake up, or at least help calm her nerves. Once finished, she dried off and finished her morning routine. Quickly dressing in the black outfit, she pulled her long brown hair back into a ponytail.

Finding her purse lying on the desk, she rummaged through it and was thankful for the small makeup kit she always kept inside for touch-up emergencies. She didn't feel the need to be glamorous, but she felt a little powder and eyeliner wouldn't hurt. It made her feel more confident, like putting on war paint. Shaking her head, she laughed at herself in the bathroom mirror at the thought of needing war paint to meet the dragons.

A knock on the door sounded as she was finishing up. *Was it 7:00 am already?* She opened the door, her breath catching in her lungs. To her shock and horror, there stood the man who had haunted her dreams for well over six years.

Shane was tall with a thin but muscular frame, dressed in the same black uniform as everyone else around here. Like the picture upstairs, his hair was a little darker, no longer the sun-kissed blond of his youth, but a deeper golden hue. His eyes, those striking blue eyes, were the color of a beautiful, clear ocean, almost teal. His eyes had been what she had seen in her dreams—the way he used to look at her with such love. At one time, she could have drowned happily in those eyes.

"Sh-Shane?" She asked in surprise.

"Hey, Liz," he said with a hesitant smile. She thought for a moment that she saw a flicker of emotion in his eyes, but it was gone before she could figure out what it was.

"It's been a while. What brings you here?" She tried to play it cool, as if his surprise appearance didn't affect her.

"Liz—" he started, but she cut him off when her emotions got the better of her.

"You know what? I really don't have the time for this right now. I am expecting Chad to show me where to get breakfast."

At the mention of Chad's name, he seemed to stiffen up a little, and the smile disappeared. "I know, and I'm sorry for showing up here unannounced." He ran his hand through his hair and let out a deep breath. "Uncle told me you were here, and I wanted to see you, or rather, see how you are holding up." He took a step closer to her. She didn't move. "He filled me in on what happened with the trolls and your grandmother." His voice lowered to a whisper as he mentioned her grandmother. "I'm really sorry."

"Thank you."

"I told Chad that I would escort you to breakfast. Hope that's okay," he said with a hopeful smile. "I guess I needed to see for myself that you were still in one piece."

"Why would you care?" she whispered, unable to stop herself. Some of the anger and hurt from his abandoning her boiled over. Her rational side knew he'd had no choice in the leaving part, but at some point, in the past few years, he could have reached out. He had known where she lived. Surely, they had phones in London or wherever the hell he had been. He could have called. But no, nothing. After everything they had meant to each other, after everything they had said and planned, he had disappeared. He had ghosted her for years.

Now, here he was, standing in front of her and acting as if he hadn't abandoned her all those years ago, as if he cared about what happened to her now. He even had the freaking nerve to ask her to breakfast. Elizabeth fought back tears that she desperately wanted to let fall, but she didn't want him to see; he didn't need to see the effect he had on her, even after all these years.

"Liz, I'm sorry." He looked at her with those damn blue eyes of his. This time, she could see the hurt and regret in them. "I should have tried to reach out to you. I know that, and God knows, I wanted to a million times. There is so much you don't know, so much I want to tell you... so much I *need* to tell you."

He reached for her hand, but she pulled away, stepping back from him. She wasn't ready for this conversation, and she definitely wasn't ready for his touch. She had to get her emotions in check. She could feel the fire burning in her chest. No matter how hurt and angry she was, she didn't want to burn Shane with her newfound and not-yet-controllable dragon fire.

She had things to do today. There was no time for this. "Shane, I can't do this. We can't do this right now. I have to go; I can find my own way to the cafeteria." Pushing past him, she ran down the hall. She couldn't hold the tears back anymore. The fire in her chest had at least stopped, so she wasn't about to set anything on fire, or worse, accidentally burn someone. Of all the freaking days for Shane Black to show back up in her life. It had to be today, seriously?

She found a women's restroom and ran into it. Panting and trying to catch her breath, she looked in the mirror. Most of the eyeliner was now running down her cheeks thanks to the tears. What was he doing here, anyway? Shouldn't he be in London or anywhere else but here?

She splashed some cold water on her face, then wiped the smeared makeup off with a little soap and water. She took a few calming breaths before exiting the bathroom and continued her quest to find the cafeteria.

Elizabeth could smell the bacon before she entered the cafeteria. Noticing several other people lined up to get their food, she fell in behind them. There was a mix of people dressed in all-black uniforms, along with those in normal office attire.

Feeling a little out of place, she tugged at the top of her leather bodice. The outfit Luna had provided was all black, but it made her look like an extra from that warrior princess TV show she watched reruns of as a kid. The outfit sported knee-high leather boots, soft leather pants, and a form-fitting, corset-type top, which thankfully didn't show any cleavage. However, she was sure if she bent down too low, it would be a different story. It had sleeves that covered up her elbows, and the material was lightweight and fit like a glove. Regardless of how it looked, it was comfortable. There were even spots for stashing knives and other weapons.

Despite her appearance, no one seemed to notice her, and as hungry as she was, she doubted she should care. The comforting smell of bacon helped to ease her emotions after her encounter with Shane.

Grabbing a tray, she proceeded through the line, filling her plate with bacon, cheesy eggs, home-style potatoes, and toast. She then snatched the largest cup of coffee she could find. When she got to the cashier, she realized she had left her purse in her room when she ran out. *Crap*, she thought to herself, but before Elizabeth could say anything, she heard a familiar voice behind her.

"I got this," said the male voice. Turning around, she saw Chad offer his card to the older lady at the cash register. He smiled at her and tilted his head to show that she should follow him.

Following Chad, she weaved through the crowd of hungry people to an empty table in the back, where they each took a seat. His warm smile and friendly demeanor put her at ease instantly.

"Thank you," she said. "You didn't need to pay for my breakfast."

"You're welcome," he replied with a smile, flashing those dimples. "But honestly, I can't take credit for it. Commander Black provides all soldiers and office employees with a meal card. So, technically speaking, the company paid for it." With a wink, he added, "Although, I would have assumed Captain Black would have taken care of this for you since he did inform me quite early this morning that he would be escorting you to breakfast."

Elizabeth grunted. "Can we not discuss Shane? Wait, did you say Captain Black?"

"Yes, ma'am," Chad spoke between mouthfuls of cheesy eggs. "He's the captain of my squad."

"You mean like a military captain?"

Chad nodded while sipping on his coffee.

Elizabeth had no clue how to respond. She had thought

Shane was a CEO, not a soldier. But then again, she had thought the same about Uncle Nicky. She wanted to ask questions, but didn't want to get Chad in trouble, especially if Shane was his superior officer.

"I'm glad to see you got a nutritious breakfast there."

She blushed as she looked at the enormous plate of food sitting in front of her. What must he think? "I'm starving?" she offered nervously, shrugging her shoulders.

He let out a laugh. "No, it's a good thing. You are going to need your energy today. Plus, breakfast is the most important meal of the day." His smile was genuine, and it lit up the room.

"Thanks. I'm trying not to think too much about it, honestly."

"Hey, I get it. It's a lot. But you really have nothing to worry about. I went to school with a few dragons. They're just like you and me."

This admission shocked Elizabeth. What kind of school had he attended? She was about to ask when he started doing that thing again, where he looked like he was talking to himself, but in reality, he was talking through the communicator in his ear.

"Sorry, Small Fry, but it looks like I need to go," he said as he stood up. "The commander said he will meet you here in a few minutes. You shouldn't be alone too long."

Elizabeth offered a weak smile as she watched Chad walk away. He had been splendid company and not bad to look at with his dark hair, crystal blue eyes, and deep dimples, but her eyes kept scanning the room looking for ocean blue in a sea of black uniforms.

What was wrong with her? Her emotions were all over the place. She should be happy to be eating her breakfast in peace, not looking for Shane. In her heart, she knew a conversation with Shane was needed at some point. He wanted to clear the air, and she needed... what? Answers? Maybe closure. Regardless, she needed to get him out of her system so she could push past all these negative feelings she had kept bottled up all these years.

Perhaps she could seek Shane out when she got back from visiting the dragons. Then they could finally get everything out in the open. But today, she needed to concentrate on her journey and whatever the hell was going on with her and her new magical gifts. There was no time to think about Shane. He would be a distraction that she didn't need right now.

She needed to deal with things one at a time or risk having a serious mental breakdown. That was, if she wasn't already. This could all be a figment of her overactive imagination, right? One could only hope.

Walking over to the trash cans, Elizabeth threw her trash away, put her dirty dishes in the bin, and added her empty tray to the tray pile to be cleaned. Hearing her name being called by a familiar voice, she turned and saw Nicholas Black walking in her direction.

"Good morning, I hope you slept well."

"As well as can be expected," she shrugged.

"I might have something that can help."

"Okay." Elizabeth eagerly followed Nicholas Black out of the cafeteria.

He led her into a large open space that smelled like sweat. They walked past cushioned mats where men and women were practicing various forms of hand-to-hand combat. She continued to follow him as they passed soldiers practicing with swords, staffs, and chains. As they arrived at an exit door, Nicholas held it open for her.

The smell of fresh flowers hit her as soon as she stepped through to the other side. Before her was a small grass-covered clearing surrounded by beautiful flowers. "I was hoping you were going to teach me how to fight when we went through the gym."

"Perhaps, but not today."

"Um... okay... are we going to have a picnic or learn basket weaving?" she smiled.

He laughed. "No, we, my dear Lizzy, are going to work on balancing your inner self."

"My what?"

"Your inner self, your inner spirit. Some refer to it as Chi. Regardless of what you call it, your center has been thrown out of balance. Your world has been turned upside down, causing great turmoil in your life."

"Okay, and how will balancing my inner self help with all the craziness that is going on?"

"By returning balance, it will help you to absorb your new reality, allowing you to better handle the emotions that come with such an upheaval in one's life. It will also hopefully help you connect, too, and channel your magic."

"You talk about magic like you're inviting me to afternoon tea."

"Magic is a part of our everyday life. True, it was hidden from you, but it has always been there. Your magic is still a part of you, whether you knew it was there or not."

"You think meditation is going to help me control the infernal I can now release from my hands?"

"Meditation, no. Tai Chi, yes."

"Tai Chi, you mean as in Kung Fu?" She looked at him curiously.

"No, as in Tai Chi. Now please, take a deep breath, relax your body, and do as I do. The movements will help you balance your center."

Elizabeth rolled her shoulders, attempting to relax her body.

"Stand with your feet together, slowly lift your arms up, and breathe in and out." He spoke in a hypnotic tone. "Now bring your arms down, slowly. Bring your arms up slowly, as if you have the wings of a bird, and back down."

She followed as his arms, hands, and legs all flowed in slow, deliberate movements, mimicking the way he breathed in and out with precise timing. The moves were not difficult, and she was soon following his instructions with ease, as if they were participating in a choreographed dance.

"That's good. Breathe in and out, hug the tree, now close the door, and hands down." He said as they came to an end.

When they finished, she found her mind was quiet, her emotions were calm, and for the first time in a long time, she did feel at peace. "Wow, that was amazing." She took a bottle of water he offered her.

"Tai Chi has often helped me gather my thoughts and proceed with a clear head."

She took a large sip of the water, wiping her mouth with the back of her hand, "Thank you for sharing it with me."

"Of course. I encourage you to practice this routine daily. It will help you in the coming days."

"You mean because of the dragons?"

"No, I mean because war is coming, Lizzy, and I believe you are meant to play a large part in it."

Elizabeth spit out her water. "What? War? Me? You can't be serious."

"Your magic is awakening. There is no way to shield you from this path any longer. The fact that your grandmother hid all this—" He shook his head. "I'm sorry, Lizzy, I truly am. But the fact of the matter is, you are meant to overshadow the darkness. It's your destiny."

"Yeah, you... clearly have the wrong girl. Did you forget who you're talking to? This is me, plain old Elizabeth Madison." She paced in front of him, running her hands through her hair. "I recently graduated from college. My life is just beginning. I'm not signing up for any wars. Why would you even suggest that?"

"I know this is a lot to take in at once. It's only a matter of time before Lilith finds out about you. I'm sorry, and we should have better prepared you for all this. Your grandmother thought we had more time. But we don't, and with her still missing, it's my job to make sure you're prepared."

"I can't do this. You're talking crazy. War, magic, a freaking demon goddess hunting me. I don't want this. I don't want this magic, and I most definitely don't want to be a part of a freaking war."

"I know—" Nicholas started to say, but she cut him off,

holding up her hand.

"Thank you for the Tai Chi lesson, but I need to go. I don't want to talk about this anymore. I need a very large, very strong coffee," she said, walking away.

"Okay, Lizzy, but please don't forget the meeting to discuss your travel to Fireside. I'll send Chad to assist you."

Chad found Elizabeth a few minutes later and walked with her to get the largest to-go cup of coffee she could find before he led her to an empty conference room. "This was where the commander advised us to wait for him and the others."

Elizabeth nodded and took a seat. Inhaling the aroma of the coffee, she contemplated all that had happened to her in the last twenty-four hours. She wasn't sure how much more she could take.

Hearing voices, she glanced at the door as Luna entered, followed by Nicholas, who offered her a sympathetic smile. They both sat across from her at the large wooden table and continued their conversation, which Elizabeth wasn't paying any attention to.

They were in a larger conference room than the one she had previously been in. This table could seat thirty people easily. The room had a similar setup, with plain white walls, a white counter, and cabinets along the back wall, with a small kitchenette.

Taking a swig of her warm coffee, she nearly choked on it when she saw Shane walk in. He gave a slight nod to Elizabeth before taking a seat next to Nicholas across the table from her.

Damn him for being calm and looking so good. Fate could have at least given him a pot belly or maybe a wart or two. Seriously, something. Elizabeth felt her heart race, and her palms became sweaty. She rubbed them against her leather pants. *What the hell*? Why did she still find him so damn attractive? *Good grief, I need to pull it together*. Thankfully, no one seemed aware of her internal struggle. How was she going to make it through this meeting with Shane Black sitting across from her.

# EIGHT

Commander Nicholas Black stood tall and confident as he addressed the room. "Thank you, everyone, for being here on such short notice. As you all know, they hit us on several fronts last night. Lilith has Dimitri looking for weaknesses in our defenses, and he is clearly finding them. There are also reports of black-market slave trading, although these reports have not yet been confirmed. This is more proof that war is inevitable. Lilith is looking to strike, and probably sooner rather than later."

Elizabeth shuddered at the thought. She raised her hand and asked, "Who is Dimitri?" The room went silent for a moment as everyone seemed to look in Shane's direction and then back at Elizabeth.

"You do know what Lilith is, correct?" Luna asked.

"There are lots of speculations. Some scholars believe she was a demon, and others say she was the first vampire. Then, there are those who believe she was misrepresented by historians," Elizabeth responded.

"I didn't ask what scholars know. I asked if you knew." Luna sat back in her chair with arms crossed over her chest, waiting for an answer.

"My grandmother told me the story of Lilith. I guess I always assumed she was a vampire since she drank Eve's blood when she killed her."

"You would be wrong."

"Luna, seriously?" Shane snapped at her.

"What?"

"No one knows for sure what Lilith truly is now," Nicholas filled in. "She started out as an immortal, the same as Queen Dianna and Adam. But somewhere along the way, she became lost, allowing her heart and soul to become dark and twisted."

"Well, if the story I heard is correct, I'm sure having Adam choose Eve, and then banishing her son to roam in darkness, might do that to someone," Elizabeth remarked.

"Are you defending her?" Luna shot up out of her chair and glared at Elizabeth.

"No, I'm saying there might be more to her story," Elizabeth glared back. "A broken heart can really mess with someone." She glanced at Shane, then back to Luna.

"We are getting off-topic here." Nicholas brought the attention back to him. "Elizabeth asked who Dimitri is, and that's a valid question."

"Fine. Dimitri is Lilith's second in command and the most ruthless vampire in her army. It's believed that he was the first person she turned into a vampire. He is strong, deadly, and ancient.

Nicholas leaned his back against the counter, crossing his arms. "He was born an Egyptian prince named Dakarai over three thousand years ago, the second son of a powerful pharaoh. Dakarai felt his older brother was too weak and undeserving to be the next pharaoh."

All eyes turned to the commander as he spoke. "Lilith used the young prince's ambitions, tricking him into thinking she was the goddess Isis. She seduced him and convinced him he was destined to be the next pharaoh. She even convinced him to kill his father and brother, allowing him to assume the throne, and she, his queen."

"As if Lilith was going to share the power," Luna said sarcastically.

"Regardless, the prince was foolish enough to believe her. Dakarai called a meeting with his father and brother under some false pretense where he slit both their throats. What he hadn't planned for was his younger brother Nakia coming and finding Dakarai holding the blood-covered knife. Nakia called the guards and then attempted to restrain Dakarai. The two brothers fought. In the end, Nakia mortally wounded Dakarai by stabbing him in the gut. Not yet dead, Dakarai got away to find his goddess. Lilith offered the dying prince eternal life if he would pledge to serve her for eternity. The rest is history; he agreed. She turned him into a vampire who has served her faithfully all these years."

"Wow, that's sad. Did Nakia become Pharaoh?" Elizabeth asked.

Commander Black shook his head. "No, Lilith turned Nakia into a monster as well."

"What? That's horrible. Where is Nakia, now?"

"That is a tale for another day," Commander Black said as he walked across the room and returned to his seat. "We have more pressing matters to discuss. Captain, has there been any news?"

Everyone turned their focus to Shane. "No sir, as of now, we are still unclear as to why the trolls were at Lady Lorraine's last night. My gut said they were looking for something they assumed she had in her possession, or maybe had knowledge of." He glanced at Elizabeth apologetically. "Sorry, there is still no news about what happened to Lady Lorraine."

Elizabeth nodded.

"That is my thinking as well. Lizzy, do you ever recall your grandmother mentioning something called the dragon stone?"

"I never heard Lady Lorraine speak of it, no, but from my studies, I am familiar with the legend of the dragon stone. You can't seriously think someone thought she had knowledge of it? It's a myth." Elizabeth shook her head. "It's not real."

"And up until yesterday, I'm sure you thought trolls and vampires were myths as well," Luna said, tapping her nails on the table.

Chad raised his hand. "Um... what is the dragon stone?"

"It's a black stone said to have been the petrified heart of one of the first dragons. It's believed to have magical healing powers—powerful enough to bring back the dead," Elizabeth explained. "It's mentioned in many ancient texts from around the world, from Egypt, Greece, Babylon, and many more. The last believed sighting, or at least the last mention of the dragon stone, was during the time of King Arthur. King Arthur's half-sister, Morgana Le Fay, was searching for the dragon stone in the hopes that it would heal her brother after Mordred mortally wounded him in battle."

"Cool," Chad said.

Elizabeth turned to the commander, a frown scrunching her brows together. "Do you honestly think my grandmother found the dragon stone and didn't tell anyone? That doesn't make any sense. She is an archeologist. A find like that would be monumental for her career. Even bigger than her finding Camelot."

"Not everything is about notoriety. Some finds should be kept secret." Luna rolled her eyes.

"We can't be certain, either way." Nicholas tapped his fingers on the table. "She never mentioned finding it to me. I know your father spent years researching its possible locations. Maybe she thought it had something to do with his disappearance."

"My father was looking for the dragon stone?"

"Yes, but this is only a theory. We don't know for certain what the trolls were after," Nicholas said.

"Let's hope that if she had found it, she managed to hide it before the trolls visited her. We won't stand a chance against

Lilith if she gets her hands on the dragon stone." Luna glared at Elizabeth before taking a drink of her coffee.

"Why? Besides its believed healing abilities, why would the dragon stone make Lilith unstoppable?" Elizabeth asked.

"The legend you spoke of where Morgana searched for the dragon stone to heal her brother is correct. In fact, the dragon stone would have been the only thing that could have saved King Arthur since Excalibur caused the fatal wound. The sword of power is the only weapon we are aware of that can kill an immortal. It's believed that even the slightest scratch from the legendary blade would be fatal. The exception to this rule, reportedly, would be the one who is wielding it, and only a member of the Pendragon family line can wield Excalibur," Shane offered.

"Arthur and Mordred were both Pendragons." Elizabeth chewed on her thumbnail as she pondered what all this could mean.

"Yes, which allowed Mordred the opportunity to issue a fatal blow to Arthur when he swiped the sword from him." Nicholas picked up his coffee mug, taking a sip.

"Yup, if Lilith gets her claws on the dragon stone, she will be invincible with no way to stop her and her blood-thirsty vengeance." Luna held her coffee mug up toward Elizabeth before she took a swig.

"Great, just what we need—an invincible, demented, power-hungry immortal. Freaking fantastic." Elizabeth was going to need something much stronger in her coffee mug.

"Why would Lilith need the dragon stone?" Shane asked, looking at his uncle. "It's common knowledge that she killed all the Pendragons years ago. Even if Excalibur were found, there is no one who can wield it. She wouldn't need the dragon stone."

"Perhaps, but who knows what goes on in the mind of a soulless creature?" Nicholas asked, looking at Elizabeth. "However, fate has a funny way of intervening when the need is great. Regardless, knowledge is power, and we are sadly lacking in that department at this time."

Elizabeth was familiar with the King Arthur legend, but she had never heard of how deadly his mythical sword was. One cut could be fatal. That was a scary thought.

"We will continue to look into what happened at Greystone Manor. For those of you in this room, I have another mission." Nicholas looked around the table.

The commander leaned forward in his chair. "I have selected you to travel with Elizabeth to Fireside. She needs to learn how to control the dragon fire. I also hope that Queen Surraya will have some useful information regarding the dragon stone's last known whereabouts.

"What? You can wield dragon fire? Since when?" Shane

looked at her, shocked.

"Um... since yesterday," she shrugged.

The commander stood and walked over to stand behind Elizabeth, putting his hands on her shoulders. "Yes, and it is imperative that no one outside this room learns of Elizabeth's power besides members of the dragon royal family. I shudder to think of the consequences if Lilith were to find out about this. She would stop at nothing to control Elizabeth and her power. Her safety is paramount."

Elizabeth felt all eyes suddenly on her, and heat rose to her cheeks from the attention.

"Along with the fact-finding mission regarding the dragon stone and Elizabeth's powers, there is another reason for this trip." He walked to stand behind Shane. "We need allies. There is no way around it. War is coming, and we need the dragons on our side if we are to have any hope of winning."

The commander put a hand on Shane's shoulder. "Shane has some connections with the dragon royal family, so he will be our ambassador. Hopefully, he will bring them over to our cause. It will not be easy; the dragons tend to keep to themselves, but they need to know that Lilith's thirst for power will not stop with the humans. It is only a matter of time before she tries to conquer all the realms."

Elizabeth wondered how Shane was acquainted with members of the dragon royal family. She wanted to ask but didn't want to draw any more attention to herself.

She remained lost in thought until she heard Nicholas calling her name. "Elizabeth—Lizzy—are you okay?"

She snapped back into focus. "Yes, I'm okay. It's a lot to take in." She attempted a reassuring smile. "Until yesterday, I had no idea dragons, magic or any of this even existed. And now, it's a lot."

Nicholas nodded his head in understanding.

"You're the chick who can wield dragon fire. You should be more than okay," Chad said with a huge grin on his face. "If I'm going into battle, I'm making sure I'm in your group, Small Fry." With that, he winked at her.

She heard a grunt, which came from Shane's direction. When she turned, she found Shane glaring at Chad like he was about to jump across the table.

"Chill, dude," Chad said nonchalantly to Shane. "We are all on the same side, and from where I'm sitting, Ms. Small Fry here does not seem to be involved with anyone. She's fair game. Unless I'm wrong?" Chad turned to Elizabeth with a megawatt smile and his dimples flashing.

Elizabeth hated being the center of attention. "Um, no, I mean yes, I'm single." She struggled to get the words out, suddenly feeling uncomfortable and wanting to change the topic

ASAP. "I'm not really looking for anyone, and that has nothing to do with why we are here." She glanced at Luna, who just rolled her eyes.

Thankfully, Nicholas interjected. "That is enough, gentlemen. We are on the same side. Can we please dial back the testosterone for a minute? We have a war to prepare for. I'm entrusting you both to make sure Elizabeth is safe. Do you both understand?"

Both men looked at Elizabeth and then back at their commanding officer before answering, "Yes, Sir!"

"Very well. Let's get back to business," Uncle Nicky said as he handed Elizabeth a beautiful silver bracelet with pink, white, and purple stones.

"Thank you," she said, looking at him, confused.

He smiled. "It's not your typical bracelet, my dear. The pink stone is a communication device. While wearing it, you can speak directly to any member of your team telepathically."

"Do I need an implant in my ear as well?"

"No, the technology in the bracelet works with your auditory nerve through energy waves. It's temporary and doesn't need to be surgically implanted."

"Hey there, Small Fry, can you hear me?" a voice said in her ear. Elizabeth looked over at Chad and saw him smirking at her.

"Yes, she can, as can the rest of us, lover boy," Luna said sarcastically. This conversation occurred in her head; neither of their lips moved.

"Wow," Elizabeth said, and she glanced at Shane, who was again glaring at Chad.

Nicholas ignored them and continued. "The white stone will provide a powerful bright light source if you need one, and the purple stone is an emergency transporter. It will automatically transport you to your desired location or a predetermined safe space within any realm. However, use this only in case of a dire emergency because you only have three jumps programmed."

"How do I activate them?" Elizabeth asked.

"You tap the stone you want to use two times," Nicholas responded.

"Wow," Elizabeth said again, looking at her bracelet. "And they say diamonds are a girl's best friend."

The meeting appeared to be coming to a close when Nicholas asked if there were any more questions. Elizabeth looked around and then raised her hand like she was a kid in school.

Nicholas smiled. "Yes, Lizzy?"

"How are we getting to Fireside? How does one travel to another realm?"

"Excellent question. If the borders are opened to us, such as Avalon, where Queen Dianna lives, or even the Misty Isles, which are home to the Druids and Celtics, then we can use a transporter device to travel there. However, in this instance, the dragons keep their borders protected and do not allow our transporters to open in their lands. We can transport from Fireside, but not directly there. We must go a little old school for this trip and find a gateway."

"A gateway?" Elizabeth perked up.

"Yes, there are gateways scattered throughout the realms that we can use to travel between. They are all protected and hidden by magic, and most have forgotten where they are located, especially now that we have transport technology. The most popular gateway was, of course, Stonehenge in England."

"Wait, what?" Elizabeth stopped him. "Stonehenge, the huge standing rocks in England, are a gateway between realms?"

"Yes, but it's also the most obvious choice because that is the only one most people remember. I'm sure Lilith will have her minions there waiting for anyone trying to flee to another realm. Unfortunately, we cannot use that one."

"Ok, I am assuming you know of another one of these gateways we can use."

"I do, but I don't have access to open them. That's why Jdril is here," Nicholas said.

Elizabeth looked at the door to see if someone else had entered without her realizing it. But there was no one. "I'm sorry, who?"

There were a few snickers from the room.

"Jdril is Chad's real name," Luna said, irritated. "He decided he wanted a more human-sounding name."

Elizabeth looked at Chad. There was so much to unpack from Luna's statements. "Wait, you're not human? And you chose Chad as a name?"

"What's wrong with Chad? I like it," he shrugged.

"It's like the most douchebag name of all." Elizabeth shook her head, trying not to laugh.

"I think it's fitting," Shane smirked at Chad, or rather, Jdril.

"I don't care what he chooses to call himself. The lieutenant is a highly skilled soldier who happens to also be a gateway fae."

"You're a faerie?" Elizabeth asked with some amusement.

"I am fae," Chad said, smirking.

"You do not look like a faerie or fae," Elizabeth said. Not that she would know what one looked like.

"I know, Small Fry. My ruggedly good looks and extreme sex appeal do not scream fae. Believe me, I get it." He laughed, "But alas, I am indeed fae."

"I'm sorry, Chad," Elizabeth smiled, "but when I think of a faerie—or sorry, fae—all I can think of is Tinkerbell, and you definitely don't look like her." With that, everyone in the room burst out laughing.

“Oh, Small Fry, you are a delight,” Chad said amusingly. “I apologize. I don’t look like Tinkerbell, but again, I am fae, not a faerie. There is a difference between the two. That said, I can shrink. I also have wings when I need them.” Chad winked again. She was starting to think he had a tick in his eye.

“More importantly,” Nicholas continued, “he has the power to locate and open any gateway.”

“Unfortunately, there aren’t too many left in the human realm. Most have been destroyed or blocked by a skyscraper. Or, like Stonehenge, they will be guarded by Lilith’s guards,” Chad said. “I do know of one that I’m sure they have no clue about. It’s a little tricky to get to, but if you trust me, Small Fry, I’ll have you in dragon territory before you can say, ‘Toothless.’”

# NINE

A few hours after the meeting had concluded, Elizabeth found herself with Shane, Luna, and Chad staring over a canyon. But it wasn't just any canyon—it was the Grand freaking Canyon. It was Elizabeth's first time seeing this wonder of nature in person. Its beauty was beyond anything she had ever seen in person. It felt like a painting had pulled her into it. The red and orange layers of the canyon walls were so vibrant, they couldn't possibly be real. The sun was setting, causing its light to reflect off the river below like little starburst on the surface.

The four of them had stepped through a portal created by a transporter, and here they were, looking down at a sharp drop-off where the bottom was very, very, very, far away. Elizabeth kept her distance from the ledge. She was not a fan of heights at all.

Elizabeth looked at Chad and asked, "Where is the gateway?" She still couldn't believe he had picked the name Chad for himself. She really liked his real name, Jdril, but he insisted on keeping Chad, so she figured he should honor that.

He did his usual smirk while pointing to the middle of the Grand Canyon. Sitting down on the ledge, he began chanting in a lyrical language she had never heard before. After a moment, a purple circular cloud appeared in the middle of the canyon. As Chad continued to chant, the purple cloud grew bigger.

"There it is. Isn't she a beauty?" Chad finally spoke up, clearly pleased with himself.

"Great job!" Shane said as Luna nodded in agreement. They were excited, however, Elizabeth remained skeptical.

"There *what* is?" she asked.

"It's the gateway to Fireside," Chad responded.

"Um, okay, and how do we get to it? Can you conjure a magical bridge?" Elizabeth was afraid of the answer.

"Well, Small Fry, it's simple. We jump," was Chad's response.

Elizabeth's heart sank as her body started to shake. "Are you freaking crazy? Do you have a death wish? Because I sure as hell don't. Not all of us can fly, shrink down, and have wings like a faerie. I can't jump all the way over there." A sharp stab of fear punctured her heart, and she sank to the ground.

"It's fae, not faerie," Chad mumbled. Then, noticing the death glare he was getting from Shane, he held up his arms in mock surrender. "Fine, fine, I'll be over here, waiting my turn to jump."

Shane walked over to Elizabeth, concerned. He squatted down to her level. "I'm guessing you still have a fear of heights?" Elizabeth looked away from him. "Hey, don't do that. There is nothing to be ashamed of here. Please look at me." She turned back to him. "I promise I won't let anything happen to you. You will get across this canyon and into that gateway unharmed. Do you hear me? I will not ever let anything bad happen to you, Elizabeth Madison. Never." She looked up into his ocean-blue eyes, and she felt the truth of his words.

She wiped the tears from her cheeks and nodded in understanding. Shane helped her stand up. Her legs were still a little shaky. She had to lean on him for support.

"Aww, Small Fry, please don't get upset. It's perfectly safe, I assure you. It's meant to look scary to deter people from abusing this gate. That's also why it's probably a forgotten gate. It's too scary for most."

Luna said, "It's okay; I will go first and show you how it's done. I can't fly or grow wings like fae boy over there, either."

Elizabeth smiled slightly, nodded her head, and watched as Luna took a running jump off the side of the Grand Canyon. Elizabeth's hand covered her mouth as she instinctually gasped in fear. She watched as Luna somersaulted in the air before doing a perfect dive into the center of the purple clouds, looking like a seasoned gymnast.

"See, easy peasy. Ready to give it a try?"

Elizabeth let go of Shane, calmly walking over to the ledge. Glancing over briefly, she turned back to them. "Hell, no. I am trying to be an adult about this. I really am. But I still think you're out of your minds if you think I can make this jump. Luna is literally a freaking cat. She has nine lives. I'm pretty sure I only have one. There has got to be another gateway."

Chad said, "Well, Small Fry, I'm afraid because of our time restraints. It's this, or we could try to catch a ride with a dragon. But sadly, I don't see any dragons around." Chad looked around dramatically and called over the edge of the canyon. "Hello, down there. Are there any dragons we can catch a ride with? *Helloooo*?" Chad waited a minute before shrugging and saying, "Oh well.":

Elizabeth glared at him. "Smartass."

"I'm really sorry, but this is our only option. If you like, I will gladly carry you."

Shane stepped between them. "If anyone is carrying her, it will be me. I am the senior officer here, and it's my responsibility to ensure the safety of all on this mission. Got it?"

"*Yes, Sir*!" Chad said, standing straight and doing a salute with a sheepish grin. "I will be on my way. I will see you both on the other side, Sir, if that's okay, Sir." Chad winked at Elizabeth and flashed her a smile.

"Yes, Lieutenant, I think you moving along now is a great idea," Shane responded.

"Okay, wait for it, Small Fry. I think you will like this." Chad snapped his fingers and immediately shrunk down to about three inches tall. He sprouted beautiful blue and green iridescent wings. His normally dark brown hair changed to various hues of green and blue, and his aura glowed, changing colors as he fluttered around her. He was simply breathtaking.

"I take it back; you do look like Tinkerbell," Elizabeth smiled.

"Ha ha ha, look who's being the comedian now."

"Enough. We are wasting time," Shane said sternly.

"Aye, aye, Captain," Chad saluted and then took off like a jet plane flying through the center of the gateway.

Elizabeth was suddenly aware that she was now alone with Shane. Silence hung in the air, and both stared at the purple clouds in the middle of the Grand Canyon. Shane broke the uncomfortable silence by clearing his throat. "Liz, I know I haven't always been there for you, and that's on me." He took her hand in his. "There is so much I want to tell you—so much I need to tell you. There is a reason I was gone for so long, and I was afraid to reach out to you. I was afraid you wouldn't understand."

"You were my best friend. We used to tell each other everything." Kicking a rock over the edge, she couldn't face him.

"I know. But this was different."

"Did I do something to make you stop trusting me?"

He moved in close to her. "Gods, Liz, no. It was never about me not trusting you." He moved his knuckles gently down her cheek, then tilted her chin to look up at him. His thumb grazed her lower lip. "It's that I didn't want to hurt you, at least, not more than I already had. I didn't trust myself to not—" Shane paused as his communicator interrupted him.

"Hey, boss man, Luna and I are here patiently waiting."

"Affirmative, we will be following shortly," Shane said.

"Hopefully, very shortly, Sir, because I'm not sure how much longer I can keep this gate open."

Shane looked at Elizabeth with a silent question in his eyes. She nodded, knowing their time was up. Shane responded, "We are on our way lieutenant, give us a second." He took both her hands in his. "I guess this conversation will need to be put on ice for the moment, but there will be a conversation. I just—"

Elizabeth stopped him, putting her hand to his lips. "It's okay. We have a mission to do right now, Captain, and that requires you to focus and help get me across this damn canyon alive like you promised. All that other stuff can wait. It's waited this long. What's another few hours?"

"I can do that," Shane responded. "But I am going to need you to trust me. Can you do that?" Elizabeth nodded. "Okay, then I need you to wrap your arms around my neck tightly and then wrap your legs around my waist."

"Um, come again?" Elizabeth put her hand on her hips.

"I said I needed you to trust me, Liz. Please, trust me and do as I ask," he said firmly.

"Okay, but if we don't make it, I will track you down in the afterlife and make it most unpleasant for you, mister. Do you understand?" She jabbed a finger in his chest.

Shane grinned from ear to ear and said, "Yes, ma'am!"

Elizabeth then did as Shane asked, wrapping her arms tightly around his neck. He hoisted her up so she could wrap her legs around his waist. "Is it wrong that I like you in this position?" He whispered in her ear. She gasped at his words. He smirked. "Hold on tight; I got you!" Then he took a running leap off the side of the Grand Canyon.

She buried her head in his shoulder and closed her eyes tightly, taking in his warmth and the comforting scent of sandalwood.

Into the air they flew, attempting to make it to the purple cloud in the middle of the Grand Canyon, which would lead them to Fireside or their untimely death if they missed.

# TEN

Elizabeth felt a jolt when Shane touched down on the hard ground. Holding on tight, she remained attached to him like velcro. Shane whispered in her ear, “It’s okay, Liz. We made it.”

Slowly, she loosened her grip. Shane helped her to the ground, and Elizabeth looked around, taking in the sights. She inhaled sharply at the picturesque surroundings. She was standing on a road that looked like diamonds. It shimmered and shone in the sunlight. Bending down, she ran her hand over the cool surface. It was hard and smooth like glass. Colors filled her vision as the sun’s rays reflected off the surface.

Further down the road sat a small orchard with fruit that was unfamiliar to her. The fruit was the size of a large apple but was green with pink spots. She noticed a magnificent waterfall in the distance with a rainbow shooting out from it as if the waterfall itself was the treasure at the end. There were fields of wildflowers of every color imaginable all around them. The air was warm with a sweet fragrance. What she didn’t see was any sign of civilization.

They found Luna and Chad relaxing under one of the trees, munching on a piece of the fruit.

“Glad you could finally join us,” Chad said with a wink, as he offered Elizabeth a piece of fruit. “It’s a dragon melon. They are delicious. It’s a cross between an apple and watermelon from your realm.”

Elizabeth’s stomach was still unnerved by that crazy, death-defying jump. She politely declined, shaking her head. “No, thank you.”

Luna stood, wiping dirt from her butt, “Well, now can we get a move on?”

Shane nodded in agreement, starting down the road. “Yes, we should get moving.”.

“Where exactly are we going? I don’t see a single building. It’s beautiful, but we are in the middle of nowhere.” Elizabeth observed.

“Well, you see, Small Fry, that’s the beauty of magic,” Chad said. “The entire village is under a concealment spell to keep it hidden from outsiders.”

Shane looked at Elizabeth. “Dragons don’t really like outsiders. They prefer to keep to themselves. Concealing their village makes it hard to find them if you don’t know where you’re going. Thankfully, we know where we are going, and they are expecting us.”

They continued to walk down the glass-like road. It was unnerving, yet beautiful at the same time to see no signs of humans. The world was untouched and remained wild and breathtaking.

Suddenly, a tremendous gust of wind nearly knocked her over. Thankfully, Shane was there to steady her. Elizabeth looked up and saw three gigantic flying beasts. Dragons, she realized, mesmerized by the sight before her. They were magnificent. Shane and Chad positioned themselves in front of Elizabeth as Luna stood beside her. The larger of the three landed right in front of them. It had beautiful, dark green scales that shone like emeralds in the sunlight, with a stripe that looked like black diamonds trailing from the spikes on its head, down its smooth back, to the spikes on its tail.

Two smaller dragons landed behind the first one. The dragon on the left was red like rubies, with a similar black stripe down the middle of its back. The one on the left was a beautiful teal color with a purple stripe down its back.

Elizabeth staggered away in surprise but found that her fear had gone. Quite the opposite remained. They intrigued her. She felt a strange draw to the beasts, her body moving on its own as she gravitated towards the brilliant creatures before her. As she walked slowly to the dragons, her hand rose up automatically with a need to touch them.

Shane shot his arm out to halt her as a blue-green mist, similar in color to her dragon fire, surrounded the dragons.

“What’s happening?” she whispered.

“Wait for it,” Shane smirked.

When the mist cleared, the dragons were gone, and in their place were three humans dressed in armor that appeared to be made from the scales of the dragons that had disappeared. There were two males, one in vibrant green armor and one in red. Then there was a female in teal armor.

The one dressed in jewel-toned green approached Shane. He had short, wavy, reddish-blond hair with distinct verdant eyes. He was quite handsome, especially with the huge smile he wore. It lit up his entire face. He held out his arm to Shane, who bowed before reaching for the elbow of the extended arm and brought him into a hug. "Shane, it is good to see you, my friend. Mother informed me that you had requested a meeting with her and would arrive today. I decided to come and greet you and your party myself."

"I am glad you did, old friend. You, of course, already know almost everyone. This is Elizabeth Madison." The man's eyes grew large and his smile even larger as he glanced from Elizabeth to Shane. "Elizabeth, may I present His Royal Highness, the Crown Prince, Drake, of the Emerald Island Dragon Clan."

"Oh my, your shifters, aren't you?" Elizabeth asked.

"We are," he nodded. "It is a great honor to make your acquaintance, Ms. Elizabeth." Prince Drake looked amused as he bowed, and then, taking Elizabeth's right hand in his, he brought it to his lips and kissed it.

"Apologies, Your Highness." Elizabeth performed an awkward curtsy. "I have never met—I mean, I never knew dragons could be shifters. Well, I really didn't know you even existed until recently," she rambled nervously.

"No apologies necessary." His smile was warm and welcoming. Elizabeth liked him instantly.

Turning back to Shane, the prince asked, "Surely this cannot be the same Liz you spoke of often when you first arrived at the academy, can it?"

This caught Elizabeth's attention. Shane had talked about her after he had left. What had he said? What had they talked about? Shane cleared his throat and turned to answer Prince Drake, but before he could say a word, Chad walked over to the prince.

"What am I, chopped liver? I only saved your butt a million times at the academy, and I don't get so much as a, 'Hey, how's it going?' I see how it is. You're this big-shot prince, now, and you have already forgotten the little people... literally. I am hurt," Chad said as he dramatically put his hand on his forehead. "I may never get over this rejection. Did you see, Luna, how I was just rejected and ignored?"

"Same old Jdril. The most dramatic fae I have ever met," Prince Drake said with a smile as he reached for Chad and hugged him. "I apologize, old friend. You know how I can get distracted when there is a beautiful woman around." Prince Drake smiled and winked at Elizabeth. Shane once again cleared his throat but said nothing else.

"I certainly don't wish to neglect any of my guests. Luna or Elizabeth, would either of you lovely ladies require a hug as well?" Prince Drake looked at Elizabeth and Luna with pure enjoyment.

"No," Luna responded curtly. Elizabeth smiled as she shook her head.

"Well then, how about we move along inside the gates before they send out a search party for us?" Prince Drake suggested as he turned and nodded to the other two dragons, whom Elizabeth had forgotten, were even there.

"We can discuss the reason for your visit once inside."

The red-and-teal-clad soldiers raised their arms above their heads and chanted something, but Elizabeth was unfamiliar with the language. Just then, it was like a curtain had fallen. Where Elizabeth had once seen a field of wildflowers, she now saw an enormous stone wall with a gigantic arched doorway, tall enough to fit a dragon. She followed as Prince Drake led them through the archway.

On the other side, an open market buzzed with life. Elizabeth felt she had walked back in time or was at some sort of reenactment. There were vendors selling potions and elixirs, leather-clad clothing and armor, some with dragon scales, and jewelry, also made of dragon scales in every color.

There were the smells of delectable foods—cakes, pies, and pastries of all kinds, as well as a fire pit with some kind of animal roasting on it. Produce vendors with exotic fruits and vegetables trying to sell their wares to all who pass by. Elizabeth's stomach rumbled. She was starving, and she realized she hadn't eaten since breakfast. *Damn*, she thought to herself. *I should have eaten one of those dragon melons when Chad offered it.*

A group of children ran past her, giggling. It was hard to believe they were dragons, and she wondered at what age they could shift. At some point, Shane grabbed Elizabeth's hand to help her along the way. It was innocent, instinctual, and familiar to them both. Hadn't Shane done that same thing a million times in the past? Something so simple as holding her hand and helping her through the crowd. But it wasn't simple. Elizabeth looked up at Shane as they walked, hand in hand. He seemed oblivious to the action. It had been less than twenty-four hours since he had returned to her life, and they were falling back into old habits. But was this what she wanted? For things to go back to the way they were. She thought she had always longed for that, but now she wasn't so sure.

After navigating through the open market, they finally arrived at an elegant, Italian-style villa. The confusion on Elizabeth's face must have said it all because when she looked over at Prince Drake, he had a huge smile on his face.

"Welcome to my home," the prince said with wide arms. "I assume by your confused expression that this is not what you were expecting."

Shaking her head, she looked around. Before her was a beautifully tiled courtyard with a large fountain in the center. There was an open-air kitchen with a brick pizza oven next to an open and inviting dining area with a large table that looked like it could seat about twenty people. A fire pit area, along with several other more intimate seating areas, had been placed around the courtyard. The open area teemed with life before they had even reached the stone staircase leading into the massive villa. She felt like she had stepped out of the Dark Ages and into Tuscany.

"I apologize, Your Highness. I guess I was expecting something with more stonework," Elizabeth said, her cheeks reddened from embarrassment.

"We do have your standard, rather enormous stone castle a few miles away. While it is lovely to look at, it's not very comfortable. It's rather drafty and is a pain to keep warm in the winter and cool in the summer."

"I bet," Elizabeth said, still taking in her surroundings.

"Of course, I would be more than happy to arrange a private tour of the castle later if you wish?"

"I think we might all enjoy that, Drake, after the business at hand has been taken care of," Shane said rather severely as he glared at the prince.

"Of course, we can arrange that."

"You know what Chad needs," Chad chimed in. "Chad needs food, and lots of it. I don't know about anyone else, but I'm starving over here." He rubbed his stomach while offering a pouty face.

"Of course," Prince Drake said, still staring at Shane as he tried to read him. "But who, might I ask, is Chad?"

The tension was broken as the group broke out into laughter at the prince's confusion.

"Chad is Jdril, and Jdril is Chad. I believe he's having a mid-life crisis. We're just going with it." Luna waved her hand at Chad.

"Well, okay, then." Shaking his head, the prince walked over to one of the seating areas. "Let's sit. I'll have some refreshments served while you tell me what brings you here."

Shane explained the reason for their impromptu visit, while they all munched on sandwiches, chips, and tea cake.

"Really?" The prince turned his attention to me. "Dragon fire; are you sure?"

"Yes, I saw it. It was definitely dragon fire," Luna confirmed.

"May I have a demonstration?"

"Um... well... I'm not sure," Elizabeth hedged.

"She claims she has no idea how she did it," Luna shrugged.

"Interesting."

"My uncle was hoping you could help her. Maybe teach her how to control it." Shane asked.

"I have never encountered one who could wield dragon fire who was not, well, not a dragon. There have been stories of one who could do the same, but I never met them."

"Could someone have suppressed her dragon?" Shane asked.

"She's no dragon. She doesn't have a dragon to shift into. My dragon would have sensed it right away, even if someone had managed to suppress it."

"Do you mind if we try something?" Prince Drake looked at Elizabeth.

"No, I guess not," Elizabeth said.

"Good. Hold out your hands and close your eyes," said Prince Drake.

"Okay," she replied slowly. She did as he asked, unsure of what he was planning.

"Take a deep breath and relax. Good. Now, go back to right before the dragon fire appeared. What were you feeling?" Prince Drake asked.

"Terrified." She really didn't want to relive the fear of almost becoming a troll's dinner.

"How about physically? Any pain or sensation of hot or cold?"

"Yes, there was a warming sensation in my chest."

"Good, now concentrate on that feeling. Try to feel it again."

Elizabeth jerked back and opened her eyes. "What? No. What if I accidentally burn one of you?"

"There is nothing to fear. I can help you control the fire. You won't hurt anyone, I promise. However, if it helps, we can ask everyone else to move out of the way." Drake nodded at Shane, who directed the others to walk to one of the other sitting areas away from them.

"There, now it's just us, and I can assure you, I'm fireproof. Feel free to do your worst. Let's try that again, shall we?"

Elizabeth nodded. Holding out her hands, she took a deep breath, closed her eyes, and tried to focus on the warming sensation she had felt before the flames shot from her hands. Blocking out everything else around her, she focused solely on the warmth that now filled her core. It was like a firm hug, comforting, and inviting.

Hearing a gasp come from beside her, she opened her eyes and saw Prince Drake staring at her hands. Looking down, she noticed the blue-green flames dancing in her palm. It was beautiful.

As she moved her hand, the flame wrapped around it. A laugh escaped her lips as the flame danced around her hand in a playful manner. Normally, Elizabeth would have freaked out about the fire around her hand. But there was something about this flame; it called to her. She knew it wanted to protect her.

Shane and Chad inched closer, which was fine with Elizabeth. She was no longer afraid of the magic she held. She knew she could control it.

"Well, that is dragon fire," Shane breathed with a sigh. "Wow, Liz."

"Who are you?" Prince Drake asked in wonder.

"She is Lady Lorraine's granddaughter," Shane answered.

Something sparked in the prince's eyes, but Elizabeth wasn't sure what it was. "Perhaps my mother will have some answers for you." Elizabeth nodded. "In the meantime, would you be up for some sparring practice? I would be happy to teach you how to wield your fire defensively."

"Yes, I would love that. Thank you."

# ELEVEN

Prince Drake took Elizabeth behind the villa to his private training yard as Shane, Chad, and Luna followed. For hours, they worked on her proper fighting stance, how to call the dragon fire at will, and how to create a fire shield, a fire lance, and even a fire whip, which made Elizabeth feel like Indiana Jones. Who knew training could be fun?

Elizabeth found it surprising how quickly she mastered each task. However, neither the prince nor Shane seemed as surprised. When she asked why, the prince told her that even without a dragon, the fire was part of her. Once she had stopped being afraid of it, she had been able to connect to it, allowing her to mold the flames to her desired outcome.

“I’m starving,” Chad said as he dramatically collapsed to the ground, holding his hand over his eyes.

Luna rolled her eyes at his antics.

“I could definitely use a shower.” Elizabeth didn’t think she had anymore sweat left in her drenched body.

“I have taken the liberty of having rooms prepared for each of you. You can all freshen up, and then we will dine out here under the stars and enjoy our evening.”

“That sounds amazing.” The prince had taken Elizabeth's arm and put it through his as they walked around to the front of the house.

“There is nothing more enjoyable than good food and good company, especially before we discuss business tomorrow when my mother arrives,” Prince Drake said. He then clapped his hands and two servants appeared. “Please escort our guests to their rooms to freshen up.” He gestured toward the stairs leading into the villa.

“Thank you, Your Highness,” Elizabeth smiled. She

followed a young woman who appeared to be in her early twenties. Her long blonde hair was pulled into a loose braid down her back, and she wore an all-black uniform-style dress that fell below her knees. She silently directed both Luna and Elizabeth to follow her. Another servant led Chad and Shane in an opposite direction.

Elizabeth was escorted to a gorgeous guest suite with Luna's room situated across the hall. "Thank you, and what is your name?" Elizabeth asked the servant.

"Apologies, Milady. My name is Skye. I will be your lady's maid while you are here. Please ring that bell on the table if you should require anything," Skye said before she curtsied and exited the room.

Elizabeth drank in her surroundings. The room was beyond elegant. There was a king-sized four-poster bed with fluffy, inviting, cream-colored bedding, along with tons of pillows piled high on it. Elizabeth couldn't help herself. She took off in a run and leaped onto the bed, landing in the middle of the super soft pillows. There was something about large, fluffy beds that made Elizabeth want to act like a five-year-old kid.

From the bed, she noticed a beautifully carved wooden desk and a chair in the room's corner, situated in a sitting area. Two cream and gold-colored couches and a matching armchair were positioned on the other side.

She reluctantly rolled to the edge of the bed and sat up before walking over to an open door. She found a luxurious en suite, and her attention was immediately drawn to the huge soaker tub that she could swim laps in. She was in heaven.

There was a knock at the door, and when she opened it, Elizabeth found Skye holding a garment bag. "Hello, Milady," she said with a curtsy. "His royal highness thought you might want something more comfortable to wear to dinner this evening."

Skye entered the room and laid the garment bag on the bed. She opened the bag to reveal a stunning light pink dress. It was sleeveless with a high neckline, tight at the waist, and then flared out to below the knees. The material was soft and expensive. Skye also produced a pair of matching sling-back flats.

"It's gorgeous, thank you."

"I'm sure his royal highness will be pleased to hear you like it. Will you require help drawing a bath, milady?" Skye asked.

"No, I'm just going to jump into the shower."

"Of course, Milady. I can wait here if you will require assistance dressing."

"Um, no, thank you. I think I can get it from here. I appreciate it. The dress is perfect," Elizabeth said sincerely. *A girl could get used to this kind of treatment. Minus the help to dress, of course.*

"Please ring if you require anything else," Skye said with a curtsy before exiting the room.

After the most glorious shower of her life, with water the perfect temperature and pressure, Elizabeth stepped out and wrapped herself in a towel. The one thing that wasn't perfect was her dripping wet hair. She searched through all the drawers and cabinets, looking for a blow dryer. But there was none. There was no way she was going to walk downstairs to dinner in a beautiful dress and wet hair.

She thought of ringing for Skye to see if anyone had a blow dryer she could borrow. Even the most basic of hotels had a blow dryer in them. Then, it occurred to her that she was no longer in the human realm, and that everyone here was a dragon and was probably capable of drying their hair with their dragon fire.

*Could I? I did really well at practice today. Drying my hair, in theory, could be much simpler than producing and maintaining a fire shield. Right? Surely, it couldn't be that difficult? But what if I burn all my hair off? Then again, it's my fire. I can control the damn thing. Right?*

After a long debate with herself, she deduced that it was worth a try. Sitting on the edge of the bed, she closed her eyes and concentrated. She willed her magic to dry her hair. She assumed the fire would sprout from her hands like normal, and she would run her hands over hair like she would a blow dryer. However, that was not what happened. To her amazement, she felt the warming sensation move from her chest to her head, and then out through her hair follicles. It was like a warm scalp massage. Once the warming sensation had faded, she touched her hair, and it was completely dry.

Jumping up, she ran to the mirror, taking in her appearance. Her hair had that salon blow-out look, the one you can never normally achieve on your own.

"Wow." She really wanted to share this with someone, but who would get it? She doubted any of her traveling companions would understand why the simple act of drying her hair with dragon fire would excite her.

Then her excitement died as her thoughts drifted to the one person whom she would have told, and she suddenly wished she could talk to her right now. Her grandmother. What would her grandmother think about all this?

"No!" She was not going to go there, not today. Since no body had been found, there was no use jumping to conclusions. Besides, she needed to finish getting ready. Now that her hair looked fantastic, she needed to finish getting dressed.

Elizabeth checked out her appearance in the floor-to-ceiling mirror. Thankfully, she had found some unopened cosmetics in the bathroom, which perfectly matched her skin tone. She finished off her look for the evening with a natural look.

Elizabeth jumped when there was another knock at the door. She smiled as she wondered what surprise Skye had for her this time, or perhaps it was Luna telling her it was time to go downstairs for dinner.

Elizabeth opened the door, surprised to find a tall, elegant-looking woman with long red hair pulled up in a loose bun. Her stunning green eyes, the color of springtime, were shining as she smiled. The woman wore an impeccably tailored black suit and a white dress shirt, which she had opened around the neckline to reveal an expensive-looking emerald necklace. She was obviously not a servant.

# TWELVE

"Hello, Elizabeth, I am Queen Surraya. May I come in for a moment?" she asked as she walked into the room.

"Of course, yes, please, it's your house," Elizabeth said, fumbling with her words and feeling unsure if she should bow, curtsy, or run away. The queen smiled warmly as she looked at Elizabeth.

"I do hope you like your accommodations. This has always been one of my favorite guest rooms in the entire villa."

"I do, thank you," Elizabeth said as she fidgeted with her hands.

"Wonderful," Queen Surraya said with a smile. "Please, let us have a seat, shall we?" The Queen motioned to the sitting area. Elizabeth followed obediently. She watched as the Queen sat gracefully on the cream and gold couch. The queen motioned for her to take a seat beside her. Elizabeth sat down as instructed on the couch next to the queen of dragons, still in shock that a queen was in her room to visit her.

"I apologize for dropping in on you unannounced like this, my dear. I heard you were here, and I simply needed to see you right away," Queen Surraya said, smiling.

"Now?" Elizabeth asked, confused.

"Yes, dear, I have been waiting a long time to meet you in person. I am delighted that you are finally here," Queen Surraya said warmly. Elizabeth looked at the queen with wide eyes. She didn't know what to say. The queen of dragons not only knew about her, but wanted to meet her. "I have a lot to tell you, and I am afraid we have little time. Sadly, you are not safe here. Lilith has spies everywhere, and I fear they have infiltrated Fireside as well, perhaps even my court," Queen Surraya said with sadness in her voice.

"Is this because I am a human who can call upon the dragon fire? Is that why they would want to hurt me or use me? That's what Uncle Nicky—I mean Commander Black—told me."

Queen Surraya reached for Elizabeth's hands. "I told your grandmother she should have been honest with you when you turned sixteen. That's when our kind comes of age. I never felt she was doing you justice by keeping you in the dark, and now look where we are. Your powers are manifesting. She's missing. Dangerous people will be after you if they aren't already. It is quite a pickle you are in, my child."

"You know my grandmother?"

"Yes, and in her defense, when your father, well, you know.. . It changed her. She felt the need to protect you more fiercely. I guess she felt that keeping you away from all things magical would do that. No matter her reasoning, she should have been the one to tell you when you turned sixteen. Not someone else, and not when you are already in your twenties. But here we are," Queen Surraya said with a weary smile.

"Tell me what?" Elizabeth asked.

Queen Surraya studied Elizabeth for a moment, squeezed her hands, and then let go of them. "My dear, there is no easy way to say this. You are not human; you are of dragon blood, like me," Queen Surraya said softly.

Elizabeth's mouth fell open, but no sound came out. How do you respond to something like that? She knew she had dragon fire, which made her different. But she never imagined she could be an actual dragon.

"Did you just say I am a dragon?" Elizabeth lifted her gaze to the ceiling before returning it toward the queen.

"No, I said you were of dragon blood."

"Um... okay. What's the difference?"

"My son is going to be expecting you for dinner at any moment, and I must provide you with some hard truth before you leave. Your life could depend on it. The hard part is that you have lived in the dark your entire life, knowing nothing of your family, the power that runs through your veins, or the responsibility you hold." Queen Surraya stood and walked over to a small bookshelf nestled in the corner.

Elizabeth watched the queen, listening, but not sure if she was dreaming or if her entire world was shifting before her eyes.

"All right, let me start from the beginning and tell you what I can." Queen Surraya turned back toward Elizabeth, and in her hands, she held an old leather-bound book. She handed it to Elizabeth as she sat back down. She opened the first page and pointed to a portrait of a rugged-looking man wearing a dragon scale crown. "My father, King Drakus, lost my mother during the Great Dragon Wars. He was lonely after that, and he found comfort in the arms of a human servant who lived in the palace."

Turning the page, she pointed to the portrait of a handsome young man with piercing green eyes. "She gave birth to a son, my half-brother, Uther. Since Uther was not full-blooded, he was born without a dragon inside him.

"However, he possessed all the other traits of our dragon line. Uther was strong, brave, loyal, and an outstanding leader. He was a great warrior, quickly rising through the ranks of the Britannia army." She turned the page to another portrait of the same young man, a little older now and wearing a crown and holding a sword. "Eventually, he became king."

"Wait," Elizabeth stopped her. "Are you talking about Uther Pendragon, as in King Arthur's father? That Uther Pendragon?"

"Yes, the same."

"Wow," was Elizabeth's only response.

"Uther could also call upon dragon fire. He was the first ever without a dragon to call upon it. And you, my child, are the second. You are a direct descendant of my brother Uther, which makes you a member of the royal family of the Emerald Island Dragon Clan. A Duchess of our clan, to be exact." Queen Surraya paused a moment to allow Elizabeth to soak in this information.

"So, let me get this straight—I got my dragon fire from Uther Pendragon, who is my actual ancestor? And I'm a duchess?" Elizabeth asked, shaking her head in disbelief.

"Yes, dear, that is correct," Queen Surraya said with a smile.

"Is this some kind of joke? Are there hidden cameras around somewhere?" Elizabeth jumped to her feet.

"No dear, this is not a joke, and why would you think there might be cameras in your room?"

"Um, never mind. Anyway, does that mean I'm a great-great-great-great-whatever child of King Arthur?" Elizabeth asked as she paced around the room. "I didn't think he had any kids besides Mordred. Oh my God, please tell me I'm not a descendant of Mordred."

"No, dear, Arthur would be your uncle, somewhat removed. You come from the line of his sibling, a child Uther had before he became king," Queen Surraya replied.

"I'm confused. According to history, Uther Pendragon only had one blood child, Arthur, and a stepchild or stepchildren, depending on which story you happen to read. There is no mention of another full-blooded Pendragon," Elizabeth said skeptically.

"That is why you are here. You can't always rely on history books. Had knowledge of Uther's other child been known, Lilith would have tracked them down and killed them and any descendants they may have, like you. Lilith fears the Pendragons, and she decided a long time ago to wipe the Pendragon bloodline from all the realms." Queen Surraya looked at Elizabeth with sympathy. "She killed Uther and cast an evil spell to make sure Arthur's wife, Guinevere, was barren. She poisoned the mind of Arthur's only son, Mordred, against him."

"Why?" Elizabeth asked. "Wiping an entire bloodline from existence out of fear is a tad extreme."

"Because of Uther's unique heritage, being both of human and dragon blood, he was tasked with protecting human and supernatural alike. To aid in this task, Queen Dianna gifted Uther Excalibur, a magical sword that has no equal. Excalibur is the only weapon known that can kill an immortal. The slightest scratch from its blade is fatal for all creatures. Excalibur is connected to Uther Pendragon's bloodline. Only a Pendragon of his line can wield it, and only a Pendragon can destroy Lilith. Do you understand what I'm telling you?"

Elizabeth halted her pacing.

"My dear, you are the last Pendragon of Uther's lineage and the only one who can kill Lilith."

She looked at the queen in utter shock. "*What?* No disrespect, but are you insane?" She started to pace again. "Even if I wanted to, let's say, *kill* the immortal, blood-sucking, crazy, evil queen, I don't have that kind of power. I certainly can't wield some magical freaking sword from the dark ages."

"I know. It's not fair to spring all this on you. I can't even imagine how you must be feeling."

Elizabeth sat back down on the couch and lowered her head into her hands.

"You mustn't fret. All will be well."

Elizabeth looked up. "Really? How? How can it all be well? You just sat here and told me the fate of the world rests on my shoulders."

"Elizabeth..."

"No, don't you see?" Tears welled in her eyes. "I can't do it. I can't kill someone. I'm not a trained warrior."

"Darling, we can get you training."

"I am not a warrior or fighter–I'm an archaeologist. I can't do this. I can't do what you are asking me. There must be another way, someone else. I'm not that girl. I can't be this Pendragon."

"It's a lot, I understand."

Elizabeth let out a humorless laugh. "No offense, Your Majesty, but I don't think anyone can understand how I feel right now."

"Please call me Surraya." Reaching for Elizabeth's hands again, she held them tight. "You're right. There is no way for me or anyone to fully understand how you're feeling. You have been told your entire world is a lie, and now you are being asked to fulfill a role that you knew nothing about."

Elizabeth nodded her head as she listened.

"I can relate on a small level. You see, I was rather young

when my father died unexpectedly, making me queen. At that time, I was also pregnant with Drake, and his father was not around anymore. I felt completely alone, not knowing who I could trust. I was being pulled in many different directions. I, too, felt like the weight of the world was on my shoulders. But I realized I had no other choice but to rise to the challenge, as will you."

"What if you're wrong?"

"Wrong about what?"

"What if I can't rise to this challenge?" Elizabeth whispered.

"I have no doubt in my mind that you will."

Elizabeth took a few deep breaths.

"Fate would not have put this in your lap if it was not certain you could handle it."

"Wait," Elizabeth frowned. "You said something about Excalibur."

"Yes, Uther's and Arthur's sword."

"It's required in order to stop Lilith, correct?"

"Yes, it is," the queen replied calmly.

"The sword has yet to be found. Which means there is still no way to kill Lilith, regardless of whether I'm this last Pendragon or not."

"You are the last Pendragon, and from what I know about Excalibur, it will find you when you're ready."

Elizabeth laughed. "I am pretty sure that I am never going to be ready."

Queen Surraya moved closer to Elizabeth, gently tilting her face up. "Elizabeth, you have more power running through your veins than you could possibly understand. The dragon fire is the first to manifest. Fate worked its magic to ensure that you would be you. I know that doesn't make sense right now, but one day it will. You are destined to restore the light."

"What if I fail? What if you are wrong and I'm not this person, or the sword never finds me? What happens if Lilith goes unchecked?"

Queen Surraya took in a deep breath. "If Lilith continues on her current path, and if the Pendragon is unable to stop her, then darkness will overtake all the realms. She will allow the evils of the world to prosper, and life will hold no joy for anyone who survives the bloodbath that will ensue. No realm will be free."

"Oh." Elizabeth had no idea how to respond to that.

There was a knock on the door as Luna shouted from the hall, "I'm starving. Are you ready to go eat?"

"Yes, give me one minute, I'll be right there," Elizabeth said as she swiped the tears from her eyes.

"Have faith in yourself as I have faith in you," Queen Surraya said.

Elizabeth shook her head. "I'm sorry, Your Majesty, thank you for the history lesson, but I'm not that girl. I can't be. My life has been a crazy shit show for the past few days. No, if I'm being honest, it's been a shit show since long before that. And all that was before you confirmed the fact that I'm not even freaking human."

"Elizabeth," Queen Surraya whispered.

"This is a lot to take in. I can see why my grandmother waited to tell me."

"Elizabeth, I am sorry to cause you this distress."

"No, it's okay, it's not your fault I was born into all this, I guess." Elizabeth dramatically waved her arms around. "But as you mentioned earlier, your son, the crown prince, is expecting me for dinner, and I don't want to be late. I need food and a drink—no—make that more like twenty drinks. If you would, please excuse me." Queen Surraya nodded, and Elizabeth walked toward the door.

"You are not alone, Elizabeth. I am here, and you have many on your side"

Elizabeth nodded, then shut the door to her room and found Luna standing there, leaning against the wall with her arms crossed.

"It's about time," Luna said, pushing herself off the wall.

"Sorry," Elizabeth said as she looked back at the closed door to her room.

"Something wrong?" Luna asked, noticing Elizabeth's distraction.

"Honestly, I don't know but," Elizabeth started to say, and then stopped as she took in Luna's appearance. She was wearing an off-the-shoulder lavender dress that made her blue eyes pop. It flared out at the waist and hit above her knees. It even showed a peek of cleavage. Her long hair was flowing down her back. She looked stunning. "Luna, you look incredible," Elizabeth said with a huge smile.

"Whatever," Luna said with her usual dose of sarcasm and an eye roll. "That lady's maid said it was best if I dressed in something besides battle gear for dinner. Now, let's go. I'm starving," Luna said as her pace quickened. "Drake, better have wine."

"I hope he has something much stronger," Elizabeth grumbled.

# THIRTEEN

Elizabeth followed Luna down to the open courtyard. There, they found Shane and Chad in deep conversation with Prince Drake. They, too, had upgraded their wardrobe. They were all in black dinner jackets, white dress shirts, bow ties, and black slacks. All three men looked up as the girls walked down the stairs and over to greet them.

"You both look stunning," Prince Drake said as he offered Luna his arm.

Shane did the same for Elizabeth. Bending down to her ear, he said, "You take my breath away."

Elizabeth blushed and said, "Thank you. You clean up nice, yourself." They followed Prince Drake and Luna to the table where Chad quickly found his spot and began munching on hors d'oeuvres.

Dinner was a pleasant distraction from all the doom and gloom, which now seemed to be a constant part of Elizabeth's life. She had little appetite, even though the artisan pizzas looked delicious. She picked at it, mainly, forcing herself to take a few bites of a slice of plain cheese pizza so as not to offend the prince or his chef. The wine, on the other hand, Elizabeth couldn't get enough of. It was amazing. Elizabeth had never been much of a drinker, but she found the dragon melon wine to be the best thing she had ever tasted. She had to force herself to sip it casually like everyone else, so she didn't look like a glutton.

Elizabeth sipped her wine, listening as the others talked. They reminisced about their days at the Royal Military Academy and all the crazy antics they had gotten into as students. Luna, to her surprise, even cracked a smile. This was what she needed. To feel normal, even if it was just for tonight. She would deal with all that other crap tomorrow.

During dessert, which was some kind of fruit tart and ice cream, Elizabeth started to feel a little strange. She found herself laughing. She couldn't stop herself. Her uncontrolled laughter filled the room, and Shane looked at her with concern.

Luna asked, "How much wine did you drink?" Elizabeth had no clue. Her glass never seemed to be empty. She felt amazing, like she was floating on a cloud. No worries, no stress.

"I need to dance!" Elizabeth yelled, jumping up and grabbing Shane's hands, attempting to drag him away from the table. Shane allowed her to pull him a short way where he stood with a harsh expression on his face.

"Liz, I think you might have had too much wine. Perhaps it's best for you to call it a night."

"Oh, Shane, don't be such a party pooper," she said as she tapped the tip of his nose with her finger. Elizabeth ran over to Chad. "Chad, will you please dance with me, since Shane is being an old fuddy-duddy?" she asked, with her bottom lip sticking out in a mock pout.

"Of course, Chad will dance with you. I'm fae; we live to dance," he said, grinning from ear to ear. But as soon as he stood up to join her, Shane pushed him back in his seat and grabbed Elizabeth by her waist.

"Liz, please, this isn't you. I think it's time for you to get some rest," Shane said, pleading for her to listen to him.

Elizabeth's expression turned stony. "How would you know this isn't me or what's best for me? You left me without saying goodbye. Remember?" After she shoved him away with both hands, he released her. "You never once tried to reach out to me. I guess they don't have phones in London or the royal whatever academy. Don't you dare stand here and tell me what's best for me!" Hurt flashed in Shane's eyes, but she continued. "You're not my father. He's dead. And you know what? I'm probably next. Let me have a little fun before I'm toast. Okay?"

Shane's scowl deepened. "What do you mean, you're next?"

"Oops," Elizabeth hiccupped, turning away from Shane and looking at the others, her hand over her smiling mouth. She put her finger to her lips and said, "Shh, I probably wasn't supposed to say anything because of the spies." Elizabeth hiccupped and started laughing. "If no one wants to dance with me, I can dance by myself." She twirled around and around.

"That's it." Shane stalked toward Elizabeth. Seeing him heading her way, she ran, avoiding his outstretched arms. "Elizabeth Lorraine Madison... Come here!"

"You know what? How about you go to bed, Mr. Grumpy Pants Shane Ignatius Black!"

"Enough!" he shouted, and without Elizabeth even seeing him move, he had her up and over his shoulder. "I'm taking you to bed."

*Ok, is it possible to be pissed and turned on all at the same time?*

Elizabeth heard Shane offer his apologies to Prince Drake as he sped up the stairs with Elizabeth over his shoulder. She hadn't even had time to protest.

Shane opened Elizabeth's door and walked in. He gently placed her on the bed.

She looked around the room before saying, "Good. At least the doom and gloom queen is gone."

Shane, who had been rummaging through her closet looking for something, stopped what he was doing and spun around to look at Elizabeth. "What queen? Who are you talking about?"

"You know what queen, the one who lives here, silly," Elizabeth said, lying back on the bed. Shane walked over to the bed, handing her a pair of pajamas, and then sat down next to her.

"What did she say to you?" he asked with concern.

"Oh, you know, the usual." She sat up. "That I'm the last of some dragon bloodline that can kill the queen bitch with Arthur's magical sword. And of course, if she finds out, then she will want to kill me, too," Elizabeth said before turning to Shane and once again becoming serious. "Shane, I don't know what to do. I'm scared. I don't know how to fight." Elizabeth cried into her pillow. "I didn't ask for any of this." Shane pulled Elizabeth into his arms and held her.

They sat, Elizabeth cradled in his arms for a bit. Shane rubbed soothing circles on her back as she cried. He continued to hold her even after her sobbing stopped, almost like he didn't want to let her go.

"Liz," he finally said, breaking the silence. "I won't let anyone hurt you, I promise. I know I have given you plenty of reasons to doubt me after not being there for you, but I am now, and I'm not going anywhere."

Elizabeth turned her head so she could look into his eyes. In this moment, she felt safe with his arms around her. She missed his touch, missed him and all that they had once been to each other. Above all else, she missed her best friend, and she needed him.

Elizabeth sat up, her gaze never leaving his. Moving and situating herself, so she was now straddling his lap. She ran her fingers through his dark golden hair and placed her hand on the back of his neck. She pulled him closer, only stopping for a brief second before her lips touched his. At first, he didn't move, but then he parted his lips and allowed her access.

She needed this distraction. Not wanting to think about anything else, she allowed the warmth of his closeness, his familiar scent of sandalwood, to transport her back to a simpler time—before he'd left her and before magic, supernaturals, and destiny had invaded her life.

She deepened their kiss as she reached for his dinner jacket. She frantically pulled at it to take it off him, but he grabbed her wrist, stopping her. He broke off the kiss. She looked into his eyes and saw only blackness, not a hint of blue. She gasped and looked away. He quickly stood, dropping her on the bed as he turned away from her. He ran his hands through his hair in frustration.

Suddenly feeling cold, she reached for a throw positioned at the end of the bed. Wrapping herself in it, she watched as he slowly turned back to face her. She noticed his eyes were back to their normal shade of blue.

His gaze bore down on her, but he didn't say a word. He was making her feel more uncomfortable than she already was. Shaking his head, he finally broke the awkward silence that had fallen between them. "Liz, I'm sorry, I can't. Not like this. Not while you're drunk and not before we can talk about... well, everything. About those years I was away, and the real reason I was sent to the military academy." He sunk down into a plush chair that was sitting in the corner of the room, head in his hands. "Why did I never call? I was afraid, Liz, and I need you to understand that." He sounded broken.

Elizabeth put her hand up. "Stop, please, just stop, Shane." Rejection, anger, and embarrassment flared to life in her chest. "You don't want me. It's okay. I understand. You didn't want me back then, and you don't want me now."

Desperately holding back tears that wanted to fall like a winter rainstorm, she said, "Please, leave." Her voice shook with both hurt and anger. How could she have been such a fool? Why did she try to open that door again? *Stupid, stupid, stupid!*

"Liz, please, it's not like that. You need to know the truth first," Shane said pleadingly.

"I don't want to hear it. I don't need some lame-ass excuse from you, trying to make me feel better. I get it, I really do. I'm sorry; I don't know what I was thinking." More hurt and embarrassed now than angry, and feeling really stupid, she turned from him, not wanting him to see the tears she could no longer hold back.

"Liz, please let me explain."

Wiping the tears from her eyes with the back of her hand, she turned back to face him. "There's nothing to explain. I saw the magazine covers. I know you moved on. I was being foolish."

"What magazine covers?" he asked, taken aback.

"Shane, seriously, do I look like an idiot? You're the playboy CEO, after all. With the movie star looks and a different model on his arm every week. I saw the article."

He flinched. "Liz, it's not like that."

"I was a fool to think that you would, I don't know, maybe wait for me or come back for me. I don't even know what I thought would happen when you left." Shaking her head, she stood from the bed and walked to the door.

"Only in fairytales or an Irene Bahrd novel do two people find love again after being apart for years. I don't know what I was thinking. It was stupid."

"Liz, can we please take a step back?" He stood up.

Opening the door, she motioned for him to leave. "I need to be alone, please," she said, once again trying to hold back the tears.

"Wait, Liz, it's not what you think. I'm not the playboy CEO. If you could just give me a second, to explain—" Shane started toward her.

"Like I said, no explanation is needed. I was just being stupid. Now, please go," she said sternly.

"Liz..." he started to reach for her. But she surprised him when both her hands lit up with blue-green dragon fire. Looking defeated, Shane lowered his head and walked to the door. "I really am sorry about tonight, Liz." He walked out, and she slammed the door behind him.

Leaning back against the closed door, she slowly slid to the floor. She wrapped her arms around her middle, the tears streaming down her face. Why had she kissed him? Why had she tried to open that damn door again? She had barely survived it the last time. He was familiar; he reminded her of home. But it was a home she didn't have anymore.

She stood up, and the room spun a little. Grabbing for the bedpost to help her navigate to the bed, she sat down hard on the bed.

Would she have wanted to kiss him if she hadn't been drinking? No, it wasn't the drinking; it was the conversation she had prior to the drinking. She was hiding; she didn't want to face what the queen had told her, and she had been willing to use her best friend to help her forget. She hadn't cared that he had just popped back into her life, hadn't considered that she had never been with a man before when acting that rashly. Yes, she was a twenty-three-year-old virgin, but no one needed to know that, and sure as hell not Shane.

She had used her heartbreak as a shield to block out the world. She was tired of the people she loved leaving her. Her mother had left shortly after she had been born, dropping Elizabeth off on her father's doorstep. Then, her father had disappeared and was presumed dead. Shane had left, and now her grandmother. It was too much to bear. It was easier to not develop feelings at all. A broken heart was too much pain, and it was pain she had suffered too many times to count.

Rubbing her eyes with her hands, she realized none of this

was Shane's fault. He had been right to stop them from going any further. Standing up once more, holding onto the bedpost to make sure the room didn't start spinning again, she headed for her door. She wasn't sure where Shane's room was, but she knew it was on the other side of the villa. She needed to find him and apologize.

Still feeling a bit unsteady on her feet, she opened the door to exit her room. She proceeded down the dark empty hallway, holding onto the wall for support, walking in the direction she hoped Shane's room was in. If she got lost, she could ask the first servant she saw for directions.

The hall was darker than she had assumed it would be. She guessed that dragons probably had exceptional night vision and didn't need extra light to see. The hallway was deserted, not a servant in sight, which meant it was much later than she had originally thought, or everyone was still attending to the prince at dinner.

As she felt her way down the hall, the sudden sensation of being followed made goosebumps appear on her arms. But she hadn't seen a single person since she'd left her room, nor had she heard any sounds of movement.

Almost forgetting in her still drunken state that she had hands that could glow, she called forth her dragon fire and used it to illuminate the hallway. The fire wasn't as bright as normal because she was having trouble concentrating. She was still able to make enough light to glance over her shoulder and confirm she was still alone.

Trying to shake the uneasy feeling, she continued down the hall. Shane's room had to be around here somewhere. Right?

Figuring she had to be getting close to the other side of the villa, she continued on. Suddenly, she heard angry whispers coming from down the hall in the direction she was headed. She doused the small flame she had in her hand and proceeded to move slowly towards the voices. She peeked around the corner. To her shock, she found two large, extremely scary, and not entirely human looking men. Black horns protruded from their heads. One had an unconscious Luna over one of his shoulders, his freakishly long fingers wrapped around her leg. The other had Skye in his grip, with his nasty hand covering her mouth. She was struggling, trying to get away.

They were talking with one of the kitchen staff. He was the one who had kept refilling her wine.

"Where is he? This spell won't mask our presence much longer, and we need the Pendragon!"

*What? How did they know about me when I had just found out? No, wait, he said he. They think the Pendragon is a man.*

"I'm s-s-sorry. I don't know where the Pendragon is. I heard that he's here. I overheard the queen saying it herself."

"If you're wrong, maggot, then these two won't be the only offerings I take with me. Do you understand?"

"Y-y-y-yes, Sir. I will find where he's staying." The kitchen staffer then ran off in the opposite direction of Elizabeth.

Elizabeth backed around the corner, out of sight. Where were the guards and any other servants? She needed to help Luna and Skye, but how? If she yelled for help, they could hurt them or worse. But if she did nothing, they would get away, and then what?

She tried not to shake with the fear, but. She was no warrior, no great hope, no bringer of the light or whatever had been said about her. Elizabeth couldn't even figure out how to help her friends. If only she had a way to call for Shane or Prince Drake. She didn't want to have to do this on her own. She had no idea what to do, anyway.

She was running out of time, and she needed to do something. She couldn't stay here feeling sorry for herself when Luna and Skye were the ones in big trouble. Elizabeth took a deep breath and prayed to whomever was listening for some divine help.

Gathering what little resolve she had, she ran around the corner and yelled for the two beasts to stop. She hoped that by making a big enough commotion, that it would attract some guards to come help.

The two men stopped and looked at her with surprise, and then amusement.

"Well, would you look at that? Ain't she a purdy little thing?" one snorted.

"Let my friends go, and no one needs to get hurt." She tried to sound brave.

"I don't think so," said the one holding Skye.

"Excuse me?" Elizabeth asked.

"I said, 'No.' We are going to take your friends as planned." He sniffed the air in her direction. "Interesting. You have no scent. What are you?"

"Again, with that? At least I don't smell like dog shit. Sadly, I can't say the same for some here." She put her hands on her hips, trying to look intimidating. *And where the hell is this bravado coming from?* She was talking crap to what she was pretty sure was a freaking demon.

"Doesn't really matter to me, and I don't think them vamps care much about what kind of blood they drink as long as it's fresh and warm. I'm sure you'll do just fine, darling."

Figured that the one time someone called her *darling*, it was a freaking gross-ass demon threatening to kidnap her. "What's this about vamps and blood?"

She needed to keep this banter going to buy some more time. Someone would have to show up at some point, right?

“Look, sweet cheeks, we can do this the hard way or easy way. You can come willingly, and no one gets hurt, or we can do it the hard way, and I make no promises about how that will end for you. You just need to be breathing and still have some blood to offer the vamps.”

“Or… counteroffer, I light your asses on fire and call it a day.” She smirked as she called forth her dragon fire. Her hands started to glow, but before she could get a good flame going, she felt a sharp prick in her neck.

Elizabeth turned around and found another demon standing behind her, holding a now empty syringe in his hand. She heard all three cackling as her world went dark.

# FOURTEEN

Elizabeth's head throbbed like it was going to split into pieces. Her eyes didn't want to open. She felt a hard dirt surface under her curled-up arms where her aching head was cradled. She realized this was not her bed at the dragon's Italian villa. It smelled like she had fallen into a sewer. The foul odor of human waste and vomit surrounded her. Bile rose in the back of her throat, but she managed to swallow it back down. Hearing her name being whispered, she tried to move toward the voice. Someone tapped on her shoulder. Slowly opening her eyes, she found a disheveled and dirty-looking Luna along with their lady's maid, Skye, standing above her. Carefully, Elizabeth sat up, taking in her surroundings.

"Where are we?" Elizabeth gasped as she took in the metal bars that surrounded them. Looking out further, she noticed even more metal cages—hundreds of other cages, all filled with people. The cages were neatly arranged in rows with several people in each. There were men, women, and children of all ages. Some looked like they had been there for weeks with the amount of filth they were covered in. Elizabeth heard crying and children begging to go home. Her stomach turned as the bile in her throat came back. What was this place?

"Shh," Luna whispered. "We don't need to draw attention to ourselves." She pointed to the guards, who were stationed in the distance. Luna looked around before continuing to speak in a hushed tone. "This is a slave auction where creatures of the lowest kind come to purchase slaves for whatever deviant purpose they have in mind, and it's never good." Luna squatted down next to her. "Vampires purchase blood and sex slaves. Trolls like to buy slaves their hellhounds can hunt and then tear apart to eat. Demons like to... never mind. I don't even want to go there."

"I thought these have been outlawed for over a hundred years," Skye whispered.

"Apparently not," Luna replied. "We can't be here. We need to get out of here quickly."

"How did we get here in the first place?" Elizabeth asked.

"You don't remember?"

"It's a bit hazy, and my head is killing me. No pun intended," Elizabeth grumbled.

"I guess I'm not surprised. Demons drugged us and dragged us here."

"Someone had to have helped the Demons gain entry to the villa. They probably used a transporter device to get us here after they drugged us. These people pay big money to anyone who brings them potential slaves. No questions asked," Luna said with disgust.

Skye looked up and said in a shy, scared voice, "It was a servant from the kitchen. He was new; I don't know his name. Mr. Shane asked me to look in on Ms. Elizabeth because she had too much to drink, and he was concerned. When I headed to your room, I saw the kitchen servant speaking with one of the demons. He had Ms. Luna over his shoulder. I turned to run out the door, but someone grabbed me from behind seconds before you came running around the corner."

Luna paced around the small cage. "I, too, was jumped from behind and stabbed with a syringe." She rubbed a spot on the side of her neck.

"Why were you singled out?" Elizabeth lowered her voice.

"I don't know," Luna shrugged. "We seem to be in this place with the general population. Everyone seems to be human or a small shifter. I think they were opportunists and just got fucking lucky. They clearly grabbed whoever they came across."

"How can you tell there are shifters here?" Elizabeth asked.

Luna looked at Elizabeth like she was dense or something. "I can smell them."

"You can tell what type of people are shifters from the smell?" Elizabeth asked.

"Yes, I'm a feline shifter. I have heightened hearing and a sense of smell like all shifters," Luna said, like it was common knowledge. Which, it probably was to everyone who hadn't been raised in the human realm, like Elizabeth.

"Hello...new to all this...remember?"

Luna let out a sigh. "How could I forget?"

"Can you smell any magic on me?" Elizabeth asked in curiosity. Queen Surraya had told her that her power ran through her veins. Could Luna smell it? Maybe she could tap into it to help them escape.

"No," Luna responded. "I can't smell you at all, which is

weird." Luna crossed her arms as she leaned against the cage, staring intensely at Elizabeth. She looked like she was trying to solve a puzzle. "All living things have a scent that is a unique mix of them personally and of their species. Whether they are humans, shifters, vampires, or whatever, they have a smell. You do not. I can smell your shampoo and soap. I can even smell Shane Black all over you." Luna raised an eyebrow. "But as for your actual scent, no, I can't smell anything."

"You can't smell if I have any magic in me or not?" Elizabeth asked.

"No, but we know you have dragon fire, and we might be able to catch them off guard with that. But we need a plan."

"Okay, what about Skye? You're a dragon shifter, right? You can shift and break this cage open," Elizabeth said, looking at Skye with some hope.

"No, I'm no dragon, milady," Skye said as she looked down at the ground. "I'm an orphan who was taken in by the dragon clan. I have no magic."

"Well crap," Elizabeth said, biting on her thumbnail, trying to stop the fear and the reality of their situation from sinking in. Last week, her biggest concern had been what to do with her life now that she had graduated from college. Now, she was probably going to be sold off to some supernatural scumbag as a freaking chew toy.

Charlotte had told Elizabeth that she was stronger than she knew. She had also mentioned the funny-shaped cross necklace was powerful and would protect her. Elizabeth reached for the cross, thankful it was still there. She held the small piece of jewelry in her hand. "Well, now would be a great time to show me what you got—if you indeed have any magic or a way to help us." She whispered to the cross.

Elizabeth, Luna, and Skye tried brainstorming ideas, but with no luck. They couldn't seem to figure out how to get out of the cage. Elizabeth even tried to use her dragon fire, moving it through her hands, trying to melt their way out, but it had no effect on the bars or the lock. On the bright side, Elizabeth was feeling more confident about calling upon the dragon fire at will instead of waiting until she was terrified or in mortal danger.

"They must spell the cages against magic," Luna said as she looked out past the bars. "That would explain why there are shifters here. They can't shift, either."

"Okay, I know this is probably going to sound like a stupid question… but magic newbie here. Is there a way to break the spell?"

"Yes, but we would need a more powerful mystic than the one who cast the original spell."

"And mystics are witches or sorceress, right?" Elizabeth asked.

"Wow, you really are clueless about our world, aren't you?" Luna shook her head. "Hard to believe you were raised by Lady Lorraine, and yet you know nothing."

Elizabeth pulled a face. "Yeah, I know."

Luna crouched down to the ground and began to draw in the dirt with her finger. "Consider this your first magic lesson."

Elizabeth and Skye crossed their legs in an attempt to get more comfortable as they watched Luna draw two large circles.

"A mystic is slang for anyone who can wield magic." She pointed to the two circles. "Mystics typically fall into two categories. Sorcerers and wizards who have magic in their blood." She pointed to one of the circles which she had drawn an A in. "And then witches and warlocks who use rituals or spells." She pointed to the other circle, which now had a B drawn in it.

Elizabeth took it all in with interest.

"Group A are born with magic, and it flows naturally from them. Like your dragon fire, Elizabeth." Elizabeth nodded. "Group B is taught magic. It does not come naturally. They have to use magical items, rituals, or spells to wield their magic."

"Who do you think spelled these cages?" Elizabeth looked around at the metal bars, which looked normal to her. But she wasn't really sure how to spot magic, anyway.

"Someone from group A. No way would the vamps hire a simple witch for a job like this."

"Okay, do you think I could remove it? You said I was from group A."

"I did, and you might be able to, but I have no idea how to remove magic from an item, and I'm assuming neither do you."

Elizabeth shook her head as she stood up. She still felt off thanks to the drugs they pumped her with. She walked over and ran her hands up the bars, touching the smooth, cool metal that held her prisoner.

She heard a *clank* as something on her wrist knocked into the metal bars. Elizabeth noticed the bracelet that Uncle Nicky had given her. Glancing at Luna, she pointed to the bracelet. "Can we use the transporter device to get us all out of here? Or at least, get a message out?"

"Ooh, how does it work?" Skye asked, looking at the bracelet in wonder.

"I press on this stone two times to activate it."

"Pretty and functional," Skye nodded.

Luna paced around the small cage for a minute. "I don't know if the transporter would be strong enough for all three of us. Two, maybe, and that would be stretching it."

Luna wrapped her hands around two of the bars and peered out, deep in thought. "You could use it to get out of here. I'm not sure where it would take you. I know in theory it should have a programmed safe destination for most realms." Luna glanced at

Elizabeth, then back out through the bars. "But I'm not even sure what realm we are in, let alone if there would be a safe destination for you to get to. The tech is relatively new, so I am not sure how far it can take you."

"I'm not leaving without you guys," Elizabeth said adamantly. "How about the communicator? Can we get a message out?"

Luna shook her head. "Our communicators are not designed to work across realms. If some of our people were in this realm, then yes. But I think we would have heard from them by now. Besides, I already tried using mine with no luck."

"Back to square one," Elizabeth said, deflated.

The guards suddenly scurried to get into a uniform formation. They stood alert. *Was there a prison break?* Elizabeth thought to herself.

Then she looked over at Luna, who was trying to hear what was going on. Luna held up her hand, instructing them to wait a minute. Luna's expression then turned bleak. Turning, she looked at Elizabeth and Skye, all color draining from her face. "Shit, Dimitri is here," Luna whispered.

Elizabeth's blood ran cold at the mention of the ancient vampire.

Dimitri walked through the aisles of cages, peering through the bars as if he was inspecting cattle. He would occasionally point to one prisoner, and a soldier walking with him would write in a notebook. He slowly made his way toward where they were being held. Elizabeth could see him more clearly as he approached.

He was tall and walked with authority. He had shoulder-length black hair and black eyes that had a tinge of red around the iris. Elizabeth hated to admit it, but he was attractive. He possessed the aura of power and strength which surrounded him. There was also something familiar about him, but she couldn't quite put her finger on it. She knew she had never met him. That was something she would have remembered. Nevertheless, there was something about him.

Dimitri looked at Elizabeth and her companions, glancing over them with the same disinterest as all the others. He turned towards the soldier. "Include these three with Lot One for the Vampire Elite. Cleaned up, they might fetch a pretty penny," Dimitri said as he walked to the next cage.

Elizabeth exhaled in relief. She then felt a gust of wind and saw Dimitri turn sharply her way. Before she could take the next breath, the cage door was slammed open, and Dimitri had Elizabeth pinned between his tall frame and the cage bars. His long, claw-tipped fingers held her up by her neck as he inhaled, smelling her like a dog.

"What do we have here?" His fangs showed through the

creepiest smile. Elizabeth changed her mind. He was most definitely not attractive at all—quite the opposite.

"What type of magic is this? I can't smell you. It's like you're not even here." He sniffed again. "But I do smell someone of interest all over you. What is your name, human?" Dimitri sniffed below Elizabeth's ear, making her feel very uncomfortable.

"E... Eliz... Elizabeth," she managed to say.

"And how are you acquainted with my son?" Dimitri asked, his voice smooth as silk.

His question shocked her. "Your son? I don't know your son. I don't know any vampires. Unless he was the asshole who drugged me and brought me here against my will."

Dimitri laughed, and Elizabeth tried to turn her face away from his. "I can assure you my worthless son would not have brought you to me. He's a disappointment, thanks to that traitorous brother of mine. But I find it interesting that you wear his scent like a blanket, and it's fresh, only a few hours old. Which means you were in his company recently. Interesting." His dark eyes roamed over Elizabeth's appearance as he licked his fangs.

Elizabeth was confused. She thought about all the people she had been around recently. And then she remembered what Luna had said about her smell not that long ago. Realization hit her like a lightning bolt, and she felt bile rising in the back of her throat yet again.

Up close to him, it now dawned on her as to why Dimitri had seemed familiar. He had the same eyes. Just a different color from both Shane and Nicholas. But now she could see it, the family resemblance. It was plain as day, and it was making her feel sick.

The only man she had ever loved, her best friend, was the offspring of pure evil. She prayed to whoever listened that she was wrong and that the name that was about to come off the lips of this monster was not that of her best friend.

"Are you of importance to my disappointment of a son, I wonder?" Dimitri continued, unaware of Elizabeth's internal struggle and downward spiral. "I do not see where he has fed from you," Dimitri said, as he ran his icy cold fingers down Elizabeth's neck and stopped above her cleavage. "Nor do I see where he has mated with you. Perhaps you are just a plaything to him, someone he was toying with." Dimitri appeared to be in deep thought. "Perhaps I will take you for myself. We could have lots of fun together," Dimitri said coldly, smirking, as he put his lips on Elizabeth's neck and kissed her. "Maybe I'll return you to Shane when I have had my fill of you." His evil, blood-curdling laugh filled Elizabeth with absolute terror.

He let Elizabeth fall to the ground as if she was nothing but a rag doll before he exited the cage. “Have this one cleaned. I will be taking her personally. The other two can go with Lot One,” Dimitri said to his soldier, who was writing everything down in his little notebook as they both walked away.

Elizabeth sat motionless on the ground, tears streaming down her face. Luna and Skye rushed to her side.

“Oh my God, Elizabeth, are you okay?” Skye yelled as she hugged a still motionless Elizabeth.

“He said his name,” Elizabeth barely whispered.

“What?” Luna looked at her questioningly.

“Shane. Dimitri said his name. Shane is Dimitri’s son.” She still couldn’t believe the words as she spoke them out loud.

“What if he is?” Luna asked.

“What, Luna, he’s the son of a monster?”

“Okay, but that’s not his fault.”

“He never told me.”

“Are you upset that he’s Dimitri’s son, or that he never told you about it? Because from where I'm standing, you two recently reconnected. It's not really first date material to talk about his insane, blood-sucking daddy.”

“You knew, didn’t you?” Elizabeth scowled.

“What does that matter?"

“You knew.”

“Yes, everyone under his command knows. It’s important that we know everything about each other to have trust. So, yeah, my commanding officer has daddy issues. But he never once let me down nor showed me any reason not to trust him.”

She didn’t know which part upset her. Maybe the fact that Shane was not the man she thought he was, after all. Luna was right; they had just reconnected after years of being apart. Curling up in a ball, she felt defeated. They were never going to get out of there. She was going to be taken to that monster to have him do whatever he pleased with her, and there was nothing she could do to stop it.

When Elizabeth was about to give in to the darkness and accept her fate, she felt a warming sensation coming from the funny-shaped cross necklace around her neck. She grabbed it and felt its warmth and its strength. Elizabeth looked around and found everyone was frozen in place. Time was at a standstill, but how and why? *Did I do this?*

She turned to face the cage entrance, and there, standing in front of her, was a large man with flaming red hair, which fell below his shoulders. He had a long red beard, large shining green eyes, and a tattoo of a dragon wrapped around his neck.

# FIFTEEN

The man walked around the cage, touching the bars, and then waving his hand in front of Luna's frozen face. Elizabeth stared at him, unsure if he was real or she had finally reached her limit on sanity.

He appeared to be middle-aged, in his late forties or early fifties, and dressed like a warrior from the Dark Ages. A long-sleeved tunic in a dark green flowed down to his worn, knee-high, black leather boots. Metal armor adorned his shoulders, and metal vambraces covered his wrists and forearms. The Pendragon crest of two golden dragons, with their backs to each other, decorated his chest. A thick, black leather belt was around his trim waist, with a leather pouch and a short sword at his side.

"Stand, child," his voice boomed. "It's quite a predicament you find yourself in, wouldn't you say?" She glanced around, terrified the guards would see him. However, when she took in her surroundings, she was no longer sitting on the dirty ground of the cage; Luna and Skye were nowhere in sight. She was now in a clearing, surrounded by lush greenery and tall trees.

"What? How? Where?" *Was she dreaming?* She ran the palms of her hands across the lush, green grass she was now sitting on. It was soft to the touch. It felt real. Closing her eyes, she felt the warmth of the sun beating down on her face and the cool breeze that washed across her bare arms.

Had she passed out? No, that wasn't it. She wasn't dreaming. This was real, he was real, and she was alone in the middle of nowhere with a medieval knight.

"Am I dead?" she asked, slowly rising to her feet. She dusted the dirt and grime which had accumulated on the pink evening dress.

"No, little Pendragon, you are not dead. Your magic called to me, and I answered."

"And you are?" She stared at him, waiting for an answer.

"I am Uther Pendragon."

"Wait, you said I wasn't dead."

"You're not."

"But you are?"

He laughed. "Aye, for many years now."

"Can magic really bring back the dead?" she questioned out loud to herself.

"It's a gray area, but I wouldn't recommend it. It tends to get a wee bit messy. What you bring back is never the same as what died."

"What... what are you talking about?" She was lost at this point.

"You asked about magic bringing back the dead."

"No, I asked if..." Elizabeth shook her head. "You know what, never mind. Let's try again. How are you here? How can I understand you? I don't speak Middle Age Celtic warrior, or whatever language you spoke back then."

"You need me," he said matter-of-factly.

"And the language part?"

"You're an astute one, aren't you?" He smiled like a proud father would. "My child, I am a guardian spirit. More accurately, I'm your guardian spirit. It would make sense that we should understand each other. My ear hears my language while yours hears yours."

"You're like my guardian angel?"

"Oh, Little Pendragon, I'm no angel." He huffed out a laugh.

"Um, okay." Elizabeth looked at him, wondering if she had finally lost her mind. Not dead, but maybe she was hallucinating?

"Where are my friends and all the other prisoners?"

"You needed a moment to gather yourself."

"Okay, but that doesn't really answer my question."

Uther smiled. "Your physical body is still in the cage, I am afraid, but your mind is here in this safe place, created by magic."

"Okay," she mumbled to herself. "Are you here to get me out of this hellhole? And please tell me you're not a hallucination," Elizabeth said, looking up at the king who towered above her.

Uther's laughter echoed all around her. "You have the power to get out of here on your own, and we will get to that. And when you do return, I ask that you take a moment and look around. You need to see these atrocities and bear witness. You will need to advise the supernatural leaders of what you have seen and what is happening in many other realms. They have all grown weak. In my day, we helped each other. They can no longer sit and wait for Lilith to attack. You must make them see that the only way to save all the realms is to come together."

Elizabeth thought about the many cages she had seen around her. She recalled the faces of small children cradled in their mother's loving arms, dirt covering their small faces, and the fear in their mother's eyes. She remembered the men who looked beaten down with no fight left in them. Elizabeth thought about it all.

Until now, she had only been worried about herself, her own pain, and her own loss. She had been single-minded and selfish. Every single man, woman, and child was going to die in horrible ways. Not only those currently in cages, but those back home in Madison, throughout the human realm, and beyond, to other realms. Her own life no longer held the same value it once did.

"I think I understand. I don't know how I can help, but I know something needs to be done."

"That's the Pendragon spirit, girl," Uther said with a warm smile. "Nicholas Black is a good man. He has been protecting the realms for centuries for Queen Dianna. But the other leaders will not follow his lead or heed his council, despite his vast knowledge of Lilith and her followers. They do not trust him simply because he's a vampire, and an ancient one at that. They judge him, not for his character, but for what he is on the outside."

Hearing his confirmation that Nicholas was, in fact, a vampire, brought back her anger and sadness about Shane. They had both lied to her. Two men she trusted and loved, considered family, had lied to her. How could she get past that? "How can I convince others to trust him when I'm not sure I trust him anymore?" Elizabeth asked, turning her back so the powerful king did not see the tears running down her face.

"No need to hide your pain from me, child." He walked over to her, putting a firm hand on her shoulder, which was surprisingly warm considering that he was technically dead.

"You have been given a great shock today. But tell me, is your lack of trust because of their character or because you now fear what they are, what they have always been?"

She turned back to face him, wiping her tears with the back of her hand.

"Or, is it because they have hurt your pride by not sharing their deepest secret with you?" Uther put his large finger under her chin, tilting her face to look into his bright, forest green eyes, not unlike her own. Using his thumb, he wiped away a stray tear.

"Perhaps your reaction to this news is what they both feared and is why they have kept their secret. Even the strongest of men have fears." Uther gently released her chin. "There have been many who have kept secrets from you. Some for your protection, and some for theirs. You will learn, in time, to trust your instincts. Do not judge someone by their secrets without knowing the reason they kept them. The reason may be bigger than you realize."

"I understand that. Honestly, I do, and I hate feeling this way. I didn't even know vampires were real until the other day." She wrapped her arms around her waist. "But Shane is that monster's son. Dimitri's DNA runs through him. How can I trust him?" More tears streamed down her face.

"To experience love, one must also be willing to experience pain. One does not choose their parents. Nor should we judge a child for the sins of their parents. Being a vampire does not mean Shane is evil or a dangerous man." She looked up at Uther as he smiled at her.

Logically, she understood what he was saying, but emotionally, she wasn't there yet.

"What if you found out one of your parents wasn't exactly the hero of their story? Would that change who you are?"

"What? Is one of my parents a villain?"

He shrugged. "That's not the point. There is good and evil in all living things. It is up to us to decide which side we are on. Who or what your parents are doesn't have to define you."

"Is that why I was never told about my mother? Was she some evil, vile creature?"

Uther shook his head. "You are missing the point. What I'm saying is that no one is defined by their heritage alone. If you truly care for him, then let him speak his truth. You will know deep down if he speaks from the heart or not. That goes for both men named Black. Because they will need you and you will need them in the coming days."

"You also didn't answer my question about my mother."

"All things come in divine timing. Remember, families come in all shapes and sizes, and they are not always blood related."

"You're being evasive as hell, but I guess you're right. I need to speak to them both, and I will." Uther nodded his head in acknowledgement. "But I don't understand why you think anyone would take my word on anything. I'm nobody to them. Why would anyone care if I think they should follow Nicholas Black or not? Surely, there has to be someone better, someone people know and trust to convince them to follow him."

Uther's booming laughter filled the air once again. "They will not follow Nicholas, little Pendragon. They will follow you. You will inspire hope, renew faith in what is good. You are a Pendragon who wields dragon fire and the mighty Excalibur. The blood that runs through your veins is both royal and magical. Connect with your people and they will follow you to the gates of Hell and back. This is why Lilith fears you. Not because you wield Excalibur, but because you wield inspiration and hope for the many."

"Um... I'm not really good at public speaking and doing speeches. I'm more of a sit on the sideline's kind of girl," she shrugged.

"I have faith you will rise to this challenge. You are a Pendragon, and the last known of my bloodline."

"Ok... maybe, but unfortunately, there are a few major hiccups about all that." She said, waving her hands in the air. "First, I am just learning to wield the dragon fire. Second, I don't have Excalibur in my possession. No one has even seen that sword in well over fifteen hundred years."

Uther opened his mouth to speak, but she cut him off.

"And even if I could find the sword, I have no clue how to use it." Elizabeth looked straight at the ancient king. "Sword Fighting 101 isn't really a required class for an archaeologist these days. I'm not freaking Obi-Wan." She started pacing around, pulling at her hair.

"Is this Obi person a great sword fighter in your time?"

"What? No, he's not even real... he's a ... never mind. Anyway, what I'm saying is... I mean, what I'm trying to say is..." Putting her hands on her hips, she stopped pacing and faced Uther again. "Honestly, I don't know what I'm saying."

"Fear not, little Pendragon. The dragon fire chose you for a reason. As will your other magic. Once you trust in yourself and your abilities, then the magic will flow through you effortlessly. You need to believe in yourself and trust in it."

"Wait... did you say other magic? As in, more than the dragon fire?"

"Of course, you could unlock any of the elements and maybe even some of the celestial magic," King Uther replied.

"There are different types of magic?"

"Yes." He looked at her sternly. "The blood and magic of great sorcerers flow through your veins. Once you learn to trust the magic, you will be as powerful, if not more so, than those who came before you. Excalibur is also magic, but harder to explain."

"I know I'm new to all this magic stuff, but how can a sword be magical?"

"Excalibur has a soul, a consciousness, and powerful magic beyond even my understanding."

"Okay, but we have a problem. No one has seen the sword since Arthur. It's been lost for centuries."

Once again, Uther's laugh filled the air. "Little Pendragon, you have had Excalibur with you this whole time."

"*What?*" Elizabeth shouted. "Where?"

"It sits around your neck on that silver chain, waiting for you to call it into service," Uther said with amusement.

*Of course*, Elizabeth thought to herself as she touched the funny-shaped cross which rested above her collarbone. *It's not a cross at all, it's a freaking sword.* The very sword everyone and their brother had been looking for…for over fifteen hundred years.

Elizabeth caressed the small, funny-shaped cross in her hand. "How do I call Excalibur into service?" She could hardly believe she had had a magical sword secured around her neck this whole time.

"Do you feel the warmth, the energy radiating from the sword?" Elizabeth nodded as Uther spoke. "Good, that's Excalibur. Now, open your mind and allow your consciousness to connect with that of the sword."

Elizabeth closed her eyes and took a deep, cleansing breath, clearing her mind. She sensed something like another consciousness at the back of her mind. One that felt foreign, and yet familiar at the same time. The sensation became stronger. It was warm and comforting, like a hug from a loved one. She didn't fight it; instead, she welcomed it.

In her mind's eye, Elizabeth could see a bright light that morphed into a beautiful woman standing in front of her. Long, silver hair streamed down her back, and she wore a dress that was the purest white, almost blinding. Her eyes looked like shimmering sapphires and seemed to hold a deep wisdom. Her ears were pointed, and on top of her head was a crown of elegantly braided silver.

"Hello, Elizabeth." Her voice sounded angelically musical. "I have been waiting for a long time to meet you."

"Me? You've been waiting to meet me?"

"Of course. I have been watching you your whole life, waiting for when you would be ready."

"Ready for what?"

"I think you already know the answer to that.

She did; she knew. She had been fighting the inevitable since this had all started. The fates had chosen her, and it was time she accepted that.

"Your mind is heavy. Come, let's talk."

As if summoned by magic, a chair appeared. Walking over to the chair, Elizabeth ran her hand over the worn cracks of a brown leather recliner, savoring the touch of the aged leather. The sight of it brought tears to her eyes. How many times had she curled up in this same chair as she had watched her father work? She could even smell the familiar spice of his aftershave. Could this be the same one that had sat in her father's office? But how? Surely, it had been destroyed in the fire?

"How? Who are you?"

"Sit please." A plush, creamed colored armchair appeared behind the woman as she took a seat. Elizabeth did as she was asked and sat down.

"My name is Nimue."

Elizabeth knew that name. "As in, the Lady of the Lake?"

Nimue smiled and nodded. "I am known by many names, the Guardian, Keeper of Magic, Soul of the Sword, and, yes, Lady of the Lake."

"You gave Arthur the sword, ensuring he would be king."

"I have been a messenger for the fates for eons. Ensuring Excalibur was delivered to Arthur upon Uther's death was one of many tasks throughout time. As a sentinel, I knew it was his time, just as I now know it is your time."

"Time for what? I'm no warrior. I'm not even a leader. I don't understand why the fates would choose someone so ordinary." Elizabeth rubbed her temples. "I'm not fighting it anymore, but I'm trying to understand. Why me?"

Nimue's angelic laughter filled the space. "I can assure you; you are anything but ordinary."

"Great, I don't know if that makes me feel better or not."

"You're nothing like the Pendragons who have come before you." Nimue snapped her fingers, and their surroundings morphed into Elizabeth's father's study. Nimue stood and walked over to a bookshelf which held Elizabeth's father's collection of books on Alexander the Great and a few mystery novels.

Cautiously, Elizabeth followed. "That's what I have been trying to tell you. You have the wrong girl."

"No, we don't."

"Wait... what? But you said..."

"I said you're not like the others. I didn't mean to imply that it was a bad thing. Quite the opposite."

"I don't understand what you want from me. I am nobody special. I'm not a warrior or royalty. I can't even hold a sword, let alone fight with one. How could I possibly be of any help against evil like Lilith or Dimitri?"

"I am essence, I am magic, and I am the soul that is Excalibur. How I came to be has been lost through the ages, for I have taken many forms. I have helped many men rise to power. I have helped conquer and destroy their enemies. I have been the instrument in many wars and taken many lives. Many kings have risen and fallen with me by their side. I am now linked by blood to those in the Pendragon bloodline. Only a true Pendragon can wield my power."

"Um, okay."

Nimue took both her hands in hers. "But through all the centuries, I have waited, knowing there would come a time when a woman of the Pendragon bloodline, one with great strength and compassion, would rise. That woman is you, Elizabeth Lorraine Madison Pendragon."

"I don't know why." Elizabeth shook her head.

"You don't need all the answers. You won't be doing it alone. Others will come, for you are not the only one fate has called upon. You are meant to bring the light. You are meant to inspire and provide hope in the darkest days to come."

"I don't feel like I'm enough. I don't understand any of this."

"No one is ever ready when fate calls upon them. Even Arthur struggled in the beginning. He was a scrawny squire who could barely hold a wooden sword, let alone Excalibur. But he stepped up and learned how to be a warrior. He learned through trial and error how to be a king. And, most importantly, he didn't do it alone. He had his trusted knights and Merlin helping him along the way."

Elizabeth looked up at the angelic being before her. "Will you help me?"

"It would be my honor."

"Okay, so how does all this work with the sword?" Elizabeth asked, uncertainty in her voice.

"It's different with each person. The sword's magic will amplify your greatest skill. Arthur, for example, was a great swordsman. Excalibur aided him by providing extra strength to his sword arm and increased stamina. Uther possessed the dragon fire. The sword's magic helped amplify that fire."

"Okay, wow. And you live in the sword?"

"I am the sword and the magic that you will feel flowing from it. I will guide you and help you as much as I can."

"I still don't really understand any of this."

"And that's okay. You will learn and you will grow into the Pendragon you are meant to be."

"I know I keep saying it, and I'm sorry. I just don't understand. Why me?"

"Oh, Elizabeth, you are refreshing. Many men have fallen under the spell of want versus need. Once they get a taste of true power, that is all that drives them. Their wants and their desires become all-consuming. You are the first woman chosen by fate to wield the sword of power. I have waited for you."

"But why? Surely there have been others in all these years that would have been better prepared."

"Merlin saw you in a vision. He knew there would come a day when a woman of the Pendragon bloodline would wield the sword of power, not for conquest, but for freedom. Your heart is pure. You were the woman in his vision. Merlin made sure you would appear at this time when he knew you would truly be needed."

"Do you mean the wizard Merlin? Sword in the Stone,

Merlin, Arthur's teacher and guardian? That Merlin? How did he make sure I would be here?" Elizabeth asked.

"The same," said the angelic voice. "However, I am afraid that is not my story to tell, and sadly, our time is up. I enjoyed our time. Know that I will be with you, and you must trust in yourself and those whom fate sends to you."

"Wait, no, what do you mean by that? Who is being sent? How will I know them? I still have questions."

# SIXTEEN

Elizabeth followed Luna down to the open courtyard. There, they found Shane and Chad in deep conversation with Prince Drake. They, too, had upgraded their wardrobe. They were all in black dinner jackets, white dress shirts, bow ties, and black slacks. All three men looked up as the girls walked down the stairs and over to greet them.

"You both look stunning," Prince Drake said as he offered Luna his arm.

Shane did the same for Elizabeth. Bending down to her ear, he said, "You take my breath away."

Elizabeth blushed and said, "Thank you. You clean up nice, yourself." They followed Prince Drake and Luna to the table where Chad quickly found his spot and began munching on hors d'oeuvres.

Dinner was a pleasant distraction from all the doom and gloom, which now seemed to be a constant part of Elizabeth's life. She had little appetite, even though the artisan pizzas looked delicious. She picked at it, mainly, forcing herself to take a few bites of a slice of plain cheese pizza so as not to offend the prince or his chef. The wine, on the other hand, Elizabeth couldn't get enough of. It was amazing. Elizabeth had never been much of a drinker, but she found the dragon melon wine to be the best thing she had ever tasted. She had to force herself to sip it casually like everyone else, so she didn't look like a glutton.

Elizabeth sipped her wine, listening as the others talked. They reminisced about their days at the Royal Military Academy and all the crazy antics they had gotten into as students. Luna, to her surprise, even cracked a smile. This was what she needed. To feel normal, even if it was just for tonight. She would deal with all that other crap tomorrow.

During dessert, which was some kind of fruit tart and ice cream, Elizabeth started to feel a little strange. She found herself laughing. She couldn't stop herself. Her uncontrolled laughter filled the room, and Shane looked at her with concern.

Luna asked, "How much wine did you drink?" Elizabeth had no clue. Her glass never seemed to be empty. She felt amazing, like she was floating on a cloud. No worries, no stress.

"I need to dance!" Elizabeth yelled, jumping up and grabbing Shane's hands, attempting to drag him away from the table. Shane allowed her to pull him a short way where he stood with a harsh expression on his face.

"Liz, I think you might have had too much wine. Perhaps it's best for you to call it a night."

"Oh, Shane, don't be such a party pooper," she said as she tapped the tip of his nose with her finger. Elizabeth ran over to Chad. "Chad, will you please dance with me, since Shane is being an old fuddy-duddy?" she asked, with her bottom lip sticking out in a mock pout.

"Of course, Chad will dance with you. I'm fae; we live to dance," he said, grinning from ear to ear. But as soon as he stood up to join her, Shane pushed him back in his seat and grabbed Elizabeth by her waist.

"Liz, please, this isn't you. I think it's time for you to get some rest," Shane said, pleading for her to listen to him.

Elizabeth's expression turned stony. "How would you know this isn't me or what's best for me? You left me without saying goodbye. Remember?" After she shoved him away with both hands, he released her. "You never once tried to reach out to me. I guess they don't have phones in London or the royal whatever academy. Don't you dare stand here and tell me what's best for me!" Hurt flashed in Shane's eyes, but she continued. "You're not my father. He's dead. And you know what? I'm probably next. Let me have a little fun before I'm toast. Okay?"

Shane's scowl deepened. "What do you mean, you're next?"

"Oops," Elizabeth hiccupped, turning away from Shane and looking at the others, her hand over her smiling mouth. She put her finger to her lips and said, "Shh, I probably wasn't supposed to say anything because of the spies." Elizabeth hiccupped and started laughing. "If no one wants to dance with me, I can dance by myself." She twirled around and around.

"That's it." Shane stalked toward Elizabeth. Seeing him heading her way, she ran, avoiding his outstretched arms. "Elizabeth Lorraine Madison... Come here!"

"You know what? How about you go to bed, Mr. Grumpy Pants Shane Ignatius Black!"

"Enough!" he shouted, and without Elizabeth even seeing him move, he had her up and over his shoulder. "I'm taking you to bed."

*Ok, is it possible to be pissed and turned on all at the same time?*

Elizabeth heard Shane offer his apologies to Prince Drake as he sped up the stairs with Elizabeth over his shoulder. She hadn't even had time to protest.

Shane opened Elizabeth's door and walked in. He gently placed her on the bed.

She looked around the room before saying, "Good. At least the doom and gloom queen is gone."

Shane, who had been rummaging through her closet looking for something, stopped what he was doing and spun around to look at Elizabeth. "What queen? Who are you talking about?"

"You know what queen, the one who lives here, silly," Elizabeth said, lying back on the bed. Shane walked over to the bed, handing her a pair of pajamas, and then sat down next to her.

"What did she say to you?" he asked with concern.

"Oh, you know, the usual." She sat up. "That I'm the last of some dragon bloodline that can kill the queen bitch with Arthur's magical sword. And of course, if she finds out, then she will want to kill me, too," Elizabeth said before turning to Shane and once again becoming serious. "Shane, I don't know what to do. I'm scared. I don't know how to fight." Elizabeth cried into her pillow. "I didn't ask for any of this." Shane pulled Elizabeth into his arms and held her.

They sat, Elizabeth cradled in his arms for a bit. Shane rubbed soothing circles on her back as she cried. He continued to hold her even after her sobbing stopped, almost like he didn't want to let her go.

"Liz," he finally said, breaking the silence. "I won't let anyone hurt you, I promise. I know I have given you plenty of reasons to doubt me after not being there for you, but I am now, and I'm not going anywhere."

Elizabeth turned her head so she could look into his eyes. In this moment, she felt safe with his arms around her. She missed his touch, missed him and all that they had once been to each other. Above all else, she missed her best friend, and she needed him.

Elizabeth sat up, her gaze never leaving his. Moving and situating herself, so she was now straddling his lap. She ran her fingers through his dark golden hair and placed her hand on the back of his neck. She pulled him closer, only stopping for a brief second before her lips touched his. At first, he didn't move, but then he parted his lips and allowed her access.

She needed this distraction. Not wanting to think about anything else, she allowed the warmth of his closeness, his familiar scent of sandalwood, to transport her back to a simpler time—before he'd left her and before magic, supernaturals, and destiny had invaded her life.

She deepened their kiss as she reached for his dinner jacket. She frantically pulled at it to take it off him, but he grabbed her wrist, stopping her. He broke off the kiss. She looked into his eyes and saw only blackness, not a hint of blue. She gasped and looked away. He quickly stood, dropping her on the bed as he turned away from her. He ran his hands through his hair in frustration.

Suddenly feeling cold, she reached for a throw positioned at the end of the bed. Wrapping herself in it, she watched as he slowly turned back to face her. She noticed his eyes were back to their normal shade of blue.

His gaze bore down on her, but he didn't say a word. He was making her feel more uncomfortable than she already was. Shaking his head, he finally broke the awkward silence that had fallen between them. "Liz, I'm sorry, I can't. Not like this. Not while you're drunk and not before we can talk about... well, everything. About those years I was away, and the real reason I was sent to the military academy." He sunk down into a plush chair that was sitting in the corner of the room, head in his hands. "Why did I never call? I was afraid, Liz, and I need you to understand that." He sounded broken.

Elizabeth put her hand up. "Stop, please, just stop, Shane." Rejection, anger, and embarrassment flared to life in her chest. "You don't want me. It's okay. I understand. You didn't want me back then, and you don't want me now."

Desperately holding back tears that wanted to fall like a winter rainstorm, she said, "Please, leave." Her voice shook with both hurt and anger. How could she have been such a fool? Why did she try to open that door again? *Stupid, stupid, stupid!*

"Liz, please, it's not like that. You need to know the truth first," Shane said pleadingly.

"I don't want to hear it. I don't need some lame-ass excuse from you, trying to make me feel better. I get it, I really do. I'm sorry; I don't know what I was thinking." More hurt and embarrassed now than angry, and feeling really stupid, she turned from him, not wanting him to see the tears she could no longer hold back.

"Liz, please let me explain."

Wiping the tears from her eyes with the back of her hand, she turned back to face him. "There's nothing to explain. I saw the magazine covers. I know you moved on. I was being foolish."

"What magazine covers?" he asked, taken aback.

"Shane, seriously, do I look like an idiot? You're the playboy CEO, after all. With the movie star looks and a different model on his arm every week. I saw the article."

He flinched. "Liz, it's not like that."

"I was a fool to think that you would, I don't know, maybe wait for me or come back for me. I don't even know what I thought would happen when you left." Shaking her head, she stood from the bed and walked to the door.

"Only in fairytales or an Irene Bahrd novel do two people find love again after being apart for years. I don't know what I was thinking. It was stupid."

"Liz, can we please take a step back?" He stood up.

Opening the door, she motioned for him to leave. "I need to be alone, please," she said, once again trying to hold back the tears.

"Wait, Liz, it's not what you think. I'm not the playboy CEO. If you could just give me a second, to explain—" Shane started toward her.

"Like I said, no explanation is needed. I was just being stupid. Now, please go," she said sternly.

"Liz..." he started to reach for her. But she surprised him when both her hands lit up with blue-green dragon fire. Looking defeated, Shane lowered his head and walked to the door. "I really am sorry about tonight, Liz." He walked out, and she slammed the door behind him.

Leaning back against the closed door, she slowly slid to the floor. She wrapped her arms around her middle, the tears streaming down her face. Why had she kissed him? Why had she tried to open that damn door again? She had barely survived it the last time. He was familiar; he reminded her of home. But it was a home she didn't have anymore.

She stood up, and the room spun a little. Grabbing for the bedpost to help her navigate to the bed, she sat down hard on the bed.

Would she have wanted to kiss him if she hadn't been drinking? No, it wasn't the drinking; it was the conversation she had prior to the drinking. She was hiding; she didn't want to face what the queen had told her, and she had been willing to use her best friend to help her forget. She hadn't cared that he had just popped back into her life, hadn't considered that she had never been with a man before when acting that rashly. Yes, she was a twenty-three-year-old virgin, but no one needed to know that, and sure as hell not Shane.

She had used her heartbreak as a shield to block out the world. She was tired of the people she loved leaving her. Her mother had left shortly after she had been born, dropping Elizabeth off on her father's doorstep. Then, her father had disappeared and was presumed dead. Shane had left, and now her grandmother. It was too much to bear. It was easier to not develop feelings at all. A broken heart was too much pain, and it was pain she had suffered too many times to count.

Rubbing her eyes with her hands, she realized none of this

was Shane's fault. He had been right to stop them from going any further. Standing up once more, holding onto the bedpost to make sure the room didn't start spinning again, she headed for her door. She wasn't sure where Shane's room was, but she knew it was on the other side of the villa. She needed to find him and apologize.

Still feeling a bit unsteady on her feet, she opened the door to exit her room. She proceeded down the dark empty hallway, holding onto the wall for support, walking in the direction she hoped Shane's room was in. If she got lost, she could ask the first servant she saw for directions.

The hall was darker than she had assumed it would be. She guessed that dragons probably had exceptional night vision and didn't need extra light to see. The hallway was deserted, not a servant in sight, which meant it was much later than she had originally thought, or everyone was still attending to the prince at dinner.

As she felt her way down the hall, the sudden sensation of being followed made goosebumps appear on her arms. But she hadn't seen a single person since she'd left her room, nor had she heard any sounds of movement.

Almost forgetting in her still drunken state that she had hands that could glow, she called forth her dragon fire and used it to illuminate the hallway. The fire wasn't as bright as normal because she was having trouble concentrating. She was still able to make enough light to glance over her shoulder and confirm she was still alone.

Trying to shake the uneasy feeling, she continued down the hall. Shane's room had to be around here somewhere. Right?

Figuring she had to be getting close to the other side of the villa, she continued on. Suddenly, she heard angry whispers coming from down the hall in the direction she was headed. She doused the small flame she had in her hand and proceeded to move slowly towards the voices. She peeked around the corner. To her shock, she found two large, extremely scary, and not entirely human looking men. Black horns protruded from their heads. One had an unconscious Luna over one of his shoulders, his freakishly long fingers wrapped around her leg. The other had Skye in his grip, with his nasty hand covering her mouth. She was struggling, trying to get away.

They were talking with one of the kitchen staff. He was the one who had kept refilling her wine.

"Where is he? This spell won't mask our presence much longer, and we need the Pendragon!"

*What? How did they know about me when I had just found out? No, wait, he said he. They think the Pendragon is a man.*

"I'm s-s-sorry. I don't know where the Pendragon is. I heard that he's here. I overheard the queen saying it herself."

"If you're wrong, maggot, then these two won't be the only offerings I take with me. Do you understand?"

"Y-y-y-yes, Sir. I will find where he's staying." The kitchen staffer then ran off in the opposite direction of Elizabeth.

Elizabeth backed around the corner, out of sight. Where were the guards and any other servants? She needed to help Luna and Skye, but how? If she yelled for help, they could hurt them or worse. But if she did nothing, they would get away, and then what?

She tried not to shake with the fear, but. She was no warrior, no great hope, no bringer of the light or whatever had been said about her. Elizabeth couldn't even figure out how to help her friends. If only she had a way to call for Shane or Prince Drake. She didn't want to have to do this on her own. She had no idea what to do, anyway.

She was running out of time, and she needed to do something. She couldn't stay here feeling sorry for herself when Luna and Skye were the ones in big trouble. Elizabeth took a deep breath and prayed to whomever was listening for some divine help.

Gathering what little resolve she had, she ran around the corner and yelled for the two beasts to stop. She hoped that by making a big enough commotion, that it would attract some guards to come help.

The two men stopped and looked at her with surprise, and then amusement.

"Well, would you look at that? Ain't she a purdy little thing?" one snorted.

"Let my friends go, and no one needs to get hurt." She tried to sound brave.

"I don't think so," said the one holding Skye.

"Excuse me?" Elizabeth asked.

"I said, 'No.' We are going to take your friends as planned." He sniffed the air in her direction. "Interesting. You have no scent. What are you?"

"Again, with that? At least I don't smell like dog shit. Sadly, I can't say the same for some here." She put her hands on her hips, trying to look intimidating. *And where the hell is this bravado coming from?* She was talking crap to what she was pretty sure was a freaking demon.

"Doesn't really matter to me, and I don't think them vamps care much about what kind of blood they drink as long as it's fresh and warm. I'm sure you'll do just fine, darling."

Figured that the one time someone called her *darling*, it was a freaking gross-ass demon threatening to kidnap her. "What's this about vamps and blood?"

She needed to keep this banter going to buy some more time. Someone would have to show up at some point, right?

"Look, sweet cheeks, we can do this the hard way or easy way. You can come willingly, and no one gets hurt, or we can do it the hard way, and I make no promises about how that will end for you. You just need to be breathing and still have some blood to offer the vamps."

"Or... counteroffer, I light your asses on fire and call it a day." She smirked as she called forth her dragon fire. Her hands started to glow, but before she could get a good flame going, she felt a sharp prick in her neck.

Elizabeth turned around and found another demon standing behind her, holding a now empty syringe in his hand. She heard all three cackling as her world went dark.

# SEVENTEEN

Slowly, the world around Elizabeth began to move again. She watched in fascination as everything transitioned from frozen, to slow-motion, and then back to normal. She had just enough time to return Excalibur to its resting spot around her neck before Luna and Skye were moving at normal speed. She wasn't ready to reveal her secret to the world. Especially not while she was being held in a cage by the same creatures that would kill her even sooner if they knew who she really was. No, she would not call upon the magical sword, at least not until things got desperate.

Luna and Skye ran to Elizabeth's side. "Are you okay? Did that monster hurt you?" Sky cried.

Luna scanned over Elizabeth as if looking for any sign of injury. "Your neck is bruising from where he held you up, but that will heal."

Looking on in confusion, it took Elizabeth a few seconds to realize where their concern was coming from. It was regarding her encounter with Dimitri. Luna and Skye had both been frozen during King Uther's visit. Feeling her neck, she winced. Sure enough, it was tender and was going to be a lovely shade of purple by tomorrow. That vampire did not have a gentle touch. The very thought of him made Elizabeth's skin crawl. They needed to get out of here.

Elizabeth held Excalibur in her hand, feeling its warmth and the magic radiating through it. Nimue had said she could tap into the power of the sword to increase her own. She felt confident she could call upon the dragon fire as needed, thanks to her recent training with Prince Drake. But would it be enough to get them out of here? Uther said she had everything she needed and to use her resources to her advantage.

Surveying her surroundings, she noted the positions of all the guards, who, she assumed, were either demons or vampires. She couldn't tell the difference; they all looked shady to her. Only seeing four guards patrolling the encampment made her feel a little more confident. If they could break out of this cage somehow, then surely, they could take on four supernatural guards, right?

Elizabeth turned to Luna who, with her enhanced sight and hearing, would hopefully be able to verify if there were any other guards. "Luna, I only see four guards. Do you sense any others?"

Luna closed her eyes for a moment, listened, and then sniffed the air. "No, I only sense the four, but they are all vampires. They won't be easy to get by unnoticed." Luna tilted her head in the other direction. "I don't believe Dimitri is still in this area. However, on a not-so-pleasant note, I heard the guards talking about sorting the prisoners out per Dimitri's orders, which means they will be back to collect you and move us to Lot One soon."

"Okay, I have a plan," Elizabeth said, feeling optimistic. "Luna, you can change into a jaguar, right?"

Luna nodded. "Yes, but this cage is spelled against shifting, and even if I could shift, I wouldn't be much of a match for four vampires. Maybe one or two."

"If I create a diversion with my dragon fire, do you think you can get past the guards, out of this cage, and then shift?"

"Maybe," she nodded. "They will have to open the cage doors to get us out."

"Once you've shifted, I'll back you up with my dragon fire. I will gladly set those assholes on fire." Elizabeth did a one-eighty turn as she took in all the other cages around them. "We can't leave them; we need to find a way to set them free."

"Look, I understand your feelings, I really do, but we aren't even sure if we are going to be able to get ourselves out of here, let alone free hundreds of others," Luna said.

Elizabeth turned to Skye. "If we take care of the guards, do you think you can help free the other prisoners?"

"How? I have no way to open the cages. I have no magic or strength," Skye said, looking at her feet.

"We will get you the keys and keep the guards away from you," Elizabeth said with more confidence than she felt. They could handle four scary vampires. Right?

"Okay, Miss, I can... I can do that," came a timid response from Skye. The poor girl was visibly shaking, and Elizabeth knew it wasn't from the cold, even though she was only wearing her black uniform dress from the previous night. Her long blond hair had long since fallen out of her original braids. Her big blue eyes filled with tears and trepidation. However, Elizabeth also saw determination, and she could work with that.

Reaching over, she hugged the terrified young woman. She knew how she felt. Elizabeth felt the same way, but she was keeping it buried deep inside. She could have a proper breakdown once they were far away from this hellish place.

Pulling away, she looked into Skye's eyes. "You got this, and we have your back. We are all getting out of here today." Skye nodded in response.

"Get ready, ladies. Two of the guards are heading our way," Luna whispered to her companions.

Sure enough, two guards stopped at their cage a few moments later. The guards were both dressed in crimson and gold uniforms with white, frilly, high collars. One had long white hair, while the other vampire's hair was long and black as ebony. Each had pulled their hair back with a leather string. Their eyes were cold, hard, and deep, dark red. Both looked like they had stepped out of the sixteenth century. For all she knew, they might have.

"Okay, slaves, move to the back of the cage, keeping your eyes front and center at all times. No sudden movements or I'll have an excuse to kill you and drink you dry," the dark-haired vampire said while laughing and flashing a fang-filled grin. He opened the cage door.

Elizabeth gave a slight nod to Luna before she unleashed dragon fire on the two vampire guards. Luna, using the distraction, ran past the guards. Turning once, Luna was free of the spelled cage, and she shifted into her jaguar form. Her pale skin was replaced by golden fur with black and white spots. Her small human frame transformed into her lean, muscular, feline form. The majestic cat let out a loud roar before jumping into the air toward the vampires. Using her powerful body, Luna knocked the white-haired guard to the ground, catching both vampires off guard. Luna positioned her sharp teeth around the white-haired vampire's neck, ripping with her teeth until his head fell from his body. She immediately leaped onto the dark-haired vampire, whom Elizabeth had distracted with her dragon fire. Without hesitation, Luna tore his head off as well.

Elizabeth had read once in a book of mythology that separating the head from the vampire's body was the best way to ensure they stayed dead. She supposed that was correct and worth remembering.

Elizabeth tried to ignore the blood and gore as she searched the now headless vampire's pockets. Finding the keys to the cage doors, she quickly moved to the next dead guard. Sure enough, they both had sets of keys on them.

Elizabeth handed one set to Skye, who rushed to the other cages and opened the doors before hurrying on to the next.

Before Elizabeth could catch her breath, more guards appeared, and there were more than the two they had been expecting. She wasn't sure where they had come from, but suddenly, there was a small army of vampires.

This had not been part of her original plan, but there was nothing they could do about it now. She lit vampires on fire and Luna systematically ripped their heads off. They were like a finely oiled machine of retribution raining down on the vampires.

Through the smoke-filled air, Elizabeth could see that they were no longer fighting alone. Some of the stronger prisoners had joined the fight. They had picked up swords from the fallen guards, and now they were helping Luna behead the vampires.

Shifters, no longer held back by the magic of the cage bars, transformed into their animal forms. Elizabeth watched in amazement as people shifted into foxes, warthogs, and small cats of prey. All joined in on the fight, ripping and tearing their way through the onslaught of vampires. Soon after, demons joined the chaos.

Wiping the sweat from her brow, Elizabeth could feel her energy waning. She had been running on pure adrenaline, which seemed to be fading. However, the barrage of vampires was not. They were like a never-ending swarm of killer bees. She wasn't sure how much more she could take. This was the most fire she had ever called upon, and she was using the extra boost from Excalibur to keep her afloat.

Using the skills she had learned from Drake, she kept a fire shield in front of her as she shot fire balls from her other hand. The smell of burned flesh and ash filled her nose.

Spotting Luna in a clearing not far from her, she could tell that even the jaguar shifter wasn't moving as quickly. Her once agile movements were less graceful. They couldn't keep this up. They needed to find a way to retreat. But where? The enemy was everywhere. There was no place to run or hide. It was fight or die, and Elizabeth didn't know how much more fight she had left in her. Her dragon fire was weakening, as was she. She was surprised by how much she had been able to use as it was.

Suddenly, Elizabeth heard a scream, and the sound filled her with terror. Of course, there was lots of screaming and shouting already—it was a battlefield, after all. But this was different. This was the sound of pure fear and helplessness, and it rang with a chilling familiarity.

Turning toward the direction she knew the scream had originated, Elizabeth peered through the smoke. Her legs moved on their own, pushing through the fighting forms of vampires, demons, and shifters. Her attention remained only on the scream, scanning around her as she walked. Then she saw it, the source of the scream. Her blood ran cold, and fear raced through her core. There, in a clearing, away from the rest of the battle, Dimitri stood, holding a terrified Skye by her neck. His gaze landed on Elizabeth as his malicious grin turned to pure delight. His fangs extended.

# EIGHTEEN

Elizabeth froze when her eyes met Dimitri's dark gaze. His eyes were pure black and soulless, and he had an expression of haunting delight upon his face. Dimitri held Skye tight against his tall frame, one hand firm around her neck and the other groping at her breast. Elizabeth wanted to vomit. He was enjoying this, toying with them both. Skye struggled, frantically trying to break free, but Dimitri was too strong. The look of terror in her bright blue eyes gutted Elizabeth.

"Let her go!" Elizabeth yelled. Anger and adrenaline were the only two things keeping her standing at this point. Elizabeth took off running towards Dimitri. She was firing dragon fire left and right, trying to hit him while avoiding Skye, but he was too fast. Elizabeth couldn't keep up, partly because of his vampire speed and partly because her dragon fire wasn't nearly as strong as it had been. She was running out of energy. She was no match for him, and he knew it, laughing and smiling as if this was all one big game to him.

"Not quite the mousey little human I had assumed you are now, are you?" Dimitri sneered.

"Let her go!" Elizabeth was desperate. She knew she couldn't keep playing his game, but if she could somehow get Skye away from him... What she would do then, she had no clue. One step at a time.

"Now, why would I do that? All this exercise is making me hungry." He flashed his long fangs.

Elizabeth didn't know what to do. She was no warrior. Her only fighting experience had been a mandatory self-defense class on campus where they did not teach Vamp Vanquishing 101. Looking around, she confirmed there was no help in sight. Luna and the other prisoners were still fighting off the hordes of vampires and the demons who had joined the mix. There was no one to save her, no one to help Skye. She was utterly alone, but she couldn't give up. Even if she had no clue what to do.

"Come now, pet, don't stop now. Our little game is just getting started."

"What do you want?"

"What do I want? Oh, pet, I want many things. However, the question is, what do *you* want? If you want your delicious little friend here, then you need to come and get her." He smirked as he ran his tongue up Skye's trembling throat.

The look of terror on Skye's face almost made Elizabeth's knees buckle. Remembering what Drake had taught her, she formed a shield and whip out of her dragon fire. Keeping her eyes on the demented vampire in front of her, she advanced toward him with caution.

"So much power, yet little skill. Seriously, pet, how do you plan on besting me?"

Elizabeth ignored his taunting.

"I could teach you."

"I'm not falling for that line of crap. You know as well as I do if I was stupid enough to fall for that line, which I'm not, your first stop would be to Lilith." They continued to circle each other.

"Maybe," he shrugged. "But maybe not. Maybe I want you and your power all to myself."

"No, thanks."

"Suit yourself, pet. However, I grow tired of this little game." He looked at Elizabeth with a crazed smile as he flashed his fangs. "I'm hungry, and if I can't have your blood, I'll settle for your little friend here."

Elizabeth screamed, "No!" But before the scream even left her lips, Dimitri sank his fangs into Skye's tender neck. Blood dripped from where he inserted his fangs. The look of amusement in his eyes as he held her stare filled Elizabeth with rage. Something in Elizabeth snapped into place as she raced toward Dimitri. She launched herself into the air, and her body and magic worked together on instinct alone.

A shocked Dimitri withdrew his fangs from Skye's neck, letting her body drop to the ground like a rag doll. Blood dripped down his chin. She caught Dimitri off guard as a gust of intense wind shot out, forcing him away from Skye's lifeless body.

Elizabeth wanted to rush to Skye, but she couldn't turn her back on Dimitri. Instead, she positioned herself in front of Skye, protecting her from further harm. She didn't have time to marvel at the fact that she had produced wind magic from her hands. She had unlocked a new skill, but she couldn't think about that now. Besides, she had no idea how to call the wind to her again.

No, she focused her gaze on one man— a monster who had killed an innocent young woman for his pleasure. Skye, a woman who had had her entire life before her. Elizabeth couldn't grieve, not yet, because the monster before her had his gaze and dark purposes focused solely on her.

Dimitri picked himself off the ground, dusting the dirt from his pants. His menacing eyes filled with mirth. "Well, well, well, you are a refreshing toy, aren't you, pet?" He started to walk to her slowly, eyeing his prey.

She froze in place, realizing she was way out of her depth. Elizabeth knew she needed to end this game of his, but she didn't even know how to play. He wasn't going to let her go. No, she knew that look in his eye. He wanted her; he wanted to unlock the mysteries that surrounded the enigma before him. But she was not going to become his next plaything or his slave. She would not go down without a fight.

The element of surprise was her only play. She had a secret, and all she needed to do was get close enough to him to strike without being caught in his grasp. Gathering all the energy she had left, she ran toward him. Relinquishing her fire, she called forth Excalibur before reaching him. Raising the legendary sword high above her head, gripping it with both hands, she prepared to strike Dimitri down. She didn't need to kill him; she just needed to scratch him, and the magic of the sword would hopefully take care of the rest.

Dimitri's eyes grew large as realization hit. He saw the sword, and he had to realize what that meant. Just as Excalibur was going to strike, Dimitri raised his own sword, blocking the attack. The force of it sent Elizabeth falling backward onto the ground, landing hard on her backside.

"Oh, pet, you are even more surprising than I had hoped." He circled around her, his sword held at the ready. She hadn't even seen the sword on him. Where it had come from, she had no clue. "You're a Pendragon. Most interesting. I haven't had the pleasure of drinking Pendragon blood in many, many years. I am going to savor you... all of you."

"Um, tempting, I'm sure, but no thanks. I have no desire to become your next plaything." Elizabeth struggled back to her feet.

"Oh, my sweet, you will not merely be a plaything. You will be my crowning glory. Once we have had our fun—and trust me, I plan to enjoy every delectable piece of you—I will present you to my queen, and she will reward me most handsomely."

He was stalking closer as he rambled on, trying to distract her with his plans for her. Looking around, Elizabeth was at a loss about how she was going to get out of this situation. She knew if Dimitri managed to take her, there would be no escape.

She could use her bracelet, but what about Luna? And she couldn't leave Skye's body behind. No, there had to be another way. There had to be a way for all three to get out of here. But where was Luna? She hadn't even come to look for them. Was she dead? No, Elizabeth couldn't let her thoughts go there.

Suddenly, Elizabeth blinked, and Dimitri was on top of her, having knocked her back to the ground. His blade held Excalibur down, and she could not raise it to strike him. This vampire was quick, tricky, and very strong. He had his other hand around Elizabeth's neck, holding her in place. His legs squeezed firm against her, his knee holding her other arm to her side. She couldn't move.

"See, my pet? Isn't this better?" Dimitri spoke, his words smooth, seductive, and menacing. Elizabeth tried to move. "Now, now, pet. We wouldn't want me to accidentally snap your pretty little neck, now, would we?" Elizabeth glared daggers at him. "My queen will be so pleased to meet you. We haven't had the pleasure of entertaining a Pendragon in centuries." Dimitri laughed and then lowered himself, his lips brushing against Elizabeth's ear as he whispered, "However, like I said, I think I am going to take my time and enjoy all that you have to offer before I introduce you to my queen."

Elizabeth shuddered as Dimitri's gaze crudely glanced over her body. He moved his hand from her neck and let it slide over her chest and down her abdomen until it rested on her thigh.

"You sick bastard," Elizabeth yelled, spitting in his face.

Dimitri laughed as he wiped the spit from his cheek. "We don't kink shame, here."

"You're really a fucking monster."

"Oh, my dear, you have no idea. But you will."

"Get off me!" Elizabeth tried in vain to break free from his hold.

"You have a strong spirit; I like it. I am going to enjoy breaking you and molding you into my perfect pet. You will grovel at my feet, calling me master and begging me for mercy." Dimitri leaned in to kiss Elizabeth.

Elizabeth struggled, but he held her hands bound to her side. All she could do was move her head so that his lips would miss hers. She knew it was futile; he was much stronger than her, but she would not give him the satisfaction of submitting to his will. She would rather die.

She closed her eyes as he laughed. Then she felt his tongue along her neck. His lips kissed a disgusting path up to her ear. "No!" She struggled against his iron hold. This was not going to happen. She couldn't let him do this to her.

She felt the dragon fire stir in her chest. It wanted to help her. It wanted her to call on it, but she was running low on strength. She tried to block out Dimitris's touch and focus on connecting with the sword. Energy returned to her body, and the warming sensation of her dragon fire grew hotter in her chest.

Quietly, she returned Excalibur to the silver chain, freeing up her hand. She hoped Dimitri wouldn't notice as she slowly positioned her palms facing him. Disgust filled her when she smelled his foul breath and as he released a moan of pleasure, continuing to work his way down with his lips to her collarbone. Her fear spiked as she felt his fangs graze against her neck. It was now or never. Pulling strength from the sword, she shot a stream of fire from both her hands.

Dimitri leaped away from her. His body was now engulfed by her dragon fire. "You stupid bitch! Do you think a little dragon fire will stop me?" His manic laughter filled the air as he hopped around, trying to extinguish the flames.

Remembering Skye, she jumped to her feet and bolted over to where Skye's body still lay on the ground. Her eyes stung and tears started to fall. Dropping to the ground, she wrapped her arms around the young woman. Skye's long blond hair fell softly onto Elizabeth's lap. The wound on her neck had stopped bleeding, but the blood had pooled beneath her as evidence of what Dimitri had done. Elizabeth couldn't stop sobbing as she thought about the timid young woman and how brave she had been.

This was her fault. She had failed Skye despite having promised this young woman they were getting out of here. But she had been wrong. Skye wouldn't be going anywhere—not ever again.

Elizabeth was supposed to be the Pendragon, the wielder of dragon fire and the mighty sword Excalibur. But she was useless, and Skye had paid the ultimate price. All this so-called power, and she couldn't do a damn thing with it. She couldn't save Skye, couldn't save herself. The fates had picked the wrong girl.

Elizabeth dropped her head to Skye's chest, her tears flowing. She couldn't win, not against Dimitri. She had failed them all. But then, was that...?

Elizabeth went still. Yes... it was a light thump, and then another, and then another. It took her a moment to realize it was Skye's heartbeat. Skye wasn't dead. Elizabeth felt a pulse. It was faint, but it was there.

"Skye, I'm here. Oh my God, hold on, please, hold on," Elizabeth whispered in her ear.

"Milady," Skye's voice was weak. Elizabeth shot upright and found Skye's piercing blue eyes fixed on her.

"Don't talk; you have to save your energy."

"Don't fret over me; you must get out of here. Use your bracelet and save yourself."

"No, I'm not leaving you. We all get out, or none of us do."

"That's foolish, and you know it. The fate of the world is at stake. They need you. Not me and not Luna, but you. Please, go."

"Don't ask me to leave you."

"Oh, my pet, you're not going anywhere," Dimitri sneered. Elizabeth looked up to find Dimitri's naked, charred, and smoking body slowly walking toward her. Accelerated healing was already working to repair the damage she had caused. "You need to be taught a lesson and punished for setting your master on fire."

"Next time, I'll aim for your head," Elizabeth gritted out.

"I do love it when you talk dirty. The more you fight me, the more turned on I become."

"Ew." Elizabeth's face twisted in disgust.

"What can I say? I'm a predator. I'll admit, you caught me off guard, but rest assured, it won't happen again. But please, feel free to run. I do love a good chase." He flashed his fang-filled smirk, looking down at where she sat next to Skye and practically daring her to try to make a run for it.

Elizabeth's gaze was fixed on Dimitri, waiting for his next move. She barely felt it when Skye grabbed her wrist, squeezing it. It wasn't until the purple mist of the portal surrounded her that she realized what Sky had done.

"You must survive, Milady." Skye's words were barely audible over Dimitri's outraged scream.

Elizabeth managed an adamant, "*No*!" before the portal took her away. She left behind a defenseless, dying Skye at the mercy of a monster.

The portal dropped her right into the middle of Black Industries' front lobby. She was on her knees, crying. She needed to get back there; she could use her bracelet. But then she realized she had no idea where "there" was. Skye had sacrificed herself to save her.

Despite her tears, she heard voices. Someone was talking to her, but she wasn't sure what they were saying. The adrenaline that had helped Elizabeth this far was now gone, and everything was finally catching up to her. She thought someone was shouting or saying her name, but Elizabeth felt like she was in a bubble. Someone put their hands on her shoulders. They were trying to help her sit... no, she was already sitting. Maybe trying to help her stand? She didn't know, and nor did she care.

Doors burst open as Nicholas Black came rushing into the room. Poor Uncle Nicky. The worry and concern on his face was clear as he looked over at Elizabeth.

She wanted to reassure him that the blood covering her torn and tattered pink dress wasn't hers—that she was okay. But was she okay? Her head was fuzzy, like she was underwater, and Elizabeth wasn't even sure if she was standing or sitting at this point. Then, suddenly, as if all her remaining energy had gone, the world fell into darkness.

# NINETEEN

When Elizabeth came to, she was unsure of what had happened. She felt a firm mattress under her and a light blanket covering her from neck to toe. Machines and monitors softly beeped off to the side. She noticed the tight squeeze of a blood pressure cuff around her arm, and then stiff tape that held an IV needle in place on her left hand. Lifting the blanket gently so as not to disturb the IV, she found someone had changed her clothing. Gone was the tattered pink dress, replaced by a sweatshirt with the Black Industries logo on it, along with matching black sweatpants.

She stared blankly at the gray Black Industries logo that went down the left leg of the pants. *How long was I out, and who changed my clothes*?

Rustling from the other side of the room caught her attention. She wasn't alone. Her heart nearly stopped when she saw Shane asleep in an armchair. He looked peaceful, despite being way too big for the chair he was currently resting in. His long legs spread out before him while his head rested against the wall. He wore a casual outfit consisting of dark jeans and a black T-shirt instead of his military uniform.

She had to be in the Black Industries medical facility. Weird that she was in a sweatsuit instead of a hospital gown. She wasn't complaining; at least her butt wouldn't be on display for all to see.

Quietly, she attempted to adjust herself, to move to a more comfortable position without waking Shane. She tried in vain not to make a sound. However, his eyes fluttered open, and then she was staring into his ocean-blue eyes. It took him a minute to realize where he was, but then he rushed over to Elizabeth's side. Relief washed over his face, and his hard features softened.

"Thank the stars you're awake! You had us worried," Shane said with a warm smile as he reached for Elizabeth's hands, careful of the IV port.

"What happened? How long was I out?" Her voice sounded rough, like it hadn't been used in a while.

Without saying a word, Shane walked over to a small table where there was a pitcher of water and some paper cups. Shane poured water into one of the paper cups, and then he walked back over and handed it to Elizabeth. He dragged the armchair he had been sleeping in closer to the bed. "About a day. What do you remember?" he finally asked her.

Elizabeth sipped the water from the paper cup. "I didn't get a head injury, Shane." She rolled her eyes at him. "I remember everything, whether I want to or not." Elizabeth paused before she continued. This time, her voice was shaky. "Oh, my God, Skye! She was near death, and I left her. I tried to stop him before he could hurt her. I tried to. And Luna, and all the other prisoners—I don't know what happened to them..." Elizabeth trailed off.

"It's okay, she's okay; Luna is alive." He gently squeezed Elizabeth's hand. "She lost a lot of blood, but thankfully, Black Industries has plenty of synthetic blood in stock, so the doctors were able to use that to help her get stable quickly."

"Oh, thank God! I was so worried." Elizabeth took another sip of her water.

"The demons who kidnapped you used a concealing spell to hide their presence. Thankfully, the spell had a short duration, and once it ended, we detected their presence. They escaped with you before we could stop them."

"They had help," Elizabeth added. "One of the kitchen staff was working with them."

Shane nodded. "He was caught in the act of trying to escape with a bag of the queen's jewelry. He confessed everything pretty quickly once faced with the angry dragon prince."

Elizabeth let out a snort as Shane continued, "You, thankfully, did not receive any injuries. Despite being kidnapped, put in a freaking cage, and not given any food or water, you were unharmed." His voice spiked with anger. "That alone would have been enough to make anyone collapse from exhaustion. According to Luna, you both held off the vampire guards while Skye freed the prisoners."

Elizabeth cleared her throat. "We tried to, anyway."

"You did more than try. Over half the prisoners were able to escape, thanks to you."

"Only half?" She sounded defeated. "What happened to the others? Where is Skye?"

"Your transporter brought you back here. Uncle

immediately had the signal traced, and we were able to travel back to where you had come from. We found Luna and the other captives tending to their wounds."

"I'm confused. What happened to the other prisoners, the ones you said were not freed?"

"That's the crazy part. According to Luna, right before we got there, everyone else vanished. The vampires, demons, and prisoners all disappeared. Even the empty cages, all gone."

Elizabeth sat up straighter. "What do you mean, vanished? Wait, where is Skye? Did your men find her? "

"No, I'm afraid the lady's maid was not found."

Elizabeth pushed the cover off her legs as she twisted, putting her feet firmly on the ground. She stood slowly but was hit was a dizzy spell.

"Whoa, where do you think you're going?"

"To get Skye. Your men didn't know where to look."

Standing up again, she started to pull at the IV. Shane grabbed her hands and gently pushed her back on the bed. "Liz, you need to stay in this bed, at least until the doctor says you can move."

"Shane," she growled.

"I can assure you, my men searched the entire area."

"No, you don't understand," she said in frustration. "Dimitri used her to lure me away from the others. When I fought him, we could barely see the cages in the distance."

"What? You fought him? What in all the hells were you thinking?"

"I was thinking I didn't want to be his slave."

"You thought it was a good idea to engage the most ruthless, vile vampire all on your own." Shane shook his head, covering his eyes with his hands. "Liz, you could have... I don't want to even think about what that monster would have done to you." Sitting back in his chair, he reached over, reclaiming her hand in his. "If I had lost you, I don't know... I can't even go there." He ran his left hand through his hair in frustration.

"Shane, I'm okay. But Skye is not. She saved me. She pushed the damn button on my bracelet, sending me here. I need to find her."

"You don't *need* to do anything. The queen already has her best trackers looking for her."

"Dimitri has her. They need to find her."

"And they will."

Elizabeth wasn't sure. She prayed to whoever was listening that Skye was still alive, and that she was found before it was too late.

"This should never have happened," Shane said, startling her as he stood and paced around the room. "They all knew what the fucking vampires and their demon stooges have been up to.

They all knew that those raiding parties were to gather slaves for the black market. This is not new information, but the leaders of the supernatural communities have been refusing to act. They will have no choice now. They took guests of the royal dragons from their rooms. I don't know why—it doesn't make any sense. They are having no problems procuring captives. Why break into the castle? Surely the risk outweighs any reward. Are they trying to start a war?" Shane's expression was hard.

Elizabeth knew why they were in the castle. They were looking for her, and she already knew the war was coming. King Uther had told her as much, and she had a large part to play. She needed to talk to Uncle Nicky about what she had learned from King Uther, but right now, she needed to talk to Shane about what Dimitri had told her. They needed to clear the air. She knew deep down he cared for her, but she also knew he was keeping an enormous secret from her. He was a vampire, and not just any vampire; he was the son of Dimitri.

# TWENTY

Elizabeth motioned for Shane to come sit back down in the armchair beside her. She took a deep breath and looked into his beautiful ocean-blue eyes. She needed to understand why he had kept this enormous secret from her.

She had loved him since she was thirteen years old. How could she not have known what he was? How could he have kept that from her all these years?

"Is Dimitri your father?" Elizabeth asked softly, still looking directly at him. Shane didn't answer right away. The emotions of such a heavy question played out on his handsome face. She saw fear, sadness, and anger. Moments passed, and it seemed like he wasn't going to answer her, but then he stood up and walked to the other side of the small hospital room. Shane turned away from her. The room was still dark, and only a little light from the full moon outside shone in through the window. She could only see the silhouette of his tall, muscular frame leaning against the wall.

"Yes," he finally said in a whisper, almost too faint for her to hear. "But it's not what you might think. I want him dead more than anyone else."

Elizabeth didn't know what to say. Instead, she listened.

"He didn't love her—my mother—or anything like that." The pain was clear in his voice. "She was one of many blood slaves. They weren't even people to him. More like cattle." He slid to the floor and put his head in his hands. His voice came out muffled as he continued. "They were his property to do with as he liked." He stopped for a minute, taking a deep breath.

Elizabeth nodded and continued to listen. It was evident it had been weighing on him for a long time.

"You see, it's rare for a human and a vampire to conceive.

She didn't tell Dimitri for fear that he would kill her or the baby." Shane looked at the ceiling. "To think, after what that monster had done to her, she was still concerned about the child he had forced upon her."

Elizabeth felt tears running down her cheeks. His poor mother.

Shane ran both his hands through his hair. "Some vampires had become tired of all the violence. They wanted to live normal, peaceful lives."

Elizabeth patted the mattress. "Please come sit with me."

Shane stood, then shuffled back over to the armchair next to Elizabeth's bed and took a seat before he continued. "Nicholas had seen what a monster his brother had become. It disgusted him. He remembered being human. He never wanted to be a vampire. Lilith took that choice away from him and then forced him to serve her. He realized other vampires felt the same way. He also fell in love with one of his brother's blood slaves."

Elizabeth gasped again. "No! Your mother?"

Shane smiled at Elizabeth's reaction. "Yes, my mother."

Her thoughts drifted back to the story of Dimitri's Egyptian roots and his younger brother. *Could Nicholas have been Nakia?*

"Dimitri found out about the pregnancy. I guess he had some big plans for me, the first half-breed. He planned to move my mother to one of his other strongholds away from Nicholas."

"That would have been horrible for your mother."

"Yeah, pretty sure he would have disposed of her after I was born." Shane leaned back in the chair as he ran his hands through his already messy hair.

A shiver ran up her spine. His poor mother, a pregnant blood slave.

"Uncle came up with a plan. Working with the other rebel vampires, they organize a prison break. During the chaos, he was able to escape with my mother and took her to Avalon, where they pleaded for sanctuary. The Immortal Queen is a pure immortal, and she has many gifts. One of which is the gift of truth. She's able to read someone's soul and know if they are true or not. Seeing that Nick was true and had no deceit in his heart, she offered my mother and him sanctuary, but on one condition."

"What?" Elizabeth sat up straighter.

Shane smiled at Elizabeth's reaction. "The queen needed a general for her army. She asked him to head up her military, which, of course, he did, and still does."

Elizabeth crossed her arms. "Okay, I guess that's not too bad."

"I was born in Avalon, and from what I am told, my mother truly loved me despite who my father was."

Elizabeth took both of Shane's hands in hers. "Of course she did. It seems like everything she did was for you. That is truly love."

Shane nodded. "We were a happy family for a while until my mother got sick. The years of being a blood slave had taken their toll on her body and weakened her heart. Despite the healer's best efforts, her heart couldn't be fixed. Nicholas tried to convince her to get a heart transplant. He promised to create a new heart just for her, but she refused, saying it was her time." Shane bowed his head, trying to hide his tears from her.

Elizabeth's heart was breaking for him.

"Before she died, she made Uncle promise to take care of me and to keep me safe."

Elizabeth pulled closer, wrapping her arms around him. He hugged her back, and they stayed in each other's embrace for a long while.

"I'm sorry," Elizabeth whispered in his ear.

"It's okay. I mean, it's not, but you know what I mean. I will *be* okay."

"Yes, you will. Of that I have no doubt. But what about all the other lives that Dimitri has destroyed? All those still being held captive. We can't let this continue. I can't go on as normal knowing that atrocities like that are happening every day."

"Liz, it's not your fight. Let Uncle and our people handle it."

"Ouch." His words stung. Granted, he had no idea how much it was her fight. But his lack of faith stung a bit.

"Liz, you know what I mean."

"No, Shane, I don't think I do. I wasn't given these crazy powers for no reason. I am meant to train and learn how to fight back. I know that now." She released her hold on him so she could look him in the eyes.

"Maybe, but the thought of you getting hurt..." He looked away.

"Okay, I agree. I'm not ready to take on Lilith or Dimitri today. I barely made it out with my life, and only thanks to Skye. I need training."

"And who are you going to get to train you?" Shane asked.

"I don't know. Who trained you?"

"A former Knight of the Round Table trained me in Avalon at the Royal Academy. But I don't have magic, and my training was different. You need to be trained in magic."

"Any suggestions?"

He shrugged. "I have no idea. The fae? We could ask Chad if he knows anyone in this realm. There are a few outcast elves who might be able to help. The dragons, of course, if you feel comfortable going back there."

"What about going to the elf kingdom?" Uther had mentioned something about going to the elves for help to find the Black Knight. Perhaps that was where she needed to go next.

"No, that's a crazy idea. It's too far. We can bring someone here to help train you."

"Um... okay." She could ask whoever came to help about the elf king. "This way, I will be ready for next time."

"*No,* Liz, there isn't going to be a next time!" Shane jumped off the bed and shoved at the armchair in frustration. "I will protect you. You don't understand this world yet and the types of monsters that inhabit it."

"Shane, there are monsters everywhere, even in the human realm."

"Not like us."

"Us? What are you talking about?"

Shane averted his gaze. "It's okay; you can ask me now."

"Ask you what?" Elizabeth wasn't sure what he wanted her to ask. This conversation had taken a crazy turn at some point, and she had missed it.

"Ask me if I'm a vampire. If I suck blood or if I crave blood? Ask me if I'm a monster like him," Shane spat out.

She already knew he was a vampire, didn't she? Or had she assumed? Did she really want to know? Of course, she didn't *want* to know, but she needed to anyway, didn't she?

"Are you?" Elizabeth whispered.

He began to slowly pace as he talked. "Yes. I'm a vampire, or rather, a hybrid. I have their abilities, but not all their weaknesses."

What weakness did a vampire have? she wondered.

"I only need to ingest blood once a week to keep up my strength. The synthetic blood from Black Industries is all I use."

"Have you ever had human blood?" She asked, not looking at him.

"Yes, but only once when I first learned what I was. But never again, not since... not since..."

"It's okay," she cut him off. "I understand."

He shook his head. "You really don't understand, Liz."

"Wait, you didn't always know you were a vampire?" Elizabeth asked.

"No, not until... um... not until..." He looked away from her as he cleared his throat. "I didn't know for sure till Uncle told me."

"Growing up, you had no clue."

He shook his head again. Still not looking at her.

"Okay." She thought for a minute. "If you only need blood once a week, does that mean you can still eat human food? I mean regular food. I don't mean it like that, I mean. Oh, you know what I mean." She gave up, throwing her arms up dramatically.

He stopped pacing, and stared at her expectantly, like he

was waiting for her to kick him out or yell, "*Get away from me!*" But she did neither. She smiled reassuringly. He then nodded and returned to the armchair.

"My human side requires regular food as well to survive. Pizza is still one of my favorites." He smiled. "I don't suffer from bloodlust or cravings unless I have been badly injured and lost a lot of blood."

"Okay, and what can you do?" Elizabeth asked, amused.

"What do you mean? What can I do?"

"You're a vampire, right? Or at least half. Vampires are supernatural, with special abilities."

"Yes." He arched an eyebrow.

"So, what can you do?"

He laughed, which made Elizabeth smile. She felt for him, for all his pain. She also felt guilty for not trusting in him and understanding how hard all this must have been for him.

"Well, I have enhanced hearing, speed, and strength. However, despite some rumors, I do not turn into a bat or have wings," he smirked.

"Well, thank God for that," Elizabeth cringed. "Bats creep me out."

"Same." His smile widened, but as quickly as it came, it was gone again, replaced with a hardened expression. "But yes."

"Yes, what?"

"Yes, I am a monster. I have his DNA inside me. That alone makes me a monster. I try not to be, but there is always the chance I will become like him." Shane crossed his arms over his chest and looked away from her again.

"Oh, Shane, you're not like him. I have looked into his soulless eyes, and you are nothing like him." She reached for his hand again. "Shane, look at me, please." She waited for him to turn her way. "You are not a monster. I know you; I know your heart. You would never hurt anyone who didn't deserve it."

"Liz, you don't know that," he said, pleading. "You can't be sure; I can't be sure. That's the reason I can't trust myself around you or be with you. That's why I never called after I left." She could hear the sorrow in his voice.

"Shane, I trust you. You would never hurt me. I know that," she said, squeezing his hand.

"But that's just it. I did," Shane whispered. "I hurt you, and you don't even remember it. Liz, I almost killed you."

# TWENTY-ONE

"Wait, what?" Elizabeth's eyes widened in shock.

"I hurt you, and you don't even remember it." He threw his hands up in the air. "I almost bloody well killed you, and you don't remember a damn thing! Stars, Liz, for that, I can never forgive myself." Looking down at his feet, he shook his head. "I'm so sorry."

What was he talking about? Shane had never hurt her. He had broken her heart, yes, and had tormented her dreams for years. But he had never physically hurt her.

"Shane, you're talking nonsense. I don't understand. You never hurt me; you would never," Elizabeth said hesitantly.

Shane walked over to the window overlooking the courtyard of Black Industries. He looked at Elizabeth and then returned his gaze to the window. "Liz, I don't even know where to start."

"How about you start at the freaking beginning?" He was starting to scare her.

He looked at her again with worry in his eyes and a sense of sadness that nearly caused Elizabeth to reach out to him. "Do you remember that last night we were together before they sent me away?" Shane asked her.

Elizabeth thought for a moment. "Of course, I do." Although, those memories had always been too painful to recount.

He faced her but stayed near the window. Crossing his arms over his chest. "What do you remember?"

What did she remember? She shifted her sitting position, wanting to yank the damn IV from her hand. Once she settled, she glanced past Shane out the window, trying to recall the last time she had seen him. They had been teenagers, and it had been a few days before the prom. Elizabeth remembered being super excited. She had planned everything down to the last detail.

"We were getting ready for prom—last details and all that. I wanted to make sure your tux coordinated with my dress." Shane nodded, encouraging her to continue. "I had ordered the corsage and boutonniere because I had been afraid you would pick a clashing color." She smiled at the memory.

"Okay, but what do you remember about the last time you saw me in person?"

Rubbing her temples, she tried to recall the actual events that occurred that last evening. Images of her and Shane laughing and kissing flashed through her mind. At one point, Shane had pressed her back against the base of a tree, kissing her passionately. She recalled how dark his eyes had become. Elizabeth had been sure at the time that it had been leading to something else. She had been ready, ready to give Shane everything. She had already planned to sleep with him on prom night, anyway, and if it happened a few days earlier, then all the better.

Elizabeth winced; a sharp pain shot through her head. Rubbing her temples, she tried desperately to remember what had happened next. How could she not remember something that significant?

The bed shifted. Shane sat beside her, rubbing comforting circles over her back. "Take your time, Liz."

Her next memory had been waking up the next morning in her bed. But how had she gotten there?

"I don't know! Shane, why don't I know? How do I not remember that night?" Her head hurt every time she tried to push the memories to the surface. She recalled Lady Lorraine coming into her room and telling her Shane had gotten into some trouble and had been sent to military school overseas. But what kind of trouble? Why hadn't she thought to ask more questions?

"I remember going from wanting to have sex with you to waking up in my bed the next morning, alone." Elizabeth looked away from him, her face turning fifty shades of red.

When she glanced back over, Shane had a knowing, mischievous grin on his face. She hit him with her pillow. "Don't look at me that way. From the bits of memories I have, you were thinking the same thing," she said, somewhat amused.

"Oh, I was," Shane said, smiling. "It's just nice to know that you remember that much."

"Anyhoo," Elizabeth continued. "What happened next? For some reason, I get the feeling that you rejected me. But I don't remember it."

"Never. I would never have rejected you. I wanted you more

than I could ever express. We were planning our life together, and I did not lie to you. I wanted that life, too. I didn't know what I was at that point," Shane said, still holding onto Elizabeth's hands. "I didn't even know about Nicholas. I thought we were a normal human family. Okay, maybe not normal," Shane said, smiling. "But human, at least. I had no clue about the supernatural. Since I had never shown any vampire characteristics, Uncle had assumed I took after my mother and was more human. It wasn't until that night, with you, that the monster came out for the first time." Shane looked away from her.

Elizabeth could see the shame and hurt in his eyes. "It's okay," she whispered, waiting for him to continue.

"It's not, Liz. I lost control. In the heat of passion with you, my fangs elongated on their own, and I bit into your neck." Shane shook at the memory.

Elizabeth gasped, putting her hand over her mouth in shock.

"I could have drained you dry, Liz. I wanted to. The monster inside took over, and it was like I was someone else." Running his hands through his hair in frustration, he stood from the bed and turned from her. "Finally, I realized what was happening. I was able to stop myself. We both dropped to the ground. You were lifeless. I was horrified. There was so much blood, and I was sure that I had killed you. I called Uncle. I was afraid I didn't know what else to do."

Elizabeth was too shocked to say anything.

"I held you in my arms, putting pressure on your wound. Waiting. Nicholas finally arrived with your grandmother."

"What? Lady Lorraine was there? She saw me like that? She knew what really happened?" Elizabeth felt a chill go up her spine.

Shane nodded. "She wrapped you in a blanket and put some kind of healing ointment on your wound. The puncture marks healed instantly with no scars. She put her hand on your head and said some words. I don't remember what they were. She told me you were going to be okay, but it was best if you didn't remember what happened, and it was best if you didn't see me again," Shane said, still visibly shaken, with tears on his cheeks.

"Oh, Shane." She wanted to comfort him, to tell him it was okay. But was it? Was it really okay? It wasn't his fault, not really, but still.

"Wait, go back. You said Lady Lorraine said some words. Do you mean like a spell?"

"Um... yeah. I think so."

Was Lady Lorraine a sorceress or a witch? How had she wiped Elizabeth's memories?

"I knew that would probably be the last time I would see you." He sat back on the bed, but this time he was at the foot of it, away from her. "It broke my heart, but at least you were alive. I needed to stay away; I needed you to be safe."

Elizabeth wiped a stray tear that had fallen down her cheek.

"When Uncle said I would need to go away for a while, I didn't fight him. I needed to learn to control my urges. We left that night for the Royal Military Academy in Avalon, and I tried not to look back." Shane paused for a moment before he continued. "I couldn't forget you, Liz, no matter how hard I tried. No matter how hard I worked, or how many hours I spent in the gym, you were always in the back of my mind."

Tears blurred her vision. All the pain he had suffered, and she had never known.

"Then, when I heard about your encounter with those fucking demons, I couldn't stay away anymore. I needed to see for myself that you were okay. I'm sorry for hurting you, for everything. I understand if you want me to go. I will, and I will stay away if that's what you want." Shane wiped at his own tears.

Elizabeth motioned for him to move closer. When he did, she took Shane's tear-stained face into her hands and made him face her. She looked into his eyes, filled with regret and sadness. Her own eyes filled with love and compassion. She brought his face toward her as she leaned in and lightly kissed his lips. He froze for a moment, apparently surprised by her action. But then he pulled her into an embrace and kissed her back.

She could feel her heartbeat picking up, but not from lust—from nerves. This kiss was nice, but it wasn't earth-shattering. She should be feeling more, wanting more. *Definitely not the time to be over-analyzing,* she thought wryly.

Elizabeth tried to lose herself in Shane's warm embrace and kisses, but then the monitors in her room all started going off. Loud alarms and beeps filled the air.

The door to her room crashed open as the nurse rushed in. An embarrassed Elizabeth buried her now crimson-colored face in Shane's chest as she realized their kissing had caused her heart rate to jump and the monitors to go crazy. The nurse was a young woman. She had short-cropped, dark brown hair and warm, mahogany-colored skin. Her dark eyes let on that she was more entertained than cross as she checked the monitors and shut off the alarms.

"Glad to see you awake. You had more than a few people concerned," the nurse said with amusement as she glanced at Shane with a raised eyebrow. Looking back at Elizabeth, she added, "My name is Veronica, but please call me Roni. Everyone else does. I'll be assisting Dr. Link with your care this evening." She gave Shane an unimpressed glance. "As happy as I am that this was a false alarm, I would like to advise you to rest. You had a rough night, and rest is the best medicine. I'll have some food sent in, and Dr. Link will be in shortly to check on you. But if there is anything you need in the meantime, don't fret. Just ask."

"Thank you," Elizabeth said, looking up from Shane's chest but still feeling her cheeks flushed with embarrassment.

"Push that little button on the side of your bed if you need anything." Walking toward the door, Roni then turned back and looked at Shane. "Oh, and Captain, please refrain from raising my patient's heart rate too much." She smirked, barely holding in a laugh as she walked out the door and shut it behind her.

"That was mortifying," Elizabeth groaned.

"No, that was entertaining. Besides, Roni doesn't care; she's cool like that. She has been around here for years. I'm sure she has seen much worse than a little kissing." He looked at Elizabeth with pure amusement and a mischievous grin.

Slapping his chest playfully was her only response. It was good to have this easy vibe between them again. She had missed this, had missed them. She wasn't going to read too much into the kiss. After all, she had been through a lot in the past week. She was tired. That had been why the kiss lacked any passion on her part.

Hearing a knock, they both looked up in time to see the door open. In walked an attractive, tall man with movie-star quality brown hair and sun-kissed skin. He was decked out in a tailored, designer pantsuit, no tie, and the top few buttons left undone on his fitted dress shirt. He looked more like he had stepped off the GQ cover instead of working at a military medical facility.

He was looking down at Elizabeth's chart as he entered, but Elizabeth still recognized him immediately. "Tyler?" She whispered.

# TWENTY-TWO

Tyler's gaze met hers. "Lizzy, glad to see you're awake." He looked down at the chart in his hands.

"Um, okay. Maybe I did hit my head. I am clearly hallucinating." Elizabeth rubbed her eyes.

Shane looked from Elizabeth to the newcomer and back to Elizabeth. "Liz, do you know Dr. Link?"

Instead of answering Shane, she sharpened her gaze on the good doctor. "You're Dr. Link, the on-call doctor, who is supposed to be checking on me? You freaking work here?"

"Lizzy, no need to get excited; I can explain." Dr. Link spoke low as if to prevent her from going all rabid animal on his ass.

"Please, do tell." She motioned for him to continue. "Please, do explain to me how a newly graduated medical student is already working for a secret supernatural military which has ties to my family that I didn't even know about until a few days ago."

"Okay sweetpea, it does sound bad when you say it that way. But I can assure you, there is a reasonable explanation for all your confusion here."

"I'm confused, too." Shane rubbed his temples. "You two know each other."

"Well, I thought I did," she said sharply as she turned to face Shane. "Dr. Link here looks an awful lot like a guy who lived in my building off campus at Johns Hopkins University and who graduated from medical school a few weeks ago."

"You graduated from Johns Hopkins?" was Shane's surprised response. "I didn't know you were going to medical school. That's great, Liz. I would have assumed you would pursue archaeology."

Elizabeth groaned and let out a long sigh. "I did pursue

archaeology."

"At Johns Hopkins?" Shane asked.

"Yes, they have other degree programs, not just the medical ones. But can we please discuss that later? Right now, I want to know why my neighbor of four years, and someone I thought was a friend, clearly lied to me about a lot... including his last name, which I thought was Barret?"

"Link is one of our finest doctors and has been for years. Wait, did you say he was your neighbor?"

Both turned to Tyler.

"It was all a lie, wasn't it?" Elizabeth whispered.

"Lizzy," Tyler breathed out.

"Where's Jonathan? Or was he a fake boyfriend, a plant to make it look more convincing? To have more eyes on me." Irritated, she attempted to cross her arms, but the IV was making it difficult.

"Jonathan is many things, but fake is not one of them. He is currently on a mission to find out what happened to your grandmother."

"Oh, has he found anything?"

"Not that I have heard, sorry," he said as he checked her vitals on the monitor.

"You were there on Nicholas Black's orders, weren't you? To what, spy? Befriend a lonely, clueless girl?"

"I was hoping to check over your injuries, but clearly we need to do this now." He put her chart at the foot of the bed.

"Yes, some answers would be nice. I'm clearly not dying, at least not yet. So, I think we have a few minutes."

"Look at you, Ms. Thing, with the attitude and a newly minted backbone. Good for you."

She raised an eyebrow as Shane took in the exchange dumbfoundedly.

"Okay, first off, I was a student; I was going for my third medical degree in this century, which is also why I was using an alias. I didn't want the medical board to get suspicious about my immortal youthfulness and all."

"Third medical degree?"

"Well, yeah, they become outdated. People invent new technologies."

"You're not human, are you?" She questioned.

"Sweetpea, I know you're new to all this, but you never ask someone if they are human. It's considered rude." Tyler put his hand on his hip. "But to answer your question, I'm an elf hybrid."

"A what?" *Did he say elf? Was this a sign?*

He chuckled. "I'm half-elf, half-human."

"Really? But your ears..."

"Half human, remember? Which is why I'm here and not in

the Elf Kingdom. They aren't the biggest fans of mixed breeds like me. The elf elders, or council, are all about the purebreds." He rolled his eyes.

"Link," Shane groaned, "can you get to the point?"

"Fine, yes, sorry. In short, I am not human, and yes, I was asked to keep an eye on you. However, love, I was never told I had to be your friend. That was all natural. I never meant to deceive or keep anything from you, but we have strict laws about interacting with humans."

"I'm not exactly human either, apparently."

"Well, I can see that now." He pointed to her chart. "But I didn't know that then, and I was asked to keep an eye on you, and report back on anything strange, not educate you on the complications of the real world." He shrugged.

"Anything strange, like what?"

"I don't know. Perhaps something like, say, shooting dragon fire from your hands, for one? Thankfully, none of that happened on my watch," he smirked.

"Nicholas knew that I had powers?"

"Or that you had the potential to have powers. I honestly don't know—that knowledge is above my pay grade."

She glanced at Shane, who held up his hands in mock surrender. "This is all news to me, I swear."

"Okay." She grabbed at her hair in frustration. "I feel like everyone in my life has been keeping secrets and keeping me in the dark regarding my own life." Again, she attempted to move to a more comfortable position, but the stupid IV kept getting in the way.

"Lizzy, girl, you can be mad if you like. Personally, I feel it's a waste of energy, but you do you, boo. I'm still your friend, but more importantly, right now, I'm your doctor. I need to take care of your medical needs because that is my job, and from what I see here, you have had one hell of an evening. Plus, I don't need you ripping that IV out of your arm, causing even more damage. We can continue this drama if needed after. Okay?"

"Fine," She agreed as she crossed her arms over her chest.

"Good, now let's have a do over, shall we?" Tyler turned around and walked back out the door.

Elizabeth and Shane turned to each other, not sure what was happening.

Then there was a knock on the door and Tyler walked back in. "Good evening, Ms. Madison." He smiled at her. "It's good to see you awake. I'm Dr. Link. I'm the on-call doctor for this evening,"

"Good evening, Dr. Link." Elizabeth smiled at his attempt to be professional.

Tyler did a full examination, checking her vitals and then

going over the various bruises and lacerations. Feeling around her neck, he touched a tender spot, and she winced. He grabbed her chart from the foot of the bed and made a few notes in it.

"Good news; you will make a full recovery. Thankfully, there was no serious damage. Looks like you have a nasty case of dehydration, exhaustion, and that bruising around your neck seems to be the worst of it."

"Okay, that's good. When can I get out of here?"

"It *is* good. It's quite amazing considering you came in after being abducted and held prisoner. You are one lucky lady," Tyler said as he put down Elizabeth's chart. "You are going to need to take it easy for a few days. I'm keeping you here overnight to continue administering fluids."

Elizabeth groaned.

"I know... I know, but I want to err on the side of caution. We can reevaluate in the morning. Rest, and lots of it, is going to be your best medicine." He offered a pointed glance at Shane.

Shane held up his hands in mock surrender, laughing as he said. "I get it, no exhausting the patient." Shane winked at Elizabeth.

Elizabeth blushed. "Thank you, Tyler. I will take it easy."

Tyler smiled and then turned his attention to Shane. "Captain, visiting hours are over. I think it's best if we let her get some sleep. Besides, the commander has been calling every hour on the hour, wanting updates on this young lady. Can you please go reassure him she will be fine? I would appreciate that."

"Sure thing, Link," Shane said with a half-hearted salute. Tyler shook his head and smiled.

"Lizzy, I am happy you're okay. I will check in on you later. Until then, please get some sleep." He patted her leg. "The nurse can give you something if your neck is sore, or if you need help sleeping." Tyler said, smiling. "I'm serious, Captain. I don't want to see you in here bothering my patient until morning," Tyler said as he exited the room.

Shane waited a few minutes after the doctor left before he looked at Elizabeth seriously. "How did you get the bruising on your neck?" He lifted her chin lightly and examined the bruising himself.

"It's nothing." Elizabeth tried to brush it off. "It doesn't even hurt. Probably looks worse than it is."

Shane let out a loud growl. Through gritted teeth, he said. "He did this, didn't he?"

Elizabeth knew who he was talking about without him having to say the name. They both knew it was Dimitri. "He grabbed me by the neck and held me up." She touched the tender spot on her neck. "Somehow, he smelled you on me."

"Damn him!" Shane yelled, slamming a fist against the wall. Elizabeth jumped. Elizabeth could feel Shane's anger permeating off of him like an aura. "I wish I could kill that bastard!" Shane hit the back of the armchair he had been sitting in earlier. "Fuck! It's all a game to him, and now you are his target. He smelled me on you, and that is why he was taunting you. He will come after you to hurt me." Shane ran his hand through his hair in frustration. "Once again, you are in danger because of me."

Laughter slipped through her lips. Shane looked at her, failing to see the humor.

"Shane, my life has become such a shit show as of late, and you are not to blame. Honestly, I'm not sure who to blame, if anyone, except maybe the damn fates. Yes, Dimitri smelled you on me, and that may have brought me to his attention a little sooner than it otherwise would have. But it was only a matter of time until the big baddies of this world realized that I possess this lovely gem right here." Elizabeth held up Excalibur in its full, enlarged form.

Shane didn't move, didn't speak. Elizabeth wasn't even sure if he was breathing. *Wait, do hybrid vampires need to breathe?* She gave him a moment to process the information. Finally, he looked at her and shook his head. He then walked around the small hospital room before stopping in front of her and taking a seat in the armchair beside her bed.

He finally asked, "Is that...? How? When? Why?" He couldn't seem to form a complete sentence or coherent thought.

Elizabeth almost laughed again. It was funny seeing Shane the soldier, a big strong guy, forget how to talk. "Yes, this is Excalibur, the Sword of Power. Before you ask, I am apparently a descendant of King Uther Pendragon, and according to his ghost, I'm the last Pendragon. Please stop beating yourself up about Dimitri because I already have a target on my back that has nothing to do with you." Elizabeth silently sent the sword back to the chain around her neck. She didn't want to risk accidentally cutting Shane or someone walking in and seeing the sword.

"I have so many questions right now, Liz, that my brain is overloaded. King Uther's ghost? What does that even mean? You can magically call forth a sword that has been missing for fifteen hundred years." Shane was shaking his head in disbelief.

Elizabeth was about to explain, or at least try to, without sounding like an insane person, but she was halted when a knock sounded on her door, and it swung open. There stood a not-so-happy-looking nurse, Roni. Holding a tray of food, she had a pointed gaze staring right at Shane.

"Captain Black, on the battlefield, you are in command, and I respect that." She walked over to Elizabeth's side and pushed a button. A small table materialized over Elizabeth's lap, where Roni placed the tray with a bowl of warm broth. "But here in this hospital, Captain, I am the one in charge, at least where my patients are concerned. I know for a fact that the good doctor has already told you to get on out of here and let this young lady get some rest." Nurse Roni said with both hands on her hips. Shifting her softened gaze to Elizabeth. "And some food in your system."

"You know, Roni, I think you could be my secret weapon on the next battlefield. You would charm our enemies with your beauty and then strike them down with your words," Shane said with a mischievous grin and wink he sent toward Nurse Roni.

"Oh no, sir, you don't. Don't you dare try to pull your charm on me, mister. I got your number. Now get on out of here before I drag you out," Nurse Roni said seriously, but with a glint of humor in her eyes.

Elizabeth couldn't stop herself from laughing, which she tried to cover with a cough. Nurse Roni glanced over at her with a knowing expression. Shane might be right; she could be a secret weapon. Part of Elizabeth wanted to see Roni drag Shane out by his ear.

Shane sensed he would not win this battle. Putting his hands up in mock surrender, he nodded, then turned back toward Elizabeth. "This conversation is far from over. But Roni is right, you need to eat and rest. We can talk more in the morning. Besides, I need to let Uncle know you are going to be okay." Bending down, he lightly kissed her lips.

"So much to talk about," he whispered so only she could hear. He kissed her again. Shane reluctantly turned to walk away when he heard Roni clear her throat, letting him know her patience with him was running thin.

Elizabeth smiled as she watched him walk out the door.

"Okay, Ms. Elizabeth. You drink this broth and then try to get some rest. I'll bring something more filling in the morning. Until then, do you need anything for pain or to help you sleep?" Roni asked as she fluffed Elizabeth's pillows.

"No, thank you," Elizabeth responded as she scooched back into the newly fluffed pillows, a smile on her face as she reached for the warm broth.

# TWENTY-THREE

Elizabeth awoke with a jolt as something small and furry jumped on her stomach. "What the Fu—!" she yelled. Bolting up, she noticed a cute little gold and black cat sitting at the foot of her bed.

"Um... hello... little kitty." Where had this animal come from? Was it feral? Was it looking for food? "Are you hungry, little guy? I don't really have any food to offer you." The cat appeared to roll its eyes at her and put its paw on its head. The cat started to glow like it was nuclear. "What the ...."

Luna now sat at the foot of her bed where the cat had been, her legs crossed and hands in her lap as if she had been sitting there the whole time. "Morning, superstar. You're looking well."

"Luna! I'm so happy you're okay! I'm sorry, I never meant to leave you there, but... Dimitri—then Skye pushed the stone, and I—"

"Take a breath. It's okay. I believe I told you to leave," Luna said in her normal, calm way.

"I know, but still."

"The prisoners and I were able to fend them off for the most part."

"Did you see Skye? No one knows what happened to her."

Luna looked down at her fingers as she picked at a loose thread in the blanket. It was weird to see her looking unsure. "Dimitri took her."

Elizabeth gasped. That was her worst fear.

"I saw him carry her through a portal before everything vanished."

"Do you think she could still be alive?"

"Probably, at least for now."

"I hope the dragon trackers find her." Elizabeth pulled her

blanket-covered knees up to her chest and wrapped her arms around them.

"What are you talking about? Dragon trackers?"

"Shane told me the dragons sent their best trackers to look for her."

Luna shook her head and laughed. "And you believed him?"

"Um... yes. Why wouldn't I?"

"You're naïve." Luna looked at her like she was about to tell a child that Santa wasn't real. "Skye is only a lady's maid. She is no one to anyone, and she's expendable. No one, not even the noble dragons, are to spare the manpower to find one person when all the realms are on the brink of war."

"No, that can't be true. Shane said..."

"Shane told you what you needed to hear so you wouldn't worry, or worse, try something stupid. Like go after her yourself."

"He wouldn't," Elizabeth said, shaking her head.

"He wouldn't, what, lie to you? Tell you what he felt you needed to hear to keep you safe?" Luna crossed her arms over her chest and cocked an eyebrow.

"Shane would never lie to me."

"If you say so," Luna shrugged. "It's no sweat off my back, what you believe. I'm sure he's exactly the same person he was back then. Right?"

Elizabeth glared daggers at Luna. She hated that she was right. Shane was not the same sweet young man she had known. He had changed; they both had. But she didn't need to sit here and have this conversation with Ms. Prickly. Pushing off the blankets, she swung her legs off the side of the bed.

"And where do you think you're going?"

"To get answers. Is the commander in?"

"Oh, you're adorable. You think either of them will tell you the truth? In their minds, you are a liability that they need to keep safe."

Elizabeth halted. Damn, Luna. To them, she was weak, little Elizabeth, who needed to be shielded and protected. She still needed to talk to Nicholas, to tell him about the sword and her conversation with Uther. Once he realized she was the Pendragon, surely, he would help get her the training she needed. Then she would find Skye and free all the other slaves.

"Doesn't matter what you think. I need to speak with him right away." She stood up and immediately sat back down as a wave of dizziness hit her.

"Good grief, here." Luna shoved a paper cup filled with water at her. "Drink this."

Reluctantly, she reached for the cup of water, and then she downed it in one gulp.

"Wait here. I'll go see if the Commander is in." She

grumbled as she walked out the door.

If Luna thought Elizabeth was going to sit here and wait for her to return, she had another thing coming. Elizabeth was tired of everyone telling her what to do—tired of being treated like a child. She was going to find Nicholas herself.

Standing up more slowly this time, she waited to see if the dizziness would come again; it didn't, thankfully. Taking that as a good sign, she slowly moved her way toward the door, only to be stopped when she felt a painful tug in her hand. The stupid IV. She had forgotten about the needle in her hand. Pulling the IV out of her hand, she winced at the pain. Blood dripped down her fingers from where the needle had been inserted.

*Damn, not my smartest move,* she thought to herself.

She looked around for a band-aid or some kind of bandage. After opening drawers and cabinets, she finally found a drawer of first-aid supplies. Wiping the blood away with a cleansing cloth, she then ripped open a self-adhesive bandage and gently placed it over the wound.

Continuing toward the door, she slowly opened it, peering out into an empty hallway. On the wall across from her, there were arrows painted in different colors. A blue arrow said, "Nurse's Station," a red one said "Emergency," and a black one said "Headquarters."

Thankful once again that she was in a sweatsuit and not an open-back hospital gown, she casually walked down the hall with her head down as she followed the black arrow, hoping it would lead her to Nicholas's office.

Familiar voices caught her attention as she was about to round a corner. She stopped and peeked around. Standing in front of a closed elevator were Shane and Uncle Nicky. She was about to speak up when she heard her name.

"Of course, she's the Pendragon," Nicholas said.

"What, you knew?" came Shane's shocked response.

"Yes, and that's why I have had people watching her all these years."

*What? He knew and never thought to tell me.*

"It was her father's wish that she live a normal life for as long as possible."

"She needs to be trained. How can she save the world if she is unprepared?" Shane asked.

"I agree, but I'm not sure she's ready."

"Uncle, is that really your call?"

"Perhaps not. But it's my job to keep her safe—at least until Lady Lorraine is found. Then we can plan our next steps."

"She wants to start training now."

"That's not her call. She has no clue what she needs."

*What the...? If not my call, then whose?*

"Plus, we have a bigger problem. Dimitri is trying to find

her. We intercepted a communication. He's placed a bounty on her head."

*A freaking bounty on me? What the hell.*

Shane let out a long breath. "Every demon in this realm will be trying to cash in. What can we do?"

"We keep her here and keep her safe."

"She's not going to like that."

"I don't care what she likes. She's too important to let Dimitri get his hands on. Have Link come up with a reason to keep her in the hospital for a few extra days. I need time to figure out what to do."

The elevator doors opened, and they walked in, ending what she could hear of their conversation.

*Okay, now what?* She couldn't sit around here waiting for the "grownups" to decide what to do next. Skye's life and many others were in danger. She was the Pendragon; it was her duty to help them. But in order to help them, she needed training. Uther had told her what to do. It was time for her to put her big girl pants on and do it. She needed to get to the elves, and hopefully, they could help her find the elusive Black Knight.

# TWENTY-FOUR

Elizabeth tried to concentrate and use her bracelet to portal directly to the elf kingdom, but it didn't work. Then she noticed a sign on the wall that said the hospital was a portal-free zone. Of course, it couldn't just go her way for once and be easy. Now she needed to find the nearest exit and pray no one spotted her first. She knew she was running out of time. Luna would be back in her room soon, and she needed to be gone before Luna alerted them to the fact that she was missing.

Following a green arrow that said exit, she rounded a corner to where the nurse's station was located. She froze. The nurse's station, which would normally be the hub of activity in a hospital, was completely empty, and there was a heavy feeling of wrongness in the air.

She walked over to the nurse's station. The monitors were all static, with nothing but white bars going across the screen. Patient charts were stacked neatly in a pile with a sticky note that said, "please file." Picking up a half-full cup of coffee, Elizabeth noticed it was still warm.

*What the hell is going on here?* No sign of a struggle anywhere. It was like everyone had disappeared. Then she heard a crash coming from one of the patient rooms behind her.

Having seen too many thrillers in her day, she wasn't going to wait around and see what made the noise. She was going to get the hell out of Dodge. She needed to get outside and portal to the elves, like now.

This was not going to be her day. She stopped dead in her tracks as a demon emerged from the room. His skin was gray with bulging black veins, his eyes solid black. He turned towards her, and a smirk appeared on his lips, yellow fangs protruding from them.

"Well. Hello there, love," he said with a heavy accent. "You're the little darling I've been looking for."

"What? Oh, I doubt that. I'm no one of importance." She tried to sound convincing as she looked around for a place to run.

Just as she was about to dart down the hallway, a second demon came strolling down the hall towards her.

"Hey, you found her," the new demon commented.

"Of course I found her," the first one said smugly.

*Wait, how did they know I was here?*

"The master would like a little of your time. Don't even bother trying to use any of your hocus pocus. The master made sure they gave you a little something to keep you calm and magic-free, there, love."

"What?" She had been feeling off, but she assumed it was dehydration. Elizabeth tried to call her dragon fire, but nothing happened. *Oh crap*. Somehow, they had drugged her and suppressed her powers.

And, of course, she was still in the damn portal-free zone. She thought about calling forth Excalibur, but then thought better of it. She was useless with the sword, which was the main reason she needed training. Whoever heard of a Pendragon who couldn't even wield their own magical sword? She really needed to get to the elves; she did not have time for this.

"Now, love. We can do this the easy way, and you won't get hurt."

"At least, not by us, ain't that right, Bates?" The second demon burst out laughing.

"Shut it, Ox," the first demon, who she assumed was named Bates, yelled. Turning his attention back to her, he said, "Or, the hard way, where I make no promises. Our master is waiting for ya, and we don't like to keep the master waiting."

"Master? Who's your master?" She had no sooner asked the question than realization hit her like a ton of bricks. Words came back to her as she recalled Dimitri telling her she would call him master. These demons were trying to take her back to Dimitri. Oh, hell no, that was definitely not happening. She had just gotten back from being kidnapped. This was getting ridiculous. *Can't a girl catch a break?*

Elizabeth looked at her surroundings. There had to be a way out. *Think, Elizabeth, think*. There wasn't much around her—nothing that could be used as a weapon. She noticed an open laptop; it wasn't much, but maybe...

She picked up the laptop, threw it at the demons, and took off in the opposite direction. Running as fast as her exhausted legs could carrier her, she ran towards a door at the end of the hall. She prayed to whomever was listening that it was a way outside.

She reached the door and leaped through it, hitting a hard wall of muscle. She looked up and saw the sharp-tooth grin of Ox. He bent down, lifting her up over his shoulder.

"Let me go!" she yelled.

"Now, now, deary. We can't do that. You have a date with your new master," Bates chuckled. "We don't want to disappoint him, now do we?"

Ox's grip was tight on her, and she still couldn't call upon her magic. She would have to wait for an opening. These two didn't seem like the brightest bulbs in the bunch. She just needed to get away before they took her to Dimitri.

"What did you do to everyone in the hospital?" She was concerned that they had hurt everyone else just to get to her.

"Oh, that. It was a simple illusion spell. Any baby witch could have cast. You were hidden from them, and they were hidden from you. Made retrieval much easier. We didn't want to worry about your protectors and all that drama."

"A spell," She breathed out. "Everyone is, okay?"

"Sure, and none the wiser that you're missing. The illusion should hold a few more hours. Plenty of time for us to get you to the master."

Well, that bought her a little time. She just needed to get away from frick and frack and then be on her way. Now, to figure out how to escape them. She had no plans of allowing them to take her to Dimitri.

They came to a stop, and she heard the unmistakable sounds of a cage door being opened. Ox then tossed her like she was a sack of grain. She landed on her butt with a thud.

"Not another freaking cage!" If only she knew how to pick a lock. She would add that to her list of things she needed to learn.

"I wouldn't exhaust myself trying to call that magic of yours. The potion you were given should still be in effect, and if it wears off, the cage is spelled to dampen all magic. You might want to save your energy for what the master has planned for you." He winked and then walked to the front of the wagon the cage had been set on.

"That's not going to happen," she grumbled under her breath.

They rode for a ways. Elizabeth was tossed, turned, and thrown against the cage bars. She was sure the bruising would cover the majority of her body by the time they stopped. They had been traveling on a deserted road, or at least she assumed it was deserted. She wondered if they were using the illusion spell, they had spoken of to keep her hidden as they traveled.

Elizabeth tried multiple times to call on any magic with no success. She couldn't even call forth Excalibur to help her get out. She tried to meditate to reach Nimue, the soul in the sword, and that didn't work, either. She was running out of ideas. There was no way she was going to let Dimitri turn her into his little plaything.

"Well, little Pendragon, it appears you are in yet another pickle."

Elizabeth's gaze shot up. Sitting on top of the cage, his leather-booted legs dangling down in an unkinglike like manor, sat Uther Pendragon.

"Tis the season for kidnapping, apparently." She rolled her eyes. "Please tell me you are actually here to help this time."

"Of course, I'm here to help. You wound me. I helped you last time, did I not?"

"No, you did not help me get out of the last cage you found me in."

"I beg to differ; did I not help you find Excalibur? I believe I also advised you to use your resources, which you did beautifully." Uther clapped before jumping down to stand beside her.

"Fine. You helped. Now, can you help me open this cage?" Elizabeth examined the large iron lock.

"I'm afraid that's against the rules."

"The... what now? There are rules to being kidnapped?" She glared at him.

"No, of course not. Kidnapping is a free-for-all. There are rules to being a guardian spirit."

"Okay. How about you tell me how you can help me out of this mess. Preferably, before I'm handed over to Dimitri on a silver platter." She crossed her arms over her chest and waited for his response.

"I am more of a guide or a cheerleader who roots for you from the sidelines. I can't get my hands dirty."

"You're a freaking warrior king. You wielded swords, not pom-poms! Surely, you can do something." She was irritated.

"I can't interfere because you need to learn to have faith in yourself and your own abilities. You're not supposed to be the damsel in distress; you're supposed to be the hero of this story. Stop thinking like the damsel."

"Seriously, that's all you got? Stop thinking like the damsel?" She ran her hands through her hair, pulling at a few strands in irritation.

"Little Pendragon, you are much more than you give yourself credit for. Those two," he pointed towards the front of the wagon, "are low-level demons. You can easily outsmart them. You need to think and remember to use all the resources at your disposal. You got this." Uther then shot her a thumbs up and disappeared.

"Well, thanks for nothing. What is the point of a guardian ghost if he can't do anything to help?" She yelled after him.

Suddenly, the wagon stopped, and a chill ran up Elizabeth's

back. Crap, was she out of time. Uther's words came back to her. *Use all at your disposal.*

The cage door ripped open. There stood Bates with his usual smirk. "Need a potty break?"

"What?"

Ox grabbed her, pulling her from the cage. He sat her on her feet, holding onto her arm a bit too tightly, probably adding another bruise to her mounting collection. He pulled her hands together behind her back, wrapping a coarse rope around them.

"Hey. What's this for?" she yelled.

"We can't risk you running off, now, can we?"

"How can I run off? I don't even know where we are." She rolled her eyes before glancing at her surroundings. They were standing in front of what she assumed was a tavern called the Bloody Brew. It was a charming stone structure, something straight out of an Irish folktale.

"I could use a bit of refreshment," Bates rambled on, "and I'm sure you could use a moment to relieve yourself. I don't need you showing up at the master's smelling of piss and human waste."

"And how am I going to relieve myself with my hands tied behind my back?"

"If you play nice, I'm sure Ox here will be more than happy to give you a hand with the matter."

"Um, gross. I don't need *a* hand. I need *my* hands."

Ox grinned with anticipation, while Bates shrugged. "Maybe, and maybe I'll even let you have a wee sip of water—wet that pretty little whistle of yours."

"Gee, don't go out of your way on my account," Elizabeth drawled.

Ox dragged her toward the doors of the Bloody Brew. If she could just get to the purple stone on her bracelet...

Now that she was away from the portal-free zone and the spelled cage, it should work. However, trying to reach for the purple stone was not easy thanks to Ox's rough treatment and her hands now being bound. Hopefully, she could convince them to untie her so she could use the bathroom.

The smell of stale beer hit her nose as soon as Bates opened the door. Inside, the Bloody Brew looked like a typical medieval tavern straight from Middle Earth. The walls were the same stone as the exterior, with a few animal heads mounted as decoration. The center of the tavern had several long, wooden tables with benches, while a few smaller round tables were nestled in the corners.

"Bates, what the bloody hell are you doing here?" A woman appeared behind the dark wooden bar. She had her black hair pulled up in a messy bun, and her breasts practically spilled out of her low-cut, ruby-colored T-shirt with the Bloody Brew logo on it. The logo appeared to be lips with fangs and a tongue sticking out. Throwing the rag she had been using to wipe down the bar, she put both hands on her hips, her lips forming a frown as she glared at the kidnapper.

"Why, Mary, my love, to see you, of course." Bates looked her up and down as he licked his lips.

Elizabeth had to look away from the disgusting display or she was going to vomit all over the already sticky floor of the tavern.

Mary pointed to Elizabeth. "Looks like your hands are already full. Are you into bondage these days?"

"Her? She's nobody—a new blood slave. We are delivering her to the master."

"And you thought it was a good idea to stop here first?"

"Of course, my sweet, it's on the way."

Elizabeth cringed at the demon's obvious attempt to woo the barkeep. She needed to activate the purple stone so she could get the hell out of here. However, she couldn't touch the stone while Ox was holding her, and her wrists were bound behind her back. She needed her hands free. She needed to move things along.

"Excuse me, Miss?" Elizabeth asked Mary. All eyes turned towards Elizabeth, and Bates glared, almost daring her to say something to start trouble. "Do you have a restroom I could use?" Elizabeth tried to look embarrassed. She was hoping to gain a little sympathy from this other woman.

Mary angrily glared at Bates, then turned back to Elizabeth, smiling. "Of course, dear. It's down that hallway."

Elizabeth shyly turned to show her binding behind her back. "I might need some help."

Bates glared at Elizabeth. "I already told you that Ox would assist you in that area."

"He will do no such thing!" Mary yelled. "She's about to be a slave to the Lord of Pain. The least you can do is allow her a few minutes of dignity before you deliver her to that monster."

"Now, now, Mary, my love, you know not to speak that way about the master."

"Cut her loose and let her relieve herself in peace." Mary stared him down intently. "Or you won't be getting what you came here for."

Bates held up his hands in defeat. "I'll let her go to the toilet alone, but I won't be removing the bindings. She will have to ask for help or figure it out on her own. That's all I can do." Bates shrugged.

*Perfect.* Elizabeth thought to herself. She could already feel her powers coming back now that she was away from the spelled cage. It would be enough to burn through the bindings.

"Sorry, girly, I tried. I would cherish the next few minutes of alone time. I'm afraid that once you're in the lord's hands, you won't be getting any more of that."

Elizabeth nodded and slowly walked down the hallway towards the restroom. Once she was inside the small room, which housed a dingy-looking toilet and small sink, she called on her dragon fire. It was still weak, but it was doing the job. She knew she wouldn't have too much time before one of the demons came to investigate.

She almost had the bindings burned through when there was banging on the door. "Time's up, love! Open up, or I bust the door in."

"Just a minute! It's a bit awkward with my hands being behind my back," she grumbled.

The door flew open just as her bindings fell to the ground. Bates stood in the door, sniffing. "I thought I smelled something burning." He then noticed her hands were free.

"Oh, no you don't." He lunged for her. She twisted and moved behind him. She managed to slam what was left of the door in his face. Reaching for the purple stone, she felt the warmth of it, but before she could press it to activate the portal, her hand was yanked back by Ox.

She stomped as hard as she could on Ox's foot, and he flung her through the air. Stumbling to the ground, she fell hard. The pain was instant as her legs hit the wooden floor planks, tearing her pants and the skin on her knees. Sucking in a breath, she tried to ignore the pain. This was her only shot.

"Please give my regards to your master," she spit out in disgust. "But I will not be spending any time with him now or in the future. Also, let him know that kidnapping is so last century." Elizabeth pressed the purple stone and prayed that it would get her to the elves. A bright purple light flared up around her. It reminded her of the purple gateway that Chad had opened to get to Fireside.

She heard Bates yelling for her to stop as they leaped toward her. The demons and her surroundings faded away as she found herself engulfed in the bright purple light.

# TWENTY-FIVE

Elizabeth used her arm to shield her eyes as the purple faded into a blinding white light. It took Elizabeth a few minutes for her eyes to adjust to her new surroundings. She blinked several times. All white surrounded her in every direction as far as the eye could see.

"Snow," Elizabeth gasped. Pure white, beautiful snow surrounded her, but she wasn't cold. Her bare feet were not wet or freezing. She was completely comfortable. She looked down at her bare feet and realized they weren't even touching the ground. Elizabeth stretched her hands out in front of her, hitting an invisible barrier. She was in a floating, invisible bubble in the middle of nowhere, which was covered in snow.

"What the hell? How do I get out of this thing?" Elizabeth asked in frustration. "And where am I? Maybe I didn't concentrate on the elf kingdom hard enough, and the portal opened in the wrong place."

Sitting down cross-legged and taking a deep breath, she held onto the purple stone and concentrated on the elf kingdom. "Please, take me to the elf kingdom," she chanted. The stone warmed up. Magic tickled her senses, and then it stopped.

When she opened her eyes, her heart dropped. Nothing had changed. White, glittery snow still surrounded her in every direction. *Well, okay, then.*

Elizabeth felt around for any kind of controls, anything to help her get out of the bubble, but there was nothing. "Well, isn't this freaking fantastic," she groaned.

Reaching for her bracelet again, she planned to use the pink stone to contact Uncle Nicky or Shane. But then she stopped herself. They would only lock her up under the pretense of keeping her safe. They didn't seem to understand that she needed to do this. She was no longer a child. She needed to prove to them and herself that she could be the Pendragon the realms needed her to be.

Now she just needed to figure out what to do next, since she appeared to be stranded in the middle of a glacier with no signs of civilization in sight.

She rested her arms on her bleeding knees. Her pants were torn, and her stomach was growling. What was she supposed to do now? She could try her dragon fire to pop the bubble, but then she would probably freeze to death. Maybe there was a way for her dragon fire to keep her body warm. But how long could she sustain that? Who knew how far she would have to walk before she found any help? Plus, she had yet to fully recover from her first kidnapping mishap, let alone the second. She had to give it to Dimitri; he was persistent, unfortunately for her.

At least she appeared to be safe at the moment. She was warm and comfortable in her floating bubble. She decided it was best to stay put for now and rest, at least until her magic fully recharged. She could try to get out of the bubble and pray that her dragon fire would keep her warm, at least until she found some of the inhabitants of his wintry realm.

Elizabeth was starting to fall asleep when, in the distance, she heard a noise, and it was getting closer. They were snowmobiles. *Oh, thank God*, she thought. *Please don't let this be a dream*. She started yelling, "Help! Help!" and waving her hands. She activated the white stone, and a bright light appeared, marking her location. Hopefully, it could be seen amongst all the white snow.

Sure enough, two snowmobiles stopped right in front of her, each with one driver. Both were wearing white snowsuits and heavy white winter coats with white fur-trimmed hoods. The white helmets they wore covered their faces and ears, making it impossible for her to tell if they were elves or not. She wasn't even sure if they were male or female, and nor did she care, as long as they were friendly and not going to try to kidnap her. She was so over kidnappings at this point.

"Hey, can you help me?" Elizabeth yelled. But neither driver responded to her. She wasn't sure if they could hear her or not.

Elizabeth watched as one driver walked to the back of their snowmobile and retrieved what looked like a rope with a hook at the end. Then they walked over to where Elizabeth was in her invisible bubble. The driver touched the bubble, and a panel opened up. Elizabeth couldn't see what was on the panel, but she saw the driver take the hook end of their rope and attach it to whatever was in the panel, tugging on the rope to make sure it was secure. They looked at Elizabeth, offered a quick nod, and ran back to the waiting snowmobile.

*What in the world is going on?* Elizabeth thought to herself. The other driver looked at Elizabeth and motioned for her with two outstretched hands to sit down. Elizabeth hadn't even realized she had stood up. She had no clue what was going on, but she sat down with her legs crossed at the bottom of the bubble, and the driver nodded their approval, giving her a thumbs up.

The snowmobiles then took off with Elizabeth's bubble in tow. She let out an involuntary scream as her bubble raced along behind the snowmobiles. She bounced up and down with the snow, flying up and hitting the bubble in all directions. Elizabeth felt like she was going to be sick. She had never been one to suffer from motion sickness, but this was intense.

She tried to look around as she bounced along, but all she could see was white, white, and more white. Finally, they were slowing down. Still, there was nothing but snow surrounding them. Then, out of nowhere, a small village appeared. It must have been under a concealment spell, like the market in Fireside.

This village was straight out of a fairytale. Cute little stone and wooden cottages surrounded her. Christmas lights adorned each house even though it was nowhere near Christmas time. The snow-covered rooftops all had smoke billowing out of the chimneys. The inhabitants all appeared to be snug in their warm homes, oblivious to her arrival. There was a forest of snow-covered pine trees that seemed to circle the village, offering it an extra layer of protection. Elizabeth had a sudden craving for peppermint hot chocolate with lots of marshmallows.

They continued past the village through the pine tree forest until they arrived at a large wood cabin. No, cabin was the wrong word for this—it was more like an enormous lodge or a ski chalet. Her degree was in archaeology, not architecture. Whatever this was called, it was huge and gorgeous while also being homey, and that was just from the outside.

It had an exposed wood exterior at least four stories high, and each floor had a covered balcony. A covered front porch wrapped around the bottom floor with several rocking chairs along its deck. Christmas lights covered the outside, and the snow-covered roof had several smoking chimneys. She had a sudden sense of déjà vu, like she had been here before. But she was sure she would remember this picturesque place.

The two mysterious drivers parked and then dismounted their snowmobiles right in front of the main entrance to the lodge. The driver who had attached the rope to her bubble removed his helmet and strolled over toward Elizabeth with purpose. She could tell now that he was all male. He had shaggy white hair, which covered his ears, pale, shimmering skin, like he had millions of tiny snowflakes or ice crystals embedded in his skin, and his clean-shaven face had sharp angles with large, lavender-colored eyes. He gave Elizabeth a stern look.

Elizabeth was so taken by his lavender eyes and his serious expression that she jumped when the other driver appeared at his side. She had long, flowing pink hair and similar, sharp features, but with a feminine softness to them. Her skin was also pale and sparkly, but her eyes were a bright teal. Her expression was warmer and more welcoming than her companion's. His lavender eyes were still fixed on Elizabeth, his arms now crossed in front of his chest.

And boy, didn't his broody expression just add to his sexiness. *Wait? What?* Elizabeth shook her head. Where had that thought come from? She needed to keep her wits about her. She had no idea if these people were friendly or not.

"Welcome," the female said in a cheery voice. "We don't get outsiders often." She was bouncing with excitement. "I'm Riley, and this is my brother, Ryker."

Elizabeth flashed a weary smile. "Hello, I'm Elizabeth. Where am I, and do you know how to get me out of this thing?"

"Well, hello there, Elizabeth," Riley said, smiling from ear to ear. "You should be able to tap the stone you used to get here three times, and it will retract the protective bubble."

Elizabeth did as Riley suggested and tapped the purple stone three times, and sure enough, the bubble disappeared. Of course, Elizabeth forgot she was barefoot and had no coat. She closed her eyes, waiting for the cold to hit her bare feet, but it didn't. Instead, she felt two powerful arms grab her. She opened her eyes and saw those harsh lavender eyes staring back at her again, this time much closer since she was in his arms.

"Welcome to the North Pole," Riley said energetically.

# TWENTY-SIX

"Where?" Elizabeth was sure she had misheard Riley, because the North Pole was uninhabitable, *right*? But before she could question it, Ryker carried her through the front door of the lodge. He was warm and smelled like peppermint and pine, two of Elizabeth's favorite scents. It took everything in her to not snuggle into his broad chest.

Her cheeks bloomed with color as she tried to look everywhere but at the man, who was now carrying her bridal style over the threshold of two intricately carved wooden doors. Worried that he could tell the many dirty thoughts running through her head—starring him—Elizabeth mentally hit herself in the forehead. What was wrong with her? She had never had such an intense reaction to any guy before, not even Shane, and he was supposed to be the love of her life, *right*? Or he had once been, anyway. That last kiss had been more awkward than passionate. But even before that, he had never made her feel like this. And all this man had done was carry her into a building. He hadn't even spoken yet.

Trying to get her thoughts off the tall, brooding stranger, she looked around the room they had stepped through in awe. There was a fire glowing brightly in the stone fireplace, filling the room with warmth and a soft glow. Two large brown leather couches were at either end of the massive room. There was a wooden rocking chair in the corner and a light brown recliner. They had turned one corner into a reading nook with a dark wood bookshelf filled with books. There was a comfortable, dark blue wingback chair and matching ottoman with a tall silver lamp behind the chair, offering the reader perfect light. It had a comfortable, homey feel to it.

Suddenly, a memory flooded Elizabeth's mind. She

remembered sitting on her father's lap in that same reading nook when she had been about five. They had found an old book about elves, and he had been reading it to her. She shook the memory away as a tear fell down her cheek.

She then heard a woman's voice calling from the other room. "Ryker, dear, you can put her on the couch. I will be there in a moment."

Elizabeth had almost forgotten she was still in Ryker's arms. Her cheeks flushed a bit darker as he gently lowered her to one of the leather couches. A woman walked through an open doorway carrying a silver tray topped with steaming mugs. The lovely woman was of average height, with a curvy shape and dressed in a stylish, form-fitting forest green sweater and jeans. Her soft, wavy gray hair fell above her shoulders. Her cream-colored skin was smooth, with only a few wrinkles, and her smile was bright, lighting up the room as she entered.

Elizabeth took in the aroma. Her mouth watered as she realized it was hot chocolate. "I do hope peppermint is still your favorite, dear, with lots of marshmallows, right?" The woman asked as she handed one mug to Elizabeth.

*What is happening here?* Elizabeth looked at the woman, speechless as she took the mug then silently nodding her head in agreement. The woman froze as she took in Elizabeth's frazzled state. "Oh, my stars, you're hurt."

"It's not that bad, really," Elizabeth said as she sipped her cocoa, letting the warmth and smell of peppermint comfort her.

"Nonsense, child, we will fix you right up." She smiled, then turned to Ryker. "Did you not think about healing her?"

Ryker looked startled. He glanced at Elizabeth, then back at the woman, who had sat the tray down on a nearby end table and was now glaring at him with her hands on her hips.

"She's human," he spit out, almost as if in disgust. "You know the rules."

Riley jumped up next to her brother. "Ryker, just this once shouldn't hurt anything."

"We have rules for a reason. It protects us," Ryker scowled at his sister.

"*But*... Ryker, look at her; she's no threat to us. Besides, Mrs. K seems to know her. Surely, you can make an exception this one time?"

"Riley..." His expression softened, and damn, if it didn't do things to Elizabeth's insides. "You know that I, of all people, cannot go around breaking the rules."

"This conversation is pointless. I do know Elizabeth and her family." The woman smiled.

"You do?" Elizabeth asked, suddenly full of questions. Like, why hadn't she remembered this place until just two minutes ago? It seemed to be a childhood dream come true; how could she have forgotten spending time here?

"I do, and Ryker, I am surprised by your reaction. I am fully aware of the rules when dealing with humans. But the fact that you, of all people, haven't picked up on who she is... well, now that's surprising." The woman, who Elizabeth assumed was Mrs. K, flashed a knowing smile.

"What?" He looked at Elizabeth in confusion.

"I'm not sure why you are not a fan of humans, but, yeah, apparently, I'm not one of them. Sorry to disappoint." Elizabeth shrugged.

Everyone turned and looked at her.

"What? Is it a secret? Granted, I did just find out about it myself. Besides, clearly neither of you are human if you have some kind of healing magic. Right?"

"I knew I liked you!" Riley bounced next to Elizabeth. "Go ahead, Ryker; heal her already. Then we can have some of Mrs. K's hot cocoa."

He nervously moved toward Elizabeth. When he touched her arm, a static shock shot through her. Ryker jerked back in surprise. His lavender eyes looked alarmed, yet he tried to play it off as nothing. "You know, Ri, I think this would be a perfect time for you to practice your healing. You should heal her."

"Really?" She jumped up and hugged her brother, oblivious to the weird exchange Elizabeth was having with him. Turning to face her, Riley said, "This won't hurt, I promise. I'm getting much better at weaving the skin back together." Elizabeth shot her a glance; Riley broke out laughing. "Oh, by the stars, I'm kidding." She sat down next to Elizabeth, patting her arm. "I'm an elf. I could heal you in my sleep, and it would be perfect."

"You're an elf?" Elizabeth was relieved. She had been portaled to the right place. She glanced at Ryker, who was staring at her, arms crossed over his chest in a defensive stance. *Definitely more Legolas than Hermey, she* thought to herself.

"Not what you were expecting, huh?" Riley's musical laughter filled the air, and a pink glow emanated from her hands, which were hovering above Elizabeth's ripped up knees. After healing Elizabeth's knees, Riley removed the bandage from her arm and healed where she had torn out the IV as well.

"Honestly, I don't know what I was thinking. I only recently learned that elves and supernaturals are actually real. But maybe I thought it would be a little greener here—less of the white fluffy stuff outside."

"Oh wow, really? I can't even imagine what a shock that must have been. You grew up in the human realm, right?" Before Elizabeth could respond, the spunky elf continued, "You're lucky. I have always wanted to go to the human realm, or really, any other realm."

Ryker cut off his rambling sister. "That's enough, Riley. Are you about finished healing Mrs. K's guest?"

"Oh, yeah, I'm done. Take a look."

Elizabeth glanced down at her knees, which looked perfectly healed. Not even a scratch or a spot of blood had been left behind.

"Sorry. I don't get to meet too many new people, and I tend to get excited and ramble on and on and on," Riley said.

"That's okay. I know how you feel. But thank you for this. It doesn't even hurt anymore." Elizabeth motioned to her knees and smiled at Riley.

"Well, now that, that unpleasantness is out of the way." Mrs. K handed mugs to Riley and Ryker before she took a seat on the couch next to Elizabeth. "What brings you all the way up here, and who had the nerve to hurt you?" Mrs. K asked with concern in her voice.

"I'm sorry," Elizabeth spoke hesitantly. "I don't mean to be rude, but how do you know me?"

"Oh my, where are my manners? Of course, this is a lot for you to take in. You were a little thing the last time you were here. Silly of me to think you would remember. Well then, let's start afresh, shall we? You have already met Riley and Ryker." She motioned their way. "Everyone here calls me Mrs. K. I live here with my husband, whom you will meet shortly. I know it will thrill him to see you again. We don't get a lot of outsiders visiting."

"Is this a hotel, or do you all live here?" Elizabeth asked.

"Oh no," Riley laughed. "Ryker is the—" She stopped abruptly when Ryker stiffened beside her and flashed her a warning look. "I mean to say, we live in the village," she said, looking at Ryker's severe expression as she spoke. "We passed through the village when we brought you here, but someone was moving rather quickly, and you may have missed it." Riley smirked as she jokingly punched her brother in the shoulder. "Mr. and Mrs. K live here in the big house."

Elizabeth wasn't sure how much she should tell these strangers. Should she tell these people she was there to see the king or ask about the Black Knight? Uther seemed to think they could help, but he had also mentioned that Queen Dianna wouldn't be happy about her finding him. Maybe not everyone would be thrilled about her attempt to find the knight.

"You look exhausted," Mrs. K said, patting Elizabeth's hand. "Perhaps we should let you get some rest. We can discuss what brought you here tomorrow, if you like. You are safe here, and your room is all ready for you."

"Thank you. I think you are right. I am quite exhausted and could really use a shower."

"Of course."

Elizabeth's stomach growled as loud as a beast, causing her

to cringe.

"Oh my, I am a horrible host. You are clearly starving, you poor thing. Let's get you up to your room and bathed. Then I will send a tray of food to you right away."

"That would be lovely, thank you." Elizabeth sat her now empty mug on the coffee table, and as she was about to stand, the front door swung open, allowing snow to drift in on the wind, followed by two people. The first was a tall, attractive, muscular man in a burgundy winter coat. His shoulder-length, white hair peeked out from the sides of his fur-trimmed hood. A white goatee and mustache framed his bright smile, and his hazel eyes were filled with warmth and amusement.

Behind him was a familiar, strikingly beautiful woman with long, graying, raven-black hair, which she wore down and framing her delicate features. She was in a long black cloak that covered her trim frame, but it was her bright blue eyes that caught Elizabeth's attention. Eyes, she never thought she would see looking at her again.

The newcomers were laughing about something when they walked in. Neither noticed Elizabeth sitting on the brown leather couch.

"Kris, dear, please take off your wet boots before you track snow throughout my clean house. Then come see who's here," Mrs. K said, smiling warmly and gesturing toward Elizabeth.

The other woman, who had been removing her wet boots, stopped and looked at Elizabeth. They locked their eyes for what seemed like an eternity. Then the woman gasped and whispered, "Lizzy," before she put her hands over her mouth. Tears flowed down her cheeks as she rushed over to where Elizabeth was sitting. Elizabeth jumped to her feet, her own tears now streaming down her face as the woman pulled Elizabeth into a tight embrace.

"Gram," Elizabeth whispered.

# TWENTY-SEVEN

"Oh, my dear, sweet girl, thank the stars that you're okay," Gram cried.

"Me? What about you? I'm not the one who got blown up in our house. How are you even here right now?" Elizabeth asked in surprise as she looked over her grandmother's seemingly healthy form.

"Ah, yes, those despicable trolls and their smelly hellhounds. Unfortunately, I did not get out of there unscathed. I have been here recovering. I knew Nicholas would take care of you in my absence," Lady Lorraine said as she looked over at Elizabeth. "How did you get here?"

Elizabeth shook her head as a small, unamused laugh escaped her lips. "How did I get here? Well, that's a bit of a long story. Two demons tried to kidnap me for Dimitri from my hospital bed at Black Industries. Since they drugged me, I couldn't use my magic, and I had no desire to go with them. I knew I needed to get to the elves. Uncle Nicky gave me a bracelet with a purple stone on it, which I used to get away from them and transport here. Then I ended up in a bubble in the middle of a winter wonderland. Thankfully, Riley and Ryker found me. They brought me here, and that's where we are now."

Lady Lorraine looked at Elizabeth with horror-filled eyes before she sank into the seat next to her, which Mrs. K had vacated. "Dimitri? Hospital? Magic? What?" Lady Lorraine asked in a strained voice.

"Lizzy, dear, perhaps you should start at the beginning?" Mrs. K suggested, looking encouragingly at Elizabeth. "And Kris, dear, I think some of us are going to need a stiff drink." She looked at her husband, then tilted her head toward Lady Lorraine. He nodded in understanding and stepped out for a moment, coming back in with a bottle of whiskey and a few glasses. He poured some of the amber liquid into a glass and handed it to Lady Lorraine, who, to Elizabeth's surprise, gulped it down in one go.

"Thank you, Kris. I needed that," Lady Lorraine said after draining her glass. "Keep it close. I have a feeling I might need another after I hear what my granddaughter has to say. Alright, Lizzy. Last I heard, you were meeting with Nicholas regarding the job he had offered you. Please start from there."

Elizabeth looked around the room at all the faces staring back at her, waiting for her to tell her story. However, a lot had happened since she had last seen Lady Lorraine. Things she desperately needed to talk about. But not in front of all these strangers.

Mrs. K, sensing Elizabeth's trepidation, spoke up. "How about we give these two some privacy?" She ushered everyone out of the room. "If there is anything we need to know, I'm sure Morg will fill us in."

Elizabeth waited till they were alone before she asked, "Who is Morg?"

Lady Lorraine laughed. "It's a horrible nickname that Kris started when we were young, and his wife has picked up on it."

"Why would he call you Morg? That makes no sense," Elizabeth said with amusement.

"I will fill you in on why they call me Morg after you tell me what is going on with you," Lady Lorraine said as she grabbed Elizabeth's hands. "Start talking, young lady."

"Wow, yeah, um... okay, so... so much has happened in such a short time."

"Yes, I gathered."

"I guess it all started when I found this." Elizabeth pulled Excalibur out on its chain.

Lady Lorraine nodded for her to continue.

Elizabeth filled her in on how she had found the funny-shaped cross in the package, which had been left on the table, how Luna had picked her up that morning, and about the office tour. She spoke of the warning from Uncle Nicky, the visit to the town, and the encounter with the vampires at the bookstore with Charlotte. She described Luna escorting her to Greystone manner and the blue light—how she had seen the manor explode. She told her about the encounter with the trolls in the field with Luna, discovering her dragon fire, and the trip to Fireside. She recounted her meeting with Queen Surraya, and then went on to describe being kidnapped and taken to a vampire slave auction, her encounter with Dimitri, the visits from King Uther, and learning about Excalibur. She told her grandmother about the battle with Dimitri, where she discovered her wind power. And finally, she ended with the encounter with the demons in the hospital. She even talked about all that had happened with Shane, including him telling her the truth about the night he had almost killed her and how she now knew Lady Lorraine had altered her memories of that night.

"Well," Lady Lorrain said, grabbing the bottle of whiskey, pouring the amber liquid into two glasses, and handing Elizabeth one as she downed the other. "The fates sure have a funny way of making sure things happen on their timetable, don't they?" Grabbing the bottle again, she poured more into her glass. She was about to refill Elizabeth's, but noticed it hadn't been touched yet. She shrugged her shoulders as she put the bottle back down.

"We had always planned to tell you. Your father and I, that is." She stood, walked over to the fireplace, and looked into the fire as she spoke. "We wanted you to live as normal a life as possible for as long as possible. I never wanted either of you dragged into all this. I was hoping we could avoid it if we didn't talk about it."

"Why didn't you tell me? If magic is a part of me, then why hide it all these years?"

"Being a part of our family, having magic, it comes at such a high cost. A price I didn't want you to have to pay."

"And dad agreed with you?"

"No, not at first, anyway." She turned to look at Elizabeth. "But I convinced him to wait until you were older. He agreed that you needed to have a normal childhood."

"What changed? I've been an adult for years. Hell, Daddy's been gone for years. You should have told me. Surraya said you should have told me at sixteen."

"Your father disappeared. That's what happened."

"A freak accident. It could have happened to anyone."

"No, sweetheart, it wasn't a freak accident. I'm not sure what happened, exactly, but there was never a body found. If it had been a freak accident, and your father had really fallen to his death, there would have been a body, blood, his pack, a scrap of clothing, anything to prove he had been there. But there was nothing. Christopher and all his belongings vanished! That is not normal."

"You think what happened to Daddy was supernatural?" Elizabeth grabbed her own glass of amber liquid, taking a swig. She made a face of disgust before wiping her mouth with the back of her hand.

Lady Lorraine shrugged. "Honestly, I'm not sure. But after that, I didn't want you involved. Not knowing who or what could have gotten to your father, I couldn't lose you, too. But I also realize that you couldn't be kept in the dark about who you are. Not indefinitely. I knew I couldn't hide you forever, no matter how much I wanted to."

"Okay, again, Daddy's been gone for years, and you still never mentioned anything about any of this."

"I was waiting for you to complete school and come back home."

Elizabeth ran her hands through her hair. "You were getting ready to tell me. Is that what you're saying?"

"Of course. Probably in the next few years. I wasn't sure if you were going to go for your master's, and maybe your doctorate."

"Okay, I guess none of that really matters now, because the cat is clearly out of the bag."

"Fair point."

Elizabeth pulled her feet onto the couch, resting her chin atop her knees. "Do you think Lilith had something to do with Daddy's disappearance?"

"No, if she had a Pendragon, she would have announced that to all the realms. This was someone or something else."

"Do you think... I mean, is it possible..." Elizabeth was afraid to ask, but could it be possible? "Could Daddy still be alive?"

Lady Lorraine grabbed onto the mantle. "Oh, Lizzy, I don't know what to think. I have had so many people looking for him. He vanished, and that's not normal. Even if he had passed, I know a few angels on both sides who would have come across his soul in the afterlife."

"What? Angels?"

"Not the point, dear. The point is, if he was in any realm, I should have been able to find him by now. I have even requested to have a meeting with Lucifer."

"Wait? You think he's in Hell?"

"No, sweetheart. Someone is hiding him from me—someone powerful. I don't know why or who, but I also don't think it has anything to do with his Pendragon side."

"You think it has something to do with George Madison? I thought he was human."

Lady Lorraine grabbed another drink and sat down on the couch. "I have so much to tell you. I don't even know where to begin."

Elizabeth took the seat next to her.

"I knew your powers would come in eventually. It was too much to hope that you were born without any. I had always hoped the prophecy was not about you, even though in my gut I knew it was. I wanted you to enjoy your life without the burdens of family responsibility." She stared at the bottom of her glass for a few seconds.

"Wait, there's a prophecy?"

"Isn't there always?" Lady Lorraine threw up her arms

briefly. "I knew Excalibur would choose you. You always had this air about you, even as a baby. So serious. Like you were born knowing the fate of the world rested on your tiny shoulders."

Elizabeth reached for her grandmother's hand. Lady Lorraine looked up and smiled.

"I have been hiding a long time, keeping so many secrets." Lady Lorraine let out a humorless laugh. "I have spent so many years pretending to be someone else to keep my family off Lilith's radar."

"I am so confused. You said you didn't think Lilith had anything to do with Dad's disappearance."

"I don't think she did. But she is not the only one who would want to get their hands on someone with the bloodline of your father. I know you have tons of questions, and I will answer them all. It's time you know the full truth about our family and who you are. But for you to understand who you are, you need to know who I really am."

# TWENTY-EIGHT

Lady Lorraine sat back on the leather couch. She twisted and moved until she found a comfortable position. It took her a few minutes to gather her thoughts before she spoke.

"First, let me say historians have gotten a great many things wrong over the years. I honestly have no idea where they came up with half of their stories."

"I can understand that."

Lady Lorraine nodded. "Okay, good. Now, as you know, I was born in England, the daughter of the Duke and Duchess of Cornwell."

Elizabeth didn't understand why her grandmother was nervous. She always assumed she had been born into nobility. She was *Lady* Lorraine, after all.

"The man I had thought was my father wasn't really my father. But you don't need to know all the gory details. They hid the truth from me for many years to protect me. Just as I have kept things from you to protect you. The irony of our histories is not lost on me."

Lady Lorraine was babbling. Elizabeth had never seen her babbling. She was usually calm and collected, no matter the situation. "This is harder than I thought. Alright, I am just going to say it."

"Gram, it's fine. I'm sure whatever you have to say—"

"My real name is not Lady Lorraine Madison. It's Morgana Cornwall Pendragon Le Fay."

"—is fine. Wait. What?"

"It's a lot, I know. And most things that have been written about me are false, but I know you're going to have questions."

"But how? That would make you..." Elizabeth tried to remember when Morgana had lived in history.

"Old."

"Arthur?"

"My brother."

"Wow." Rubbing her temples, Elizabeth felt like her head was about to explode.

"Maybe we should stop there. Let you get some rest."

"No, I'm good," she smiled.

"I had a dream childhood. My father, Gorlois, spoiled me rotten. When my uncles and aunt passed, my parents took in their two daughters, my cousins, Morgues and Morgain. Their stories have mingled with mine over the years, causing some of the confusion."

"I can see why; your names were similar."

"Morgain is the one who drugged and seduced Arthur, producing Mordred."

"Oh, wow, that really did happen."

"Unfortunately, yes, and I have always felt it was Lilith pulling her strings, but before all that, we were happy. Before Lilith waged war. The High King of Britain, King Ambrosius, called his war counsel to assemble at his summer palace in Wales. My father brought the entire family so we could see the countryside."

Elizabeth shifted in her seat. She couldn't believe her grandmother had experienced living history.

"It was in Wales that I was first introduced to Uther Pendragon. I was only seven and not privy to what was going on. But in a few short weeks, my life was completely turned upside down. The father I adored had died, Uther Pendragon was crowned High King, and my mother, Igraine, was made his queen. We were all moved into the palace, and a few months later, Arthur was born."

"Did Merlin really cast a spell on Uther to make him look like your father to seduce your mother?"

"Lizzy, I already told you not to believe all the stories you have heard. I do not know where that ridiculous story came from. No, he did not. Merlin wasn't even around until Arthur, and I were much older."

"You honestly knew Merlin? What am I saying, you're freaking Morgana Le Fay. Of course you knew him. Didn't he train you or something?"

"Hardly. I apprenticed with the Immortal Queen to become a high priestess of Avalon at seventeen. The name La Fey is not a surname; it is a title. It means 'one with the fae.' It was a high honor that only a few received. Technically speaking, I out ranked Merlin." Lady Lorraine smirked with pride.

"I believe my cousin Morgain trained alongside Merlin for a time. Again, another story historians misinterpreted."

"Didn't he train Arthur?" Elizabeth asked, wondering if any

of the stories were right at this point.

Lady Lorraine shook her head with a smile. “No, Merlin was like a brother to Arthur. Along with Lancelot, the three were inseparable.”

Elizabeth's interest was now piqued. She had always been drawn to Lancelot.

“Merlin was a wizard of the highest order and only a few years older than me. No one except a pure immortal like Queen Dianna was more powerful than him.”

“Even though you out ranked him. Right?”

“Of course,” Lady Lorraine laughed. “There were whispers that in time, Merlin would grow to be more powerful than her. Even my skills paled in comparison to his. He was magnificent, and we fell madly in love.”

“You and Merlin?” Elizabeth asked.

Lady Lorraine nodded. “Unfortunately, our union was frowned upon. I was a princess, the sister of the future High King. My role was to marry a prince or king from a neighboring kingdom, forging an alliance. My feelings didn’t matter.” Lady Lorraine’s eyes showed the sadness she must have felt. She saw the concern on Elizabeth’s face. “Don’t fret. It was a different time back then. Thank the stars that things are different for you. You won’t have to choose duty or family obligations over love.”

“Maybe.”

“Uther, Arthur, and Merlin were called to war. I wanted to help. I knew I could help protect them with my magic. However, Uther forbade me from going. He feared for my safety and felt I would be more a distraction than any help.”

Elizabeth shifted in her seat; her butt was starting to go numb from all this sitting.

“I was angry; I didn’t even say goodbye or see him off. Instead, I screamed at him and ran to my room, acting every bit a child.” Lady Lorraine stopped as tears streamed down her face. “From my room, I watched them ride off. That was the last time I saw Uther. The man I would later find out was my real father. The man who raised me.”

Elizabeth wiped at the tears now running down her cheeks.

“A man I thought of as indestructible was killed by Lilith. I was never told the details, but I know it must have been horrible, because my brother could never speak of it, and nor could Merlin. I regret my actions that day more than I can say. Even now, I am ashamed of how I acted.” Lady Lorraine looked away from Elizabeth as she wiped the tears from her eyes.

“He loves you, you know. He told me to tell his children he loved them and that he was proud of them. He is proud of you and who you have become,” Elizabeth said as she wrapped her arms around Lady Lorraine, embracing her.

“Thank you, Lizzy. I’m glad you got to meet him and talk to

him." Wiping another tear away, she continued. "When my brother came back, he was different. His carefree prince days were behind him. He now had the weight of the world on his shoulders. To secure his kingdom and create a powerful alliance with Scotland, Arthur took Princess Guinevere to be his queen."

"What was she like?"

"Evey bit his equal. She was a warrior and sorceress in her own right. She was the perfect queen. Camelot was in high spirits, for a time."

"What about Merlin and you?"

"We kept our relationship secret. I hoped, in time, Arthur would warm to the idea. But then Mordred showed up, claiming to be Arthur's son and demanding his birthright. Arthur refused to make Mordred his heir, which infuriated both Mordred and his mother, Morgain. Both vowed to destroy Arthur."

"Arthur's queen could not bear him a child. He became distant. We then learned that Lilith was planning yet another attack, this time with the Saxons, who were a brutal people to the north. Arthur arranged an alliance with a powerful kingdom to our west, which would have provided us with troops and supplies for the coming battle, in exchange for my hand in marriage to their crowned prince."

"Oh, wow." Elizabeth said.

"I refused. I was in love. He didn't seem to care, and he gave me one week for my goodbyes and refused to see me."

"What happened?"

"We eloped. When Arthur found out, he banished both Merlin and me from the kingdom."

"That's horrible!" Elizabeth yelled.

"No, it was generous of him. We had committed treason; he would have had every right to sentence us both to death. I broke my brother's heart that day. It's something I carry with me still. Soon after, he learned of Guinevere and Lancelot's affair. Within days, Arthur lost his sister, his wife, and both his best friends. When I say Arthur was not ready for the battle, I mean it. He was not mentally ready. He no longer knew what he was even fighting for."

"Poor Arthur," Elizabeth whispered.

"I convinced both Merlin and Lancelot to go into battle with Arthur, even though he had banished them. I knew it would go a long way for him to have them by his side. It was a brutal battle. Our forces were fighting against the Saxons, as well as Lilith's army. I requested aid from the dragons. The dragons' arrival helped turn the tide in our favor, but not before Mordred struck Arthur down with Excalibur. Arthur reclaimed the sword and thrust it into Mordred's heart, killing him instantly. I arrived only moments later. Arthur was dying, but I knew the dragon stone could save him if I could buy some time. I cast a time spell that froze Arthur at that moment. I encased him in quartz for protection."

*A time spell. That sounds pretty awesome,* Elizabeth thought to herself.

"I hid him in the cave system underground. I also fortified the cave with a blood-cloaking spell, ensuring that only a member of our blood family could remove the spell. When I returned to the battle, the dragons had pushed the Saxons and Lilith's army back. I didn't realize Lilith was there, but she saw me. Even though she did not know I was a Pendragon, I was still a powerful sorceress who was a threat. She sent a powerful, magical surge toward me that would have killed me on impact. I didn't have the time to counter it. However, Merlin had the gift of sight. He knew this moment in time was coming and he had prepared for it. He cast his spell, which reached me a second before Lilith's did."

"Wow, thank goodness for Merlin," Elizabeth said.

"Indeed. To anyone who was there, it looked as if Lilith had killed me, when, in reality, Merlin had sent me fifteen hundred years into the future."

"Merlin, not George Madison, is my grandfather, then?"

"Yes, dear, Merlin is your grandfather," Lady Lorraine responded with a slight smile. "As for George, he was a lovely young soldier who I befriended. I told him my baby's father had been killed in the war. As an only child, he was worried about his aging parents in the States. They were well off and had the means to hire plenty of help, but he was afraid of them being taken advantage of. Plus, I had no one. He proposed marriage to help us both out. I could claim a father for my child and watch over his parents until he came back. It had already been months since I had arrived. With no sign of Merlin, I was desperate, alone, and pregnant, so I agreed. I set off for the States and George for the front lines. I never saw him again, but I kept my promise. I cared for his parents until the end. George Madison gave me a family and a new life. For that, I am eternally grateful to him."

Elizabeth yawned, and then her stomach let out a loud growl. "Oh, excuse me," Elizabeth grimaced.

Lady Lorraine smiled. "It's okay, dear. It's a lot to take in. How about we take a break and see what Mrs. K has in the kitchen? Then, off to bed with you. We can discuss what Uther suggested about training later."

Elizabeth followed Lady Lorraine into the kitchen, eager for a snack, and then some rest.

# TWENTY-NINE

Mrs. K was a godsend. Her love language appeared to be food. She seemed to really enjoy cooking and feeding everyone comforting, delicious dishes, and Elizabeth was here for it. Elizabeth loved food and didn't mind that it made her a little more on the curvy side. Although she couldn't cook her way out of a paper bag if her life depended on it. Her version of a gourmet meal was buying name-brand sauce and pouring it over fancy pasta.

After her long day and then the draining conversation with her grandmother, Elizabeth was both starving and exhausted. She needed food and a bed, ASAP. Venturing into the kitchen, she was delighted to find a feast. Mrs. K had a delicious dinner of roast beef, mashed potatoes, honey carrots, and fresh bread all ready for them. Elizabeth devoured it in a rather unladylike manner, but she did not care.

When Elizabeth was stuffed, unable to eat another bite, she asked to be excused. She needed a shower and much needed rest. After all, in the last twenty-four hours, she had been kidnapped, almost enslaved by a deranged vampire, met her great-grandfather's ghost, found a magical sword that had been missing for fifteen hundred years, discovered her best friend was half-vampire, had been kidnapped *again*, and then found out her entire family history had been a lie. Needless to say, she needed a minute to herself.

Lady Lorraine showed her to the guest suite where they would be staying. The suite had two bedrooms, each with a private bathroom, a sitting room, a small kitchenette, an eating area, and a balcony. Elizabeth went straight to her bedroom and flopped face-first onto the four-poster, queen-sized bed. Maybe the shower could wait till tomorrow. Wrapping herself in the

Christmas-themed quilt that adorned the top of the bed, she quickly fell into a peaceful slumber.

The next morning, Elizabeth felt refreshed but stinky. Rushing to the bathroom, she rummaged through the cabinets and drawers, finding gingerbread-scented shampoo and soap. She also, thankfully, found a new toothbrush and toothpaste. Grabbing a towel and washcloth from the linen closet, she set out to make herself somewhat presentable for the day.

After stepping into the warm, relaxing spray of the shower, she realized she didn't have any clean clothes, and what had she'd had on yesterday was in no condition to wear again.

Wrapping herself in the fluffiest towel she had ever seen, she proceeded toward her grandmother's room, her bare feet slapping against the cool wood floor. Then she noticed the door was ajar.

*Good.* Hopefully, her grandmother had brought her something to wear.

"Gram, do you have anything I can—" She froze mid-sentence when she saw it was not her grandmother standing by her empty bed. Her stomach began to flutter as she took in the lean, masculine form in front of her. Ryker turned to face her, his lavender eyes widening in shock as he took in her appearance. His cheeks flushed as he gazed at her from head to toe.

Horror and embarrassment set in when she realized she was standing there in front of him, wearing only a towel and nothing else. She screeched, "What are you doing in here?"

Quickly, he turned his still reddening face away from her. "My apologies. Your grandmother asked me to bring these for you. I was going to lay them on the bed." He held out a cream sweater and black leggings, along with a pair of black flat slip-on shoes, for her to see.

"Um, okay, thank you," she awkwardly replied.

"Just... hurry up and get dressed. Mrs. K has your morning meal waiting." Laying the clothes on the bed without a second glance in her direction, he stormed out of the room, slamming the main door to the suite in his wake.

Once she heard the door to the suite shut, she released a breath she didn't even know she had been holding. "*Ugh,* I can never face him again," she said out loud as she flopped on the bed, covering her face with a pillow.

After wallowing in her mortification for a few more minutes, she decided it was time to get moving. As she sat up, her stomach started to growl, a reminder that she was starving.

"Traitor." She looked at her stomach. "Maybe I was going to hide up here forever."

Walking to the bathroom, she planned to take as much time as possible to get ready. She slipped the soft, cream-colored sweater over her head. It was the softest material she had ever felt. Then she put on the black leggings and stepped into the flats. Everything fit her like a glove. She wasn't ready to face Ryker again just yet. Her cheeks flushed thinking about their encounter.

Slowly, she made her way toward the kitchen, when suddenly, she heard voices. Stopping short, she realized one of the voices belonged to Ryker. She was about to turn back when she heard Mrs. K calling her.

"Lizzy, is that you? Come on in dear; breakfast is ready."

"Good morning," she said as she walked into the kitchen. She smiled at Mrs. K and then her grandmother, who was sitting at the table. She completely avoided Rykers' intense gaze at all costs.

"Perfect timing, dear. We were just discussing you."

"Oh?"

"Yes, your grandmother was informing us that Excalibur has finally made its presence known to you," Mrs. K said as she placed a plate full of gingerbread French toast in front of her.

Elizabeth glanced at her grandmother in surprise.

"It's fine, dear. Both Ryker and Kris were knights at Arthur's round table. They know all about the sword and us being Pendragons."

"You were a knight?" Elizabeth couldn't help the shock in her voice as she finally looked over at Ryker.

"Another lifetime ago, yes." Ryker briefly looked at her before turning his attention to Lady Lorraine. "However, I am unclear as to why I am needed in this conversation. I do have other matters to attend to."

"Ryker, don't be rude," Mrs. K chastised him.

"The truth is not rudeness, milady."

"You're here because Elizabeth needs training. She needs to learn how to unlock and control her magic."

"Agreed, and these are things you should have been teaching from day one. Again, I ask, why am I here?"

"Ryker!" Mrs. K gasped.

"It's fine, Jessica." Lady Lorrain held up her hand. "He's right. I should have ensured that she received proper training. Instead, I allowed fear to cloud my judgment."

"Gram... it's okay."

"No, it's not. But it will be. You are not prepared for what lies ahead, and that is on me. You should have known about your magic, about our legacy." Elizabeth, feeling the pain in her grandmother's words, reached for her hand to offer comfort.

"As touching as this family moment is, I again must wonder why I am here?" Ryker crossed his arms over his chest and glared at Lady Lorraine.

"I need you to train her." Lady Lorraine waved in

Elizabeth's direction.

"What?" Ryker looked between Elizabeth and Lady Lorraine in disbelief. "That's absurd."

"Wait… what? No. He can't train me. Uther said I should go to Avalon to be properly trained." There was no way this grumpy elf was going to train her.

"In a perfect world, yes, that would have been ideal. However, time is not on our side. Dimitri knows about you, which means so does Lilith."

"I still do not see why you would ask this of me. You are among the most powerful sorceresses ever to emerge from Avalon. Plus, you are the child's family. It seems clear that you should conduct the training."

*Did he seriously refer to me as a child?* "Excuse you, I am not a child." She glared at him with her hands on her hips.

"Really? Because from where I'm standing, it looks like you're about to throw a temper tantrum."

"Wow, I guess they didn't teach you manners or common civility in knight school."

"I will not apologize if the truth wounds your fragile pride." Ryker uncrossed his arms and rested his hands on the counter behind him. He crossed one long, boot-clad leg over the other to appear relaxed. His eyebrow raised, his lavender eyes sending her a pointed look.

"Who the hell do you think you are?"

"Enough of this." Lady Lorraine stood and faced Ryker. "Her magic is different from mine—more powerful. She is connected to the elements and the world around her. She needs a master elemental to train her properly."

"I can notify Avalon and request a prompt dispersal of a proper instructor," Ryker said, never taking his eyes off Elizabeth.

"We talked about this. Time is not on our side. We do not have the luxury of waiting for Avalon to send someone," Lady Larraine huffed out.

"Then, I suppose we are back to you as her trainer." Ryker's stern gaze shifted to Lady Lorraine.

"Why not you? You can train her," Lady Lorraine said, exasperated.

"I can do no such thing," Ryker responded matter-of-factly.

"Why not? You're the most powerful elemental ever." Lady Lorraine threw her hand in the air in frustration.

"She's not an elf," Ryker spat out.

"No, she's the Pendragon." Lady Lorraine pinched the bridge of her nose.

"But still not an elf." Ryker recrossed his arms over his chest.

"Your people and their silly archaic ways. If Elizabeth is not prepared, then Lilith will win. You know as well as I do that your people will be next after the humans. Her obsession with you is legendary, Ryker. Please, don't be foolish."

Ryker's face darkened as he stood from the counter. "Do you honestly think I don't realize what is going on in the world around our little bubble? That I have forgotten all that Lilith has taken from us, from me?"

"No, of course not. But you can help ensure that your people are never targeted again. That they are safe. Surely, even your council of elders must agree to this course of action. Ensuring Elizabeth is ready is our only hope." Lady Lorraine said, her eyes pleading with him.

"Ryker, dear, she is right. You are the best option we have," Mrs. K said as she put her hand on his shoulder.

"The council will not approve of such an action. Not for a non-elf." Ryker's expression softened slightly as he glanced at Mrs. K.

"Funny, I always thought the council was simply there to offer advice to the monarch. When did they become the voice of the elves instead of the king?" Lady Lorraine glared at Ryker.

"You forget your place, madam." Ryker whispered harshly.

"No, I have not, but I think you have. What happened to the Ryker I once knew? The knight who fought by the Pendragons' side? Who knew of the devastation Lilith could reap into the world and vowed to stop her?"

Ryker looked at Elizabeth and then back to Lady Lorraine with a defeated expression, which broke Elizabeth's heart. This man had been through something. She recognized the pain of loss in his eyes. It was a pain she knew all too well.

"You know what happened to him. Now, if you will excuse me, I do have other matters to attend to." He then turned his back on them and walked out of the kitchen.

"Ryker, where are you going? We aren't done here."

"Let him go, Morg," Mrs. K whispered. "Give him some time. He might come around."

"No, he won't." Lady Lorraine turned to face Elizabeth. "I am sorry about all that. I will find someone to train you, I promise."

"Uther told me to seek out the Black Knight to help with my sword training. He said the elves could help me find him."

"Perhaps, but I feel your magic training should be our priority. I can help you with the basics. I left a few books on beginner magic in your room. This should at least get you started. I also reached out to Nicholas. I sent him word last night that we were both alright. Perhaps he will have some insight on an instructor for you."

Elizabeth nodded, only half listening. That look on Ryker's face before he left made her want to chase after him. She wanted to know what caused the pain she had seen in his eyes. Which was crazy. He had been nothing but a jerk toward her since she had arrived. However, she felt there was something more to his crappy attitude. She felt a need to be near him, despite his rudeness—a pull she didn't quite understand.

# THIRTY

With nothing better to do, Elizabeth sat in her room reading the books on magic her grandmother had left for her. She was attempting to get through a chapter on magical theories when an annoyingly consistent tapping sound broke her concentration.

She tried to ignore the sound and continue with her reading. However, after the third time, she begrudgingly got up to investigate. She found a way-too-chipper Riley peering through the glass door which led to the balcony. Elizabeth walked over and opened the sliding glass door, inviting the young woman in.

"Are you up for some fun?" Riley asked, practically jumping up and down.

"I don't know. I should probably stay and rest," Elizabeth said, faking a yawn and stretching out her arms in an attempt to show she was exhausted.

"Nonsense. Let's go. You are way to wound up and in desperate need of fun!" Riley said as she dragged Elizabeth toward the balcony.

"Wait!" Elizabeth shouted. "I'm not really dressed to go anywhere."

"You're right. We will find you something warm to wear. We don't need you freezing to death. Not that you would. You do have dragon blood and all," Riley said as she looked around the room. "Ah yes, this will work." Riley grabbed a red and green sparkly throw blanket from the sitting room. "Okay, wrap this around you."

"Huh? I don't think this is going to work." Elizabeth looked at Riley with confusion.

"Did you know that Cinderella's fairy godmother wasn't

really a fairy?" Riley said as she wrapped the blanket around Elizabeth.

"Well, no, I guess I never thought about it." Elizabeth was unsure of what was happening. "Not really sure what Cinderella has to do—" But before Elizabeth could finish her statement, a pink glow surrounded her. The blanket was molding itself around her body. Elizabeth looked at Riley, whose eyes were closed and whose hands were moving around like she was conducting an orchestra.

When the pink glow faded, Elizabeth found herself in a red Christmas-themed snowsuit complete with silver fur trim on the hood and red, fur-lined boots.

"As I was saying," Riley said with a mischievous grin. "Cinderella's fairy godmother was actually an elf."

"Oh my gosh, that was amazing!" Elizabeth exclaimed. "I have never seen anything like that before."

"Elves can manipulate matter. It's pretty simple." Riley shrugged and continued to drag Elizabeth toward the balcony door. "Now, let's go have some fun!"

Elizabeth followed Riley out the balcony doors. She stopped for a minute when she realized they were on the third floor and there was no way down from there. "Um, do elves fly, also?" She looked down at the snow-covered ground below them. "Because I'm pretty sure I don't. Dragon blood, yes. Actual dragon no," Elizabeth said dryly.

"We aren't going to fly, silly. But how awesome would that be if you did have a dragon? I have never seen a dragon, but some of the other elves have. I'm jealous. I bet they are amazing." Riley excitedly rambled on before saying, "We are going to take the stairs."

Elizabeth looked around again and was about to ask what stairs when she noticed the pink glowing light coming from Riley as she moved her orchestra hands again. Looking down, she noticed the snow was rising and swirling all around. Elizabeth stood there in awe as the snow transformed into a staircase leading from the balcony to the ground.

"Let's go!" Riley said enthusiastically. "Everyone else will be there already." She grabbed Elizabeth's hand and led her down the magical staircase made from snow.

"Be where? Where are we going?" Elizabeth asked as she followed the bouncing Riley.

"To go reindeer racing, of course," Riley said, laughing as she led the way toward a large, snow-covered hill.

When they got to the base of the hill, Elizabeth saw about ten other figures. They were all dressed warmly in winter gear, but Elizabeth could see small glimpses of pale, glittering skin that sparkled in the moonlight. Strands of brightly colored hair escaped from their fur-lined hoods, and like Riley had said, several were racing reindeer down the hill.

Elizabeth didn't see the stone-faced elf with pure white hair and piercing lavender eyes. "Is your brother here?" Elizabeth asked as she looked around, unsure why she cared.

"No, he doesn't do fun," was Riley's giggly response.

*Why does that not surprise me?*

"I don't think he likes me very much," Elizabeth said, unsure why it mattered if he liked her or not.

"Oh, don't worry about him," Riley said, waving a hand. "He doesn't like anyone. I love my brother, but he needs to remove the stick from his you-know-what now and then and enjoy life. But heavy is the head that wears the burden, as they say."

Before Elizabeth could ask what she had meant by that or comment that she was pretty sure that wasn't the actual saying, Riley dragged them toward two elves who had dismounted their reindeer. "Wanna race?" Riley asked with pure joy and excitement in her voice as she pointed to the two riderless reindeer.

A few minutes later, Elizabeth couldn't believe she had allowed Riley to talk her into this as she sat on top of a reindeer. There were no reins or saddles, just huge antlers, which they advised Elizabeth to hold on to. The smell of campfire and pine surrounded her. Not the smell of a wild animal, which she had expected.

Riley and she were next up to race. Elizabeth had no clue what she was doing. She wasn't even sure if this would be considered fun in her book. Suddenly, Elizabeth heard someone yell, "GO!" and her reindeer took off. Everything was a blur as the reindeer raced down the hill. Elizabeth held onto the antlers for dear life. Her heart was pounding, her pulse was racing, and adrenaline flooded her system. Elizabeth had never felt terrified or more alive in her life. Trees passed by in a blur. Riley and her reindeer were a little ahead of them, but then Elizabeth's reindeer huffed, and, in a burst of speed, overtook them. When they reached the bottom of the hill, she took a few minutes to catch her breath. That had been exhilarating. She kissed her reindeer on top of the head, thanking him before jumping off his back. Riley raced over to Elizabeth, her excitement and joy clear on her face.

"You were amazing," Riley yelled. "Most people, elves included, fall off their first few times racing. Wow, that was just—wow!" Riley gave Elizabeth a big hug.

"I'm sorry, what? You failed to mention that little tidbit before the race," Elizabeth whispered in Riley's ear. Riley shrugged and turned with a grin toward the other elves, who were now gathering around Elizabeth. The elves were all offering Elizabeth congratulations and patting her reindeer, whose name she now knew was Bolt, on the back. Apparently, Elizabeth and Bolt had won the race.

They watched a few more races before Riley led Elizabeth over to a campfire where some of the elves had gathered. They were passing around a bottle of what smelled like peppermint schnapps. Elizabeth took a swig and instantly felt warm and relaxed.

Riley and Elizabeth sat by the fire and listened to the elves as they shared tales, using their magic to create little figurines out of the snow to animate each story. It was like watching a live action cartoon, if that was a thing. The story where the Elf King outsmarted Lilith to save his people fascinated Elizabeth.

At one point, Lilith had been a beautiful, loving mother and guardian of the earth. Sadly, the heartbreak of Adam's betrayal turned her heart black and caused her soul to wither. She demanded vengeance and craved power. Her lust for power caused her to turn to the elves, attempting to trick them into doing her bidding and feeding her their magic. The elves were a peaceful race. Their magic was nurturing, not vengeful. They refused to use their magic for her evil purposes. The elves wanted to live in peace and use their magic to nurture and care for the earth.

Elizabeth was seeing a repeat pattern where Lilith was concerned. Like Adam, The Elf King broke her heart by tricking Lilith into thinking he was under her spell and madly in love with her. For a while, it seemed to work, and for a while, Lilith believed she was happy, forgetting her vengeful plans.

The sad part was that the king used himself as a distraction. He never meant the sweet words he whispered to her or the loving caresses. He made false promises to her each night for weeks, allowing his people time to escape unnoticed. With the help of his friend, Mr. K, they led the elves through a portal to their new home, a land covered in snow and ice, which they would turn into a magical winter wonderland, safe from Lilith.

Elizabeth hated to admit this, but she felt sorry for Lilith on some level. Granted, she did go about things in the worst ways. But was it possible that she was just a woman looking for love to repair a broken heart? Could it be that simple? It could never excuse her choices or the fact that she had tried to kill Elizabeth's entire family for generations. Still, it made her think.

Thankfully, the next story was a funny folktale about an elf boy and his magical pet bunny who went on a grand adventure.

Elizabeth remembered Uther had told her to seek the Elf King, that he could help her find the Black Knight. She had forgotten to mention the part about the Elf King to her grandmother. Was it possible that it was the same Elf King? Elizabeth wanted to ask Riley about him, but the elf had apparently had too much peppermint drink and was now passed out beside her, using Elizabeth's shoulder as a pillow. Looking around, Elizabeth was trying to figure out what to do about the pink-haired elf. She didn't know where she lived, just that it was in the Elf Village somewhere. She didn't want to leave her there. The other elves seemed like they were all friendly, but Elizabeth did not feel comfortable leaving Riley unconscious and defenseless.

"Need some help?" came a familiar voice as Ryker appeared out of nowhere. His typical, stony gaze took in the sight of Riley passed out on Elizabeth's shoulder.

"Um, yes, it seems like your sister has slightly trapped me."

"It would seem." As he walked toward them, she noticed his expression softened a little as he gazed at his sister. It surprised her how much more attractive he was when he wasn't scowling at her. The caring way he looked at his sleeping sister was heartwarming.

*What the hell? How do I keep finding him attractive? Am I asking for trouble? Isn't one annoyingly, confusing, and attractive supernatural enough for me? Good grief! Get a grip, girl!* She found herself yelling at herself. *Besides, he doesn't even like you.* "Riley said you wouldn't be coming tonight."

Ryker stepped toward his sleeping sister. He cocked an eyebrow. "Oh really? Asking about me, are we?"

"No, of course not," Elizabeth shot back, heat rising to her cheeks.

"Mm-hmm." "I didn't, you know, ask about you... Anyway, what brings you by?" Elizabeth asked, trying to regain some composure, unsure why Ryker was making her feel flustered.

"Riley is rarely out this late. I needed to make sure she was okay. It looks like I came just in time."

"We had a good time. I really like your sister."

"She seems quite enamored with you as well." Reaching down, he picked up Riley's limp body. His warm hand brushed against Elizabeth for a split second, sending a jolt of electricity up her arm. He glanced at Elizabeth. Had he felt that, too?

He momentarily froze, meeting her eyes. She was sure he wanted to say more, but he didn't. Instead, he shook his head, then started to walk toward the lodge, Elizabeth following close behind. He stopped when they reached the front door. "Get plenty of rest tomorrow. You're going to need it for the next day." Not looking back, he headed toward the elf village.

"Why, what's happening?"

"We start your training bright and early the day after tomorrow. And I won't go easy on you just because my sister kept you out all night." He looked over his shoulder at her. *Wait, is that amusement I see in his eyes? No, I probably just imagined it.*

Elizabeth stared dumbstruck into the night as he walked

away with a still-sleeping Riley in his arms. Ryker was going to train her. What had changed? He had been against it a few hours ago. She wasn't sure how she felt about that. Excited and a little unsure, perhaps. Was this a good idea? She decided not to overthink it. This was why she was here. To get trained. To help Skye and the other captives.

Elizabeth climbed up the snow staircase, which thankfully was still there, leading up to her balcony. When she entered her room, she found Lady Lorraine sitting on her bed, waiting for her. "I thought you were resting."

"That was the plan, until Riley showed up and insisted I go have some fun," Elizabeth said, smiling as she took a seat on the bed beside her grandmother.

"I'm glad. Sadly, there may be few chances for fun in the coming days," Lady Lorraine said with sadness. "I am sorry for the burdens that have been laid at your feet. But know this: you are not alone; you will never be alone. I am here if you need to talk. I hope you know that."

"I do, and I did want to ask you about something." Elizabeth paused, not sure how to approach the subject but needing to know the truth. "Shane. Why did you never tell me about Shane? Why did you wipe my memories of what happened? And before that, why were you against us being together?"

Lady Lorraine got up from the bed and paced for a few minutes before she spoke. "You are my only grandchild. I would move heaven and earth to protect you," Lady Lorraine said, not looking at Elizabeth, but staring into the fire burning in the stone fireplace across the room. "Nicholas is my oldest and dearest friend. I trust him above all others. I know he would never hurt our family, but his brother Dimitri is another story. You know Dimitri is Lilith's general, her second in command, and stars know what else."

Elizabeth nodded her head in acknowledgment.

"He knows her desire to see the end of the Pendragon line. Shane, through no fault of his own, is Dimitri's son. You are a Pendragon. There is danger there. I know you think you love and trust Shane, but he has not been a part of your life in years." Lady Lorraine walked back over to Elizabeth and sat back down on the bed. "I will never get the image of Shane holding you in a pool of your blood, while blood dripped from his fangs out of my head."

Elizabeth shivered at the thought.

"I was out of my mind with anger." Lady Lorraine tensed, and Elizabeth could hear the raw emotions in her voice as she spoke. "Had Nicholas not been there, I would have struck that boy down in a heartbeat. No regrets, because he hurt you. He put your life at risk. You didn't need to know that. You didn't need to remember that your first love almost killed you. It was in my power to take that fear and pain away."

"No, I just spent the last seven years feeling rejected and feeling like a fool." Elizabeth stood and walked away from her grandmother. Elizabeth felt the anger and sadness wash over her like a tidal wave. "Not knowing the truth affected me. It made me feel like there was something wrong with me. Like I was unlovable or undesirable."

"Oh, my sweet girl, I am sorry. I never meant for anything like that to happen. I cannot change the past. I wish I could. I know I have made many mistakes where you are concerned. Please, try to understand where I'm coming from. You were young. Shane was your first taste of love, but that doesn't mean he should be your last. He's not the only man out there. I would hate for you to miss out on something or someone spectacular out of some misguided loyalty to your past. I will try to respect your judgment in the future. However, if Shane or anyone else hurts you, I cannot be held responsible for my actions. You are my joy, and I love you." Lady Lorraine walked over to Elizabeth and took her in her arms.

Elizabeth did understand where her grandmother was coming from. She felt some of the anger and past sadness fade. She was grateful to have her grandmother back in her life. It wasn't that long ago that she had feared she was dead. She would not let mistakes from the past come between them now. Besides, she wasn't entirely sure about her feelings for Shane, either. She was an adult, but an adult who knew absolutely nothing about love and relationships.

After a few minutes, Lady Lorraine patted Elizabeth on the back. "Okay, sweetheart, you need to get some rest," Lady Lorraine said as she pulled down the covers from Elizabeth's bed.

"I guess. Ryker told me about training."

"What about training?"

"That we are going to start training the day after tomorrow?"

"Really? He said that?"

"Um, yes, just a few minutes ago."

Lady Lorraine slowly sat down next to Elizabeth. "Thank the stars."

"You didn't know?"

"I had no clue he had changed his mind. You should feel quite honored to be trained by a knight of King Arthur's Court." Lady Lorraine patted Elizabeth's hands.

"That's crazy. Ryker looks like he's... maybe twenty-five?"

Lady Lorraine's laughter filled the air. "Looks can be deceiving. Especially with those who have magic in their blood. Not all magical creatures are true immortals, like the Immortal

Queen Dianna or even Lilith. However, the magic in our veins helps us to live hundreds, if not thousands, of years."

"Are you telling me Ryker is thousands of years old?" Elizabeth asked.

"I am not clear about how old he is. Honestly, I don't even know how old I am anymore. But Ryker is skilled, so take advantage of your time with him. Now, get to bed. There are clothes for you in the wardrobe and fresh toiletries in your bathroom. Good night, my dear," Lady Lorraine said as she walked out of Elizabeth's room.

Elizabeth found a pair of red and green flannel pajamas in the wardrobe, which she quickly changed into. She finished in the bathroom and jumped into bed.

She fell asleep to thoughts of lavender eyes.

# THIRTY-ONE

The magical smell of peppermint mocha coffee filled the room. Elizabeth had been dreaming of dark, moody, lavender eyes and strong, muscular arms. The bed beneath her moved, alerting her to the fact that she was not alone. Had it not been a dream? Elizabeth shot up out of bed, relieved and disappointed at the shock of pink hair, she almost slammed into.

"Riley?" What was she doing here?

"Good morning. It's such a beautiful day. I didn't want you to waste it sleeping it away."

"I like sleep." Elizabeth threw a pillow at the way-too-chipper-for-this-early-in-the-morning elf. "Sleep is my friend, especially when my other friend keeps me up way past my bedtime."

"I thought you might feel that way. That's why I brought a peace offering." Riley waved the paper cup decorated with snowflakes under her nose.

"Hmm, coffee." She sniffed the delectable smell.

"Yes, and it's all yours once you rise and shine. I have the whole day planned."

"Okay, okay, give me one sip to get me going." Riley smiled as she handed Elizabeth the cup filled with the nectar from the Gods.

Elizabeth grabbed a pair of jeans and a soft red sweater from her closet before heading into the bathroom to get ready. She emerged a short time later, fully dressed and somewhat alert.

"Alright, what's the plan for the day?" Elizabeth asked, picking up the snowflake cup from the end table where she had left it. "Hmm, still hot."

"Well, a little birdie told me that you are going to start training with my brother tomorrow."

"Yup, that's what I've been told as well."

"That's big news. Ryker is pretty private about his magic, and never—I mean, never—trains anyone." Riley's eyes got huge as she talked. "I can't believe the council is letting him train a non-elf. They are pretty weird about stuff like that."

"The council?"

"Yeah, the Council of Elves." Riley directed Elizabeth to the balcony where the snow staircase from the night before still stood. "They are a bunch of old fuddy-duddy elves that are chosen to help govern until a new monarch comes of age to take over ruling the kingdom on their own."

"Your monarch isn't of age?" She wondered if it was the Elf King Uther had told her about.

"No, he is, and has been for some time now. I think the council is manipulating the situation to keep themselves in power. They make him doubt himself. He keeps them on as a safety net."

"And it's this council that could tell Ryker he couldn't train me?"

Riley glanced over at Elizabeth with a strange look but kept walking toward the village. "They could try, but something tells me he wouldn't listen."

"I don't want him to get into any trouble over me."

"Oh, he won't," Riley said vaguely.

"It's really weird. I know my grandmother asked him to train me, but he seemed against it. They even argued about it. I'm not sure what changed his mind." Elizabeth shrugged. "Anyway, let's not think about my training. I thought we were going to have fun. Isn't that why you woke me up at this ungodly hour?" Elizabeth yawned.

Riley laughed. "You act like I woke you up before the sun."

"Close enough."

"Anyway, I thought you might want to get out of the lodge and see the village. We have some cute shops, a bakery, and a café with coffee from all around the realms."

"There is coffee in other realms?" Riley had her attention now.

"Of course, silly, did you think only humans enjoyed it?"

"Honestly, yes."

"Well, then, prepare to have your mind blown." Riley laughed as she tugged Elizabeth along.

Riley pulled Elizabeth until they came to a covered wooden bench. "Why are we stopping? I thought we were going to the village."

"Oh, we are. It's too much of a hike to go on foot," Riley beamed.

Elizabeth heard jingle bells. She glanced down the road and found a horse-drawn carriage headed their way. A gorgeous white stallion, adorned with red and green bows in its long mane and sleigh bells on its harness, stopped in front of them. Behind it sat an elegantly carved white single-bench sleigh.

"We are riding in this?"

"Of course, silly, how else would we get there?" Riley jumped into the sleigh and waited for Elizabeth to follow.

Elizabeth, not nearly as graceful as Riley, stumbled as she climbed into the back of the sleigh. She sat down as Riley covered them both with a red fur-lined blanket.

She had only ever seen a horse-drawn carriage in movies. Her mind started thinking of how cozy it would have been if Ryker were here beside her, maybe with some peppermint hot cocoa. *What the... I seriously need to get my head out of the clouds and stop fantasizing about a man, or rather, an elf I barely know. It's not like he even likes me...*

The carriage started to move when Elizabeth noticed something important was missing. "Whoa! Where is the driver?"

"There is no driver."

"I'm sorry, what?" Elizabeth's mouth dropped open.

"The horse knows where he's going. It's fine." Riley snuggled deeper into the blanket.

The carriage was already moving, and it wasn't like she could just jump out. Right? Gripping onto the blanket with white knuckles, she prayed this ride didn't end badly.

The village came into view, and Elizabeth gasped. The entire village appeared to be straight out of a Christmas movie. There was no way this place was for real.

"Welcome to the Sinterklaas Village."

"Oh, it's not called the Elf Village?"

"Of course not. What kind of name would that be?" Riley laughed.

The horse came to a stop in front of another covered bench. Relieved that they had made it in one piece, Elizabeth let out a long exhale.

"See, I told you we would be fine," Riley giggled. "Now, come on. Let's go. I'm starving, and I want to get to the bakery before they are all sold out."

"Sold out of what?"

"You'll see." Riley's eyes sparkled as she grabbed Elizabeth's hand and led her further into the village.

Elizabeth was stunned by the aesthetic of the village. It was breathtaking. Everywhere she looked could be the cover of a Christmas card. As Riley dragged her down Peppermint Way, they passed Dashers Delivery, Prancers Pub, Tinsel Tavern, and The North Pole Post.

*This village is really into Christmas, it would seem.*

"Is the Christmas theme for tourists?"

"No, we just really like Christmas," Riley said sheepishly as she pulled Elizabeth along.

The streets were pretty much empty. They only passed a few brightly colored elves as they walked, and they all stared intently at Elizabeth as they passed.

"Where is everyone?"

"It's a workday. Most elves are at the factory, and the younglings will be in school."

"Do you work?"

"I'm more of a social ambassador," Riley shrugged. "Here we are."

They came to a stop in front of a huge gingerbread house. The smell was intoxicating; she wanted to take a bite out of the door frame.

"Is this for real?" Elizabeth was stunned. Then she noticed the sign that read "Ginger's Bakery."

"Wait until you see inside," Riley beamed as she opened the door.

Inside was wall-to-wall heaven. A rainbow of color proudly displayed every kind of baked treat one could think of, and some she had never seen before. The smells were divine, and they made Elizabeth's stomach grumble and her mouth water.

"Welcome," said a female elf, who appeared behind the counter. She looked like a cookie herself with her long-sleeved, gingerbread-colored dress and an intricate, white piping design around her collar, sleeves, and running down the sides of her dress. A matching hat sat on her head with a red pompom on top. Red buttons ran down her front, and her cheeks were painted a bright pink.

"Good morning, Ginger," Riley waved. "This is Elizabeth."

The elf's eyes widened as she dropped into a curtsy. "My Lady Pendragon, it is an honor to have you in my humble bakery."

Elizabeth was a bit taken aback by this reaction. "Um, please, no need to curtsy. This place is amazing. I'm sure I gained ten pounds just from the smell," Elizabeth smiled warmly.

"Please, you must try our famous peppermint bark scones. They are a particular favorite of the kings." Ginger flashed a proud smile.

"That's why we're here." Riley rubbed her hands together in delight.

"Well, if royalty loves them, who am I to disagree? It would be my honor to try them."

"Can we get a dozen of your gingerbread biscotti as well, please?" Riley asked enthusiastically.

"Oh, of course. I have a fresh batch about to come out of the oven. Please, make yourselves comfortable. I won't be a minute." Ginger directed them to take a seat at one of the tables.

"Thank you, and please feel free to call me Elizabeth or Lizzy."

"Oh, my! The girls at cookie club are never going to believe that I am on a first-name basis with Lady Pendragon," she said as she ran to the back.

Riley snickered as they walked over, finding a seat at one of the tables situated in front of a large display window.

"What was that all about?" Elizabeth asked.

"It's a small village. Word travels quickly," she shrugged.

"Word about me?"

"Lizzy, you're the Pendragon. That's kind of a big deal."

"I honestly don't know why." She turned to look out the window, noticing a familiar face headed their way. "Hey, isn't that your brother?"

Ryker was walking on the other side of the street; he was with an attractive female who was dressed in a fashionable black business suit that hugged her trim curvy body. On her feet, she wore ridiculously high heels— the kind that could be used as a weapon in a pinch.

As if sensing her, Ryker's head shot up, and his intoxicating lavender eyes met hers. He started to walk toward the bakery. The woman he was with touched his arm, as if to stop him. A spark of jealousy shot through Elizabeth. *What the ...* She shook her head. Ryker gave his companion a stern look, and she released his arm. He continued towards the bakers.

"Ginger, we are going to need a few more peppermint bark scones. Looks like Ryker is going to join us," Riley yelled to Ginger, who was still in the back getting their order.

"Oh, wonderful!" Ginger yelled in return.

A jingle bell chimed as the door to the bakery opened. Elizabeth's heart rate jumped as the smell of peppermint and pine assaulted her senses. Running his long fingers through his wind-disheveled hair, Ryker walked into the bakery. She was surprised that he was dressed rather casually in a pair of tight-fitting dark jeans, a white Henley shirt with the top buttons undone, and lovingly worn brown boots.

"Ladies." He nodded and then stood behind the chair next to Riley.

Elizabeth looked around but did not see the woman he was with. "Where is your friend?"

He cocked his eyebrow. "Why do you ask?"

"Um, I thought it would be nice if we invited her to join us." She flashed him a warm but fake smile. Truthfully, she really did not want that woman joining them, although, for the life of her, she didn't know why. She didn't even know the woman, and the sudden urge to scratch her eyes out was alarming.

"Bri is fine outside. I only came in to offer a quick hello. I was headed back to the palace when I saw you."

"The palace?" Elizabeth's interest had been piqued.

"Yes, I work there." He turned away from her.

"You work with the king?"

Riley laughed, which she quickly covered up with a cough after Ryker flashed her a look.

"You could say that, yes."

Elizabeth was about to ask more, but Ginger showed up with their order.

"Here you go! Sorry for the delay. I heard you couldn't stay, so I boxed you up enough scones for your entire office." Ginger blushed as she handed Ryker a large pink box that smelled amazing.

"Thank you, Ginger, I will be the hit of the office today."

She handed Riley a pink bag containing two smaller boxes of delicious-smelling treats. Ginger then handed a small pink bag to Elizabeth. "This is my special coffee twist. I hope you enjoy it, Lady Pen... sorry, I mean, Elizabeth." Ginger curtsied.

"It smells divine. Thank you, Ginger, I appreciate it. Can't wait to scarf it down." Elizabeth affectionately squeezed the woman's hand. The woman then curtsied again and ran towards the back as the group got up to exit.

The jingle bells rang as Ryker held the door open for her and Riley to exit. There, outside the door, leaning against a tree, was Bri, scrolling through her phone. She looked up, rolled her eyes at Elizabeth, smiled slightly at Riley, and returned her full focus to Ryker. "Good, Sir, we really need to get a move on if you are going to make your next meeting," she said as she took the box of treats from him.

"Well, I guess that's my cue to leave." He nodded toward Bri. Ryker leaned down and kissed Riley on the cheek before offering a slight head bow to Elizabeth.

Seeing him tender with Riley confused her. He was like Jekel and Mr. Hyde. He had a wall built up to block out everyone except Riley. But why? And more importantly, why did that make him even more attractive in her eyes? She clearly had issues.

Riley grabbed Elizabeth's arm. "Well, we have a hot date with some coffees from around the realms, so we will catch you later, brother."

Elizabeth looked back to see Ryker staring at her as Bri attempted to drag him along in the opposite direction.

"You are going to love this. I'm so excited!" Riley clapped her hands together.

Elizabeth turned back, allowing her new friend to lead the way. They stopped in front of Comet's Café, and the smell of coffee delighted Elizabeth's senses.

Inside was divided into two sections. There were cozy couches, big plush recliners, and several bean bag chairs on one side for those who wanted to relax with a warm drink and a good book. On the other side were standard smaller tables and chairs for those who were going to be in and out.

They walked over to a tall lanky elf with reindeer antlers sticking out his head, who greeted them. Elizabeth had no clue if they were real or not. His long, burnt-orange hair was pulled back into a man bun. He wore a black apron that read in glittery red script, “I Run on Coffee and Christmas Cookies” over his crisp white dress shirt and black trousers.

“Good morning, Jive. We will take the realm sampler for two, please.” Riley was practically bouncing with excitement.

“Coming right up.” Jive winked at Riley, who blushed as she turned to face Elizabeth. “We can sit over here where it's more comfortable.” They walked over to a couch which had a small, low table in front of it.

“Which of the realms has your favorite drink?” Elizabeth asked.

“Oh, I don’t know. I have never done this before.” Riley looked down. “It’s the kind of thing you do with a friend. And I don’t normally get out much.”

“Really? Why?”

“Ryker is a bit overprotective. He doesn’t really trust many people.”

“Why is that?”

Riley shrugged.

“What about your parents?”

“Our parents died when I was a baby. It's been me and Ryker ever since.”

“Oh, wow. I’m sorry. My dad went away when I was a young girl, and I never knew my mom. It's just been Gram and me. I get it.”

“Well, now we have each other,” Riley beamed.

Her energy was infectious. How could you not want to be friends with her? “Yes, now we have each other.”

Jives wheeled over a two-tiered cart filled with steaming cups. They spent the next several hours laughing and drinking strange coffee concoctions the likes of which she had never even dreamed of. The weirdest was a drink called bloody Joe, a vampire favorite which neither of them dared to try. However, the glittery rainbow brew from the fae realm was delicious, as was the dark brew from the Beast Kingdom.

They spent the rest of the day together talking, laughing, and enjoying themselves. They ate dinner at Dashers Diner and had ice cream at Santa’s Sundaes. By the time Elizabeth crawled into bed that night, she had a full belly and a happy heart. However, sleep did not come easily. She was nervous about what the next day would bring. She worried about training with Ryker and what that would mean for her growing infatuation with him.

# THIRTY-TWO

Elizabeth swatted the air, trying to knock away whatever was tickling her nose. She had been in the middle of an amazing dream, too. *Stupid bug*, she thought. Cracking her left eye, she saw a floating feather hovering above her nose. She swatted at it a few more times, but the damn thing wouldn't go away. Frustrated, she finally sat up, and that was when she noticed Ryker sitting at the foot of her bed.

She gasped and reached for her blankets to cover her from neck to toe. "What are you doing here?"

"Good morning, Sunshine. This is your morning wake-up call. Get up, get dressed, and meet me downstairs in fifteen minutes. I do not recommend you be late," Ryker said. And before Elizabeth could protest that the sun wasn't even up yet, he vanished into a puff of glittery white snowflakes.

*I really need to learn that vanishing trick*, Elizabeth grumbled to herself. She walked over to the wardrobe, thankful that her grandmother had gotten it stocked with clothes for her. She hadn't taken notice of the choices, but it seemed to be filled with clothes of all different styles in her size. Today, she grabbed a pair of black stretchy yoga pants and a matching long-sleeved shirt. She finished in the bathroom and ran downstairs with two minutes to spare.

She found Ryker sitting at the small breakfast table in the kitchen, chewing on a piece of bacon. He motioned to a plate of eggs and bacon sitting on the table in front of an empty seat. "Eat up, Sunshine. You're going to need the fuel."

She did as he suggested, and an hour later she found herself running laps in some kind of climate-controlled, open-air arena. Ryker was right beside her, however, even though she was drenched in sweat and gasping for air. He wasn't even winded, and there wasn't a drop of sweat on his muscular body. She was pretty sure she hated him in that moment.

"The first lesson is endurance. In order to maintain a spell or wield magic, one must be strong, both physically and mentally." He pointed to his head. "You are in okay shape, for a human, but you are not human, now, are you? You still have a long way to go until you are battle-ready," Ryker said as he handed her a bottle of water.

"Well, in my defense, until a few days ago, I thought I *was* human," she said before she chugged the water down.

"Hmph," was Ryker's only response as he motioned for her to continue with her laps. Elizabeth grumbled, then proceeded to run laps until she felt like she was going to die. When she couldn't run another lap, she stopped, dropped to the ground, and lay on her back as she attempted to catch her breath.

"Well, I must say, you lasted longer than I thought you would." Rykers stood above her, arms crossed over his chest.

She growled in response and covered her eyes with her arms.

"Lesson two is strength. We need to build up your upper body strength in order for you to wield a sword properly." He handed her a set of three-pound weights. "We will start small and work our way up."

The next week consisted of Elizabeth running laps until she was ready to die. Then he had her lifting weights along with leg squats. The weights increased in size every other day. By day seven, she was lifting ten pounds in each hand.

By the end of each day, Elizabeth was spent, and her entire body ached. She had enough strength to eat, then climb the stairs to her room and clamber into her bed. Sometimes Riley would be there waiting to hang out, sneaking sugary treats into her room since Obi-Wan Elf had outlawed all sweets. Which really sucked since Mrs. K was a baking fool. The house always smelled like gingerbread, cookies, or some other amazingly tasty, sweet treat. Thank the stars for Riley, who had advised that what her brother didn't know, wouldn't hurt him.

After another two weeks of the same routine, she was starting to get frustrated. She thought the training would consist of her learning magic, swords, or at least some self-defense. Not running and weights, which she could do in any corner gym. She needed to learn magic and how to fight. Skye still needed her. There had been no word about what had happened to her. Elizabeth owed it to her to find out. There was also the creepy Vampire Lord, and his evil queen to contend with. She needed to know how to defend herself.

The next morning, after her warm-up laps, she decided she had had enough. She walked over to her elf trainer, put her hand on her hips, and stared him down. When she looked into his stunning lavender eyes, she almost forgot what she was upset about.

"Did you need something, Sunshine?" he asked with lips pressed into a straight line. "If not, I didn't say you could stop running."

"This is pointless!" She waved her hands around, indicating the running.

He cocked an eyebrow. "How so?"

"Unless you're training me to run away from my enemies, this is pointless."

"Well, Sunshine, I disagree. Now, get back to your laps."

"Really, that's it? No discussion, no telling me when we are going to move on to something else?"

Lifting his gaze to the sky, he let out a sigh. "Since you seem to know more than I do, what would Your Majesty like to do today?"

"I think we should be spending more time training me how to fight, or at least, how to defend myself."

Ryker was quiet for a moment. "Okay, call forth Excalibur."

"Um... okay." She called for the sword.

"Now, raise the sword in a defensive position."

She struck the pose she had seen in countless movies.

He walked around her, looking at her form. She felt his warmth at her back, which sent a shiver down her spine. "No, stand like this." He kicked her legs wider, then adjusted her arms so they were slightly bent. He used his strong, warm hands to move her into the position he needed her in.

"Good, now don't move," he whispered in her ear, giving her goosebumps. Then his warmth was gone, and she saw him walking away.

"Wait! Where are you going?"

When he was half the length of the arena away from her, he turned back to face her, snapped his fingers, and a leather recliner appeared. He gracefully sat down, adjusting until he was comfortable.

"What the hell? This is not teaching me a damn thing!"

"Untrue. This is teaching you plenty and allowing me to take a nap while I wait."

"*Ugh,* you are such an ass!"

"Yes, I am. Now, please keep your moaning to a minimum. I'm trying to nap, here."

She wanted to throw something and spit at him. Her arm was burning, her nose itched, and her stomach growled.

"Ryker, it has been over an hour, and I can't feel my arms anymore."

He stood up from the recliner, stretched his arms above his head, and let out a big yawn. He then snapped and the recliner disappeared. "Is that your way of informing me you can't hold it any longer?"

"Yes!" she yelled, frustrated.

"You may move."

She wasted no time returning Excalibur to the silver chain around her neck, and then she stretched her achy arms and shoulders out. "What was the point of that? Or was it just a punishment for speaking up?"

His long legs ate up the space between them. Before she knew it, he was standing right in front of her, his peppermint and pine scent making her sway. "I would never punish you for speaking up," he growled. "That demonstration was for me to see how strong your upper body is. In battle, you may be required to hold your sword for hours at a time, never letting it down for fear of death. That is why we work on building it up before we advance to sword training."

"Oh."

"Oh, indeed. Now, I will admit, you are much stronger than I had originally perceived."

"You should never doubt me, Obi-Elf. I'm stronger than I look."

"Yes, well, moving on, shall we?"

"What? We aren't done?"

"No, Sunshine, we are not done. We still have plenty of daylight left. Now, I want you to take a swing at me."

"I'm sorry, what? You want me to hit you... like, punch you?"

"If you can, yes."

Elizabeth made a fist and lunged for him. Hands behind his back, he simply moved out of her way. Frustrated, she tried again, and once more, he moved with little effort out of her way.

"What is the point of this? You know I don't know how to fight."

"Yes, and I needed to make sure you knew it as well. This way, perhaps we can continue with your training without further questions. I never mind you speaking up, but you must learn to trust me." He put his hands on her shoulders and looked into her eyes. "I want you to succeed, and I will train you to be the best. Most warriors start young, so we have a lot of time to make up for in a short amount of time. But I need you to trust me to do things my way and not question my methods. Can you do that?"

She nodded. She knew he was right; she needed to trust him. But was trusting him really the problem? She chose not to think too much about the sparks she felt when they touched. Instead, she paid close attention as he demonstrated the proper way to throw a punch. *Who knew you could punch someone wrong?*

For the next few weeks, Elizabeth's days were all about

training. She ran laps in the morning, followed by weight training, hand-to-hand combat, and ending with meditation or the Tai Chi uncle Nicky had taught her. They had yet to work with any magic, but she knew better than to question the process, as he called it.

In a few short weeks, she could see her body changing, becoming stronger and leaner. Elizabeth could now run laps with less effort, and she could hold her own in fights that did not include weapons.

She missed Shane and thought about him often, as one would their best friend. However, her heart no longer longed for him like it had the past few years. Strange how now that he was back in her life, she wasn't sure what part she wanted him to play in it anymore. Lady Lorraine had assured her that he knew she was safe and that she was training. As a soldier himself, she knew he would understand. But she also felt guilty because she had this overwhelming draw to Ryker, which only grew stronger the more they worked together. Although she still assumed he was not interested in her in the same way.

There was also the fact that she had a huge target painted on her back. She needed to be able to defend herself. She could not expect Shane, Ryker, or anyone else to save her. She did not want to be some damsel in distress. Elizabeth wanted to be the one kicking ass and taking names. Fear no longer had a place in her life. She couldn't afford any distractions, especially from two tempting supernaturals.

Elizabeth's attention was brought back to her current training situation when Ryker's fist struck her in the face. Over the past few weeks, she had taken many of his punches until she learned to block them. Pain was a successful motivator.

"Your head is not in this fight, Sunshine, and that is how people get killed," Ryker said unapologetically.

She sidestepped and moved away from another oncoming punch.

"Nice footwork. Now, do you want to tell me what has you distracted?"

"Sorry, I was wondering when we would start working with my magic. I know I must trust the process, which is why I didn't want to ask or say anything." Elizabeth rubbed her bruised cheek.

"Do you feel that you are ready? Do you feel strong enough, both mentally and physically?"

"I think so, but the only way to be sure would be to try, right?" she shrugged.

"You're right, and I also think you are ready."

"Seriously?" She was so excited, she jumped right into Ryker's unsuspecting arms. With their noses almost touching, both seemed to be holding their breath, unsure of what to do next. If she moved in a little, her lips would brush against his. Time stood still, and then Elizabeth noticed how stiff Ryker's arms were. She was making him feel uncomfortable, she was sure of it.

“Sorry about that.” She looked at the ground as she backed away from him, not wanting to see his disapproving gaze.

“Nothing to apologize for. We can start magic training after lunch,” Ryker said, to Elizabeth’s surprise. “But until then, show me you still know how to block,” he said before sending another punch her way.

# THIRTY-THREE

After morning practice, they ate a lunch of sandwiches and homemade butternut squash soup. It seemed simple, but the flavors that Mrs. K could elicit from a simple sandwich were pure magic.

Elizabeth sat cross-legged on the ground in the training arena across from Ryker, thinking about how she had felt in his arms. She had spent every waking hour with the elf and still knew next to nothing about him. He was different from the others of his kind, including his sister. Riley and the other elves, some of whom Elizabeth had met, were fun and full of life. They bounced around everywhere, full of energy and color. They could be exhausting. Ryker was more reserved and always serious. Over the past few weeks, he had become someone important to her. Elizabeth found herself curious about his story. Did he have someone special? Was that why he tensed when Elizabeth had jumped in his arms? He never mentioned anyone, but then again, he never really discussed his personal life at all. Was it Bri? She was always hovering around him the rare times Elizabeth had seen him outside of training.

Had he always been the serious one, or had something happened to make him this way? She found herself wanting to make him smile. To see his face light up. She wanted to see if he had a more playful side and maybe even see what other sides of him she could bring out.

When she heard Ryker's sigh, Elizabeth's focus returned to the present. “Sunshine, did you hear a word I said?” He sent her an impatient glance.

“Um... sorry, not really,” Elizabeth said as she felt the color of her cheeks go holly berry red. Good thing he wasn’t a mind reader.

"You have been waiting for weeks to practice magic. What could have you distracted now that we are about to begin?"

Elizabeth smiled as she looked at him for a moment. "Honestly, Ryker? You," Elizabeth said with a laugh. "I find you puzzling."

"Me?" Ryker responded. "What about me could be distracting?"

*Besides the fact that you're freaking hot and don't seem to know it.*

"It's just, you're always so serious, which differs from the other elves that I have met."

"To be fair, you have only met a few of my kind. The elders and most of the population choose to live in the mountains away from the village. However, you are correct. I take a more serious outlook on life than most of my people. Mainly because of spending a great deal of time in other realms. I have seen the hardships, witnessed hatred and prejudices, seen war and death, and experienced significant loss. Those are things I never want my people to experience again. The younger generation does not remember life before this peaceful realm, but I do. I remember when Lilith tried to enslave us for our magic. I remember when she waged war on the human realm. I was there for it all," Ryker said with sadness. It was the first real emotion she had witnessed from him.

"I'm sorry. I didn't mean to upset you," Elizabeth said, unsure of how to proceed.

"You didn't; I simply have many regrets regarding the past. I wasn't there when Lilith attacked my people the last time. I was in the human realm on a mission for Arthur."

"You were one of his knights, correct? You knew Arthur, personally?" Elizabeth asked.

"I was, and Arthur was a dear friend. When he asked me to escort his banished Queen Guinevere to Glastonbury Abbey, I had to accept."

"Wow."

It was also no coincidence; Lilith attacked my people and the humans while I was away. Lilith both fears and wants me. She wishes to control me," Ryker said as he stared off into the distance.

"Why?" Elizabeth couldn't help herself from asking.

"Why, indeed? That is a question for Lilith, for I do not know the answer. Who knows what motivates a monster? I do not, nor do I wish to, dwell on it. Besides, we have little time to get you ready for whatever is coming. Shall we get back to it, Sunshine?" Ryker asked, clearly needing to change the subject.

There was more than what Ryker was saying between him and Lilith, and he was obviously unwilling to talk anymore, even though Elizabeth was fascinated with the idea of him being one of King Arthur's knights. She now had a ton more questions, but she could tell by the look on his face that he did not want to continue with the current topic of discussion. Maybe she would ask Riley about it later.

"Let's begin with the basics, shall we?" Ryker said, moving on. "There are five categories that most practitioners of magic fall into. Elemental magic is where the practitioner uses the natural elements of fire, water, air, earth, and metal. Summoners are practitioners who can call forth whatever they desire by mere thought or spell casting. Manipulation is when a practitioner can distort or manipulate the surrounding reality. Glancing is the magic a seer uses to glimpse the future. And finally, spirit walking is where the practitioner can walk amongst the spirits. Some even believe that the more powerful practitioners of spirit walking can slip into the shoes of the spirit and catch a glimpse of past events through the eyes of the spirit. There are other branches in each field, but it's best to start with the basics. We can get into the more specialized areas later."

Elizabeth wished she had thought of bringing paper and a pen to take notes. She was trying to absorb everything Ryker was saying.

"As for how one wields their magic, that is up to them," Ryker continued. "Some choose to use a wand or staff to focus the magic through, or at least to help focus their intent. Others can simply focus with no aid at all. Some use their hands to move the flow of magic. It depends on the individual user. The same idea goes with spell casting. Some practitioners can issue a command or intent with pure thought, while others need to construct a spell in which to direct their desired magical outcome. There is no wrong or right way. In time, you will learn what works best for you. From what I understand, you have already shown some elemental magic. Is that correct?"

"I have dragon fire and wind that I know of," Elizabeth replied.

"Yes, you should be able to wield all five elements. Let's start with earth. Touch the ground with both hands, palms facing down, and try to sense what is under the dirt," Ryker said as he put his own palms down on the ground.

Elizabeth did as she was instructed. She could feel the coolness of the earth under her touch, but nothing else.

"Let go of all thoughts. Feel the energy from the earth and let it flow through you."

Elizabeth listened to Ryker's words and tried to let go. It took her a few moments, but then she felt something. It was a small jolt of electricity. She felt as if the earth had a pulse of its own. Its beating rhythm matched her own heartbeat. She heard Ryker's voice in the background, but she didn't know what he was saying. She felt the earth's energy flow through her and all around her. Everything was alive and pulsating with energy, with magic. It was as if Elizabeth was connecting to Mother Earth herself. Through her mind's eye, she could see everything that lay beneath the dirt. She could see the seeds that had not yet sprouted, the roots of the trees, plants that were all intertwined together, fossils from thousands of years ago, and insects working in their communities. She could see it all, and it was breathtaking.

Elizabeth opened her eyes, and a blue-green glow surrounded her, similar in color to her dragon fire, but different in feel. She looked over at Ryker, who nodded at her approvingly.

"Now," he said. "Try to help one of the un-sprouted seeds sprout into life. Envision the seedling sprouting its roots and reaching toward the sun."

Elizabeth focused on one of the unsprouted seeds, and it came to life. She saw the seed crack open as the roots spread out like tentacles, reaching up through the dirt and clawing its way toward the surface, toward the sun. The roots burst through the surface and continued to grow and grow until a beautiful rose bush appeared. Its flowers quickly moved from bud to blossom. Elizabeth stood up and walked over to the bush, touching a blossom. The petals were soft, and the sweet smell invaded her nose. She stood in awe.

She heard a clapping sound and turned to see Ryker walking towards her, clapping his hands. "That was... impressive. Control like that usually takes years to achieve, and you did it in mere moments. Well, done, Sunshine, well done!"

All at once, Elizabeth felt completely drained. She reached for Ryker, who quickly helped to steady her.

"That brings us to our next lesson," Ryker said as he helped hold her up. "Magic always comes at a price. The bigger the task, the more energy it will require. This is why we started working on your physical and mental endurance before working with magic. The stronger your body and mind, the more magic you can wield at once. As the bearer of Excalibur, I believe you can also draw on the energy from the sword if need be. But as far as the first lesson goes, not bad. How are you feeling?"

Elizabeth, who was still holding onto Ryker for support, sent him a death glare. "You could have warned me about the energy drain, you know."

"Maybe," Ryker shrugged. "But I feel the lesson is more potent if it's experienced."

*Jerk*. She would remember this. "But, besides that," she glared at him. "I feel amazing. I can't believe I did that." She pointed to the rosebush. "What's next?" She asked.

"Well, considering you can't stand at the moment, I think that is enough for today. Tomorrow, we will work on water. I am interested in seeing what you can do with that element. But for now, let's get you back to the lodge to get some food and rest." Ryker picked her up and carried her toward the lodge.

Elizabeth didn't protest being carried like a baby. Instead, she allowed herself to enjoy the warmth of his body and the comfort that it offered her. She knew she would need to figure out what to do regarding her ever-growing feelings for Ryker—especially because she had unresolved confusion about Shane—but not right now. At that moment, she was too tired to think.

# THIRTY-FOUR

Elizabeth had been so exhausted after her first magic lesson that she must have fallen asleep in Ryker's arms. She awoke the next morning in her bed, still wearing the workout clothes from the previous day. Thankfully, feeling refreshed and ready to take on the day, she seemed to have recovered from her first magical lesson.

Her stomach growled, but she was filthy from yesterday. Deciding a shower and then breakfast was the better course of action, she quickly stripped out of her dirty clothes and jumped in the shower before rushing down to breakfast, hoping to not be late for Ryker's lessons. She really didn't feel like doing extra laps if she was tardy.

Running into the kitchen, she stopped dead in her tracks when she saw two familiar faces sitting at the table. One was stuffing his face with Mrs. K's homemade eggnog pancakes, while the other was sipping some freshly brewed coffee.

Her heart nearly stopped as those ocean-blue eyes met hers. Shane lowered his cup and immediately rose from the table and ran over to her, picking her up in a warm embrace and lightly kissing her on the lips. Chad raised an eyebrow as he noticed their exchange. Flashing his signature mischievous grin, he said nothing. Instead, he continued to stuff his face with the pancakes.

"Oh Liz, thank the stars. I have been worried about you. When you went missing from the hospital, I was ready to tear the entire demon army to shreds with my bare hands looking for you. I was afraid that Dimitri or Lilith had gotten to you." Shane's voice broke a little as he spoke, still holding her in his embrace.

"They almost did. Thankfully, I had my bracelet on. I was

able to transport here. Lady Lorraine said you knew I was safe and was here training."

"Knowing and seeing are two very different things. I needed to see you for myself," Shane said as he released Elizabeth from his embrace and led her over to the table where her usual eggs and bacon waited for her.

"Damn, Small Fry. Look at those guns! I see an arm-wrestling match in our future." Chad wiggled both eyebrows as he motioned to her newly toned arms.

Elizabeth smiled back at him and said, "You're on." Chad laughed and then returned to his plate of pancakes. She turned back to Shane. "Why are you here? Not that I'm not happy to see you guys."

Before Shane could answer, Chad spoke up with a mouth full of pancakes. "Well, Small Fry, that's classified. I don't even know."

"Uncle Nick thinks we have a traitor who is feeding Dimitri and Lilith information, so all our missions are on a strictly need-to-know basis. And right now, he does not need to know," Shane said, holding back a smirk.

"Oh, wow," Elizabeth said, but before she could ask more questions, Lady Lorraine entered the kitchen.

"Good morning, my dearest." She walked over and kissed Elizabeth on the cheek before looking at the two soldiers sitting at the table. "Gentleman, what brings you all this way?" She walked over to the coffeepot and poured herself a cup of the steaming hot brew.

"Message from the commander, ma'am." Chad stood to attention and handed an envelope to Lady Lorraine.

"At ease, soldier," Lady Lorraine said with a smile as she gracefully sat down at the table with the envelope and her freshly made cup of coffee. She opened the envelope and read its contents. Her face drained of all color.

"Gram? What is it?"

When she was finished, she held the envelope in the air and it caught on fire, disintegrating almost instantly.

"Is everything okay?" Elizabeth asked.

Lady Lorraine reached for Elizabeth's hand and patted it gently. "I'm afraid not. There has been a development. According to our spies in Dimitri's camp, they are planning on attacking Fireside."

"What? That's a village with children. They aren't soldiers," Elizabeth yelled.

"The war has begun, I'm afraid. No one is safe; not even children."

"Okay, but why target a dragon village? I thought the dragons could rip a vampire apart?"

"That's the scariest part of this report. According to the

spies, there is a great wizard working with Dimitri who can suppress the dragons, making them human. Without their dragon form, they will be easily overthrown."

"What? Is that even possible?"

"I don't know. I have never heard of such a spell or anyone strong enough to cast it." She looked at Elizabeth with a worried expression. "Nicholas is asking for my assistance in offsetting this spell."

"Can you do that?"

"I hope so. If there is, indeed, a powerful wizard who can suppress the dragon's inner beast, then they will need my help to reverse such magic."

"Or it could be a trap to draw Elizabeth out of hiding." Ryker walked into the kitchen. "What better way to draw out the Pendragon than to threaten her family?"

Both Shane and Chad shot up out of their chairs and stood at attention. This reaction confused Elizabeth.

"Guys, it's okay, this is Ryker. He's my trainer and my friend," she said, but no one seemed to listen.

"You could be right," Lady Lorraine nodded at Ryker, completely oblivious to the two soldiers who were now standing at attention. "There is no way for them to know I'm still alive. It must be about Elizabeth."

"At ease, gentlemen," Ryker said as he nodded to both men.

Both men bowed to Ryker. "Your Majesty," they said in unison. Then they both relaxed a little but were still standing now with their hands behind their backs.

"Your Majesty, we were on our way to the castle to deliver a message from Commander Black," Chad said with a serious tone in his voice which Elizabeth was not used to.

"Looks like I saved you both a trip." Ryker waved his hand dismissively. "And call me Ryker, please. I do not care about all that formal crap." He looked at Elizabeth with an expression of guilt and then back to Chad. "What does the illustrious commander need from the elves?"

"Assistance with protecting the dragons."

"Dimitri is making his first move. I'm curious if this is his idea, or his leash holders. Attacking the dragons first seems foolish. And out of character for Lilith." Laday Lorraine glanced at Ryker.

"Agreed. The commander felt the same. That is why he is meeting with his spymaster to gather as much information as possible before joining us here," Shane said.

"I will wait to speak with him directly," Ryker informed them.

Elizabeth watched the exchange, speechless. Riley's words came back to her at that moment. "*Heavy is the head that wears the burden.*" Something finally clicked into place. How had she missed it? Ryker was the freaking Elf King. Everything made sense now.

# THIRTY-FIVE

Ryker was the Elf King. How had she not known this? He did not act like a king, at least not around her. Not that Elizabeth had been in the company of many kings—or any kings, really, except for her short time with King Uther. But he was a ghost. Did that even count? Did this mean Riley was a princess? Why had Riley never said anything? Elizabeth's head was reeling, her mind going a mile a minute. From what Lady Lorraine had said, Elizabeth knew Ryker was much older than he appeared. Was he the Elf King from the story she had heard? Was he the same Elf King Uther had told her to seek or were there others? So many questions, and Elizabeth couldn't even open her mouth to speak.

Finally, Elizabeth blurted out, "You're the freaking Elf King?" Everyone stopped and looked at her as if she had grown a unicorn horn on her head.

"Yes, I am," Ryker said.

"Why... um, why did you never tell me?"

"It was unnecessary."

"Really, unnecessary for me to know that the man I was trusting to train me was a king?"

"What would it have changed had you known?"

"A lot, I'm sure."

"Exactly. You treated both my sister and me like everyone else. Riley has never had a true friend before you. Someone that cares for her because of who she is on the inside and not because of a title she received at birth. There was no ill will intended toward you. No big conspiracies. It was only a matter of time before you found out."

Elizabeth looked at Ryker in disbelief, hurt that he hadn't felt the need to tell her, and neither had Riley. But was he right?

Would she have treated them differently had she known the truth? Perhaps—okay, more than likely—and she might have missed out on getting to know the real Riley. She was hurt, but she also understood, to some degree, why they had kept it from her.

As she looked around the kitchen, something dawned on her that made her see the entire situation in a new light. Here she was in a room with an Elf King, a vampire, a fairy, and a rather infamous sorceress. Shaking her head, she started to laugh hysterically. Shane wrapped his muscular arms around her waist, thinking she needed comfort, but she didn't.

She needed to let it go. All the worry, the confusion, the stress, and constantly trying to hold on to her old life. She just laughed it all away.

She laughed, and it felt good to let go of it all. The more she thought about the past few months, the more she became aware of the absurdity of it all. She was now a real-life fairytale character. How the heck had that happened?

"I'm okay," Elizabeth said as she stepped out of Shane's embrace. "I really am okay." She looked at everyone else, and then she noticed Ryker's stern expression.

"Did I break her?" Ryker asked, cocking an eyebrow at Lady Lorraine.

Elizabeth lost it again, hysterically laughing, with tears streaming down her face. Shane reached for her again, possibly afraid she was going to fall to the floor. Even Chad had a look of bewilderment, unsure of what was happening.

"Seriously, no one else sees the humor in this situation?" Elizabeth asked, amusement still lighting up her face. "A few weeks ago, I was a normal human girl, or so I thought. Now I'm two steps away from being a character in a fantasy novel. Seriously, no one sees the humor?" Elizabeth looked at each of them. "I am friends with an elf princess. I'm being trained how to use magic by the Elf King. My grandmother is a sorceress, and not just any sorceress, but the legendary Morgana Le Fey." Elizabeth looked up at Shane. "My best friend is a vampire. Plus, I'm friends with a gateway faerie."

"Gateway fae," Chad interrupted.

"Oh yeah, sorry, a gateway fae. All of which I had no clue about until recently. The story pretty much writes itself. Oh, I almost forgot the part where I have a magical sword, which I am terrified of because it can kill with a scratch."

"Well, when you put it that way, Small Fry," Chad said cautiously, smiling, before turning to Ryker. "Yes, sir, I think you broke her. Your admission of omission did her in."

"I'm not broken. Actually, laughing made me feel better. I didn't realize how much stuff I was holding onto. I'm not upset. On the contrary, I completely understand and I'm thankful that

I didn't know you were the king," Elizabeth said, looking at Ryker. "I am glad I was able to get to know Riley and you without all the royal stuff getting in the way. I might have been afraid of being sent to the dungeon if I got a good punch in during combat training."

"As if that would ever happen, Sunshine," Ryker said.

"Are there any other secrets that I should know about?" Elizabeth asked half-jokingly.

"Tons, I'm sure, my dear." Lady Lorraine walked over to Elizabeth and took both of her hands in hers. "But unfortunately, we do not have time to get into all the things you do not yet know. You will, in due time. Let's concentrate on your training for the time being."

Elizabeth nodded.

"Don't stress about what secrets you have yet to uncover regarding a world you knew nothing about until recently," Lady Lorraine said, her eyes filled with love as she looked at her granddaughter. "Ryker, I leave her in your capable hands. Train her as much as you can over the next few days. I have a feeling, even though I hate to admit it, that Fireside will need both of you." Lady Lorraine glanced at Ryker and raised her hand in the air as if to stop him from protesting. "You may be a king, but I hold a few titles of my own. You may not see it, but you are needed as well. The other supernatural leaders do not know what we know about Lilith. They consider her a human problem, not one we should all be concerned about. But we know better, and we will need to make them see her as a genuine threat before it's too late."

Ryker crossed his arms over his chest but continued to listen.

"We will all need to come together. This is the first battle of the war. We will need all the allies we can get."

Ryker simply nodded.

Only Lady Lorraine could put a king in his place the way she did, with such poise and grace. *Wow, she is amazing,* Elizabeth thought to herself.

Lady Lorraine gestured to Chad and Shane. "Gentlemen, please alert me as soon as Nicholas arrives. I have some research to do if I'm going to combat this mystic of unknown origins."

Both men bowed and said, "Yes, milady," in unison.

"Lizzy, dear, continue with your training. There is nothing we can do until Nicholas arrives and fills us in on the latest intel." Lady Lorraine hugged Elizabeth and kissed her on the cheek before walking out of the kitchen.

"I guess I better get back to it." She glanced at Ryker, who simply nodded.

"Can I have a word before you go?" Shane asked.

"I guess I'll see you soon, Small Fry. I believe I heard

something about a bakery in the village that makes the most amazing scones." Chad winked at Elizabeth. Then he turned to Shane and patted him on the shoulder. "Better make it count, buddy."

"I will meet you at the training arena when you have concluded your business here," Ryker said as he glanced from Shane to Elizabeth, no expression on his face as he, too, walked out in the same direction as the other two.

Once it was just the two of them, Shane pulled Elizabeth back into his embrace and kissed her lips. He then whispered in her ear, "Something is going on here. We don't need to label it yet if you don't want to. I know there is still stuff we need to figure out, but know that I'm all in and I'm not going anywhere. Unless you tell me to. I lost you once; I'm not planning on doing it again."

"Shane," she said breathlessly. "What if I need time?"

"Time for what?"

"This," she motioned with her hand to indicate both of them, "is moving a bit fast. We just reconnected, and to be honest, I'm not sure of what I want. A lot has changed in a short time."

"I can understand that." His shoulders sagged.

"Can you? What if what I need is my best friend, not a boyfriend?" Elizabeth stepped back so she could see his face.

"Can't I be both?" Shane's lips were pressed into a straight line.

"Shane." Elizabeth frowned as Shane stepped further away from her.

"Is it him?" He spat out, as he ran his hands through his hair.

"Is it who?" Her voice squeaked.

"The king. Ryker. Do you have feelings for him?" Shane's face twisted in anger.

*Yes*. "No, it's not about him. It's about me and my crazy, confusing life. I don't have time to figure us out right now."

"Liz, I know I let you down in the past, but please give me another chance. Give us another chance. I promise to be the man you need me to be." He grabbed her arms, his voice pleading with her."

Wasn't this exactly what she had wanted to hear from him? Why was she not professing her love for him? Hadn't she loved him most of her life? Or was she in love with a memory that wasn't real or a dream that had never existed except in the mind of a broken-hearted teenager? She was confused. Thoughts of Ryker tried to pop into her head, but she pushed them aside. Now was not the time to be thinking about Ryker or wondering what his lips would feel like. *Good grief, what is wrong with me?*

Before she knew it, Shane's lips were on hers again. She didn't know how long the kiss lasted, and despite her internal torment, Shane was a damn good kisser. All too soon, it was over. He released her from his warm embrace, and they looked deeply into each other's eyes. A single tear escaped down Elizabeth's cheek. Shane tenderly wiped it away before saying, "I'm all in," and with one more quick kiss, he was gone. She was left standing there in the kitchen alone and consumed with conflicted feelings.

*This is what happens when you don't date in college. You are left unprepared for the real world,* Elizabeth thought to herself before heading off to training where the other man, who was starting to consume more of her thoughts, was waiting.

Elizabeth arrived at the open-air arena, which was climate controlled. The grass was green and soft, and the temperature was perfectly comfortable inside the invisible magic barrier. She found Ryker sitting cross-legged with his eyes closed. He was wearing his usual workout attire of a navy-blue T-shirt and matching sweatpants. He was the only elf she had met who didn't wear bright neon colors all the time. Riley was always in neon pink. Elizabeth needed to wear sunglasses around her sometimes, even at night.

Ryker appeared to be meditating when she arrived. Not wanting to disturb him, she just stood there and watched him for a few minutes, hardly believing that he could be thousands of years old. He was gorgeous with his glittery skin and pure white hair that shimmered in the sunlight. Suddenly, his bright lavender eyes popped open.

"You can stop ogling me now, Sunshine," he said with his usual cocked eyebrow. "Didn't you just say goodbye to your boyfriend?"

"I am not ogling you," Elizabeth said with an eye roll. She had definitely been ogling him. "Shane is not my boyfriend."

"Does he know that?"

"Anyway, you looked so peaceful. I didn't want to interrupt you."

"Hm." Ryker stared at her for a moment. "Ready to begin?"

"Yes!" Elizabeth said excitedly.

"Good. There are a few things I want to discuss with you first. Please, have a seat." He motioned for her to join him on the ground. Elizabeth walked over to where he sat. She lowered herself to the ground, crossing her legs as well. "I heard you when you mentioned being afraid of Excalibur," Ryker said with a concerned expression.

"Aren't you concerned, too? It can kill anyone with just a scratch. What if I accidentally scratched someone with it and they died? I could never live with myself if something like that happened. Look what happened to Arthur," Elizabeth said in almost a whisper.

"I understand your trepidation. I do not have the answers you seek. You would need to speak with someone who has intimate knowledge of the Sword of Power and its capabilities. The sword carries a lot of legend, but what is fact and what is fiction? I cannot tell you." Ryker ran his elegant, glittering fingers through his shaggy white hair. "Arthur would have been my first suggestion, but who knows when and if he will ever return? I know Lady Lorraine is trying to locate where she left him fifteen hundred years ago, but the landscape is different from then. She has been having a hard time."

"Does she think she can bring him back? Did she find the dragon stone?" Elizabeth asked. She couldn't believe that she had forgotten to ask her grandmother about her brother and the stone.

"I am uncertain about that. However, without a king to revive, what's the point? That is out of our hands. Our mission is to find another expert on the Sword of Power. We can't have you being afraid to wield the only weapon that can help in the fight against Lilith." Ryker tapped his fingers on his leg as he spoke.

"Does such a person even exist?" *Where is ghost Uther when I need him?*

"The sword has only been handled by the Pendragons, and from what I understand, Lady Lorraine and I are the last." Elizabeth thought about all that she had learned about the sword. "What about Queen Dianna? Isn't she the person who gifted the sword to Uther in the first place? Maybe she knows something about it." Elizabeth felt like she was grasping at straws.

Ryker's eyes got big. "Sunshine, you might be a genius."

"Why, what did I say?" Elizabeth asked.

"The Black Knight gave the sword to the queen. He was a Celtic warrior and the best swordsman to have ever lived. His people made Excalibur. If anyone would have the answers you seek, it would be him."

Memories of her conversation with Uther came back to her. "Oh, my Gods, I completely forgot. Uther told me to seek the Elf King and he would help me find the Black Knight to train me in swordsmanship. I can't believe I forgot all about that." Elizabeth shook her head in frustration. She had meant to ask Riley about it a few weeks ago, but it had completely slipped her mind.

"Leave it to my old friend to be two steps ahead, even in the afterlife."

"Are you the Elf King I was supposed to seek? Do you know where I can find this Black Knight?" Elizabeth asked with hope.

"I am the Elf King, but I do not believe I am the one whom Uther was directing you to."

"There is more than one Elf King?"

"There is another whom Uther used to call the Elf King as a joke. This is who I believe Uther was referring to. If the Black Knight is still alive, he can find him."

"Great, so how do we find this other Elf King?" Elizabeth asked.

"That's easy enough. You have been staying in his house."

"What? You mean Mr. K?" Elizabeth was confused.

"Yes. Have you not wondered what the 'K' stands for?"

"No, not really. Lady Lorraine calls him Kris. I guess I just assumed that was it. But clearly, I'm wrong."

"The K could stand for Kris. You are right, but in this case, it stands for Kringle. Kris Kringle," Ryker said.

Elizabeth crossed her arms and looked at Ryker with a serious expression before she spoke. "Are you freaking serious? Are you telling me that Mr. K, who is tall and muscular, with no sign of a belly that shakes like a bowl full of jelly, is Kris Kringle? AKA, Santa Claus, Father Christmas, Jolly Old Saint Nick?"

"Why do you find that hard to believe after everything you have seen? Dragons, vampires, elves, shifters? Why would Santa Claus be any different?"

"I don't know. But I guess now you're going to tell me he can help find the Black Knight because of his naughty/nice list, aren't you?" Elizabeth said, shaking her head. Just when she thought she had heard it all, she found out Santa was real, and she was currently staying in his guest room.

# THIRTY-SIX

Elizabeth found herself distracted. It wasn't every day a person found out that Santa Claus was real, and they were staying in his house. She had questions, but Ryker insisted she needed to continue training, and they would seek out Kris afterward. They did have an upcoming battle to prepare for. But she didn't really want to dwell on that sobering fact. Not yet.

Attempting to manipulate water was not nearly as easy as one would think. Ryker had her trying to move water from one bucket to another. Per his advice, she was trying to take a moment to connect with her magic, to feel it flowing through and around her. Elizabeth closed her eyes, concentrating, but nothing happened.

"Maybe I can't manipulate water?" Elizabeth asked, frustrated after the twentieth time, with no results.

"I do not believe that is the case. Do you have a fear of the water, or is it of your magic?" Ryker asked.

"I don't know, maybe both. I felt powerful yesterday with the earth and growing the rosebush, but afterward, I felt nervous. What if my magic corrupts me? What if I—" Ryker put his hand up to stop her.

"Your magic is as much a part of you as your right hand or your left foot. Magic isn't what corrupts the soul, but the soul can corrupt the magic. In Lilith's case, for example, her thirst for revenge was what corrupted her. You are nothing like her. Your magic is nothing to fear. It has been protecting you your whole life, whether you knew it was there or not."

"That's the problem. It only shows up when my life depends on it. Maybe I need to be drowning or something for the water manipulation to finally kick in." Elizabeth kicked the ground in frustration.

"Are you aware that you have no scent?" Ryker looked at Elizabeth. He crossed his arms as he waited for her to reply.

"Um... okay, that's random. Yes, I have heard something about that from a few people. I assumed they meant I didn't stink," Elizabeth said as she shrugged her shoulders.

"No, that is not the intended meaning. Every living thing has a unique scent that is all its own. It is how animals and, by extension, those supernatural beings with an animalistic side can identify, track, and hunt."

Elizabeth remembered Luna mentioning something about all this a few months ago.

"You wouldn't have had much need for it in the human realm. However, if a supernatural came across you while you were there, they would have known you were not human instantly from your scent."

"I am assuming that would have been a bad thing?"

"You assume correctly."

"Maybe Lady Lorraine did some kind of magic to hide me."

"I am unaware of any spell or magical remedy that can take away or hide someone's scent for longer than a few hours. Which is why I believe your magic instinctively knew you needed to be protected, and it protected you by removing your scent altogether."

"Okay, that's a good thing."

"Yes." Ryker picked a leaf off the ground and stared at it as if he was waiting for it to do something. "I have never come across another magical being whose magic works without the wielder even knowing they possess magic."

This surprised Elizabeth.

He looked up from the leaf he was twirling around in his long fingers. "I was uncertain if you could truly be the prophesied bringer of light. I also have never heard of one whose magic worked on instinct as yours does, even without your knowledge."

"Wait, go back. A prophecy? About me? Lady Lorraine briefly mentioned something about a prophecy. But she never told me what it said." Elizabeth pulled her hair out of her hair tie and proceeded to tie it back up into another bun on top of her head as she paced around. "Okay, lay it on me. Tell me what this so-called prophecy said." She made quotation marks with her hands as she spoke.

"When the blood of the four are joined into one, the evil that remains will be undone. The light will overshadow the dark. The many will follow and fight for all that is right. The battle will finally be won when the light returns the soul and the sun." Ryker spoke almost in song.

"Despite the fact that some of those words were printed on the bottom of the jewelry box I found Excalibur in, I'm not really seeing the connection with me here. Next, you will tell me I'm going to be meeting up with a wizard named Harry," Elizabeth said sarcastically as she put her hands on her hips.

"I do not know of any wizard named Harry," Ryker said, looking at Elizabeth with confusion. We could ask Lady—"

Elizabeth held up her hand, interrupting him. "Please stop. Never mind, it's a human thing. Can we get back to this whole prophecy thing, please? And why would anyone think it is talking about me?" she asked, shaking her head.

"I'm not sure of all the details. However, both Lady Lorraine and Queen Dianna felt it was about you when you were born. Something to do with the fact that you have the blood of four out of the five original immortals that came to earth running through your veins."

"Um... what?"

"I do not know the complete story. They are still trying to keep you and your abilities a secret as much as possible. It's bad enough that Dimitri and Lilith know you are the Pendragon who has Excalibur. They don't need to know that you could also be the most powerful magical being ever who also happens to be prophesied to destroy Lilith."

"I don't know what to think."

"It's not something you need to worry about at this point in time. Let others speculate. You need to concentrate on your magic and connecting with it."

"Easier said than done, but okay. I'm ready to try this water thing again," she said, taking in a deep breath. "Then we can we find Kris and maybe even a nice, hot, steaming cup of Mrs. K's peppermint mocha."

"Perhaps. Show me what you can do first."

For the next hour, Elizabeth tried to move water from one bucket to another without success. By the end of the session, she was irritated, tired, and hungry.

"I'm telling you, I can't do it! Water magic is not in me." Yelling in frustration, she kicked the empty bucket, sending it flying across the field.

"It's okay. It will come when you're ready."

He wasn't getting it. She clearly did not have water magic. He was wrong about her having all the elements.

Elizabeth sat down on the soft green grass. She closed her eyes and tried to feel the power inside her. She tried, but all she could think about now was how hungry she was. How she wanted the peppermint mocha and some warm sugar cookies. As she was concentrating, she heard Ryker chuckle. Elizabeth opened her eyes and saw a small wooden table sitting in front of her with a plate of freshly baked sugar cookies next to a mug of steaming hot peppermint mocha. "Are you a mind reader?" she asked as she grabbed a cookie.

"I did not do this. You did. I guess we can officially add summoner to your list of abilities," Ryker said in amusement.

"Oh, my God! This tastes amazing!" Elizabeth said, stuffing her face with the cookies. "I didn't think magical food could taste this good."

"I'm pretty sure you summoned these from Mrs. K's kitchen. You did not conjure them into being. We will get into the difference another time. I hope this wasn't intended for Mr. K, or you might have ended up on Santa's naughty list."

"Wait, did you just make a joke?" Elizabeth stopped mid-cookie-bite.

"I am a king. I don't joke."

"I know. That's the scary part," she smirked. Elizabeth didn't care where her snack had come from. She was starving, and these cookies were divine. She would simply apologize later.

After enjoying their afternoon snack, Ryker agreed it was time to go talk to Kris, AKA, Santa Claus, which Elizabeth still couldn't believe. Mrs. K said they could find him in the gym. Thankfully, she didn't mention a missing plate of cookies or peppermint mocha, to Elizabeth's great relief.

They walked to the gym, which was in a part of the main house that Elizabeth had never seen. The room was enormous. It had every kind of workout equipment you could think of, including a few that looked like torture devices. Past a large boxing ring in the middle of the room, there was a section where several human-looking mannequins made of wood stood. That was where they found Kris.

He wore a pair of loose-fitting red sweatpants, but was shirtless, showing off his six-pack abs and muscular shoulders and back. His feet were bare, and a brown leather cord pulled his shoulder-length white hair back. He raised a huge sword above his head before he swung toward one of the wooden mannequins, slicing its head off in one go. How the world had gotten the image of Santa Claus so wrong, Elizabeth had no clue. This was not a man who sat around consuming milk and cookies all day. There wasn't a single spot on his body that would jiggle like jelly.

Kris glanced their way, a huge smile splitting across his face. He quickly sheathed the sword and grabbed a towel from a nearby bench to wipe the sweat from his brow. He then grabbed a water bottle, chugging it completely before walking over to where Elizabeth and Ryker stood.

"Well, good afternoon to you both," Kris said warmly.

"Good afternoon, Kris. I hope we didn't interrupt your workout," Ryker said apologetically.

"Not at all. I was just finishing up. What can I do for you? I hope your training is going well?" Kris said as he looked at Elizabeth.

"Yes, um, yes, thank you. Santa, um, Kris, I mean, Mr. K." Elizabeth stumbled on the words, and she felt mortified as heat rushed to her cheeks. She was making a complete fool of herself in front of Jolly Old St. Nick himself. She had been staying in his house but had little contact with him since that first night when she had seen him with Lady Lorraine. Finding out he was Santa Claus was really doing a number on her brain.

Kris's joyous laughter rang out, and there it was, the iconic *Ho, Ho, Ho!* laugh. "It's okay, Elizabeth. Please, feel free to call me whatever is most comfortable for you. However, most call me plain old Kris, except the elves. They insist on calling me Mr. K., which is okay too," Kris said as he pulled a white T-shirt over his head. "Now that we got that out of the way, how can I help you?"

Ryker shifted his feet and crossed both his arms in front of his chest. "Uther came to Elizabeth and told her to seek the Elf King, who would help her locate the Black Knight, to train her in swordsmanship. I knew he wasn't talking about me since I have no way of tracking him."

"That cheeky bastard. He knows I hate that stupid nickname," Kris said, shaking his head and laughing. "You're their king. I provide them with gainful employment." Kris looked at Elizabeth and back to Ryker. "As for the Black Knight, I would have to check the list. I haven't heard from him in a long time. Not since before Queen Dianna banished him to the human realm. I'm not even sure what name he is going by these days. It might take me a few days, but I'm sure I can track him down."

"Thank you." Ryker bowed his head.

"Yes, um, yes, thank you," Elizabeth said, still fumbling with her words.

"You're welcome," Kris said, smiling at both of them. "In the meantime, I would be happy to assist with the training. I used to be quite handy with a sword myself."

"I saw you just now. How is it that Santa Claus can wield a sword like that? I can't imagine there are too many warrior kids trying to steal your bag of gifts on Christmas Eve?" Elizabeth asked with a smirk.

Kris's festive laughter rang out again. "No, you're right, although some on the naughty list can be a bit scary. I was one of King Arthur's knight's back in the day before I took up the mantle of Santa Claus."

"I did hear that. You weren't always Santa Claus?" Elizabeth asked, eager to know.

"No, I had an entire life before I became Santa. I was born in England to a noble family, not far from where your grandmother Morgana grew up. We were friends. At one point, I had hoped we would be more, but that was before Merlin and

Jessica came into our lives. However, Morg and I have remained friends all these years. I'm sorry; I am getting off-topic. Yes, I was a knight along with Ryker, here. We proudly served under both Uther and then Arthur."

"Okay, I have to ask—how did you go from noble knight to Father Christmas?"

Kris looked over at Ryker and had a sad expression on his face. "That, I am afraid, is not a happy tale, nor is it all mine to confess."

"I'm confused. If not your story to tell, then whose? Mrs. K's?"

"Well, yes, it is her story as well, but also..." He glanced at Ryker.

"It's a story for another day," Ryker interrupted. "We should all return to the lodge and see if Nicholas Black has arrived with the intel regarding the attack on Fireside."

Elizabeth nodded. That had been weird. She would let it go for now, but something told her Kris's story was something she needed to know, and it clearly involved Ryker.

# THIRTY-SEVEN

When they returned to the lodge, Lady Lorraine informed them that Nicholas had sent word to expect him in two day's time. So, there they were. Two days later, the commander was due later that evening, and they had all gathered for another fantastic dinner of meatloaf, creamy mashed potatoes, and sweet peas. Elizabeth had a sense that they all felt that it could be their last before all hell broke loose in Fireside.

Ryker had been quiet throughout the meal. He had also been avoiding her for the past two days. Instead of continuing with her magic training, he had insisted that she work with Kris on some basic sword work. She had been happy to do it, except Ryker hadn't even had the decency to tell her himself. No, His Royal Pain-in-the-Ass had sent a messenger with a wax sealed note. Who sent wax sealed freaking notes anymore? Oh, yeah, an ancient king, that was who. One who was obviously trying to avoid her, but why? Well, that crap was not going to fly. He couldn't avoid her forever.

It wasn't until Riley bounced in that Ryker appeared to perk up a little. Riley had that effect on everyone. You couldn't be sad or upset with Riley around. She was living, breathing sunshine and happiness. Elizabeth chuckled to herself, thinking of how Luna would respond to Riley. The two women were so different.

Elizabeth was leaning against the kitchen counter, lost in thought as she waited for the water to boil for her after-dinner hot cocoa, when Ryker walked by her.

"Hey," she said, stopping him in his tracks. "You've been avoiding me."

"No, I have been busy preparing for the upcoming battle."

"You've been avoiding me." She stared at him, hands on her

hips, as he attempted to look everywhere but at her. “Why? Have I done something to upset you?”

Ryker said nothing, his lavender eyes staring into hers and neither one moving. He glanced over to where Shane was sitting, staring at their exchange, and back at her. “It’s nothing.” His expression hardened, and then he walked away before she could ask anything else.

*What was that about?* Before Elizabeth could dwell on what his problem was, Riley bounced over to her. “Oh my God! I still can’t believe you’re going to Fireside; I’m jealous! What are you going to wear?”

Elizabeth had given no thought to what she would wear. It was a battle. What do you pack in preparation for a battle? She was planning to throw a bunch of stuff in the new luggage her grandmother had left for her, hoping for the best.

Riley took in Elizabeth’s confused expression. “You have no idea, do you? It’s a good thing you have me. Let’s go raid your wardrobe and see what we can find!” Riley grabbed Elizabeth’s arm and practically dragged her to her room, giggling the entire way.

Elizabeth sat on her bed as Riley rooted through her closet. Lady Lorraine had the closet filled with clothes and shoes when she first arrived, but Elizabeth honestly had no clue what was in there. She stuck to basic workout gear every day since training was pretty much all she had done since arriving. Even her occasional girl’s night with Riley had just been relaxing. No need to glam up.

“No… no… no… definitely not, no,” Riley said as she examined each piece of clothing. “Okay, I can work with this, and maybe this.” Riley shook her head and then turned to face Elizabeth. “Now, I need you to try on this pile.” She pointed to the pile of clothes on the bed. “Then I can make the necessary adjustments.”

“What necessary adjustments? For what?” Elizabeth asked as she took the pile of clothes from Riley.

Riley let out an exasperated sigh. “Lizzy, one does not show up to a battle in yoga pants and a T-shirt. We have a lot of work to do before you are ready to leave, and I need you to try these on, please.”

Wishing she still had her leather armor that Luna had given her before the last time she went to Fireside, she walked toward her bathroom to change as requested.

"And when you come out, you can tell me what's been bothering you all evening. Maybe even why things seemed a little awkward between you and my brother," Riley said with a smile as she continued to sort through Elizabeth's clothing.

Elizabeth groaned as she closed the bathroom door. She wasn't sure if she was ready to talk about it, especially with Ryker's sister. But Riley was fast becoming one of her best friends, if not her best friend, and she needed help to sort through her feelings where both Shane and Ryker were concerned. Perhaps talking about it would help.

She tried on the first outfit and walked out to model it for Riley.

"Lovely, now spill. I can multitask. What is bothering you?"

"Okay, but if I tell you, you have to promise it will stay between us."

Riley put her hands on her hips and looked at Elizabeth for a second. "Girl, I don't know if I'm more insulted that you think I would talk, or that you think I don't already know what is going on." She laughed.

"What?" Elizabeth asked, surprised.

"Lizzy, just because I'm bubbly and fun doesn't mean I'm clueless. I have eyes. I can see that you are torn between your vampire and my brother."

Elizabeth was speechless.

"Why don't you tell me everything that's happened between you and them, and we can take it from there?"

Elizabeth filled in Riley on everything from when she and Shane first met as kids to Ryker's weird change after they had talked to Kris. Riley listened as she made the finishing touches on a beautiful ball gown.

Riley had insisted on packing no less than three ball gowns, just in case there was an after-battle party. Elizabeth just went with it. Riley seemed happy, and it kept both their minds off of what was coming. Plus, she had to confess, this last gown was stunning. It was a shimmery ruby red, off-the-shoulder silk gown with a sweetheart neckline. It cinched in at the waist, then flared out and dropped to the floor like liquid. It was nothing less than exquisite. Matching ruby slippers made Elizabeth think of the Wizard of Oz. She could relate to how Dorothy felt about not being in Kansas anymore. She also hoped she would have a reason to wear this dress one day.

"No wonder you are a mess," Riley said matter-of-factly. "You are clearly at war with yourself."

"What?"

"It's simple. Your teenage self never got to see how the relationship with the vampire would play out. You romanticized the situation and made yourself believe he was your one true love. Instead of moving on, you held on to his memory like a protective shield. You never wanted to get hurt like that again. When he swooped back into your life, it was like your teenage fantasy playing out in real life. Except you're refusing to see the red flags that keep getting thrown on the field."

"What red flags?" Elizabeth asked suspiciously.

Riley shook her head. "Okay, let me spell it out for you. First, he doesn't bother contacting you even after he became an adult. Second, he did almost kill you and chose to keep that secret, and then use that same secret as the reason he didn't contact you. Then, he continued to keep the secret about his bio dad from you."

"I can see how someone looking in would think those were warning signs, but he was afraid of how I would react. I get it."

Riley raised an eyebrow. "Okay, I am simply saying these are things to consider." She started to pack the dresses up. "Then you asked for space, and he glossed right past it."

"No, it wasn't like that."

Riley glanced up from the suitcase. "Fine. What about my brother?"

Elizabeth let out a long sigh. "I honestly don't even know. He caught me by surprise. At first, I found him grumpy and annoying, but over these past few weeks, I don't know. I find him fascinating. He's still grumpy and annoying, but I feel drawn to him, even knowing that he is way out of my league and there is no way he would be interested in someone like me. We make no sense. Ugh! I don't know, maybe it's just me having a crush on my teacher, kind of thing. I mean seriously, he's a freaking king who's been around forever, literally. Plus, I'm not sure what happened. Things were fine until I asked Kris about how he became Father Christmas. Ryker said it was a story for another time, and then he started to avoid me. It was really weird."

"Uh-huh." Riley bit the side of her cheek.

"What do you mean by that?"

"Look, first off, do not sell yourself short. You are an amazing woman. Any man, including a king, should feel honored to have you at their side. Ryker included. I can't speak for him because he doesn't confide in me, but I can see that he has been different since spending time with you. He's lighter and happier."

"How can you tell? His face is like stone," Elizabeth laughed.

"I have even seen him crack a smile or two, which he never does. His eyes light up whenever your name is mentioned or when you enter a room. It doesn't take a genius to see there is something between you two."

"Really? Are we talking about the same elf?"

"He has walls... lots of walls."
"Why?"
"I can't get into details. He's private about it all. But Kris's story brings up a lot a trauma for Ryker, and he hates being reminded of Yavanna and her unborn baby."
"Who was Yavanna?"
"Ryker's wife," Riley said, stunning Elizabeth.
"His what?" Elizabeth gasped.
"Oh." Riley's hand covered her mouth. "Please don't tell him I said anything. He doesn't talk about her, like ever."
"What happened to her?"
"Lilith happened."
"I am such a fool." Elizabeth sank to the bed. "No wonder he has walls. He's still in love with his dead wife."
"No, I don't think that's it. She's been gone for a long time."
"What happened to the baby?"
"She was still pregnant when Lilith had Dimitri kill her."
"Oh, my God. Poor Ryker." Elizabeth's hands covered her mouth in shock.
"Lizzy, that was a long time ago. I doubt it's what's holding him back now."
"Then what?"
"Maybe because he thinks you're taken, and he's not that kind of guy."
"Really? You don't think he's still pining over his late wife?"
"Ryker's marriage was arranged."
"An arranged marriage, really? I guess I have read too many romance novels. I would have thought that elves would have fated mates or something like that."
"Oh, we do, but it is rare. Few ever find their soulmate or kindred soul, as we call them. Plus, as royals, we have even less of a chance since we usually marry for political reasons."
"That's kind of sad."
Riley shrugged her shoulders. "I don't know their story; I was too young, and he never talks about it. However, I'm pretty sure he feels responsible for her death, even though it wasn't his fault. He also grieves for the child that was taken, as would any parent. But I don't think that's what's holding him back," Riley said as she closed one of the many suitcases which were now lying around. "The question you need to ask yourself is, are you taken? Are you in a relationship with the vampire or are you open to seeing what could happen with Ryker?"
"I don't know how I feel about Shane. It's not the same, but I don't want to hurt him."
Riley groaned. "You mean, like, he hurt you? Lizzy, since that man popped back into your life, you have let him have the driver's seat. I think it's time you forget about what Shane wants, forget about what Ryker may or may not want, and focus

on what Elizabeth wants. Maybe Elizabeth doesn't want to be settled down with one man. Maybe she realizes it's okay to sample what's out there without making a full-on commitment. You're young, you're smart, you are drop-dead gorgeous, and you are learning about who you are. If either of them really cares for you, then they will be willing to wait until you know who you are and are ready to be with whomever you choose."

"You're right. I have a lot on my plate right now. Juggling a relationship is the least of my worries. Let me survive this upcoming battle first, and then I can revisit the subject of romance."

"That sounds like a plan to me. I have already started planning the Lizzy kicks butt party," Riley said with a mischievous grin.

Thank the creator for Riley. They were finally finished packing. Elizabeth now had several tailored, battle-appropriate outfits. As she gathered her necessary toiletries from her bathroom, there was a knock at her door.

"Lizzy, you have a visitor," She heard Riley yell.

Dropping the pile of toiletries into her luggage, she was shocked to find Ryker standing in the doorway.

"Apologies. I didn't mean to interrupt."

"You're not silly. I was helping her pack." Riley smiled at her brother.

"I wanted to bring you this and let you know Commander Black has arrived," he said, handing her a large box.

"Thank you. What is it?" She took the box and placed it on the bed.

"It's elven armor. I figured you might need it. I hope you don't mind?"

"Mind? No, of course not." Elizabeth opened the lid to find a glimmering set of silver-plated armor.

"Ryker," Riley said in astonishment as she looked in the box.

"It is made from elven steel, which makes it lightweight and impenetrable. I also had it warded with magic for extra protection. The same as mine."

Elizabeth didn't know what to say. "It's amazing, thank you."

"I'm sure Riley can assist you with how to put it on and adjusting the fit if need be."

Elizabeth glanced at Riley, who looked in shock, but nodded in agreement.

"Anyway, I must go. The briefing with the commander will be in an hour. See you then." He bowed and made his exit.

"I can't believe he gave you this," Riley said, running her hands on the cool metal plating.

"I know, it's gorgeous."

"No, you don't understand. It's royal armor; it was my mother's."

"Oh, wow, I can't accept this. It's too much. It should be yours."

"No, I agree with him. It will protect you. I'm shocked he thought of it."

"What does it mean?"

"I don't know. But this is going to piss the council off," Riley said with a mischievous smirk.

# THIRTY-EIGHT

The meeting to discuss the upcoming battle had been long and tedious. The plan was to leave the next day with a battalion of elves, which included Ryker. Riley would be staying behind to run things while he was gone.

Ryker had sent his battalion ahead through a portal. Elizabeth was surprised to discover that any supernatural with royal blood could open a portal. He promised to teach her when they resumed her training whenever that would be. The war had started, and she was about to take part in her first battle. Was she ready? *No!* But too many people were depending on her. She hadn't forgotten about Skye or all those other captives, especially the children.

She hoped if they could stop Dimitri here and now, then it would be easier for her to get to Skye and the others. Was she being naïve? Probably, but she needed to hold on to the hope that Skye was still alive. She owed the young woman for saving her.

She found herself filled with nervous energy, pacing back and forth in front of the lodge. Wearing the exquisite armor that Riley showed her the proper way to wear, she waited for everyone else to be ready to depart for Fireside. She had no idea how they were getting there this time; she was praying the Grand Canyon was not involved.

She was so deep in thought that she didn't hear when someone walked up behind her. She turned and walked right into an armor-clad chest with the same elven rune on the chest plate as hers. Looking up, she found herself staring into her favorite pair of lavender eyes.

"Ryker, I'm sorry. I guess I wasn't paying attention."

"No apology needed. My mother's armor suits you, as I

knew it would."

"Thank you. I can't believe you lent me her armor."

"It's yours. Knowing that the Pendragon wore her armor would have been an honor to her."

"The honor is mine. Thank you."

He bowed his head in response. "I also wanted to see how you were doing."

"Honestly, I don't know. It's a lot. I have never faced death like this before."

"You know we won't let anything happen to you, correct?"

"I know. It's strange; my fear isn't about myself. It's the thought of losing any of you." She looked down as she picked at her thumbnail.

Ryker nodded, then glanced off in the distance before looking back at her. "Would you permit me to show you something? It might help you relax a little."

"Of course. What is it?"

He grabbed her hand. The usual spark, which she hadn't felt in some time, tingled up her arm as they touched. The smell of peppermint and pine filled her senses as they ran behind the lodge. His impromptu action surprised her. It was unlike Ryker. As they ran, she relished the warmth of his long, elegant fingers wrapped around hers.

He led her to a small patch of trees, glancing once over his shoulder before opening a portal.

"Ryker, do you think we should be leaving? What if someone comes looking for us?"

He flashed a warm smile that rendered her speechless and made her heart stop. "I promise we will not be long. She nodded and followed him into the swirling purple portal. They stepped through to find a breathtaking view.

Letting go of Ryker's hand, she stepped forward, gasping at the wondrous beauty that lay before her. A dark, shimmering lake reflected the stars from above, making it appear endless. Three crescent moons, one a little higher than the other two, glowed in the night sky. From afar, she observed rings that were wrapped around other planets.

In her wildest dreams, she would not have been able to conjure something this extraordinary or magical. Never in her entire life had she wanted to be an artist so badly, to be able to capture this moment in chalk or paint.

"What is this place?" she whispered, afraid that speaking too loudly would break the spell or cause it to vanish.

"It has no name, as far as I know," he shrugged. "It is a small pocket realm I stumbled onto as a boy."

"It's too perfect not to have a name."

"Perhaps you can come up with something fitting if you like."

She beamed at the prospect of naming this amazing world. Ryker snapped his fingers. Their armor was replaced with more comfortable clothing, and a quilt with an intricate Christmas pattern appeared on the ground. He gestured for her to sit as he lowered himself to the ground.

Sitting down on the quilt next to Ryker, she never took her eyes off the view. It had such a calming effect; she didn't think she would ever want to leave this spot.

"I come here sometimes when I need to be alone, whenever I feel overwhelmed, or when I simply need to sit with my thoughts."

"I can't imagine you ever being overwhelmed. You always seem calm and put together. I envy you." She stole a glance his way. He was lying on the blanket, his hands resting behind his head. He looked peaceful—so un-Ryker-like.

Opening one eye, he glanced at her. "We all get overwhelmed at times. It's nothing to be ashamed of."

"Is that why you brought me here? You thought I was spiraling?" She let out a humorless laugh.

"Spiraling... no. Nervous about your first battle, yes." He closed his one open eye but continued to speak. "I have been where you are many times. There is no shame in being nervous or even afraid of an upcoming battle."

"How could you possibly have been where I am? You're a king. You were trained for this life, trained to be a warrior. You have always known what you were meant to be. I feel unprepared for what is expected of me." She pulled her knees to her chest, wrapping her arms around them for comfort.

Ryker opened both eyes, staring into the great beyond. She watched as he seemed to struggle with his next words. He sat up, crossing his long legs before him. His lavender eyes filled with sadness.

"I am afraid you're wrong. I was not born to be king. That title was meant for my older brother, Cirinde. We called him Ryder." Ryker looked off into the distance, a faint smile on his lips as he slipped into a memory. "He could tame and ride any beast, speaking to them, gaining their trust. He was born to be king, and he would have been amazing if he'd been given the chance."

Ryker gracefully rose to his feet, his back to her so she could not see the intense pain on his face. But she could feel it through the air, radiating off him in waves of despair.

"I was born second. My purpose was to support Ryder. I was sent to the Pendragon court to train under Uther to learn how to be an adviser, and yes, a warrior. One that would serve my brother when he ascended to the throne." He began to pace keeping his back toward her. "I was supposed to have a simple life of service, not the complex role of leadership." He turned back toward her. "I was not properly prepared for my life, either."

Elizabeth rose to her feet, reaching for Ryker's hand. "What happened to him?"

"Lilith killed him." His voice broke as he turned away again. "He was ambushed on his way to my knighthood celebration in Camelot."

Elizabeth wrapped her arms around his back. The loss of his brother still tormented him. Lilith had truly taken everything from this man, and yet, he still stood tall and continued for Riley and his people.

"When I arrived home for the memorial, I found my brother's wife, Yavanna, was with child. The future heir of our people. To honor my brother, I took her as my wife, vowing that their child would be heir to the throne as they should be. After the bonding ceremony, I returned to Camelot."

Ryker turned, her arms still wrapped around his waist as he faced her. "Yavanna was my wife in name only. She was my brother's kindred soul, bonded to him for eternity. I only ever viewed her as a sister."

Elizabeth nodded in understanding. Suddenly, to her surprise, the sky lit up with thousands of streaking meteors shooting across the sky. She pointed to the sky. "You know, in the human realm, these are called shooting stars, and it's believed that you can make a wish on one of them, and it will come true."

"Really? That seems a bit strange," he said, looking up at the sky.

"No, I think it's magical." Elizabeth closed her eyes as she stepped away from him. Tilting her head to the sky, she made her wish. *I wish for us all to survive this coming war, and then to find peace in all our hearts.*

"Did you seriously make a wish?" Ryker asked, amused.

She nodded.

"Well, what did you wish for?"

"I can't tell you that."

"Why not?"

"Because then it won't come true."

Ryker shook his head as he laughed. "What kind of nonsense is that? Who said it won't come true if you tell me?"

"Everyone said it, that's who. You never tell your wish to someone. Not a wish on a star, or a wish made on a birthday candle?"

"Wait? Humans make wishes on candles?"

"No, not just any candle. Only a birthday candle, which is usually lit on top of a person's birthday cake once a year on their birthday."

"Humans have some bizarre customs. I can assure you, telling me the wish you made on a falling rock will have no bearing on the outcome of your wish whatsoever."

Elizabeth thought about her wish as she looked up at the night sky again. "Maybe, maybe not. But I choose to believe in the magic of the shooting star and will keep it to myself."

"Sunshine, seriously, you're going to believe in this human dribble." He crossed his arms over his chest.

"I promise, if it comes true, I'll let you know." She smiled at him.

"We really should be getting back," he said regretfully.

She reached for his arm. "Wait. Before we go back."

He raised an eyebrow. "Yes?"

"I wanted to say thank you for bringing me here and for telling me about your brother. I know that wasn't easy."

He nodded. "This has always been my haven; I never had a desire to share it with anyone until you." Ryker stepped back, then lifted her chin and stared into her eyes.

Time stood still, as she was certain he was going to kiss her. She closed her eyes as she leaned forward. But his soft lips didn't brush against hers. Instead, he groaned and wrapped his arms around her again, tightly, pulling her against his warm body.

She felt his lips graze the top of her head. "Why are the fates so cruel to me? Sometimes I forget that you could never be mine."

She pulled away slightly, allowing room for her to look into his beautiful lavender eyes. "What if I want to? What if I want to be yours?"

His eyes widened in surprise. "What about Captain Black?"

"Shane will always have a place in my heart. But I realized some time ago, he wasn't the one who owned it."

His gasp of shock brought a smile to her lips. But then he shook his head, dropped his arms, and stepped away from her.

His reaction confused her. "Ryker?"

"It could never be, don't you understand?" He ran a frustrated hand through his shaggy white hair.

"No, I don't understand. What I feel, what we feel..."

"Is unimportant," he said solemnly. "I have a responsibility to my people."

"I still don't understand. Why could we not explore this?"

"My people would never allow it."

"You don't think your people would accept us?"

"No, Elizabeth, I know they would not." He looked at her with regret. "I want you with every fiber in my body. I think of you first thing in the morning and the last thing at night. You haunt my every dream. "

Tears filled her eyes as she listened to his confession. They were words she had longed to hear, yet they were breaking her heart. “But now you know my heart belongs to you, Ryker! It belongs to you!” she cried.

“It only makes this situation much harder. At least before, I thought I was alone in my torment. I am required to marry someone of pure elven blood. My people have been after me for years to take a new queen. But I have been foolish, holding out, hoping to find my kindred soul, my other half. Yet even that dream doesn’t compare to my want of you.” He dropped to one knee and bent his head.

She rushed to him, lowering herself to his level and wrapping him in her arms.

He touched her tear-stained face. “I want to kiss you right now more than I want to breathe. But I know if I did, if I allowed myself this one moment of weakness, I would never be able to stop.” She wiped at her tears and rested her forehead against his.

Time was not on their side. They needed to get back. Elizabeth knew at this moment that she could never love another. Ryker was it for her.

# THIRTY-NINE

Elizabeth found herself eager to get this battle over with. The nervous energy and the constant what-ifs running throughout her mind was enough to drive her mad. She was standing off to the side alone while Ryker conversed with Lady Lorraine, and Uncle Nicky was having a heated conversation through his communicator. Suddenly, she felt herself whipped around to face the other direction.

"Who gave you the right?"

*What the hell?* Elizabeth was greeted by an angry-looking Bri.

"How did you manage to get your grubby, mutt-blooded hands on the queen's armor?"

"Rude, what is your problem? Ryker gave it to me."

"Such disrespect for my king. He is 'His Majesty' to you. And he would never give something important that was meant for m—that was meant for our next queen, to a lowborn, mixed breed like you."

"Wow, tell me how you really feel." Elizabeth tried to walk away, but Bri grabbed her arm.

"Remove it or I will—"

"You will what, Bri?" Ryker asked, surprising them both. "Release your hold on the Lady Pendragon at once."

"My liege." She instantly dropped to one knee. "I was informing the Lady Pendragon that it is inappropriate for her to wear our queen's armor into battle."

"Is that so?" Riker rested his hand on the hilt of his sword.

"Yes, Sire." Bri responded, looking up at him.

"And who gave you the right to take back a gift which I myself bestowed upon the Lady Pendragon?"

Bri's eyes turned big and round as saucers as she realized

what he was saying. "But Sire, surely you can see the council will not approve."

"It is not up to the council, nor is it up for debate."

"Yes, Sire." She quickly lowered her gaze.

"I am certain you have more pressing things to occupy your time with as we prepare this morning. Besides harassing the Lady Pendragon." Nodding in agreement, she rose, bowed, then walked away without another word.

"My apologies," Ryker said, clearly back to being his stern self, despite confessing his true feelings for her not an hour before.

"It's fine." *It isn't.* What Bri had said was hurtful. But he didn't need to know that.

"It appears that our access to Fireside has been compromised," Nicholas announced, grabbing her attention. "Shane and Chad, who guided our elven brothers to the gateway, successfully led the battalion through, but they faced intense demon opposition."

"Oh no, is everyone okay? What does that mean for our plan?" Elizabeth asked.

"It means we will need to find another way into Fireside. Chad had to close the gateway permanently to keep it from getting breached again. And there isn't enough time for him to find another one."

"How are Lilith's forces getting in? I thought the dragon realm was impenetrable?"

"We can assume they entered the same way we did, which means they are already there."

*Oh no. That is not good. There goes our element of surprise.*

"I can get us into Fireside, no worries." Lady Lorraine waved her hand with a flourish. Elizabeth had almost forgotten that her grandmother was an infamous sorceress.

"I was hoping you would... wait, what? Hold on. I'm getting another communication." Nicholas said as he walked away from the group. I'm sorry, can you repeat that?"

"Your Majesty! Your Majesty!" A tall lanky elf with lime green hair, whom Elizabeth had never met before, came running breathlessly to Ryker.

"Haell, what seems to be the problem?"

"It is the southern border, sire." The poor elf was bent over, gasping for air. "They are here!"

"Who is here?" Ryker's eyebrows furrowed.

"Lord Dimitri and his forces."

"What!" Elizabeth and Ryker yelled in unison.

"How is that possible? Have they breached the dome of the North Pole?"

"No Sire, the magic of Christmas is holding. But that still

leaves the mountains and the low-lying villages which are not protected by the magic of the North Pole."

"Sound the alarm. Have everyone evacuated to the tunnels."

"Not to the pole, Sire?"

"No, we can't risk Dimitri getting into the pole. Where is Kris?"

"Lord Kringle went to inspect the situation for himself."

"That old fool is going to get himself killed," Ryker grumbled before turning his attention to Elizabeth. "Stay here. I will be right back."

She nodded as he disappeared in a swirl of glittering snowflakes.

Lady Lorraine came rushing over. "Where is he going?"

"I don't know. But Dimitri isn't in Fireside; he's here."

"What, are you sure?"

"Afraid so, milady," Haell responded. "If you ladies will excuse me."

"He's not alone." Ryker reappeared in a flurry of snowflakes with Kris in tow.

"He has an entire army of Lilith's forces with him, and they appear to be headed toward my workshop in the North Pole." Kris lowered his head.

"What's at your workshop that Dimitri would want?" Elizabeth asked.

"All the world's Christmas magic is stored there. Without it, the world would succumb to another dark age," Kris said solemnly.

"And... I'm guessing that would be bad." Elizabeth bit her bottom lip.

"Very bad," Kris nodded.

"We have a problem," Nicholas said, walking back over to the group.

"Yes, we know Dimitri is here."

"What?" Nicholas' gaze shot over to Lady Lorraine. "No, that's not what I was talking about. How is that possible? No, we have an even bigger problem in Fireside."

"What could be bigger than Dimitri in the North Pole?" Lady Lorraine asked.

"Merlin."

"What about Merlin?"

"The wizard working with Lilith—it's Merlin."

"No! Never! Merlin would never work with her, and he would never betray the dragons. He would never," Lady Lorraine protested.

"I'm sorry. We have several reports of him being seen with Lilith, using his magic to attack the dragons as we speak."

"No! I won't believe this nonsense."

"He's suppressing their dragons. If we can't reverse the magic, they will be slaughtered."

Lady Lorraine started to sink to the ground, but Nicholas caught her before she fell.

"Perhaps Lilith managed to brainwash him or something." Elizabeth prayed that was not the case, but they needed to be open to any possibilities. "That could explain why he never came to find you."

"No, there must be another explanation. There is no way it's Merlin," Lady Lorraine said, shaking her head, still holding on to Nicholas.

"Could there be another wizard as powerful as that?" Elizabeth asked.

"Anything is possible except for it being Merlin." Lady Lorraine looked at Elizabeth.

"Regardless of who it is, the dragons are in serious danger. They need our help," Nicholas said.

"Yes, I will go." Lady Lorraine stepped away from Nicholas.

"What? Gram, what if it's him?"

"If it is truly Merlin, then I am the only chance the dragons have at defeating him," she said, standing back up.

"They are dividing our forces, forcing us to choose between the Dragons and the Elves." Nicholas looked at Ryker.

"Elizabeth, I will go with Nicolas to Fireside. You stay here and help the elves." Lady Lorraine grabbed Elizabeth's hands.

"No, you might need me if it's truly Merlin. You said before, his powers surpassed yours. I can't lose you."

"If it's truly Merlin, he won't hurt me. There is nothing Lilith can do to him to cause him to ever hurt me. I have faith in him. If it is him, then he needs me. I can't—no—I won't abandon him." Elizabeth nodded as tears welled in her eyes. "Remember, you were chosen to be the Pendragon for a reason. Have faith in yourself, as I have faith in you."

Lady Lorraine hugged her granddaughter one last time before she opened a portal for her and Nicholas to step through to whatever awaited them in Fireside.

# FORTY

Elizabeth found herself pacing in Mrs. K's kitchen, cursing both Ryker and Kris. They left her behind to face Dimitri. Ryker had given her some bullshit story about needing her to be kept safe, *blah blah blah*. She was sick and tired of being treated like a porcelain doll that could break at any moment. How was she going to prove herself as the Pendragon if they kept leaving her behind?

"What are you going to do about it, Little Pendragon?" Elizabeth swirled around so fast at the unexpected voice that she knocked over one of the kitchen chairs.

"Uther?"

"In the not so flesh?" He grinned from ear to ear.

"What are you doing here?"

"I was about to ask you the same thing."

"What do you mean?"

"There are at least two different, yet equally crucial, battles happening, and yet here you are pacing around with a biscuit in your hand."

Elizabeth looked down at her hands. "A biscuit?" She hadn't even realized she had picked up an elf shaped gingerbread cookie at some point.

"I ask again, Little Pendragon, what are you going to do about it?"

"What can I do? I don't know where they are."

"That's a flimsy excuse if ever I heard it. You're smarter than this. Time to prove that you are the Pendragon. Now, use the boulder between your shoulders and think, girl."

"Rude." She rolled her eyes at the medieval king.

Biting at her thumbnail, she thought about what she had overheard. Dimitri had come in through the southern border.

There had been mention of the low-lying villages. But their focus was on Santa's workshop in the North Pole where all Christmas magic was held. But that made no sense. Dimitri was no fool. He was there for her; she was sure of it.

"He's using their own fears against them." Uther nodded for her to continue. "Both Ryker and Kris are going to the wrong place." She was pacing around the kitchen again.

Elizabeth's gaze shot up to Uther. "Dimitri isn't going to the low-lying villages; there is nothing there. He's not going to the North Pole, either, because that's not what he's here for. He's here for me. He's going to the main village to draw me out. He'll send the bulk of his forces to keep Kris and Ryker busy, allowing him time to sneak around and look for me."

"How astute, little Pendragon. What are you going to do?"

"I need to go to the village."

"Not alone, you don't." Elizabeth's gaze met that of a determined Mrs. K standing in full medieval armor with a sword at her hip and a crossbow at her back.

"Mrs. K?" Elizabeth looked around for Uther, but he was gone.

"Please, call me Jessica, dear."

Elizabeth nodded as she tried to absorb the sight in front of her.

"I am much more than a good cook, dear. I was also a knight of the round table, and I still know how to fight. These are my people, and right now, they need us."

Elizabeth nodded, and the two women made their way towards the village.

Once they arrived, horrified screams and the sight of hellhounds running in the street greeted them.

Hellhounds were stalking through the streets, burning buildings and attacking citizens. With the elven army protecting the Christmas magic, the elven citizens found themselves fighting off the hellhounds on their own.

Jessica pulled her crossbow from her back and took aim at a hellhound who had corned a peach-haired elf who was trying to hold it off with a large stick in one hand and a baby strapped to her back. The arrow struck true; the hellhound fell dead where it had stood.

Using her wind power, Elizabeth pushed several beasts away from their intended targets. All the while, she scoured the surrounding areas, looking for Dimitri. She could almost feel his gaze over her skin, causing goosebumps to appear. He was near, watching and waiting.

Everywhere she turned, inhabitants of the village were fighting off the beasts. Several hellhounds took notice of her and started to stalk toward her. She shot dragon fire at them, but it didn't seem to faze them. It only made them angrier. She called on Excalibur, and one of the beasts lunged for her. Turning at just the right moment, she pivoted, slicing the beast's head clean off. Blood splattered her face as bile rose in the back of her throat.

"Yuck!" She wiped her face.

Losing sight of Jessica, she ducked behind a huge tree. She needed to keep her wits about her if she was going to survive this. But how was she going to do that? Her most powerful magic was her dragon fire, and it apparently it didn't do crap against creatures born of fire. There was no way she could use Excalibur to fight off multiple hellhounds. She wasn't that skilled with a blade yet.

She peered from behind the tree. Two hellhounds were approaching a group of young elves who were shooting light beams at them and flinging handfuls of rocks. Elizabeth shook her head and ran toward the beast. Once again, she used her wind to move the beast away from their intended target.

"Hurry, get somewhere safe, or at least far away from here," she yelled. The younglings all nodded and ran in the opposite direction from where she had flung the beast.

Hearing a growl from behind her, she raised Excalibur and slowly turned. There were not two, but six pairs of red glowing eyes that were now focused on her. Looking around, she confirmed the hellhounds were no longer running after the innocent elves. No, they had found their target.

"Oh, shit," she whispered.

She was bracing for an attack when a loud roar came from the sky as dragon fire rained down onto the beasts before her. Like her dragon fire, it didn't hurt the hellhounds, but it did get their attention away from Elizabeth. Then a swirl of glittery white snowflakes appeared as Ryker and Kris materialized, swords drawn and leaping into action.

Both men slashed and fought with ease and perfection. Ryker wielded his sword with elegance and grace while Kris used his with brute force and strength. Both men were magnificent to watch, and both were terrifying to their opponents.

Elizabeth wanted desperately to be that skilled with Excalibur, for it to be an extension of her. She was still lost in thought when a hand touched her shoulder. Turning, she found Jessica's concerned gaze.

"Lizzy, are you hurt?" She calmly asked.

"No, the blood isn't mine."

"Oh, thank the stars." Elizabeth took in Jessica's appearance. She, too, was covered in hellhound blood.

"Where did the dragon come from?"

Jessica's blood-smeared face morphed into a slight smile. "It was an illusion. I wasn't sure what else to do to distract them."

"You have magic too?" Elizabeth asked.

"Like I said, I'm much more than an excellent cook." She winked, then drew her sword. "Come on, we can't let them have all the fun, now, can we?" She ran toward where Ryker and Kris were now fighting off demons who had joined the fight.

Elizabeth had just begun to wonder if Dimitri was truly there at all when she spotted him. He rode an enormous beast, and it brought him into battle with startling speed. His mount was huge, with the body of a lion and the face and teeth of a crocodile. His army of trolls, demons, and vampires followed close behind, ready to destroy anything that came in their path. How was their small army of elves ever expected to go against such a throng of savage beasts?

# FORTY-ONE

Screams, shouts, and the clanging of metal filled the air. The stench of smoke and blood filled her nostrils. Elizabeth stood frozen in place, staring at the man who had been hunting her. She shifted her gaze to Dimitri's army; his number more than tripled theirs.

"Good thing I had a warm-up," Kris said as he swung his sword and beheaded a hellhound in one swoosh.

"Avoid his beast," Ryker yelled at the elves who had gathered, preparing to meet the invading army head on. "It's a bloody Devourer."

"A what?" Elizabeth asked.

"It's a foul beast, dear," Jessica said with a shudder. "One I didn't think existed any longer. If it gets too close, it will feast on your soul. A painful way to die."

"How would it feast on your soul?" Elizabeth asked.

"It sucks it from your body like one of those modern cleaning devices." Jessica thought for a moment. "Oh, yes, a vacuum cleaner."

"What?" Elizabeth was horrified at the thought.

"Just avoid its mouth, dear, and you should be fine," Jessica said encouragingly.

"How are we going to get close enough to take Dimitri out if we can't get past his beast?"

"It would appear, Sunshine, that we need to take the beast out first," Ryker said with a very un-Ryker-like smirk.

"Agreed." Kris shook his head. "Well, let's get this over with, shall we?" Kris raised his bloody sword.

"Wait, there are so many." For the first time, Elizabeth wasn't sure they would prevail.

"I know this is a lot for you, dear. War is never an easy

thing, especially for one so young. If we don't make a stand, here and now, innocent lives will die, including women and children. Sadly, this is just the beginning of what I fear maybe a long war." Jessica offered a sad smile as she pulled her flowing gray hair back up into a bun.

"True, love, but freedom for all is worth any sacrifice we might pay." Kris then grabbed Jessica by her neck, bringing her in for a passionate kiss, making her blush. Their love was pure and beautiful. Elizabeth longed to have someone look at her like that one day.

"Don't lose hope before we even begin," Ryker said. "The fates would not have sent us the Pendragon to have us fail in the first battle. Their numbers may look daunting, but don't count us out yet. You've never seen an elf fight. They're a fierce bunch who can do a lot more than make toys."

Kris laughed as he hit Ryker on the back. "Aye, brother!"

"Remember your training," Ryker said to Elizabeth. "Connect with your magic. It's your strongest ally right now. Use the sword's power to enhance your own. You are stronger than you realize, Sunshine. Time for you to show your enemies who you are." Ryker's words spoke to her soul and ignited her spirit.

"Okay, let's do this, and may all the gods, old, new, and whoever, be on our side!" Elizabeth yelled, raising Excalibur. Then something happened that caught her off-guard. All the elves responded back with, "For the Pendragon!"

"For the Pendragon!" Both Kris and Ryker yelled as they ran towards the invading army, followed closely by Jessica.

Dimitri's army surged forward while Dimitri stayed back. That was when she noticed Dimitri wasn't alone in his saddle. Slumped in front of him was a person.

Elizabeth's breath caught in her chest. The person wasn't just anyone; it was hard to make out what condition the young woman was in from this distance, but it was definitely Skye.

"Let her go." She wasn't sure if he heard her over the fighting, but his gaze shot to where she was standing. His sadistic smile filled her with rage. Excalibur's magical energy pulsed in her hand.

Shoving and pushing her way through the crowd, Elizabeth used her dragon fire to torch two demons who came at her. She swung Excalibur, slicing the hand off of a two-headed snake demon as he attempted to grab her. With a singular mission in mind, she worked her way through the onslaught of evil, attempting to get to Skye. She would see the young woman free from Dimitri's slimy clutches if it was the last thing she did.

The thought of killing anyone, including demons, did not sit well with her. She was not a killer, but this was self-defense, she kept reminding herself. Not that she really knew if she was killing anyone. Weren't demons and vampires technically already dead?

She spared a look at the carnage. The elf village was being destroyed; good people were being cut down by monsters. There was no other choice. If she got the opportunity, it was her duty to strike Dimitri down, no matter the cost.

Strangely, the smell of burned cookies mingled in the air with the odor of burned flesh, blood, and smoke, causing her to gag. Glancing over, her heart sank as she saw Ginger's bakery was ablaze. Dasher's Diner was in ruins, and Santa's Sundaes was completely gone.

*They can rebuild, she* told herself. *We just need to make it through this.*

As she continued to work her way through the crowd, the speed and skill the elves displayed in the fight amazed her. They were skilled in both swordsmanship and archery, as well as elemental magic. Dimitri's army dwindled shockingly fast.

When she finally broke through to where Dimitri was watching the carnage he had unleashed, blood, sweat, and grime covered her. Thankfully, he wasn't looking in her direction. Taking a moment to compose herself, Elizabeth ducked behind a wagon to gather her thoughts. She hadn't really made a plan; she had a single focus: Get to Skye. Now, here she was, and she needed a plan. The sounds of battle with grunts, roars, cries, and howls of pain made it almost impossible to think.

Swirling snowflakes got her attention. Ryker and Kris were working their way through the chaos as well, moving toward the beast Dimitri sat upon. If they could work together to take the beast down, then she could go after Dimitri and free Skye in the process.

*Is it wishful thinking that I can take on Dimitri alone, perhaps? But I have to try... right? For Skye.*

Elizabeth marveled at the way Ryker wielded his magic and his sword in a beautiful but deadly dance. Wind and snow swirled around his targets, vines would hold them in place, and then either fire or his blade would strike them down before he moved on to his next target. He was a vision of perfection in motion. Smooth and elegant, yet deadly and fierce.

She hoped, if given the time, she could be as proficient with her magic and Excalibur. She hadn't even tried to use her earth magic; it was still too new. Her dragon fire and wind seemed to work on instinct, where the earth magic needed concentration, something she didn't have time for in the middle of a battle.

Then there was Kris, freaking Santa Claus, wielding his sword like the mighty knight he was. His opponents didn't stand a chance against the precision of his blade. If only the world could see this version of Father Christmas. How would the holiday change?

Dimitri didn't seem to notice how close the two warriors

were getting to him. He seemed distracted as he frantically surveyed the battle before him. Then it dawned on her. He was searching for her.

Waiting and watching, Dimitri sat upon his monstrous steed surveying the battle, looking for his chance to get to her. The bastard wasn't even getting his hands dirty. Occasionally, an elf would get a good shot and send magic his way, but with his quick vampire reflexes, he easily avoided the strikes.

Ryker had moved in closer to the beast's backside. But where was Kris? Fear that Ryker would be seen before he could strike, she acted on instinct, running toward Dimitri to get his attention, hoping to distract him long enough for Ryker to take the beast down.

Shooting her dragon fire like a madwoman, she yelled for Dimitri to get off his beast and face her like a man. The smirk he offered could have chilled the air. This was what he wanted. He wanted her, and here was his chance. As he leaped off, his beast screamed in pain.

Its thrashing tail threw Ryker into the air. Fear for him, momentarily freezing Elizabeth in place. But relief filled her as she saw Ryker regain his composure quickly, going at the beast again.

Dimitri abandoned his pursuit of Elizabeth to aid his beast. He charged after Ryker, sword poised to strike the elf king. Her heart leaped in her throat. She screamed for Ryker to move, unsure if he noticed Dimitri's trajectory. She screamed again, but a roar coming from the sky drowned her out, followed by the flames shooting from the flying beast.

Prince Drake, in his dragon form, was soaring over the crowd, roasting Dimitri's army. Lady Lorraine must have been able to reverse the spell, because high in the sky was a purple portal and more dragons were flying through.

*Thank God, reinforcements had arrived.*

Dimitri roared in anger. Ryker disappeared in a swirl of snow just as the demented vampire's sword came crashing down on his neck. Elizabeth nearly collapsed with relief.

With the appearance of the dragons, Dimitri's army started to abandon the battle. All around, demons started vanishing into black smoke, while vampires and trolls opened portals to escape. *Had they won?*

She needed to get to Skye before Dimitri fled with her again, knowing that he would be furious at the cowardice of his troops. Elizabeth feared he might take his anger out on Skye. But she hadn't seen what had happened to Skye when Ryker had attacked the beast.

Elizabeth frantically searched around the fallen beast. There, lying next to a front paw, lay a heap of blonde hair. Elizabeth ran, dodging fleeing demons. Dropping to the ground, she lifted the girl's head up.

"Skye?" Pressing her ear to the woman's chest, she listened for a heartbeat or a breath. Then the most beautiful sound came out as Skye whispered, "Milady?"

"Yes." Elizabeth let a strangled half-laugh, half-cry. "It's me." Elizabeth searched around for anyone to help; surely, there had to be a medical elf, healer, or someone on this damn battlefield who could do something. She noticed Jessica was assisting another wounded soldier.

"Skye, I'm going to get you help, but I need you to help me get you there. Do you understand?" The young woman nodded, then started to stand with Elizabeth's help.

Relief hit her as she saw Ryker sheath his bloody sword and hurry in her direction. A breathtaking smile lit up his face, causing her pulse to quicken.

A loud screech came from behind him as the Devourer's large eyes popped opened. Its crocodile-like mouth revealed huge teeth rearing in Ryker's direction. The force of the creature's soul sucking power froze Ryker in place. Elizabeth could see him grimace in pain, but he couldn't shake free from the creature's hold. His fear-filled gaze landed on her as his soul was being ripped from his body by the Devourer. His lavender eyes lost their brightness as the creature drained Ryker of his very essence. Her heart shattered. She was losing him before her very eyes.

"No!" Elizabeth yelled, dropping Skye to the ground. She ran towards Ryker and pushed every ounce of power she possessed into her wind magic, creating a tornado that pushed Ryker from the beast's grasp. He landed unconscious a few feet away.

The creature screeched in anger that its meal had been ripped from its grasp. Its large eyes then found Elizabeth. It quickly darted for her. Knowing she would not be able to fight back. She tried to scurry away, tripping over a dead demon, which halted her escape. The creature's crocodile like mouth opened. She could feel the sucking sensation and pain as it latched onto her soul. Elizabeth continued to move, attempting to flee from its grasp.

Then from the corner of her eye she saw a streak of ruby red, and a loud roar came from above as an unknown dragon swooped down and sprayed its dragon fire, roasting the beast in its wake.

A relieved Elizabeth nodded thanks to the fire breather before stumbling away from the burned carcass. Glancing at Skye, she saw the young woman was thankfully being assisted by an elderly elf, allowing Elizabeth to focus on getting to Ryker, who was still unmoving where he had landed. She needed to make sure he was okay. He had to be okay.

She used up so much of her energy trying to help Ryker and herself get away from the Devourer, that she was finding it hard to walk and only managed a few steps at a time. She was so busy concentrating on making her feet move that she walked right into a hard chest. But before she could apologize, she felt a sharp pain in her side. Instinctively looking down, she discovered a jeweled dagger protruding from her side, her hand covered in blood. *What the hell?*

Dimitri's gleeful laughter turned her blood to ice as he pulled her closer.

"Did you think I would leave without my prize?"

"Y-y-you stabbed me?" Elizabeth said in disbelief.

"How sharp of you, my pet. No pun intended." He flashed a fang filled smirk. "I only wish you were at least half a vampire. Then this silver blade would paralyze you for me, making our exit so much simpler. Sadly, you're not. Of course," he licked her ear, "I could rectify that right here and now. Would you like that, pet, to be mine for eternity as one of my kind?"

"No, please don't..." She was feeling weaker as the blood dripped from her body. There was no way she could fight him off, and Ryker was still unmoving. Where was Kris, Jessica... anybody?

"No, I think I will take you home and have some fun before I decide what I want to do with you." He wrenched the blade from her side, causing her to scream out in pain. He brought the dagger to his nose, sniffing it. "Delectable," he said before he licked her blood from the blade. "My Queen really wants you, but Pendragon blood has always been a particular favorite vintage of mine."

She heard a clicking sound in his hand. That's when she saw a portal open before them. She wanted to fight, but she had nothing left. He may have lost the battle, but he had succeeded in getting her, which had been his goal all along.

The main question was, what was he planning to do with her? He didn't seem to be in too much of a hurry to take her to Lilith. The thought of spending any time alone with Dimitri terrified her more than facing the Demon Queen herself.

He was beginning to lift her up when suddenly, his grasp on her was gone. She looked up in shock as she saw Shane tackling his father to the ground. He rained down a flurry of blows in quick succession, rendering Dimitri unconscious. Then he rose to his feet, leaving the older vampire unceremoniously on the ground.

"Are you okay?" he asked as he held out a hand for her.

She was holding her side, barely able to move. She shook her head. That was when he must have seen the wound, because all the blood drained from his face.

"We need a healer over here! The Pendragon has been

hurt!" he yelled. Shane bent down to pick her up when his face contorted into pain.

"No!" She tried to scream as Dimitri appeared behind Shane, stabbing him with the same silver dagger he had used on her. Shane stood, but then the paralyzing effect of the silver must have kicked in because Shane went rigid and still. Then, to her horror, Shane fell toward Dimitri, causing both vampires to fall into Dimitri's open portal.

Elizabeth reached out her hand toward the portal, but she could do nothing as she watched it close, taking her best friend with it.

He was gone. Shane was gone. He had been paralyzed by the silver dagger, which meant he was defenseless. What would Dimitri do to him? He was his son, but there was no love there.

She was getting weaker from the blood loss. But she needed to tell someone about Shane. Had anyone even seen him fall through the portal? Did anyone know he needed help? Black spots started to form around her vision, but she fought it. She needed to help Shane. She was the only one who knew what had happened to him.

She tried to call for help, but nothing came out. She glanced at Ryker. But oh God, he still hadn't moved. Was he dead? *Please don't let him be dead.*

A sobering thought entered her head as she lay there, bleeding out and surrounded by fallen soldiers from both sides. They had lost, after all. Shane was gone, Ryker was gone, and she was surely dying.

Would her father come to escort her soul to the afterlife? At least she would see him again.

A weightless feeling came over her. She was dying, and she had failed them all? Worst Pendragon ever, dying in her first real battle.

"Hang on, Lizzy. Stay with us! I got you." She looked up to see a blurry Santa. She tried to speak, needing to tell them about Shane. They had to know, they had to save him. It could not end like this. But before she could say a word, her world faded to black.

**The story will continue *In Rise of the Pendragon***

# ACKNOWLEDGEMENTS

Elizabeth's story has been a true labor of love. One that started over twenty years ago. It truly does take a village to release a book into the world, and I would not have been able to do it alone.

To my friend Beth for being my cheerleader for all these years, and always offering me words of encouragement.

To Shelly, whose support gave me the push I needed to take the few last steps to get this book published.

To my amazing editor Devon Atwood. Thank you for helping me find my way to the heart of this story.

To Rose, my cover artist, who helped me bring my vision to life in an amazing work of art on the cover.

To all the amazing authors, I now consider friends who I found in the craziest of places, TikTok. Your advice and unwavering support have been invaluable.

To all my beta and ARC readers for being willing to take a chance on a new author.

To my husband and children, without whose support and understanding, I would not have been able to fulfill my dream.

To my mom, who instilled in me the importance of hard work, and to my dad, who instilled in me the need to have dreams.

To all my family and friends not mentioned by name. Your love and support were no less invaluable. I truly feel blessed and honored to have had all of you along on this journey with me.

A special thank you to all the following individuals who supported me through my crowdfunding campaigns. Without your donation, The Last Pendragon would still be an unfulfilled dream. So, thank you all from the bottom of my heart.

Sheena Showe, who purchased the very first copy! Thank you!
Jade and Rebecca
Tia Ware
Tammy and Carol
Sherry Brazile
Tina Munsky
Tanya and Jenna Denchfield
Crystal Renner
Ann Cruze
Katherine Malloy
Caitlin Millsaps
Nikki T
Kieran Pritchard
Christy Laukaitis
Danae
Megan Kell
Brian Grimes
Alexandra Corrsin
Billye Herndon
Julia Fay Deutsch
Ryan Q
PunkARTchick “Ruthenia”
Dean Lambert
Kristina Atkins
ALB

# ABOUT THE AUTHOR

**Jeanette T. Queen** is a fantasy author who loves to read anything with magic and or romance. Especially those books written by her friends. She grew up in the small town of Boonsboro, MD. But now lives with her husband, two children, and four fur babies in the beautiful state of North Carolina.

Jeanette is a professional hypnotherapist and life coach, when she's not writing. She is also a food allergy parent who advocates for food allergy legislation and education.

You can keep in touch with Jeanette through her newsletter, TikTok, Instagram, Facebook, and Clapper.

Printed in the USA
CPSIA information can be obtained
at www.ICGtesting.com
LVHW060543270824
789394LV00013B/136/J

9 798330 263288